Natural Justice

By

George Donald

CHAPTER 1

He didn't know, couldn't recall when it all began to go wrong. It seemed like they had been quarrelling and bickering forever. The slightest comment, the unguarded word, all or any would set Karen's teeth on edge and lead to a tense silence that would in the end cause her to explode into a raging fury; and always end with her berating him for all their troubles.
His life with her had become a cautious walk on eggshells.
Laura with a child's keen instinct to Karen's changing moods had come to recognise the signs; quietly making her way to a safe corner of the room to play with her doll. He had tried to reassure her, hug her and with forced smile, tell her that mummy and daddy still loved her; it was just that sometimes grown-ups argued, all the time knowing that a three year old could neither comprehend, nor would ever understand the breakdown of a relationship.
For that's what it was.
The mug of tea had grown cold and he pushed it away from him. The Formica topped table still bore smears from the wet dishcloth that he'd used to dry the spilled milk.
He looked about him at the small, untidy kitchen. He hadn't foreseen this when he'd left the service. Sitting in the falling darkness, the rain softly beating a tattoo on the window, he wondered where his life had gone wrong.
Almost two years had passed since completing his military engagement; two long years of scraping by, counting the pennies, making ends meet.
Not like it had once been.
Twelve years as a Royal Marine, five as a married man.
In the beginning, Karen had loved the status, the prestige of being married to a member of the elite Corps. She had enjoyed the life of the permanent staff at the training centre at Lympstone, where they had begun married life. The living quarters were large and roomy and, as an instructor, he had been home most nights. He'd tried to tell her, explain it wouldn't last; that his instructor secondment was just three years and he was due for posting, but she dismissed his warning. She always enjoyed the social weekends, the attention she attracted with her good looks; the formal dinners in the NCO's mess and proudly celebrated with him when he made sergeant.
He hadn't known or suspected then of her possessiveness; nor her snobbery.
The first signs of her aloofness was when she began to ignore his friends wives, those who hadn't attained similar rank, preferring instead to mix with the wives of the senior NCO's; encouraging him to invite his bosses for dinner, pushing him to seek further promotion.
The pregnancy had been ill timed.
His joy was short-lived. He remembered her disgust, her shock when the doctor confirmed her misgiving. She'd slyly hinted at abortion, her attempts to persuade him she was too young to have a child. He'd laughed, immediately regretting his insensitivity as

he realised she was serious and foolishly reminded her she was two years older than he. Her black mood that time had lasted for almost two weeks.
He closed his eyes, his lips tightening when he recalled her anger when news of his posting arrived; the position he'd applied for prior to the pregnancy. Reminding her that it was at her suggestion he'd applied, her insistence the move would be good for his career had caused further fury, particularly when the deployment was approved just a few days later.
Eighteen unaccompanied months in the Province with the Detachment.
She had openly wept, begged him to call off on personal grounds, using their expected child as a lever to have him change his mind. But all to no avail. He had resisted her taunts and sneers and fought hard to be selected for the course. His boss had agreed and with his recommendation, been accepted for the gruelling six weeks secondment in London with the Security Service.
She had moaned incessantly, complaining that six weeks, let alone eighteen months, was far too long for them to be apart.
With infinite patience, he'd tried to explain to her that the Corps was not prepared to spend that amount of money training him without some form of recompense. And besides, he had been told he'd be home every six weeks for a five-day break.
Then, as he always did, he had given in to her, succumbed to her tearful sobbing.
Later, when he'd spoken with his boss and submitted his withdrawal form, he had explained Karen's fears. He hadn't expected the curt response, the veiled threat that *'Any change of mind, Sergeant Bryce, will be recorded in your personnel file and most definitely delay future advancement!'*
With a reluctant acceptance, he'd taken the hint and withdrawn his form; yet his guilt was tinged with a secret relief that the Major had coerced him into continuing with the posting.

The eighteen months in Ulster had been a physically hard, gruelling and dangerous time for him but not, if the rumours that reached him were true, for Karen. While she'd remained at the family quarters in Lympstone, pregnant or not, he learned she still found time to get out and about and not always, he'd once heard laughingly whispered, alone.
Shortly after the birth of Laura, Karen wrote him that she had engaged the services of a young, local teenage babysitter and bragged that with or without him, she intended resuming her social activities.
He had thought long and hard about it and decided she was lonely, that he wouldn't challenge her about the gossip; a cowardice that still haunted and continually tormented him.
He stood up and pushed the chair back from the table, his hand unconsciously reaching for his left cheek as he worked his jaw, still numb and smarting from her open-handed blow.
He stared at his hand, his eyes widening with surprise as he saw the faint smear of dried blood, not realising that her ring had cut his cheek. He glanced at the small mirror hung on the wall by the back door. Just nicked it really, he saw.
He stared hard into the mirror at his reflection. His brown hair, neatly trimmed and side parted, steady hazel eyes and square jaw. Back then, when he enlisted, his face could have been a recruitment poster for the marines. Now, at thirty-four, he felt as though his

life was almost over. The cut on his cheek had reopened slightly. He rubbed hard at it with his fingers, but it had stopped bleeding and the dried blood flaked off.
With a sigh he turned away, shivering as though suddenly chilled and walked into the narrow hallway to adjust the thermostat. Flicking the light switch, he blinked against the harsh light and stared at the photograph on the wall.
The picture had been taken the day he earned his sergeants stripes. Dressed in full lovat green uniform, his Green Beret sitting regulation square on his head, he was smiling at the camera. Karen, hugging his left arm, her long fair hair lying loosely about her shoulders, her light blue dress clinging to her shapely figure, head turned slightly to stare smilingly at her six-foot husband, standing almost a full head taller than his petite wife. A perfectly posed photograph.
They were happy then. Or so he had thought.
He moved through the small house, closing the curtains against the falling darkness and switching on first the front room and then upstairs for Laura's bedroom lights.
He glanced at the brightly coloured wall clock, the farm animals beating a rhythmic tick-tock to the battery driven mechanism. They'd been gone almost an hour.
He guessed she'd driven to her mother's house in the affluent Glasgow south side suburb of Newton Mearns. He knew that the short journey from their home in the small estate in Paisley's Glenburn would take no more than twenty minutes if she used the back road through Barrhead. Once there, he guessed her mother would fuss over her and Laura, reminding her daughter once more that she'd warned her against marrying someone like him, a crude and unfeeling brute.
He smiled softly at the memory of the early days, both of them laughing at her mother's description of him. Before it all began to go wrong.
His father in law, as usual, would say nothing; merely sit with his pipe and paper in the large, comfortable chair, his slippered feet resting on the grate beside the fireside in the front room of their detached and soulless bungalow. Once long ago, in a rare moment of male intimacy, he had admitted to Johnny that to argue or disagree with his wife caused nothing but hardship for days thereafter. *'I've learned to keep my mouth shut'*, he had solemnly confessed.
Johnny hadn't realised then that often the old adage was true; like mother, like daughter.
He lifted the remote for the small stereo unit and pointed it to activate the CD that was in the machine. One of his favourite songs, Savage Garden's *Affirmation,* begun to play softly from the speakers.
Sitting down wearily on the two-seater couch, he lifted the fluffy bear and puzzled that Laura would have left it behind. But then again, she wouldn't have had much choice, he grimly recalled; remembering how her enraged mother snatched the toddler from the floor and hauled her out to their ageing Ford Escort; another thing that constantly irritated Karen, who dreaded being seen by any of her former friends in the old car.
He had tried, God knows, to find some decent work when he'd been discharged. Half promises from former colleagues had fallen through or meant relocating to England.
'Definitely not!' she had vehemently told him when he suggested moving south. 'My mother wouldn't tolerate it,' she had added. He no longer argued with her when she was in that kind of mood.
The jobs available to ex-serviceman were few and far between and like many others, he'd fallen into the security industry, not through choice but by circumstance. The money

didn't reflect the long hours. But, 'What choice do we have?' he'd argued.
He knew she was ashamed of him, insisting he wore a jacket over his security company blazer lest the neighbours see what he had become; what kind of failure she was married to.
The little they had saved from his military salary was almost entirely spent on the down payment for the mid terraced, two bed roomed house; an excuse for accommodation that some enterprising sales executive described as ideal for the first time buyer. Compared to their former home, the detached three bed roomed service quarter, they had seriously downsized, a taunt Karen unfailingly delivered at least a dozen times each day.
He'd done his best, painting and decorating when he wasn't on shift, but it was never good enough.
With a sigh, he glanced again at the clock. He was on early turn; six am start the following morning at Garvey's Superstore, in the Braehead Shopping Centre; the new mall situated beside the River Clyde. He knew he couldn't be late, would have to be there to monitor the cameras from the CCTV room as the bleary-eyed accounts staff emptied the bulging forty-six tills of their previous day's takings, in readiness for the day's business.
He'd give it an hour then go to bed. If Karen wasn't home by then, he'd leave a note, telling her he was sorry they'd fallen out, that he'd phone her from work. He softly closed Laura's door as he thought what he'd add to the note, hoping that Karen wouldn't be spiteful enough to ignore reading it to their daughter. He'd end the note by telling them he loved them both.
In his heart he knew he was only half telling the truth.
But he really did love his daughter.

*

The three men in the old Vauxhall Cavalier, or more properly the two men and the youth, had shared the spliff between them. The sweet smelling smoke engulfed them all and caused the youth in the back seat to splutter as the unaccustomed strength of the weed caught in the back of his throat.
Davie Crowden and his brother Sammy who at twenty-two, was three years the younger, both sniggered at Ian Morrison's discomfort and for now, their previous argument about bringing Morrison on the blagging was forgotten. When the youth produced the cannabis cigarette, Davie relented and reluctantly agreed the nineteen-year old could accompany them.
'But mind,' he'd warned the teenager, his voice grating as he fought back a cough, 'keep your trap shut and if we get stopped by the cops on the way there, it's me that does the talking. Savvy?'
'No problems, big man,' Morrison had agreed, his hands held up in mock surrender and a huge grin on his acne pockmarked face.
'Right, here's how it's going down,' began Davie, coughing slightly as he half-twisted his body in the passenger's seat to include Morrison in the conversation. 'The Shogun should be parked in the driveway and, if it's the same as yesterday,' he glanced at Sammy who vigorously nodded his head, 'it should be facing down the driveway towards the gate. Was the gate opened yesterday?'
Sammy again nodded his head.

Davy paused for breath, involuntarily shuddering as Sammy steered the old Cavalier dangerously close to a parked van.
'For fucks sake!' he cried out loud, 'we want to get there in one piece, Sammy!'
His brother grinned and not for the first time did Davie think he was deliberately driving like a nutter simply to piss him off.
'Right, where was I?' he glared at Sammy, 'oh, aye, the Shogun. We park down the road and let you out, Ian. You walk past the entrance to the house and if the motor's still in the driveway facing towards the gate and if the gate's open, you continue to walk past without stopping. So it's just a quick shufti, understand? When you get to about fifty yards further down the road, stop and light a cigarette. We should be able to see you. That's the all-clear signal for us. Sammy and I will ditch this heap and walk into the driveway; he does his edgy to make sure nobody is hanging about that might see us and I get the motor started….'
'Will you need to break into it?' interrupted Morrison.
Davie grinned at his brother then turned his head to face Morrison, holding his hand up with a key held in his fingers.
'The Shogun got sold last week from Pat Delaney's Car Sales over in Tollcross. Guess who's got a spare key?'
Morrison began to laugh.
'Is that not where your kid sister Mary works?'
Davie slowly nodded. He had to be careful when he spoke about Mary. He couldn't have Sammy guessing what he really thought.
'Aye, she does the account books for Pat Delaney and from what she tells us, his books are that hot she has to wear asbestos gloves,' he replied. Suddenly, as if guessing the younger mans thoughts, he turned towards Morrison, his eyes narrowing.
'And another thing, wee man; you'll forget about our Mary giving us the key. We don't want her arse dragged into this, okay?'
A sudden fleeting image of the lovely Mary Crowden's perfectly formed rear end crossed Morrison's mind, but the warning from Davie was more than crystal clear.
'No worries, big man,' he hastily replied, grateful for the darkness in the car that hide the creeping blush rising to his cheeks.
'So,' asked Morrison, eager to change the subject, 'what happens after you blag the Shogun?'
Sammy, keen to include his wee pal Ian in the business, interrupted.
'While Davie and I drive off in the Shogun, you walk round the block and get yourself back to this scrapper. I'll leave the key in the drivers' sun visor and then you drive it back to the lock-up. The Shogun is going to a warehouse down by the docks at South Street in Partick. We've a guy down there that will fit new plates and then it's onto a cargo steamer and across the water to Dunlaoghaire. We've got a contact in Southern Ireland that pays good money for four by four vehicles.'
Davie inhaled deeply and tried to flash a warning at Sammy, that he was telling the kid too much, but his cocky young brother ignored him.
'What if…' Morison's mouth was dry, 'what if someone tries to stop us? Prevent us from getting the Shogun, I mean.'
Davie cast a quick look at Sammy, and then reached down between his feet. When he sat up he was holding two short lengths of metal pipe, each having one end bound with

insulating tape.
'That's why I've brought a couple of wee persuaders,' he grinned evilly.

*

Karen Bryce sat sniffling in her mother's kitchen, the box of disposable paper tissues in front of her. From the front room, she could hear her daughter laughing delightedly at her father's antics as he crawled about the floor, making farm animal noises.
'But he's such a failure, no matter what I've done to encourage him Mum,' she wailed.
'I know dear, I know. After all,' her mother haughtily reminded her, 'wasn't it I that saw his failings before anyone else? Didn't I try to warn you that he would never amount to anything? Royal Marines indeed! Grown men playing at soldiers, running around shooting off their guns. Should get proper jobs, those people, rather than have the country keep them.'
She sat her plump backside down beside her daughter, idly patting at her blue rinsed hair with one hand and secretly pleased that at last it seemed to be over; Karen would return home to where she belonged and with the added bonus of bringing her child Laura with her. It would be good for the toddler too, having a bit of discipline now and again. Yes indeed, things were working out nicely.
Her husband stood in the doorway, his granddaughter lying back in one arm; he smiling wearily as he balanced her on his bony hip.
'Guess who needs a wee drink of juice, Granny?' he grinned, his facc flushed from rolling about the floor.
'Grandmamma, if you don't mind Hector,' she tartly replied. 'We want the child brought up with manners,' she drawled, her affected accent intended but not quite suppressing her working class background.
Hector sighed and turned away, leaving his wife and daughter to once again berate Johnny; a man that he liked and secretly admired, but had never dared to openly admit such feelings.
'So, do you or do you not intend leaving.... that man,' she asked Karen, her aversion obvious at the mention of Johnny's name.
'Oh Mum,' her daughter cried, the tears running unabated but deliberately down her cheeks, 'the things I've had to suffer. Only last week he suggested that we consider putting Laura into a day nursery and me...' her eyes widening again at the horror of the thought, '.... me getting a part time job!'
Mavis was aghast.
'How dare he!' she cried out in anger. 'In all the years your dear father and I have been married, never once have I had to work! I'm fuming that he would even suggest such a thing!'
With feigned rage, she slammed a podgy hand down on the coffee table causing the china teacups and plates to rattle. Hastily she dabbed with a tissue at the small spillage of liquid on the highly polished surface.
'Why, he's not a man at all. With a child and house to keep, no man should have his wife go out to work. What a suggestion!'
This, she decided was the perfect opportunity. She stood upright and drew herself to her full height of five foot two inches. Turning melodramatically towards Karen, she set her face to reflect her determination, her tight mouth highlighted by the vivid slash of bright

red lipstick.
'Well, I'm your mother and I think I'm acting in your best interest; and your daughters' too of course,' she added almost as an afterthought, 'when I tell you that you must leave him. Leave him immediately! There will always be a room here for both of you. Do it right now. Right this minute,' she insisted, her face set, her thin lips closed tightly together.
Karen smiled through her tears. It had gone exactly as she had planned. Her mothers' outrage, real or otherwise, was the final part of the drama she had rehearsed so many times in her mind.
But there was just one more thing to do.
'You're right of course, Mum', she fawned, 'I should have listened to you all those years ago. I'll do what you say, but not tonight.'
Her mother looked puzzled.
'I'll go home tonight. Johnny will be in bed anyway. He's got an early start tomorrow at that miserable job of his, so I've no doubt he'll have turned in early. I'll use the spare bed in Laura's room and when he goes to work, I'll pick up all my things and something for Laura, and come back here tomorrow morning. If that's all right with you?' she asked, deliberately making her voice tremble and pretending to shiver slightly. It worked. Her mother reached over to stroke her shoulder. Karen was, if nothing else, her mothers' daughter.
'There, there,' Mavis replied, patting Karen on the shoulder in what she thought was a suitably comforting gesture. 'Of course, anything that you want, dear' she cooed, her eyes glistening in the knowledge that once again, she had been proven correct.

Hector, standing quietly in the hallway with Laura now gently asleep in his arms, sighed sadly as he listened. That was the problem, he knew. Johnny had given in too often to Karen's bullying ways. And now he was about to lose not only his wife, but his child also. He glanced sadly down at the cherubic face and his throat tightened.
Perhaps things might have been different, he wondered, if he too hadn't given in so easily.

*

Archie Crichton had first regretted accepting the overtime following the gruelling backshift, but with his daughters wedding due early next year and retirement in three months time, his wife was nagging him to put more by than he could really afford. Not that he was a penny-pincher; not by any means. But his frugal upbringing in the small Fife town of Cupar had instilled in him a sense of thrift; *watch the pennies and the pounds will look after themselves*, as his old granny used to tell him. That prudent upbringing had done him no harm; quite the opposite, in fact. Those first few years on the fishing boats had developed the body of the skinny young man he had been to the big and powerful police officer he had become. A little overweight, he shifted guiltily in his seat, but middle age doesn't come quietly; at least not with all the fish suppers I've had to consume these nearly thirty years, he inwardly grinned.
Besides, manning up for four extra hours overtime to three am had its attractions. The gleaming new BMW with its impressive livery had only been in service with the Traffic Department less than a week and his nightshift colleague, the busty Julia Morton with the cropped blonde hair, was easy going and no bother. Not for her the idle chitchat that so

many of these young women insisted on, he thought. Come to think of it, he reflected, it was damned hard to get a civil word out of her at all.
He cast a sideways glace at her.
'Not looking at my tits, I hope?'
He flinched with embarrassment. He had been hoping to get an unobtrusive eyeful of the department's well-known 'twin peaks' that jutted out from her blouse.
'Not at all!' he blustered, pulling on the steering wheel to adjust his sitting position and knowing fine well that *she* knew he was lying. He adjusted his weighty backside more comfortably in the seat, privately wishing that car manufacturers placed more thought into the seating requirement of the overweight, middle-aged man.
'So, any holidays planned this year?' he asked in a tight voice.
In the darkness of the car, she grinned to herself. Dirty old bugger.
'Aye, my boyfriend and me are thinking of Mexico. Seems that you can get more for your money's worth there,' she replied.
'That's nice,' he idly replied, staring through the rain-splattered windscreen as he activated a single stroke of the wipers. The darkened lay-by into which Archie had reversed the BMW was overhung with branches and effectively hid the unlit traffic car from oncoming vehicles; an ideal vantage point from where to close in and ambush passing speeders.
Patiently, the officers waited on their first unsuspecting victim.

*

Sammy Crowden drew the old Cavalier to a smooth halt in the wide, tree-lined avenue and cut the engine. The large houses on both sides of the road seemed silent enough, with just a few showing the odd porch or hallway light. The three occupants of the Cavalier looked about them, then glanced at each other as if seeking support for what they were about to do. All quiet, they agreed.
'Right,' Davie turned to Morison, 'get your arse down there,' he pointed out the driveway, 'and remember! Walk past and if it's all clear, light a cigarette. Okay?'
Morison gave him a nervous thumb up and grinned as he slid from the back seat, gently closing the door behind him. They watched as he swaggered down the avenue.
'I'm not happy telling him all our business,' Davie began, his cough irritating him as he spoke. 'I know he's your pal, Sammy, but the more people that know about the scam, the more chance that someone will let something slip to the rotten mob. One sniff of what we're up to and the cops will be all over us.'
'The wee guy's sound,' protested Sammy, 'he knows what would happen to him if he lets us down.'
'Right,' warned Davie, peering through the darkness, 'he's at the gate; he's passed it. Wait, wait,' the anxiety betrayed in his voice. Reaching down between his legs, he sat back up and handed Sammy a metal pipe. 'That's the fag lit. Right, let's go!'

In the darkened bedroom, he lay in quiet discomfort, his aching stomach grumbling and threaten to explode into a loud fart. His wife had warned him about taking a second bowl of Chilli. No, nagged him more like. But after downing a few lagers, more Chilli had seemed a good idea at the time. Now he wished he'd listened to her. As quietly as he could, he slipped from below the sheets, easing his bare feet onto the coldness of the laminate floor. As gently as his bulk would allow, he raised himself from the mattress

and stood upright. On the other side of the bed, his wife's snores caused him to grin and he involuntarily passed some wind. Suppressing a chuckle, he silently made his way on bare feet across the darkened room.
He decided against using the en-suite and made his way quietly to the WC on the half landing. The moonlight streamed through the ornate leaded window and illuminated the small room. He ignored the light and rightly guessing he was about to stink the room out, gently raising the lower sash to allow a draft of night air to sweep through.
He dropped his pyjama bottoms and sat with relief on the bowl, shuddering as almost immediately he discharged his bowels. Reaching towards the toilet roll, he stopped and held his breath and listened intently. He thought he had heard a stifled cough. A few seconds passed and then from outside came the soft but distinctive crunch of someone walking slowly on the stone chips of the driveway, below the toilet window.

Gently, Davie inserted the Shogun key and with what seemed like a thunderclap, the centrally locked door opened with a click. He climbed smoothly into the drivers seat and saw Sammy doing likewise into the opposite passenger seat.
From above them the night exploded as an abusive scream of outraged anger filled the air.

*

The car radio burst into life, urgently alerting all the Traffic car call signs and particularly those patrolling in the Newton Mearns, Clarkston and Giffnock areas of Glasgow that a Shogun four by four vehicle had just been stolen from a driveway in Belvedere Gardens and was last seen towards Ayr Road. Two suspects aboard added the voice that now repeated the vehicles details.
Julia Morton scribbled the registration number down on her pad and turned to Crichton. 'What do you think?'
Crichton's eyebrows knitted together. He knew the area intimately and figured that if these guys were professional car thieves, rather than the usual scummy teenagers that the tabloid press insisted on dubbing 'joyrider's', then it was more than likely they'd stick to the quiet backwaters rather than risk open confrontation with the Traffic cops.
'Crookfur Road,' he decided at last. 'Chances are that if they know they have been rumbled, they'll cut across westwards and head straight towards Paisley; try and avoid main roads and the police vehicles that will be attending the call.'
Experience had taught him that upon receipt of such a message, police officers invariably headed for the last known sighting of their quarry, rather than spread out in a net and thereby increase the search area.
'Either way,' he gunned the engine and took off at speed, a grin on his face at the acceleration of this beauty and quietly excited by the thought of some action, 'we'll likely be called on if there is a pursuit.'

*

'Shit, shit, shit!' repeated Davie Crowden, repeatedly slamming his hands against the soft leather of the steering wheel.
'What'll we do Davie, what'll we do?' pleaded Sammy, his head turning to look behind, expecting the cops to be on their tail any time. 'Will we ditch it?'
'No, we're not bloody ditching it!' his brother screamed at him. 'It's just a hiccup! We drive towards Paisley and they'll not find us! They'll be expecting us to go into the city,

not through the back roads and the housing estates!' he shouted, his nerves raw and his mouth dry.
'Might be a good idea to switch on the headlights,' Sammy timidly suggested.

*

'Now remember dear,' her mother told her, 'if he gets back before you leave or anything; or if he gets violent, just phone and I'll send your father down to protect you.'
She settled Laura into the car seat, pulling the straps tight. The child moaned in her sleep, her dreams fleetingly disturbed.
Hector put out a hand as though to assist, but quickly withdrew it when his wife glared at him. Never in a million years, he thought, would Johnny Bryce hit Karen. That should have been my job, when she was a child. A skelp on the arse now and then might have made the difference rather than leave her to the manipulations of her mother.
Maybe should have tried it with her mother first, he wryly considered. And me, he grinned to himself, swap punches with a lad like that, who's had all that commando and secret undercover training? Aye, that'll be the day! She must be off her head!
Karen was in the driver's seat, slamming the door closed. She wound down the window.
'And I take it you'll bring the car with you?' asked her mother glancing distastefully at the rusting vehicle, already making plans to have it consigned to the scrap heap when she had it here, under her control.
'Yes, of course Mum,' Karen replied, impatient now to be gone, 'I'll see you both tomorrow morning, bright and early,' she smiled without a trace of humour.
'Bright and early,' echoed her mother, fluttering a hand at the departing car and seeing the curtain twitch at number forty-two across the road, where that nosey old bitch was likely wondering what was going on. Let her curiosity choke her, she thought unkindly.
Karen drove away, the red stone chips of the driveway flailing under the tyres.

*

The Traffic car reversed slowly into the small, tight cul de sac and Archie Crichton switched off the lights, staring at the junction forty yards away where the main road was joined by the darkened side road; more of a wide lane really and which eventually wound its way to the nearby town of Paisley.
Beside him, Julia Morton held her breath. Her gut feeling was to be out there, driving around, looking for the stolen vehicle. It crossed her mind to suggest this, but the calm assuredness of Crichton swayed her. It was commonly whispered round the office by the younger cops that he was a fat, doddering old fool about most things. But nobody could deny his experience and his impressive list of arrests. He had an instinct for this type of work, a knowledge of the area and escape routes that was, frankly, incredible.
So she sat with him, her mouth shut. And, impatience gnawing at her, waited.

*

Karen switched on the radio, listening to the local channel broadcasting yet another rundown on the pending Old Firm match between Celtic and their city rivals, Rangers.
"Bloody football," she irritably thought, one eye on the poorly lit road and the other looking for the knob to change channels. Glancing up, she hastily corrected the steering and brought the Ford Escort back across the centre white line and into her own lane.

*

Davie Crowden took the corner of the darkened road too fast and clipped an overgrown hedge.

‘Fuck!’ he silently mouthed, grinning as he sensed his brother reach forward to brace himself on the dashboard. “Shoes on the other foot now” he smirked.

*

‘No trace of suspect vehicle meantime,’ droned the voice from the radio.

*

Johnny lay awake, listening for the sound of the old Escort’s laboured engine. The mid terraced property didn’t warrant a garage, merely on-street parking and a designated bay that was almost always occupied by one or another of the neighbours. Another of Karen’s never-ending complaints he had learned to shrug off. He sighed, turning over and trying to sleep, knowing he wouldn’t; couldn’t till Laura… No, he quietly rebuked himself; till they were both home, safe and sound.

*

Julia Morton was getting anxious.
‘That’s nearly seven minutes, Alex. If it was coming this way, don’t you think it would have been here by now?’
‘Time and distance,’ he softly replied, his fingers beating a slow tattoo on the steering wheel, ‘time and distance.’

*

Karen approached the junction and again righted the car as it swerved slightly.
“Jesus!” she cried out nervously, glancing at the rear-view mirror to confirm her daughter still slept. She thanked God that at last she’d managed to tune into something other than football.
Her mother was right, she decided. There would be life after this. After all, she sneaked a further glance in the mirror, widening her eyes and tilting her head slight as she smiled at her reflection. I’m still an attractive young woman.

*

The backs roads were unfamiliar to Davie. He’d never had the occasion or any interest in visiting this part of the city, other than to steal good quality motors and then it had always been in darkness. The road twisted and turned like a fairground ride. He accelerated through the few straight yards, braking sharply as he hit yet another bend. He fought to maintain the vehicle in the middle of the road, the lights at full beam, his intention to avoid the overgrown hedges from scratching more of the paintwork than was necessary and thus devaluing the Shogun. He grinned mirthlessly to himself. Always the profit, as Pop likes to say.
He missed the warning sign. But then again, if the very same hedges half hid the bloody thing, he would later contest, how was he to know there was a concealed junction coming up?

*

Alex Crichton stiffened when he saw the headlights approach from his side, and then relaxed when he recognised the familiar shape of a trusty old style Ford Escort.
‘Bugger!’ said a tense Julia Morton beside him; then smiling softly as she exhaled with a slow sigh.
Their attention was engaged with the bright lights from the approaching Escort and neither saw the speeding Shogun emerge from the darkened road, a lane almost. Not until their eyes opened wide in horror as they watched the Shogun collide with the Escort. That’s when all hell broke loose.

*

CHAPTER 2

It was later estimated in the official report of the accident that while the deceased Karen Bryce had been travelling between thirty-five and forty miles an hour and in excess of the thirty mile per hour limit enforced on that road, it was estimated the stolen Shogun that failed to halt at the obligatory Stop sign had been travelling at well over sixty miles per hour. Karen's slightly excessive speed, it was determined, was not particularly contributory to the final outcome.
According to the police eye witness Constable Alexander Crichton, the Shogun emerged at what he termed 'great speed', struck the Escort squarely in the drivers side and shunted the vehicle across both the road and the short grassy path way that run beside the road; both vehicles coming to a grinding halt when the Escort struck a dry stone brick wall.
The subsequent fireball type explosion was, experts were later to prove, due to the immediate rupturing of the Escorts petrol tank and ignition of the petrol fumes by a flash that was undoubtedly caused by parts of the electrical wiring of the Escort's battery becoming loose and thus creating an open spark. The damage to the rear seating area of the Escort had resulted because the force of the explosion expended itself mainly in the cab area of the Escort and consumed everything within that small area.
Fortunately for the Shogun and its occupants, the short distance between it and the fiery Escort saved it from any similar combustion.

'No,' Constable Crichton sadly confirmed much later, 'there was nothing anyone could do to save the driver or the child trapped in the rear.'

Davie Crowden came to. His head hurt and the raging fireball in front of him lit up the night with an eye searing bright light.
Beside him, lying curled in a foetus position in the foot well of the passenger side, Sammy softly moaned, unconscious but at least alive.
The door was yanked open and a hand reached in and grabbed Davie by the front of his jacket.
'You murdering bastard!' screamed a small, blonde haired woman, a hatless cop he saw by her uniform, who punched him on the side of the head and with extraordinary strength, dragged him from the drivers seat. He fell helplessly onto the ground, his chest aching from a broken rib and his face slimy with what he later learned was blood oozing from a head wound.
He looked up in time to see her booted foot crash into his side, the incredible pain against his broken rib causing him to blanch then violently throw up onto the ground. He collapsed forward into the pile of vomit.
A voice shouted from the other side of the Shogun.
'Julia! Get over here! Now!' and the female turned to leave, but stopped, nearly breaking his wrist as she viciously snapped a handcuff on his left wrist; then dragged his unresisting arm upwards, ignoring his scream and snapping the other half onto the driving wheel.
He hung, half suspended, wondering what the fuck was going on?

'I ensured that the driver of the Shogun was alive and secured him by handcuff to the steering wheel,' Constable Julia Morton afterwards informed her Inspector.
'No sir, not being a doctor I didn't know if he had suffered any injury, apart from a visible slight cut on his head, the front as I recall. Like I said, I was unaware that he was otherwise injured. No sir, I do not intend to sound flippant, but the suspect made no complaint of being injured at his time of arrest.'
'Drag him from the car sir? Me sir? No sir! With respect sir, David Crowden is about six foot tall and weighs nearly fifteen stone. I ask you sir, how could a slightly built person like me lift someone that size who wasn't being cooperative?'

The Traffic vehicle's fire extinguisher that Archie Crichton used was worse than inadequate in that it gave a false sense of purpose, but he knew that the raging fire was out of his control and the two figures within must mercifully now be dead. He backed off, recoiling at the intense heat that forced him to even step further away, unaware that his close vicinity to the flames had scorched his eyebrows and hair and the wool on the front of his NATO style police pullover.
Beside him, Julia sobbed, unable to avert her eyes, one hand to her mouth as she watched the flames lick round the shrivelled corpse of the small figure that was strapped in the child seat behind the driver. The blackened figure in the driver's seat, hair alight and clothes furiously burning, slouched over the remains of the steering wheel, one hand raised claw like as if beseeching God to spare her the intensity of the fire.
Julia hardly felt the fatherly arm that Crichton placed about her shoulder.
'Go back to the car, lass,' he firmly told her, surprising himself that his voice was so calm, 'call for back up and the fire brigade. Tell them we have a fatal RTA and give the location, there's a good girl.'
He recognised she was in shock, unable to grasp what he had told her and instead led her back to their vehicle, ignoring the Shogun, with its dazed handcuffed prisoner, and helped her sit in the front passenger seat.
He watched as with a shaking hand, she reached for the microphone; tears running down her cheeks and swallowing hard as she tried to compose herself to deliver the message.
From the back of the car he fetched an orange fluorescent jacket and shrugged into it, the consummate professional, prepared to assume control of the scene and direct any vehicles that would pass by or arrive to assist.
A head bobbed up on the passenger side of the Shogun. Not the prisoner, Crichton saw with surprise. Then he remembered. The report had said two suspects, didn't it?
He walked swiftly to the passenger door and tore it open.
Sammy Crowden, dazed and similarly with a head wound, stared up at the old cop and grinned weakly, accepting arrest but strangely pleased that the cops were here to sort this mess out.
Alex Crichton didn't smile back.
He seized the smaller man by the hair and, ignoring the handcuffed prisoner's feeble protests, dragged Sammy viciously from the vehicle.
Sammy flopped onto the ground as the two massive hands reached down and turned him onto his face, a set of handcuffs brutally slapped onto his wrists behind him.

'No sir,' admitted Constable Crichton, 'I didn't immediately realise that there was a second suspect within the vehicle, my attention being taken up at that time by the poor unfortunate victims in the Escort.'

Again Crichton seized him by the hair and dragged him upright to his feet.
Sammy squealed in pain, then found his voice, screaming:
'Let me go you bastard! I'll fucking report you!'

'Strike a handcuffed suspect, sir? Well, I'm extremely upset that you would believe that an officer with my experience and service would even consider resorting to such a stupid act!'

The old, fat cop stared at the bloodied face of the car thief and with quiet anger shook his head.
'Let's make it worth your while then, laddie,' he replied coolly, then clenched his fist and drew back his arm. But he stopped, staring at the wild-eyed car thief.
Slowly, he lowered his arm and unclenched his hand.
'You're not worth it, you piece of shit!' he shook his head, and then turned Sammy round, slamming him against the door of the vehicle.

CHAPTER 3

Johnny sat on the armchair in the small sitting room, his hands clasped tightly together and resting on his lap, head bowed, unable to grasp what he had been told, let alone come to terms with the news. The two police officers facing him, sitting awkwardly together on the narrow couch were silent. The Inspector held her cap in her hand, the single band of silver braid across the peak reflecting the overhead light, conscious that the stiffness of her leather utility belt was pressing against her, digging uncomfortably into her side. She remained still, fearful that her discomfort might in some way detract from the moment. The young probationary cop she'd had accompany her sat upright, almost at attention, his face chalk-white, not daring to breath. Like his Inspector, he was uncomfortable but rather more because this was this first death message and he thanked God it wasn't his alone to deliver.
Johnny raised his head and stared into the Inspector's eyes.
'There's no doubt?'
She hesitated, her mouth suddenly dry and unable to draw back from the steady, calm gaze of this troubled man. She was reluctant to say anything further, other than the dreadful news she had just imparted; conscious that there was still much to be done, still more details to follow that she did not yet have access to. And besides, how could she possibly explain that the message she'd received indicated burns beyond recognition?
'It seems,' she began slowly, choosing her words carefully, 'that at this time there is no doubt. The vehicle is registered to you at this address, your wife's handbag was discovered, albeit I understand with some damage, but sufficiently identifiable to enable the officers at the scene to discover credit cards, as well as some…some personal items.'
'And Laura…my daughter?'
'The child that was…' she stopped and swallowed hard. Her own daughter was excitedly

looking forward to her fifth birthday party, next week. 'The child in the rear seat…we can only presume that it… that she…. was Laura.'
He lowered his head into his hands. He remembered another time, another place. He had seen the damage that extreme heat can do to bodies.
'Can you tell me where they had been? The direction of travel would seem to indicate they were returning here, coming home, I mean.'
'Her mother's house probably. Karen's parents stay in Newton Mearns,' he replied, his voice steady and even. He didn't believe it was worth mentioning they had been arguing, that she'd run off, angry and upset with him. He wasn't to know that after answering the persistent doorbell, when he'd gone back up the narrow flight of stairs to shuffle into sweat pants and top, the Inspector had peeked a look at the note he'd earlier laid on the table; nor had she missed the slight of cut to his cheek.
God help him she'd thought. He's lost his family and now, knowing his wife has left angry with him, he'll never forgive himself.
The young cop remembered his training; some practical advice the sergeant at Tulliallan Police College had given him. He swallowed hard and licked his lips.
'Can I get you a cup of tea, Mister Bryce?'
Johnny stared at the youngster, a look of wonder crossing his face. Tea, the good old cure for all disasters and calamities. But the kid was just trying to be nice.
'Please, son,' he nodded his head, 'you'll be able to find the stuff in the kitchen. Maybe for you and the Inspector too, eh?'
The young cop left them alone, anxious to help and happy just to be doing something. With more room on the small couch, the Inspector gratefully adjusted her seating position.
'Is there anyone we can contact for you? Your in-laws perhaps? Your own family?'
He didn't raise his head when he replied, his voice threatening to break.
'Thanks, but…Karen's parents, I'll get a taxi…. visit them myself. Me?' He shook his head slowly. 'There's nobody. Well, a sister in Canada. Nobody local.'
She stared at the top of his head. When she had arrived, he seemed somehow vaguely familiar. She'd learned not to ask those kind of questions, though. Not since that embarrassing time when a familiar face at her husbands' office night out caustically reminded her she'd recently locked him up for assaulting his wife. But still?
'You work locally, Mister Bryce?'
He raised his head and nodded.
'Security guard. Garvey's in Braehead.'
She nodded, recalling her attendance at an urgent call to the store, not too long ago. Staff struggling with a violent shoplifter, the report had said. Bryce had the suspect, a well-known junkie; pinned to the floor, face down. The junkie claimed he'd been assaulted, but Bryce denied it; was very clearly holding the man down on the floor to avoid injury to him and the other staff.
She had accepted his story, recognising the thief as a junkie and knowing his violent history.
'Yes, we've met before, albeit briefly.'
He nodded again. He remembered too.
'Where will they take them, Karen and Laura?'
'The. …accident…occurred within the Glasgow boundary, so it's likely they will remove

both of them….' she paused again to collect her breath; God, she hated this, '…. to the city mortuary at the Saltmarket. Beside the High Court,' she added.
He nodded his head yet again, not trusting himself to speak. He knew where the place was.
She had to tell him, the worst part of the news.
'You'll appreciate there will probably be a post mortem, Mister Bryce?'
He sat upright and stared her in the eye, his face totally blank. He took a deep breath.
'What more can they do to them?'

They got back into the car, she driving and the young cop beside her.
'They tell you about it,' he said, clicking into his seat belt and staring through the windscreen. He swallowed hard. 'How to break the news I mean. But they don't tell you how hard it can be.'
She started the engine and slowly reversed out from the parking bay.
'The day you get used to it Frankie, is the day you want to chuck this job,' she replied.
His eyes narrowed, the question puzzling him.
'You didn't mention it had been a stolen motor that crashed into them. That we've got two in custody. Do you not think he should be told, Ma'am?'
She paused, contemplating her answer.
'At the moment, it's still an RTA. Yes, I agree, the other vehicle has been reported stolen and yes, I know there are two arrested. But right now, that poor man's got to come to terms with losing his wife and child. There's time enough for him to be provided with all the details later. It's still dark, Frankie. The dayshift CID will get the inquiry and the DI can visit and fill him in with the full story. Once we've got it all ourselves. There is still forensic work and witness statements to be done. Better having all the details before going off half cocked, that way we don't have to revisit and pester the man with constant updates. What do you think?'
He suspected she was being kind; knew that his impatience was due to his inexperience. And of course she was correct. There was no need to rush. Time was now on their side.
He remembered the photograph.
'Aye, Ma'am. I saw a picture on the wall in the hallway, when I was bringing the tea through, him and his wife standing together. He had been a sergeant in the Royal Marines, a commando.'
She remembered the ease with which Bryce had the junkie pinned to the floor.
'That,' she smiled back at him, 'isn't hard to believe.'
Frankie thought that Mister Bryce had looked quite fit in the picture. Happy and content, his good-looking wife standing beside him.
Better we've got those two car thieves, he pondered, rather than Bryce get a hold of them. God alone knows what that man is capable of, if he was angry.

*

Later, much later when the taxi had delivered him back home, he reflected on his unpleasant visit to her parents; wondering if he had done the right thing instead of having the police break the news.
It hadn't been easy.
Hector had said nothing, just sat there in his old, worn dressing gown, staring at the cold fireplace, his face pale and expressionless.

Mavis had predictably gone off her head, weeping and wailing, blaming him for their deaths. She'd stopped just short of calling him a murderer.
Then, the cruellest blow of all, as her anger turned to venomous spite.
'She was going home to get her things. Hers and Laura's,' she spat at him, her teeth clenched, her eyes blazing. 'She was leaving you, you wastrel, you…you…you good for nothing failure!'
Odd that numb as he felt, he should notice it; realising her voice had reverted to the broad, guttural working class accent of her youth.
She ranted and spat the vilest of curses and oaths at him.
He had stood there in their front room, staring at her. Refusing to be drawn, refusing to answer, her malice washing over him.
'ENOUGH!!'
She had stopped in mid-tirade, her mouth open and eyes open wide, turning slowly to face Hector.
Her husband had stood by the fire, his face tearstained.
'Enough!' he repeated, quieter this time.
He walked towards Johnny and slowly raised his hands, clasping him by the arms then briefly embracing him.
'Go home son,' he'd said, his voice low and full of emotion. 'Go home and rest. You've lost much more tonight than I think I could bear.'
She'd found her voice again and begun to speak, but Hector turned to her and with sudden fury shook a clenched fist at her.
'Quiet!' he'd ordered her through gritted teeth, his voice harsh and unforgiving. 'I'm sick to death of listening to your ranting and raving! Shut up, you *stupid* woman!'
Stunned, she'd fled the room in tears. Hector had stared after her, shaking his head.
'That was too little and far, far too late,' he sadly told him.
He'd placed his hand on Johnny's shoulder.
'Go home son,' he'd whispered, his voice breaking with emotion. 'Take time to grieve for your daughter…and your wife, if you can ever forgive her.'

*

The small and cramped room with the single overhead bulb boasted a desk and chair, a worn examining couch, a narrow side table that prevented the door from opening fully and little else. Upon the table sat the distinctive yellow coloured bin that encouraged drug addicted prisoners to deposit their used syringe needles. An ancient eye chart adorned one peeling wall. Facing it on the opposite wall was hung an AID's information poster, upon which some wag had scribbled the legend in ballpoint pen, *I don't want to catch this AGAIN.*
The elderly police casualty surgeon examined Davie Crowden, probing gently with practised fingers at the tenderness of his ribs and turned to make a notation upon the form that lay upon his desk.
'There's little doubt,' he said over his shoulder to the uniformed sergeant standing behind him, 'that the ribs broken. I can't treat him here so he'll have to be moved to the hospital. And I'd see about that cough,' he warned his patient.
The doctor politely assisted him to shrug back into his shirt.
'And while you're at it,' winced Crowden at the doctor's touch, 'I'll want to make a complaint. A wee blonde haired bitch assaulted me tonight. Punched me and kicked me,

the wee cow!'
The doctor turned with a quizzical look to the sergeant, his glasses perched on the tip of his nose.
'Let me get this straight, Mister Crowden,' said the bulky sergeant softly and taking his cue from the doctors raised eyebrow. He leaned towards Davie as the doctor stood aside to discreetly pack away his examination kit, 'you're telling me that a wee blonde haired policewoman, and I presume you're talking about the arresting officer…a wee woman,' he continued, the sarcasm dripping from his voice, 'standing about five feet three inches tall, battered a big lad like you?'
Crowden stared at him with widening eyes and a sudden understanding. If word got out, he'd be a laughing stock, his street cred in tatters.
'It wasn't like that,' he stammered, 'I mean, I was injured like. She assaulted me when I was in a daze.'
'So, after killing a young mother and her toddler….'
'That's still to be proved!' he spat back.
'After killing a young woman and her child,' repeated the sergeant, 'a big lad like you was beaten up by a wee lassie. Is that what you're telling me?'
Without a backward glance, the doctor quietly left the consulting room and closed the door behind him; content not to be present when anything else was alleged. What he couldn't hear he couldn't repeat when cross-examined, was his way of thinking.
In the room, Crowden stared sullenly at the sergeant, suddenly aware that he was alone with the hulking brute and then turned his eyes away, his bravado failing him
'I'll say nothing more till I've seen my lawyer,' he mumbled, holding his broken rib as he spluttered again at the irritating cough.
The sergeant stood back and took a deep breath. He had been close, he realised, to punching this windbag right on his sarcastic mouth. He swallowed hard and turning away from Crowden, called for the two constables standing outside the examination room.
'Have this…hard man…. taken to the Royal Alexandria Hospital,' he instructed them.
'And don't forget to tell the nursing staff why he was arrested.'

*

Ian Morrison had driven past the accident in the old Vauxhall Cavalier, seen the flashing lights of the police, the ambulance and the fire tender, whose crew were using a thin water hose to damp down the skeletal remains of a smoking Ford Escort. But what had worried him most was the wreck of the Shogun, both doors lying wide open and the front smashed seemingly beyond repair. There was no doubt, he realised it was the same vehicle that Davie and Sammy had blagged earlier. He'd almost had a heart attack when the traffic copper had stopped him and given him the evil eye, convinced that he was getting a pull because of the poor condition of the heap that he was driving. But to his relief, the cop had other things on his mind and hastily waved him through the carnage, grimfaced as he indicated for Morrison to wind down his window then curtly telling him to drive slowly over the thick fire hose that snaked across the road.
He glanced about the people who were standing around, but of Davie and Sammy, there was no sign.
As soon as he was clear of the accident he drove straight to the old, rambling house in Cardonald, anxiously keeping one eye on the road and the other on his rear view mirror, his mouth dry and his hands shaking; watching for the tell tale blue light that he was sure

was coming after him.
At last, he arrived outside the house. He checked his reflection in the rear view mirror as he nervously licked his dry lips. This would be the tricky bit.
Pushing open the wooden gate, he took a few steps forward and was almost immediately blinded, raising a hand to protect his eyes against the brilliance of the porch light as a sensor switched it on.
He used his hands to smooth back his greasy hair and wiped his sweaty palms on the seat of his denim trousers. Then, with a shaky finger, pushed the electric bell.
He could hear the strains of '*Scotland the Brave'* being electronically played from the doorbell inside the house then, after a minute or so, an upstairs light came on.
Morrison took two steps back and tilted his head back to stare upwards as a window was nosily opened.
'If this is a fucking joke,' a deep voice growled at him, 'then I'll come down there and rip your throat out, pal! Do you know what time of night it is?'
'Mister Crowden, it's me, Ian Morrison. I need to speak to you for a minute,' he whispered.
'Who?'
He raised his voice slightly louder this time.
'Ian Morrison, Sammy's pal; there's been an accident.'
'Wait there,' ordered the gruff voice.
A few seconds later, the door was heaved open and Alex Crowden stood barefooted, his huge bulk covered by a white towelling dressing gown over navy blue, silk pyjamas. Despite being almost sixty years of age, the former boxer, standing a little over six feet tall, still retained the physique of the pugilist. Now completely hairless, his face bore the marks of his former trade; almost a hundred professional fights and many more that were fought outside the formality of the Marquis of Queensbury rules. His large hands, scarred and disfigured, hung by his side from arms that testified to his daily and punishing regime of weightlifting. He was, as many an opponent discovered, as tough as his Gorbals upbringing.
'I know you,' he growled, squinting his eyes as he inspected the nervous Morrison.
'You're the squirt that's been hanging about with my Sammy right enough. Right, spit it out. What's the problem laddie?'
Morrison gulped and apprehensively looked about him. He opened his mouth to reply when a voice spoke from behind the former boxer.
'What's going on, Pop?'
Mary Crowden, her cerise coloured dressing gown held tightly about her slim figure and her long, blonde hair falling naturally in waves upon her shoulders, appeared behind her father.
'No worries,' he replied in a soft voice. 'Go back to bed, there's a good girl.'
'I know you,' she addressed Morrison, ignoring her father's instruction. 'Ian isn't it?'
'Aye, Mary…Miss Crowden,' he corrected himself; suddenly aware of the sharp glance her father gave him.
'Come in,' she invited him, one hand on her fathers arm as she ushered him to one side.
Hesitantly, he stepped across the doorway, wiping his feet on the mat and following her into the front room. God, he thought, she's beautiful!
She indicated a chair and eased herself onto the couch.

Alex had followed them into the room, standing by the doorway. He stared curiously at the teenager.
'So laddie, what is it that's so important to get me out of my bed?'

When he'd finished his story, Morrison sat with his hands neatly folded in his lap. Try as he might, he couldn't take his eyes of Mary Crowden and the way she had draped herself across the couch, her dressing gown lying open just enough to let him see her long and shapely legs and the hem of what he guessed were pale blue cami-knickers. He guessed she was teasing him, that her pose was deliberate.
He knew Mary was about twenty-four, a lot older than him, but he didn't care. He'd heard whispered stories, that she had a bit of a reputation with the men, but that didn't bother him either. One thing he did know, glancing furtively at the huge man standing in front of him; nobody boasted about shagging her, not if they wanted to keep their balls intact.
'Are you bloody deaf or what?'
'Eh?'
Morrison realised with a frightened start he hadn't been listening; he'd been lost in thought, staring at Mary's legs and trying to see up her knickers.
Alex Crowden had quietly approached in slippered feet from behind and slapped him on the back of the head.
'I said, are you deaf or what? I asked you, do you know if my boys got the jail or are they on the skite?'
'I…I…I don't know, Mister Crowden. The police were everywhere. I nearly shit myself, begging your pardon Miss Crowden, because the car that I drove back was a wreck and I've not got a licence or insurance, if you see what I mean,' he tailed off in a squeaky voice, the blush creeping from his neck into his acne pimpled face.
'So, you didn't hang about, see if they needed a lift out of there then?'
The implication was obvious. He had bottled it, got away and saved his own skin, abandoned Alex Crowden's sons to their fate. Bloody hell!
'I never thought, what I mean is….'
His throat had suddenly become dry and his stomach turned over as the older man leaned across the top of him, his stale breath washing over Morrison.
'Hang on Pops, give the wee guy a break,' interrupted Mary with a thoughtful glance at the teenager.
She stood up then, the dressing gown falling about her and, to his disappointment, closing off his view of her legs.
'Where did you park the old banger, Ian? The car you came in,' she added, seeing his confusion.
'Eh,' his uncertainty was obvious, 'just on the road. Outside the house.'
She smiled tightly at him, her expression displaying the tolerance of an adult with a thoughtless child.
'Then it might be a good idea to get it moved, don't you think? If the cops *do* have my brothers, they might be turning up here, eh?'
A sudden realisation struck him and he swallowed hard.
'Right,' he said, scrambling quickly to his feet, 'I'll be away then.'

As Morrison drove along the narrow, poorly lit Tweedsmuir Path, he turned into Wedderlea Drive and glanced in his rear view mirror, mouth gaping open as he saw the bright roof lights of the police car stop outside the house. That settled any doubt in his mind. Davie or Sammy, or maybe both, had obviously been arrested.
'Well,' grinning with relief at his close call and thinking of Alex and Mary Crowden, 'at least they're awake.'

*

Father and daughter sat together, shocked at the news.
That Davie and Sammy had been arrested; that was never a surprise or that they'd been caught stealing a car; no surprise there either.
But locked up for causing the death of a mother and her daughter, a small child?
Well, that was a first, even for that pair of idiots.
'I'll get us a cup of tea,' sighed Mary, tossing her blonde hair as she stood up.
She was angry, fuming that the torn faced bitch of an Inspector and her puppy dog constable had broken the news and, without saying so, more or less accused Pops and her of being involved. Her angry thoughts turned towards her brothers. Just because those two tosser's were family!
She emptied the teapot with savage fury into the sink and banged it down onto the gas ring, furiously shoving the kettle under the fast flowing tap and splashing water across the draining board.
'No need to take it out on the kitchen,' her father said quietly from the doorway.
'Sorry Pops,' she replied, 'I'm just annoyed at that cow thinking she's so much better than us.'
Alex Crowden loved his daughter. Yes, well, he was fond of his sons too; for family was family. But his daughter held a special place in his heart. So like her mother God rest her, from whom, he never stopped thanking God she'd taken her good looks, but her brains? Mary had most definitely inherited her intelligence from him.
'Don't worry about her,' he motioned his head towards the front door and the since departed Inspector, 'she's just an uptight bitch doing her job. Forget the tea, love. Get yourself to bed. We've a lot to do tomorrow if we're going to get that pair of buggers out on bail. People to contact; things to do, okay?'
She nodded and smiled at him. With complete certainty, Mary knew where her father held her in the family pecking order, knowing he had placed more than just his faith in her ability. When push came to shove, she was far more dependable that those two wastrels he called sons. And when it came down to it, as it most certainly it would, she knew to whom the old man would eventually entrust his fortune. She smiled again and her father's heart beat ever so slightly faster, believing his beautiful daughter's smile was meant for him.
But in those briefest of seconds, Mary's mind had wandered, already calculating how she would beat her brothers out of their so-called inheritance.
She reached up and kissed Alex on the cheek, smoothing her hand over his bald head as she bade him goodnight.

When she'd gone upstairs, he walked slowly into the front room and poured himself a stiff whisky from the small cabinet. From a drawer in the same cabinet he fetched a small electronic diary, then with stubby fingers carefully typed in the code and opened the telephone directory. Scrolling through the index, he smiled as he reached the name he sought, then picked up the mobile phone and punched in the numbers.

*

Sammy Crowden sat on the concrete plinth that doubled as a bed, in his cell, his head still aching from the collision. He wasn't so much troubled at being arrested; hell, this wasn't the first time and it was a risk of the game when he was out blagging. What worried him were the additional charges the cops had spoken of, causing death by dangerous driving. He knew from reading the newspapers that there was a determined campaign to hand down heavy sentences for drivers who were involved in death collisions. If he was convicted, it could mean anything up to ten years. Even with remission for good behaviour, he could be facing a six stretch.

Yes, that was a definite worry, but the worse thing was, he hadn't been driving. That was down to Davie. He idolised Davie who had always looked out for him. But what he needed to decide now was, just how much loyalty did he owe his older brother?

*

CHAPTER 4

The following morning, the media frenzy struck Paisley police office like a whirlwind. The headlining death of a mother and her child, caused by two unnamed males reputedly driving a stolen vehicle, filled a huge gap where there had previously been a deficit of reportable news.

The officers within Paisley police station soon found themselves besieged by newspaper reporters and camera crews, but all refused to be drawn at the blatantly open and sometimes underhand questions asked of them, though more than a few were sorely tempted to communicate their limited knowledge of the inquiry in exchange for the currency notes thrust under their noses.

Realising that his inexperienced officers were being barracked and tempted by the reporters, the Divisional Commander hastily telephoned the media room at police headquarters in Glasgow and requested the immediate dispatch of a team of three trained personnel. Upon their arrival less than an hour later, the team hurriedly assimilated what facts were known and swiftly convened a press conference within the police stations conference room.

Yes, the Superintendent leading the media team agreed, *there were two unfortunate deaths but the names were not yet being released till relatives have been informed*, he coolly lied.

Privately, he knew that the husband was already aware, but agreed to the Divisional Commander's request that a stalling action be put in place to permit his CID to collect all the facts and pay their own visit to the bereaved Mister Bryce ahead of the press posse.

Yes, the Superintendent admitted to a local journalist, *two men have been arrested in connection with the incident and will appear later this afternoon at Paisley Sheriff Court.*

No, he regretted with frown, *the names of the accused would not be released.*

'Isn't it true,' ventured one enterprising reporter, 'that one of the accused is currently being treated at the Royal Alexandria Hospital for injuries sustained in the crash?'

The Superintendent balked at the question. The last thing he wanted was a wave of press descending on the hospital, bribing and cajoling staff to discover the identity of David Crowden. He turned to his civilian assistant and whispered that she'd to advise the duty

Inspector to get more personnel up to the casualty department, and pronto.
He watched as she left the table, then he prepared himself to tell yet another lie.
'No,' he cheerlessly smiled at the sceptical reporter, 'I've no knowledge on that'.

*

The duty casualty surgeon took the call from the hospital administrator at the nurses' station.
Silently he listened to the request.
'It's not my place to judge what he's done,' he replied to the caller, 'but in all conscience I can't release a man who might have internal injuries.'
The earpiece bellowed again in his ear and the nursing staff saw the normally placid doctor raise his eyes to heaven.
Davie Crowden, lying on the bed behind the curtain, one wrist handcuffed to the metal frame of the bed, stared morosely at the two constables who sat watching him.
'You dickheads got nothing better to do,' he sneered at them, 'than watch a man in pain?'
The exasperated voice of the doctor carried over to him and he became acutely aware that it was he who was being discussed.
'That's not my problem,' he heard the doctor say, 'if you're expecting trouble, you really should consider employing more porters rather than the three that we have to serve the whole hospital!' roared the doctor.
The sound of the phone being slammed down echoed throughout the ward and was intensified by the sudden silence that indicated the nursing staff had stopped work to listen.
The curtain was roughly drawn aside and the doctor walked into the cubicle. Both the officers startled, one reaching for his baton.
'Steady on,' warned the doctor with a half smile, 'it's not a rescue attempt.'
'Mister Crowden,' he addressed him, 'it seems that the *paparazzi* or whatever you might wish to call the local media, are seriously considering invading this hospital and this ward in particular. Consequently, my administration superiors,' he said, referring to them as though with a foul taste in his mouth, 'are suggesting you be released into the custody of the officers here. How do you feel about that?'
The two cops looked at each other in disbelief. This stupid bugger was giving Crowden the opportunity to decide if he wanted to go or to stay! Worse than that, the cushy job of watching him from a comfortable chair and being off their feet for a couple of hours was in danger of disappearing before them.
Davie stared at the doctor, a sudden hope seizing him. If he could remain at the hospital then he might be able to get away a lot easier. But then again, if he appeared at court this afternoon, Pop might be able to swing bail, particularly if Pop used his contacts of which Davie knew his father had many; and most of them by the short and curlies.
'If it's all the same with you, Doc,' he drawled with more bravado than he felt, 'I'll get back to my cell. I've got court this afternoon, I think and I wouldn't want to disappoint my public now, would I?'

*

Johnny Bryce hadn't been able to get into a deep sleep, but the old military habit of napping had taken over and his body had at least enjoyed some rest through the night.
He awoke early, beating the digital alarm clock and reached over to hush his sleeping wife. With a jolt he realised the other side of the bed was empty.

He remembered then. Karen was dead.
He lay for a few minutes taking it in, the previous night's horror. In one fell swoop, the loss of his family.
He'd come home and ignored the bottle tucked at the back of the kitchen cupboard in favour of a strong coffee. He recognised and accepted that he was in shock, a state of limbo, his mind trying to come to terms with his loss. There had been no tears; those he rightly suspected would come later in a private moment. Much later.
In truth, right now he felt nothing.
He made a decision. He would run hard for a few miles, pound the streets and let the route around the estate that he favoured, numb his mind; his personal antidote to pain, both physical and psychological.
From his wardrobe he fetched an old worn, navy blue tracksuit, the Royal Marine logo on the left breast fading from a hundred washings. Moving from his bedroom through into the small, hallway landing at the top of the stairs, he reached for the second bedroom door, his intention to glance through to see his sleeping daughter, but remembered with a jolt, his throat suddenly tight that Laura wasn't there; and never again would be.
Downstairs he slipped on his training shoes and left the house through the front door, pulling it closed and hearing the lock click into place. The bracing cold wind filled his lungs and his breath formed a cloud before him. Flexing his shoulders and arms he jogged slowly to the end of the road, allowing his leg muscles to unwind before putting them into serious overdrive. A few early morning drivers passed by, staring curiously and with some sympathy at the obvious madman who'd be putting himself through this kind of punishment before seven in the morning.
The huddled figure at the bus stop watched as he approached, the khaki coloured, ex-military style greatcoat with the wide collar and garishly purple replacement buttons that were fastened all the way to her throat; a multi coloured scarf wound round her neck and a bright yellow woollen bobble hat crammed on her head that completely covered her shiny, shoulder length, auburn hair and warmed her ears. The small leather backpack slung over one shoulder allowed her the freedom to cram her cold hands inside the deep pockets of the coat.
Since moving into her new house just over a month previously, Annie Hall had seen the muscular running man, as she had come to know him, several mornings in the past few weeks. Once or twice he'd courteously nodded a greeting and curiously, she'd been thrilled that he'd noticed her. She remembered clearly the first time she had seen him. Quiet and reserved, Annie was too shy to do much more than smile, berating herself later and wishing she could be more assertive. But how do you engage a jogger in conversation, she'd asked herself countless times?
She watched as he quickened his pace, his head down as his feet beat a steady drum against the pavement, causing a small splash of water to kick up behind him from the wet tarmac. She prepared herself to smile, but he passed by seemingly without noticing her. Disappointed, she turned to watch him, then visibly startled at the heavy groan of the diesel engine as the bus arrived to stop beside her, the driver with a huge smile on his dark face, cheekily grinning that he'd managed to surprise her.

The short bus journey to the train station at Gilmore Street, then the fifteen minute walk from Glasgow Central station to the Mitchell Reference Library allowed Annie plenty of

time to daydream about the running man.
Was he married, she wondered? Did he have a family? What did he do for a living? And more importantly, where did he live and could I perhaps meet him by chance, sometime? A hundred times she had imagined herself bumping into him, she the cool librarian, indifferent to his charms and he dumbstruck that he hadn't previously saw how attractive she was. What she would say to him or how she would reply to his greeting. She sighed, a little self-consciously and silently rebuked herself, knowing that she should be past fantasising like a schoolgirl; and her nearly thirty years of age!
The cleaners were just departing when she arrived, laughing among themselves and greeting her with smiles, teasingly asking in the manner of the middle-aged women that they were, if she'd found herself a man yet.
They liked Annie, they agreed among themselves; not like the rest of them stuck up sods that thought because they worked in a bleeding library they were the bee's knees.
She greeted old Jimmy, the stoic doorman at the Kent Road entrance, sitting as usual behind his work station, his once white chipped and stained mug standing in defiance of regulations on his desk, reading the early edition of the *Glasgow News*.
The headline screamed at her: *Mother, Toddler Killed by Stolen Car*.
'Dreadful news,' he waved the paper at her, for once showing uncommon interest in something other than the football news on the back page. 'And how are you this morning Annie?'
'Just fine, Jimmy,' she pulled off her woollen hat and shook her hair loose, clawing with one hand at the itch in her scalp the wool always seemed to leave behind.
'And yourself?'
'Ach, the arthritis is kicking in again. Time I got myself another new hip for the ceilidh dancing on a Saturday night at the welfare club,' he quipped.
With a backward wave, she pushed through the turnstile, climbed the stairs to her first floor office and hung her heavy coat on the rickety peg behind the door. Annie liked this time of the morning, believing that it gave her the opportunity to get most of her work done and to clear her basket of anything from the previous day. Small though the untidy office was, it belonged to her alone and the east-facing window that looked across the busy motorway below allowed plenty of daylight to stream in and fill the room with natural light.
'Morning,' greeted a voice from the door.
Sadie Parker, the senior librarian and Annie's immediate boss beamed a smile into the room. 'Time for a coffee?'
She followed Sadie to her own, larger and even untidier room and sat in the comfortable visitors' chair, watching as the older woman worked at the rickety side table, boiling the small kettle and preparing the two mugs.
'There's a budget meeting this morning in room two seven. Thought you might like to attend, represent the department,' she said casually.
Annie was surprised.
'Isn't that your prerogative?'
'Normally, yes,' Sadie slowly replied. 'But I've other things on my mind, at the moment,' she confided. 'My better half has suggested that as the kids are gone, we might consider moving to pastures new.'
'But…but I thought that you were here forever,' burst out a stunned Annie.

Sadie laughed, pouring the boiled water into the mugs, milked and stirred them and handed one to her.
'You're such an innocent, Annie Hall. Not everyone takes his or her work as seriously as you do. Some of us like to think there's a life out there away from all these dusty old files. I mean, who cares what family lived at number blah blah street in the year dot or whose uncle married their great granny a hundred years ago? For heavens sake, girl, think about it. There's a lot more to life than filing and farting about in Glasgow's ancient archived records.'
Annie blushed, damning herself for seeming so naive.
'Look,' began Sadie more softly, realising she had hurt the younger woman's feelings, 'the reason I'd like you to attend the meeting is because if indeed I do seek early retirement, and it's not confirmed yet,' she warned, 'then I'm considering recommending you as my replacement. How do you feel about that?'
Annie was taken aback. Promotion was the last thing she had considered.
'I'd…I'd like that…. very much,' she stammered.
'Well, that's settled then,' smiled Sadie, cupping her mug in her hands, 'the meetings at nine thirty. Choccy biscuit?'

*

Alex Crowden had been busy on the phone since the police had called to reveal they'd got his sons.
His first act had been to call in a favour. Well, not really a favour, he grinned mirthlessly to himself at the memory. More a reminder to the man on the other end of the line about the time, all those months ago, when he had visited one of Alex's brothels and got a little carried away.
He could recall the incident with stark clarity.
The panicked phone call late in the evening. When he'd arrived, he had immediately sensed the hushed atmosphere within the large flat on Churchill Drive, on the north side of the city. The scrubber that he employed as his Madam to run the flat, nervously ushering him through to the rear bedroom and the bloody scene that awaited him there.
Richard Smythe, he hated people calling him Dick, Alex recalled, had been naked, curled up in a ball in the corner, weeping and crying for his mother, his knuckles torn and bloodied.
Alex had found it hard not to curl his lip in disgust, punch his head from his sobbing shoulders.
The fifteen-year-old rent boy that had been found for Smyth lay face down on the bed, hands tied behind him with a dressing gown cord and his blood-soaked body bruised and beaten. A thin leather trouser belt, Smyth's it turned out to be, was wound round the boy's neck like a leash, further restricting his irregular breathing. The silver paper with the white powder Alex found; cocaine that the Madam later admitted was part of her own private enterprise and which she had sold Smythe and now lay scattered about the floor.
The Madam had been panic-stricken, fearing the boy might die. She deserved the beating Alex later had meted out to her, for punting the drugs without his permission.
With quick and precise instructions, he had organised the girls in the flat to remove Smyth from the room, clean and tidy him up in the bathroom, get him dressed and down to wait in Alex car.
He smiled when he remembered the painstaking time he had spent collecting the small

samples of blood and using the digital camera, a Christmas present from Mary, to record everything. The police forensic people, he later laughed, would have been proud of him. The boy had seemed so small, frail and helpless as he lay there, his breathing shallow and erratic. A good-looking boy, Alex had indifferently thought, with his long fair hair and lengthy eyelashes that were probably the envy of most women. His injuries had been bad, but not so terrible that an emergency visit to the casualty ward couldn't have coped with them.

But that would have meant questions and the police taking an interest. And Alex couldn't afford to have the filth prying into his business, certainly not at this crucial time.

Left alone in the room, smothering the boy with the bloodstained pillow was so very easy and convincing Smythe that it was he who had killed the lad had been a simple task. The stupid bastard had wanted to go straight to the cops, confess what he had done.

It had taken Alex almost half an hour to calm him down, his patience eventually overridden and instead forcefully settling that argument by reminding Smyth of his position, with particular emphasis on what any sentence would have meant to someone like him, his wife and family. Besides, the idiot wouldn't have lasted more than a few days in Barlinnie prison before…. well, some guys had their own idea of sexual partners, hadn't they?

Disposing of the boys' body had been a little more difficult, but that's why he had sons, wasn't it?

*

Detective Inspector Ronnie Sutherland was in a foul mood. A shouting match with his teenage daughter, who persistently left her bloody coat, bag and shoes all over the lounge floor and caused him to stumble and throw his coffee all over himself, didn't brook for a good start to his day. That and his wife, as usual taking his daughters side…. bloody women!

The car needed petrol. His wife had once again run the thing on gas fumes. Already running late, he had to queue for nearly ten minutes at the cashiers till in the service station on Neilston Road, behind the oldest and most senile guy he'd ever had the misfortune to encounter and who obviously still hadn't grasped the concept of using a Visa card.

Added to everything else, he'd heard the local radio news broadcast and already suspected what kind of nightmarish inquiry awaited him when he arrived at his office.

'Good morning Ronnie,' greeted his Superintendent from the door of the CID office.

'Heard the news then?' he asked, his eyes daring Sutherland to say 'no', his eyes mischievously dancing in his eagerness to drop the bombshell.

'Aye, it was on the radio, the eight o'clock news, boss. Tragic for that family,' he replied, his stomach already churning as he guessed what was coming next.

'We've two locked up and downstairs in the cells, Ronnie. I've spoken with the Divisional Commander and he feels, as I do, that someone with your experience had better handle the case.'

Sutherland stopped and stared at him, eyes narrowing and mouth squinting, suspecting there was something else.

'Right, boss. But you've got that evil grin on your face. Is there something that I should know, something about this case?'

'The two that are locked up. They're Alex Crowden's sons.'

Sutherland whistled softly through his teeth. Now that he didn't expect to hear. Of course, he knew of Crowden's reputation. Alex Crowden, uncrowned king of the Glasgow city centre brothels. Reputedly the owner, though not on paper, of a half dozen or so lap-dancing clubs and with a finger in a variety of other pies, all connected to the pub and club licensed trade or the sex industry; a veritable spiders web of a criminal empire. Like Crowden, Sutherland was a native of Glasgow and had also been born and brought up in the sprawling housing estate that was known throughout the land as The Gorbals; but there any similarity ended. Crowden he considered was the epitome of evil. It wasn't possible to be in the police service for longer than five minutes and not be aware of the far-flung reach of Alex Crowden. Through the years, more than a couple of cops had been found guilty of corruption charges in cases that all seemed in some way to be laid at the feet of Crowden.

Sutherland knew of old Alex own personal history. A hard man who had begun his career in the fifties, in the backstreet and highly illegal boxing circuit before graduating in the nineteen sixties to the more lucrative money-lending racket. Once he'd made a pile of money, he'd diversified into property. But the predominantly larger type flats he purchased hadn't been for re-sale or letting to families. No, Crowden had recognised the profit to be made from prostitution and turned his flats into brothels. Rumour had it he'd control of more tenement property than the Glasgow Housing Department. It also helped that he was often photographed at official functions in the company of local Councillors, some of whom sat on the licensing boards and who likely had their own and very private arrangement with Crowden.

Sutherland recalled a purge by the police on prostitution that had taken place ten years previously, when he then served as a DS in the Serious Crime Squad. Flats were raided, prostitutes and their punters arrested, statements taken. Then it was discovered that certain clients the ladies entertained included some so-called professional people, another name for members of the judiciary and at least one high-ranking police officer. Cases were lost, charges dropped and vital witnesses disappeared. A disgruntled colleague of Sutherland's had reputedly dropped the story one night over a pint to a tabloid reporter. It hadn't done much good. The reporter wound up in the Royal Infirmary, both legs broken and steadfastly refusing to reveal how he had come by his injuries, citing "press privilege".

'So you'll understand,' the Superintendent interrupted his thoughts, 'why we'd like you to personally handle this case, Ronnie.'

He nodded his head, knowing that senior management, and not just locally, would be taking a keen interest in this inquiry. A conviction wouldn't do his career any harm, either. Suddenly, Ronnie Sutherland's day had just got a little brighter. He smiled for the first time that day.

'Indeed sir, it will be a real pleasure.'

*

Regretfully, the same enthusiasm escaped Johnny Bryce. He had just stepped out of the shower and was towelling his hair dry when the news bulletin from the radio in the bedroom boomed out the arrest of two suspects in the tragic road accident that claimed the lives of a mother and child, though it neither named the two suspects nor Karen and Laura.

He stopped dead, wide-eyed and shocked, listening intently as the broadcast continued.

Arrests? Stolen vehicle? That can't be right.
He wrapped the sodden towel about his waist and hurried down to the lounge, switching on the television and turning to the twenty-four hour news station. The newsreader was in the midst of a budget story, but the scrolling ribbon at the bottom of the screen confirmed the radio item. This time there was a name. He read that two unnamed men were arrested in connection with the death of Karen Bryce and her three years old daughter. A stolen vehicle involved, the scrolling ribbon continued. Police were refusing to release further details and then forewarning to the viewer that a press conference would be convened on the hour.
He sat slowly down on the couch, the remote slipping from his grasp. The Inspector hadn't told him any of this, yet she must have known. But why not? Was there something he wasn't to be told? His mouth felt suddenly dry.
The clock showed nine am. The television news headlines began with a brief account of the accident from a dishevelled reporter at the scene, standing dramatically in front of a yellow taped off area that cordoned off the recently scarred and smoke damaged wall behind her. He watched as she tried vainly to hold an umbrella upright while brushing a strand of loose hair from her face. The camera panned over to the reporters' background where a uniformed woman police officer could be plainly seen bending down and placing a bunch of flowers on the ground next to others that already lay there. The camera swung back to the reporter, her eyes narrowing as she concentrated on the information that she was receiving in her earpiece. Without warning, the picture transferred to a uniformed police officer, a superintendent Johnny saw, flanked by a woman and a younger man in a suit, sitting behind a cloth covered table, the logo of the police prominently displayed on the wall behind them. The screen flashed a 'LIVE' sign on the top left hand corner and the buzz of the assembled audience settled down as the superintendent spoke. The microphone faltered and he missed the few introductory words.
Johnny listened t the broadcast, yet did not hear it; snatches of the statement breaking through his thoughts.
'…two men arrested…'
''No I'm sorry, the matter is Subjudice and their identities won't be revealed till they have appeared at court.'
'As I understand it, the relatives were informed last night.'
His head jerked up and an involuntary fury seized him. *Informed*? Half the story, more like!
The doorbell rung.
He walked to the window and sneaked a look through the closed curtain. Two men wearing overcoats against the slight drizzle of rain stood outside, a maroon coloured Nissan Primera parked by the pavement. The doorbell rung again.
He made his way through the small hallway and opened the front door a fraction. The older of the two men held a warrant card in his hand.
'Mister Bryce? I'm Detective Inspector Sutherland. Sorry to call so early, but I think it's important that I speak with you.'
Concealing his anger, Johnny nodded his head and opened the door further to permit them entry. He walked back into the lounge, the hallway too tight to accommodate the three of them standing together. The younger man followed his Inspector and closed the front door behind him.

'Give me a minute till I throw some clothes on.'
He climbed the stairs and threw on a clean pair of jogging pants and sweat top. He waited a moment, time to collect his thoughts and calm down. He realised that it would serve no purpose to begin a shouting match, not when he required information from the men downstairs.
The two detectives were still standing, their attention on the television, when he returned to the lounge. The live press bulletin had seemingly ended and the budget story was again being discussed. He switched the television off.
'I was just about to make some tea,' he offered with natural courtesy, indicating they should sit down, yet thinking he needed to time to take in the news broadcast and prepare himself for what he was about to hear.
He waited in the kitchen while the kettle boiled, preparing the tray and the mugs and forcing himself to be calm. His former training kicked in. The last thing he wanted was to lose it in front of these two guys.
'So, how are you?' began Sutherland, stirring the sugar into his tea and almost immediately regretting having asked such a stupid bloody question.
Johnny shrugged.
'A little surprised when I heard the bulletin this morning,' he quietly replied, staring at the detective. 'I wasn't told the car that had struck my wife's Escort was stolen. Even more surprised to hear that you've arrested two men.'
Sutherland exhaled quietly and slowly nodded his head.
'That was…unfortunate. The Inspector that was on last night, I know her. She's a decent sort. Stayed on after her shift finished this morning to speak to me personally, tell me the circumstances rather than explain it in a written statement. She also told me that she deliberately didn't tell you last night. Thought that it would be better you heard it later, so to speak, once all the details were known, rather than receive the bad news piecemeal. I'm sorry that we didn't get here before the press released the details. To be honest, I think we fucked up, if you'll pardon my French. Big time. It was a mistake not telling you right away, but I swear to you, it was done with the best intentions.'
Johnny's face remained impassive. What could he say? Who could he rage at?
He took a deep breath.
'The two men who have been arrested, what's their story?'
He couldn't fail to spot the quick glance that Sutherland gave his sidekick.
Sutherland stirred at his tea to give him time to think, a few precious seconds. He made his decision.
'Their names are David and Samuel Crowden. They're well documented with us, car thieves in the main but happy to turn their hand to anything that will earn them money. Davie is twenty-five, a nutter who will resort to violence if he has to. Sammy, twenty-two, isn't as hard a man as his brother, but follows anywhere Davie leads.'
He took a deep breath, wondering how far he should push this.
'Have you heard of a man called Alex Crowden?'
Johnny shook his head. The name meant nothing to him.
'Crowden is a major criminal in the Glasgow area. These two are his sons. The father has been known to the police for a long time, an ex-boxer turned brothel owner. A finger in every pie, so to speak. We've tried a few times to convict him, but intimidation is second nature to these types of people and we've had problems trying to get witnesses to speak

up. Personally,' he sighed, 'I believe they have a gene missing, they don't have the same emotions as ordinary people, no conscience; seem to see the general public as theirs to use and abuse.'
'But the two you have arrested. You have a good case against them? I mean, they'll go to prison for what they have done?'
'We've a good case, aye. The court will decide if they go to prison, Mister Bryce. But if you've been reading the papers recently, you'll know there's a strong campaign to increase sentencing for drivers who kill while committing a criminal act, either drink driving, drugs or, in this case, a stolen vehicle. So, to answer your question, yes, I firmly believe that they will go to prison.'
They sat in silence for a minute, the three of them.
'Is there anything we can do for you, Mister Bryce?' inquired the younger detective.
Johnny sat with his hands clasped tightly in his lap.
'Not that I can think of just now, unless….'
'Anything at all.'
'Perhaps you might keep me informed of any developments, anything that might affect the case. And when can I…' his voice faltered, 'make arrangements, for my wife and…. my daughter,' he replied, his throat suddenly dry and tight and for the first time feeling the overwhelming need to be alone to grieve.

Later in the car, as they drove to their office, the younger detective voiced his concern.
'Do you not think that maybe it *wasn't* such a good idea telling him about the Crowden's, their backgrounds I mean?'
'Can't see that it will do any harm now,' replied Sutherland. He blew his nose noisily into a well-worn but clean handkerchief. With a sudden realisation, the high profile of the inquiry became plainly obvious.
'After all, he's going to get a lot more information in tomorrow morning's papers when the tabloids find out this afternoon that's appearing at the custody court. But first things first. When we get back to the office, I want to see every piece of paperwork connected to the case, who the witnesses are and the like. I've had personal dealings with Alex Crowden and if he acts true to his previous form, we could have a problem with witnesses. I want this tied up as tight as an Aberdeen housewife's purse before he starts putting the hammer on anyone connected to the case. I don't want these two shit's to get off on any technicalities, understand son?'

*

Mary Crowden went to work as usual, that morning.
That those two clowns of brothers of hers had got themselves arrested was no more than of passing interest to her.
Her blonde hair tied back in a tight ponytail and held with a black, velvet ribbon and wearing a smart pinstriped suit jacket over her crisp white blouse and pleated suit skirt, she looked every inch the car sales executive that the title proclaimed on her laminated badge, pinned to the left breast pocket of her jacket.
Shame, she sighed, I'm wasting my talent working in such a shitty little dump like this place, she thought as she steered her new Mini Cabriolet from the short side street off Shettleston Road into the tight piece of uneven ground that served as the forecourt for Pat Delaney's Car Sales showroom.

Parking her car against the side of a lean-to shed, she picked her way cautiously across the roughly slabbed ground towards the Portacabin that served as the office. Once again, the cheap bunting that Delaney had put up to enhance the barbed wired topped chain link fencing that enclosed the ground, had come loose and trailed across the thirty or so vehicles parked in the yard. She gave a fleeting glance at the expanse of rocky waste ground behind the forecourt.
'If only he knew,' she stifled a grin.
She stepped between the puddles of stagnant rainwater, again thinking that it never ceased to amaze her Delaney managed to run a relatively successful business from such shabby premises. She glanced about her. Though second hand, some of his stock was almost new; first class quality vehicles that would not be out of place sitting in the showrooms of the more up-market garages further along the road. And, she had to grudgingly admit, he had a good turnover with the vehicles being sold on a regular basis. But the state of this place, she shook her head. What he needed was a business partner. And that, she smiled grimly, whether he knew it or not, was what he was about to get.
'Morning doll,' the voice called to her from the Portacabin.
She squared her shoulders and forced herself to adopt a smile.
'Morning Pat, how are you today?' she asked brightly with forced cheeriness.
'All the better for seeing you,' he leered at her, winking one rheumy eye.
Though most certainly in his late fifties, Pat Delaney continued to pretend he was just thirty-nine years of age. She knew he gelled back what remained of his thinning hair and, she suspected, used a mascara pen to darken the thick moustache that badly needed trimmed. Those vanities she could cope with, but what repulsed her most weren't just his crude sexual innuendoes or the constant brushing of his groin against her, nor even his 'accidental' wandering hands. What really turned her stomach was the large amount of hair that protruded from his bulbous red nose, its colour a testament to his alcoholism and his frequent visits to the grotty little WC where she knew he constantly kept a half bottle of neat vodka hidden in the loose cistern; that, she inwardly shuddered, and his halitosis.
Mary sat down at her desk and slipped her jacket off, lacing it on the chair behind her. She smoothed back her hair with both hands, deliberately, thrusting her breasts forward as she did so.
'Might be getting a wee bit of business today,' he stood over her, watching as she removed the plastic cover from the keyboard of her computer. 'Had a guy in late last night, thought he might want another look at that Astra estate in the back.'
'That's good news,' she simpered. 'Do you have the keys to the safe?'
'Oh aye,' he tossed her the two heavy brass keys. Catching them in both hands, she smiled her thanks as she laid them on her desk.
'And how's your Pop these days?'
'Keeping fine', she replied, then realised that he'd soon hear the news. Better impart it herself, make it seem like she was taking him into her confidence.
'Had a bit of bad news last night, though,' her brow furrowing as though in worry. 'Our Davie and Sammy got themselves locked up,' she sighed. She didn't believe it necessary to impart that the crime had included the theft of the Shogun.
That was all the opportunity that Delaney needed. Before she could say more, he was standing behind and over her, bending down and rubbing her shoulders as if sympathy, his hands stroking gently downwards, edging towards her breasts.

Above her his eyes opened wide as he stared down her cleavage, seeing the full white roundness of the top her breasts straining against the cups of her brassiere.
Inwardly she winced, aware that his groping could never arouse her. His hands continue to slowly caress her shoulders, moving slower towards her cleavage and she felt nauseated, unable to look at him. But it was all part of the big picture Pops had reminded her. After all, this was one of the reasons she was here, working for him.
Just play him along, he had told her; let him think he's your type. But even Pop could not suspect that Delaney would never be her type.
As he leaned forward, she could feel the warmth of his bad breath on her neck. She almost giggled out loud. The old fart!
She waited her moment. Just as he was ready to slip his skinny hand inside her blouse, she felt him press himself against her back, his breathing a little faster and knew that he was becoming aroused. Right, she finally decided, that was enough for today.
Ignoring of his state of excitement, she exhaled and stood up sharply, causing him to jump back, his erection visible through his cheap nylon trousers.
'Ah, well,' she said with what she trusted was a sad smile, 'boys will be boys, I suppose.'
He turned away from her, trying discreetly to lift a leg and adjust his trousers.
Mary walked over to the heavy floor safe and bent over to open it, aware she was tightening the material of her skirt and displaying her neat little bum. If the old sod doesn't have a heart attack after this, she grinned mirthlessly to herself, then I'm definitely doing something wrong.
The safe swung open and she reached in for the day's paperwork and stopped dead.
She stared at the wooden board with its neatly labelled sets of car keys. Suddenly it hit her. A chill passed through her and her face went pale.
The car key that she had provided Davie with, the key to steal the Shogun. If they were caught at the time of the accident, it must still be in the ignition of the jeep. If the cops realise that it's a true key and the owners still has his, then they'll come here to inquire how Davie came to have the one he stole the jeep with!
And that, her heart sank, will lead them straight to me!

*

The duty Inspector at Paisley police office had rightly assessed the attention that the death of Karen Bryce and her daughter Laura would draw.
The fine old and imposing two-storey building, with its balconied Roman Doric loggia and situated in St James Street just off the town centre, had served as the Paisley Sheriff Court since 1885. Recently refurbished and brought back to its former glory, the fine old lady now found herself once again besieged by camera crews and photographers, hoping to get a glimpse of the monsters that had slain the young mother and her child. Local broadcasters vied with each other for a suitable position to encompass the backdrop of the building, discreetly using small, hand held mirrors to check their countenance prior to appearing on camera. Photographers jostled with each other while the reporters' nipped across the road to the much-used watering hole where the liquid golden refreshment was measured in quarter gills.
At last, the custody court list was published and in a quiet corner of the gents' toilet, a discreet ten-pound note changed hands. 'The one you're looking for,' whispered the nervous court usher to the journalist, 'is case number 05/2609 and it's set to appear before Sheriff McInally about two-forty p.m.'

But the court usher had no particular loyalty to any one reporter and the word soon got round that both accused in case number 05/2609 were to be brought to court in a closed police van. In the age-old game of competition, the photographers shrugged their shoulders at each other in despair, pretended that was that and there was nothing further to be gained by hanging about. Then, as one, they all sneaked round the back to the yard where the van would arrive, hoping against all odds to get a couple of snaps anyway.

The sombre atmosphere inside the public court, where the reporters and public alike sat impatiently waiting, was tense. Within his private chambers and as was his custom; the diminutive and sharp-nosed Sheriff McInally sat upon the large wine coloured leather sofa, his short legs dangling just above the floor as he contemplated what he was about to do, glancing once more towards the door, as if seeking assurance that his black robe still hung on the large brass hook behind it. His best horsehair wig sat upon a mannequin head, combed in preparation and recognition of the number of gentlemen of the press who were likely to be present; a recent gift from his dear wife.
Checking his wall clock against his fob watch, he dressed in his robe and wig and adopted his most severe frown, inspecting his appearance in the full-length wall mirror as he prepared to receive the usher who would escort him to his court. Satisfied with what he saw, he pressed the bell on the wall to indicate his readiness and left the anteroom. Preceded by his usher, the Sheriff slowly and sombrely made his way through the ill lit but ornate corridors, acknowledging with a nod the few staff who stood to one side as he passed, their heads slightly bowed in deference to his status. Arriving through his personal entrance into the custody court, the Sheriff discovered a large number of relatives of the many accused who were to appear before him that day, as well as an impressive array of press in the court, all of who stood respectfully upon his arrival.
He settled himself in the comfortable chair upon the raised dais, the imposing Monarch's Seal of the Crown prominently displayed upon the wall behind him. As the usher bade the assembled court be seated, the Sheriff fussed over his paperwork, situating his pens and notebook squarely upon his desk and prepared himself to deal with the cases before him, but well aware they were of little real interest to anyone. No, he knew, the real interest was in the two accused charged with the theft of the vehicle and subsequent slaughter of the mother and her child. He dabbed at his nose with a cologne infused handkerchief and once again privately regretted that for all the money spent on refurbishing the building, the dank and cloying smell remained.
With a discreet nod of his head to the usher, he instructed the first case to be called.
As the afternoon progressed, one by one the cases were disposed of.
The tall, slightly stooped Procurator Fiscal Depute reading the charges against each accused who in the main, were aware that if they pled guilty that day, would be immediately dealt with or, if they tendered a plea of innocence, a court trial date was set for a future time. Dependent on the severity of the allegation, each accused were either released on bail or detained till time of trial.
The mood of the court changed and a tension seized those present, their anticipation evident. Case number 05/2609 was dramatically called and the Crowden brothers were escorted in through the side door that led directly to the court from the cells, a uniformed police officer at either side.
Handcuffed to each other, both wore bandages on their heads. Davie shuffled along,

grimacing as though in pain, theatrically massaging his broken rib with his free hand and ignoring the buzz of whispered conversation from the public gallery. Neither brother glanced about them, but held their gaze on the bewigged and wizened figure of the elderly Sheriff, who sat high above them.
Word had got out then, Davie surmised.
As though visibly hurting, he staggered slightly against Sammy. Only he knew that there was no real pain, other than a dull ache, but considered it in his best interest to adopt the pose of the martyr, a point that was not missed by the assembled press, many of whom furiously wrote in their notebooks.
The court usher bade them stand before the Sheriff. The PF Depute stood upright from his table and glanced at the charge sheet in his hand, reading aloud the details of report in a high-pitched voice.
As if suddenly realising whom the PF was, Sammy stared open mouthed at Richard Smythe, a past memory of him sitting dazed in his Pop's car; a body wrapped in an old carpet. He turned wide-eyed towards Davie, his mouth open to reveal who the PF was when Davie sharply nudged him in the ribs to prevent him speaking; the warning immediately clear. *Keep your mouth shut!*
Blissfully unaware of the peril, Smyth continued. The charge, he intoned, was one of theft of a motor vehicle and the subsequent murder or culpable homicide of Karen Bryce and Laura Bryce.
As he sat down, the silence that followed was in itself, deafening.
A minute passed while the Sheriff, head bowed low, continued his note taking.
'How do you plead?' asked the Sheriff finally, his head still bent over as he made notations upon the pad in front of him.
'Not guilty,' the brothers mumbled in unison.
A murmur spread round the benches of the press.
The Sheriff glanced up, his eyebrows raised.
'For the defence?'
A thin, poker faced man, grey hair slicked back, gold rimmed bifocals perched on the tip of his hawk like nose and likewise dressed in wig and court gown, stood from a side table and coughed politely, as though determined to attract all attention within the court..
'Mister Mathew Gordon for the defence, M'lud.'
The reporters again scribbled frantically in their notebooks, writing the names of the accused, excitement mounting as they acknowledged that these two weren't any ordinary teenage tearaways, but the sons of a powerful underworld figure in the local crime scene. The names of their victims were hastily added to their shorthand notes, as was that of Mathew 'Gospel' Gordon, so nicknamed for his predilection to quoting the Scriptures in his defence of his clients and who was to represent the accused Crowden's. Shit, they realised almost as one, this is excellent copy!
One reporter, sure that his editor would want every detail and sick of the smug bugger constantly catching him out, turned to a female colleague.
'The guy reading the charges, the PF. Do you happen to know his name?'
'Oh aye,' she grinned impishly, 'that's our "Depute Dickie", Richard Smyth. Just don't call him Dickie to his face, though,' she warned. 'He doesn't like that nickname.'

*

He knew he should feel something. Anything. Less than twelve hours ago he had lost his

most precious possession. His family. Both gone. Dead.
But he was numb.
Was this shock? Or was it that his time in the Province had made him so insensitive; inured him to natural feelings?
He hadn't stirred since the detectives had left. It was as if he couldn't move, the sense of loss denying him the ability of motion.
He stared at the framed photograph that sat upon the small table; Laura, nine months old and crawling towards him, her face a picture of happiness, one arm outstretched and fingers in the act of wiggling to grab at the camera, her laughter evident even in the still of the photo.
A lump formed in his throat.
How had she died?
Had she been awake or asleep? Had she cried out when the stolen vehicle struck the Escort? Please God, she didn't suffer.
He blinked rapidly; trying to stave off the first of the tears that escaped his eyes.
A sliver of sunlight streamed through a crack in the curtain of the lounge window and the warmth beat upon his face. A second tear rolled unchecked down his cheek.
His lips began to tremble and he gritted his teeth against the flood that he knew was coming. But he couldn't prevent it. His shoulders shook uncontrollably as he sobbed, lowering his head onto his chest, his hands still tightly clasped in his lap.
He wanted to move towards the photograph, have something to hold, something that he could see, and something to….
No, he needed no reminder of his daughter. She was where she always had been and where she always would be.
In his heart.
It wasn't till later, much later that he realised.
When the guilt set in.
He hadn't given Karen the same thought.

*

CHAPTER 5

There was a stunned and surprised silence in the court when Sheriff McInally was requested by the Crown to grant the Crowden brothers bail. With a grim face he beckoned both the Fiscal Depute and the defence counsel, the equally bemused Gospel Gordon, forward for consultation.
'You are of course aware of the gravity of these charges, Mister Smythe. Am I to understand you are arguing that the accused be released on bail?'
There was no mistaking the bleak caution being issued by the Sheriff.
Richard Smyth swallowed hard, the phone threat from Alex Crowden still ringing in his ears.
'I don't care how you do it, but get my lads released…or else!'
'Yes, Milord,' he began, his argument already prepared, 'we know that both accused have fixed addresses and it is unlikely that they will abscond from these charges. I believe it is in the public interest that they be released in order to facilitate further inquiries by the investigating officers. Their detention might inhibit the inquiry; place the police officers under undue stress to complete their investigation within a short time

limit. There are, I believe,' he hesitated praying that the old sod wouldn't push it, 'other issues to consider.'
The aging Sheriff stared hard at him. In his water, he knew something wasn't right, that something was being kept from him. But in fairness, if what Smyth said was correct and the police had other matters to investigate and that the detention of these two reprobates would hinder that investigation, then he was duty bound to cooperate.
He shrugged his shoulder in annoyance. He turned to Gospel.
'I presume you do not intend to argue this motion?'
'I defer to my learned colleagues wisdom', smirked Gospel, still not sure what Smyth was up to but happy to accept the credit that would inevitably follow, when old Alex Crowden learned that his wayward sons had been released on bail.
The Sheriff stared hard at Smyth, watching the PF Depute squirm under his steely-eyed gaze. With a resigned sigh, he lowered his head and began noting the details in his book.
'Very well, Mister Depute, on this occasion I will accede to your request.'
He motioned with his hand to attract his clerk's attention, effectively dismissing Smyth and Gospel.
'Bail is granted,' he barked at Davie and Sammy, 'with the usual conditions. Now gentlemen,' the court hushed, all eyes turning towards the Sheriff who poked a bony finger at the Crowden's, 'I warn you in the strongest possible terms. The charges that you both face are most grave. I would *strongly* advise that should you fail to either cooperate with your bail conditions or in anyway hinder or obstruct the on going inquiry….' he paused for effect, aware that a hush had descended upon the court, 'then I will have you both brought before me and I shall *not* be lenient.'
Without waiting for any kind of response, he effectively dismissed them both when he raised his head and barked, 'Next case!'

*

Ronnie Sutherland took the news with ill grace.
'You're kidding me on,' he stared incredulously at his Detective Sergeant. 'They two murdering bastards got bailed? But we've not had the chance to parade them for a possible identification from the Shogun's owner!'
He sat down heavily in his swing chair, shaking his head and trying to work out what possible motive the PF might have for not opposing bail. Like other officers, he had heard whispers about Richard Smyth, but presumed them to be little more than tittle-tattle; the continuing enmity that usually existed between the police and the Procurator Fiscal service, upon whose instruction they were required to act in law. Still….
'Well, that only makes things that more difficult for us. The Crowden's have a reputation for intimidating witnesses. First things first,' he launched himself from his seat and strode into the corridor, beckoning the DS Kevin Wilson to follow him.
'Get yourself up to the Shogun's owner's house. I don't care what he's up to or where he is, bring him down here and obtain a statement from him and have it tape recorded.'
Wilson was about to protest that surely a written statement would suffice, but Sutherland cut him short.
'I know what you're going to say, but if I'm right, old Alex Crowden will already have the guy's details and working on a plan to cause him memory loss. That's why I want his statement on tape so that if he tries to back out of it for any reason, he can explain why to a Sheriff.'

'What about the key that was found in the vehicles ignition? I was supposed to be following that up?'
'Leave that and I'll have someone else deal with that. Just get to that witness… and fast.'

*

The early editions of the evening press headlined the Crowden brothers release and most tabloid papers carried photographs of them both, pictures that had been obtained when the brothers had previously appeared at court hearings.
Alex Crowden angrily crumpled the *Glasgow News* in his huge hands and threw the ball into the mock Tudor fireplace.
Davie and Sammy sat together pensively on the couch in front of him, silent and waiting on the wrath that was about to descend upon them. Davie consciously holding his arm across his broken rib in a vain attempt to stave off any physical retribution his father might be considering. It wouldn't be the first time their father had used to fists to put his point across.
Alex rose and strode to the large window and gazed out at the neat lawn and flowerbeds. Strange that even this early in the year, the daffodils were beginning to bloom. His wife had loved the garden but try as he did, he just couldn't keep it as neat and tidy as she could. The old tree needed trimmed too, casting its shadow across the lawn and likely stopping the sun from drying out the grass. Maybe time to consider getting someone in, a pensioner perhaps on a weekly basis. Would be worth twenty or thirty quid a week, he mused, to keep it shipshape.
He didn't turn around, but continued to stare out of the window.
'You're the oldest, Davie. Perhaps you might want to explain exactly what happened?' he asked, his voice quietly controlled.
Davie swallowed hard.
'It was my fault, Pop. The job went tits-up as soon as we got the car door open. The guy in the house must've heard something because suddenly, he's hanging out of his window screaming down blue murder at us. We took off and I thought we'd got clear. I drove along the back roads, but got a bit lost. The next thing I know is I'm coming out of a side road and there's this old Ford Escort in front of us. Couldn't help but hit it. Lucky we weren't killed,' he finished lamely, his mouth suddenly dry and his breathing spurting in short gasps. For effect, he leaned over and winced, again hoping to remind the old man that his ribs were hurting.
His father didn't turn round and ignored the pretended sigh of pain. Pain, he remembered, was being in some two bit hall with a makeshift boxing ring; bare knuckle and up against a guy that intended beating you to death and knowing if you didn't win, that's what was going to happen. And I always won.
'You killed a woman and her kid,' he spoke softly, continuing to stare out of the window. 'Three years of age she was, the wee lassie; according to the television reports.'
The silence in the room was oppressive. Sammy sneaked a glance at his brother. He needed a pee, but no way was he moving; no way was he going to attract Pop's attention. With a sudden sigh of relief, he realised that Davie was taking the blame. So he should, he thought bitterly. Stupid bastard might have got me killed.
'How good a look did the owner get at you two?'
Davie looked at Sammy and shrugged his shoulders; coughing as he did so and feeling the acid stomach bile rise to his mouth.

'It was dark. He couldn't have seen that much, maybe a couple of shadows.'
'Maybe isn't good enough, son. Maybe could get you heavy time in the jail.'
Alex run a large hand across his bald head.
'Anyway, that's been taken care of so there's no problem there.'
Davie's eyes narrowed and he licked his dry lips.
'You've had him seen to Pop?'
'Aye, it's been done. A favour called in,' he added. No need to say more, he decided. The less these two clowns knew the better.
What he didn't believe he needed to explain was that another number in his diary was followed by an early morning phone call to a nervous secretary employed at the Procurator Fiscal's office; a young lady whom he had reminded about her previous occupation and the services she provided to paying gentlemen. A previous occupation that had it become known to her employer that would undoubtedly result in her swift and immediate dismissal from her current post. He had savoured the thought of her squirming in her office when he had asked the favour, a favour she could not nor would deny him. The return phone call ten minutes later, from a telephone kiosk he presumed, had supplied him with the name of the Shogun owner that was listed on the charge sheet, details which he had then passed to an old and reliable friend, who visited the owner before he left his home for work.
'So, what do we do now, eh lads?'
A silent Davie knew that this was what his father had waited for, the opportunity to once again prove to his sons that Alex was the big man; he run the business and that they could never fill his shoes.
A wave of anger passed over him. His brother waited for Davie to respond, afraid if he made any comment then Pop would round on him and subject him to the usual verbal humiliation.
'Anything you can do Pop, anything at all,' said Davie, his teeth clenched and hating himself for his climb down. 'Sammy and I would be grateful. Wouldn't we Sammy,' he turned to his brother, glaring at him and silently urging him to agree.
'Oh aye, Pop. Anything at all,' agreed Sammy, nodding vigorously, the smirk on his face betraying his recognition of Davie's humiliation. No fatted calf for you now you big bastard, he thought.
Alex continued to stare out of the window, but now with a tight smile playing about his lips.
'Just leave it to me boys. Your old Pop will see you right.'

*

The phone call from DS Kevin Wilson caught Sutherland chomping through a bacon roll and sipping at a mug of sweet tea. Wiping his mouth, he listened as Wilson related the witness had already left his house for work and when tracked down at his office, refused to attend at the police station. The witness insisted the uniformed officer had been mistaken, that he'd not seen the faces of the two men, that they had merely been shadowy figures getting into his vehicle.
No, he replied to the DI's question, the witness refused to budge on the issue. Wilson added the witness stated quite firmly that he couldn't identify the two men.
'Has he been got at?' asked Sutherland.
The pause in the line, he guessed, was Wilson thinking about it. Sutherland knew that his

DS wasn't the brightest bulb in the box, but slow as he was to make a decision, equally any decision he did make would be with careful deliberation of the facts he had to hand.
'I believe so. Aye,' he finally decided, 'He's lying. Wouldn't look me in the eye, kept wringing his hands together and his Adams apple was working overtime; and he kept licking his lips. Yes boss, I think he's been got at. Do you want me to go back and put it to him, that he's been threatened?'
Sutherland took a swig of cooling tea and again wiped his mouth with a paper napkin.
'No, leave him be for now. We'll let his conscience work at him. According to the note I was left by the nightshift CID, his wife seemed a right decent sort of woman, so will likely know the truth; that is if we're assuming he's already told her the original story. What we'll do is leave him for a few days then visit him at home, probably in the evening when she's there. Try and speak to him when she's present. If again he denies being able to identify these two, he can do it in front of her. Maybe that'll provoke a reaction from her, particularly if we press the death of the child and leave her to pressurise him.'
He thought of his own domestic situation and sighed heavily.
'There's nothing like a nagging wife to either make a man turn to drink or come clean.'
'What do you want me to do now, return to the office?'
'You were originally to follow up the inquiry about the key in the ignition, weren't you? Do that. Get over to….'
He placed the mug down and scrambled among the paperwork on his desk.
'Pat Delaney's Car Sales. According to what I'm reading here, it's located in a side street off Shettleston Road, over in Mount Florida in the east end of Glasgow. Do you know where that is?'
'I've got wee Maria Lavery driving, so provided I don't get involved in a pile-up…'
Sutherland smiled at the expletive in the background from the outraged young detective.
'Keep in touch,' he instructed Wilson and then grinningly added, 'and tell Maria to try and stay on her side of the road, for a change.'

*

DC Lavery parked the Nissan Primera on the roadway in the narrow street, outside the metal gate that seemed to be the entrance to waste ground that apparently served as the forecourt to Delaney's Car Sales. She stared at the uneven, puddle-ridden ground and shook her head, immediately regretting wearing her new sling backs to work today.
From their car, the detectives could see a man inside the squat, metal Portacabin that presumably served as the office. A blonde haired woman, seemingly a sales rep, was standing beside and demonstrating a green coloured Vauxhall Astra to a customer.
Wilson noticed the woman looked very attractive and he wasn't sure whether the male customer was admiring the car or her. Carefully, they picked their way across the uneven ground to the Portacabin.
The detectives were unaware that Mary Crowden, smiling coyly at the customer, had already seen them and figured them to be coppers.
'Can I help you good people?' Delaney smiled broadly at them from the door of the office, his wide smile as fake as the tan on his face that Lavery could see ended just below his shirt collar.
Wilson flashed his warrant card.
'CID from Paisley. We're looking for the owner. Would that be you?'
'Pat Delaney,' he offered one hand, beckoning them into the office with the other and

anxious to get them both out of sight of the curious customer. Police and second hand cars, he knew from bitter experience, weren't a particularly good mix.
Wilson refused the offer of both coffee and a seat and briefly explained the circumstances of the previous night's accident. It didn't escape his attention that after mentioning the Shogun, Delaney seemed to be extremely nervous.
'The witness and owner of the Shogun have told us that he purchased the vehicle from you three weeks ago. You have the records of that transaction, I presume?'
'Oh, they'll be here in the paperwork,' he waved a hand at the cardboard box files that stood regimented upon a shelf against the back wall and above the heavy, black square safe that sat on the floor.
'Was there something in particular you were looking for?'
'The owner told us that when he took possession of the vehicle, there was only one set of keys. Given that the Shogun is less than two years old, isn't that a little strange, just one set of keys?'
Lavery saw the smaller mans' eyes narrow.
'Let me check the sales document,' he replied and turned towards the shelf.
'The customer for the Astra…oh, I'm sorry Pat. I didn't realise you were with customers,' smiled Mary from behind them, one foot on the step and both hands on the doorframe. The position caused her body to arch forward in the doorway, thrusting her beasts against the thin cotton blouse, a stance that couldn't be ignored by Wilson.
By his side Lavery's nostrils flared. She recognised the calculated move and immediately formed her own opinion of the sales rep. Tart!
'Ah, Mary,' replied a relieved Delaney. 'These good people are from the police. It's to do with the theft of a vehicle that we apparently had in stock what, two or three or three weeks ago?' he turned quizzingly towards Wilson.
'Three weeks,' smiled Wilson, unconsciously standing upright, now beguiled at the sight of the really attractive blonde woman.
Mary returned her most enticing smile, ignoring the lipless cow that stood behind the tall detective.
'Let me see what I can dig up from last months file,' she simpered, reaching up and with exaggerated difficulty, dragging one of the files from the shelf.
Wilson moved forward to help her and placed the file on the desk.
Lavery grimaced at Wilson's obvious distraction by the blonde sales assistant and glanced at Delaney. She was surprised to see a thin bead of sweat had broken out on his forehead.
Now why, she thought curiously, should such a simple request provoke such a worried reaction?
'Ah,' said Mary, turning the pages of the file and apparently finding what she sought, 'here's the date we took possession of the Shogun from the car market. So, what was it you wanted to know?'
'How many sets of keys came with the vehicle when it passed through your hands?'
Mary exhaled nosily through perfectly glossed lips, flashing her even white teeth as her pink tongue whipped across her upper lip.
'I really can't recall,' she slowly replied. 'Sets of keys are not something that we would normally record in the file. What I can say is that there would be no need for us to hold onto spare keys.' She shrugged as if the issue was unimportant to the business. 'Any sets

we have we usually just hand to the customer. How many did the customer tell you they received?'
'Just the one,' replied Wilson, standing so close to her he could almost feel her warm breath on his face.
'Then it's likely that's all we would have,' she responded with another dazzling smile, snapping the file closed and knowing full well that this dizzy cop would be satisfied with the answer now that she had him, at least literally, by the balls.
'Right then, I'll just note the previous owner's details and we'll be out of your hair,' replied Wilson brightly.
Lavery stood silently, her rage contained behind a blank face. She saw Wilson was obviously smitten by Mary.
Bloody men! Bloody *stupid* men!

They walked in silence to the car. Savagely, she turned the key in the ignition and roared away into the line of traffic, incurring the wrath of a bus driver who slammed on his brakes and sounded his horn.
He could sense she was annoyed or angry with him
'Whoa, Maria! You trying to get us killed?'
She slammed on the brakes and steered the car into a parking bay, then turned on him.
'I can't believe you fell for that blonde bimbo's wee schoolgirl act. Jesus, Sarge! You're supposed to be a flaming detective! Did you not pick up on what she did or was your brain lodged somewhere in your nether region, at the time?'
Shocked, he stared at her. This wasn't the quiet Maria that he knew and usually liked to work with.
'I don't have a clue what you're talking about.'
'Too fucking right you don't,' she barked at him, her derision made worse by the fact she didn't normally use foul language.
'The file,' she continued patiently, concentrating on her driving but with the sarcasm dripping from her words.
'She opened the file at the Shogun's sale receipt. She wasn't in the office when we discussed the case with Delaney and we *didn't* tell her that the car we'd come to inquire about was a Shogun! So, answer me this. How would she know?'

He watched the detectives drive off, then turned to her.
'There were two sets of keys, Mary,' said Delaney, his eyes narrowed in suspicion as he stared at her, daring her to deny it. 'I remember the car. It was minted, in beautiful condition. I'd even thought about hanging onto it for my own personal use. And I remember that there were two sets of keys, because they had been kept together by one of those wee plastic cable ties. I had to cut the cable tie with a knife because the keys were so closely bunched together and it was awkward using them that way. So, Mary, why did you lie to the cops? You must've known there were two sets and why didn't the buyer get the two sets from us?'
She smiled at him, a tight smile without humour. She'd waited on this opportunity for months, her chance to set about this skinny little prick!
'I don't think that an explanation is really necessary, do you Pat? I know you will have guessed that my brothers were caught in the Shogun and we both know they used the

second key to steal it. You got a good price for the car and the new owner will get paid out by his insurance Now the thing is, given that I know so much about your business and the scams that you've been working with the VAT, is it really in our *mutual* interest to start worrying about these wee hiccups, eh? The only losers in this are my brothers, they got the jail for car theft; so is there any need for you to worry yourself?'
'And that woman and her kid. Don't forget them!' he blustered, feigning anger.
But she saw right through his indifference to someone else's suffering. She kept her voice calm and folded her arms, raised her chin and stared back at him, daring him to challenge her.
'Nearly six months I've worked for you Pat. Six months of your fondling me, trying to slide your hand inside my blouse and brushing against me with your wrinkled Willie, hoping to get into my knickers,' she hissed at him.
'Well, no more. I know too much for this to go on. So listen to me,' she crossed the narrow distance between them, her face now inches from his; close enough for him to feel her hot breath.
'My Pop has a vested interest in me working here and he's been waiting for the chance to have a wee meeting with you. A wee business meeting, so to speak. So tonight's the night, Pat,' she hissed in his face, her eyes blazing and her spittle causing him to blanch. 'I'll be making a telephone call to set it up. Keep yourself free, Pat. And don't even think about speaking to the cops. About anything, okay?'
He blinked rapidly, and then slowly nodded. Alex Crowden's fearsome reputation was well known. His dread of Alex outweighed any outrage he might have had about her treatment of him. His shoulders slumped as he realised he didn't have the courage to argue with her.
Patting a loose strand of hair from her face, she backed off and turned away from him, her domination of him complete. Calm now, she turned again towards him, dazzling him with her smile, once again the businesslike and professional sale representative.
'Now, shall we discuss the terms that the customer out there has proposed for the Astra?'

*

His jacket slung carelessly on the chair behind him, Ronnie Sutherland chewed at a pencil end and listened patiently to Kevin Wilson's account of his visit to Delaney's Car Sales. Wisely, Wilson thought it better to omit being smitten by the blonde sales assistant and revealed her knowledge of the Shogun as a post observation noted by Lavery, rather than a gaffe by him.
'So, where's Maria now?'
'Err, she's phoning the Inland Revenue business department to ascertain this woman Mary's full details. Try and establish if there's any connection with the Crowden brothers.'
The door knocked and Lavery entered without invitation. Sutherland saw her face was flushed and her eyes bright.
'Shoot!' he told her.
Without looking at Wilson, she glanced at the scrap of paper in her hand.
'Delaney the owner and two staff, one of whom is part time and seems to be employed cleaning the cars and,' she paused and looked up at Sutherland, 'Mary Crowden.'
Sutherland glanced sharply at Wilson. His gut instinct told him he wasn't getting the full story, but time would tell.

‘One other thing, boss,’ continued Lavery. ‘The guy that I spoke to at the Revenue told me Delaney’s business had been of interest to them for some time now. Seems his tax records don’t correspond with the stock he moves through the place. They haven’t given it any priority, citing the usual ‘too busy with other things’ excuse, but would be grateful for anything that we might turn up. Also said if they can help, maybe use his records as leverage, we only have to phone and they’ll cooperate.’
Sutherland nodded his head.
‘Good work you two. At the moment we’ve no proof that Mary Crowden gave the key to her brothers,’ he sat back and placed his hands behind his head, ‘but it doesn’t take a genius to work out the scam, there. No way will those two burst to her being an accomplice, so at the moment, we use it simply as intelligence to build up the bigger picture.’
He sat forward and rubbed his chin thoughtfully.
‘Let’s see what we have. The two Crowden brothers will have to attend an ID parade or Sheriff McInally will have them banged up for non cooperation of the bail condition, but the only witnesses we have are the two cops who caught them in the Shogun and, with the way things are at the moment, police evidence in court is losing credibility with the juries. And if Gospel Gordon follows his own track record, there will be the obligatory allegation of police assault against his clients to counter as well,’ he sighed.
‘On the plus side, the Shogun’s owner…’
He waved a hand at Wilson.
‘I know, I know. The guy’s refusing to ID them right now, but time and maybe his conscience will be on our side there.’
He glanced at his notes.
‘Tentative forensic evidence indicates their blood and fingerprints inside the vehicle, so they’ll be hard pushed to deny that evidence.’
He sat back in his chair; his shirtsleeves rolled up to the elbows and placed his hands behind his head.
‘What we need to decide is do we settle for the two Crowden’s that we can probably convict or go for the family of three, try and tie their sister Mary into the charges by colluding with her brothers by providing the vehicle key?’
His face light up in a huge grin.
‘By God, that would certainly be a catch and no mistake, putting that bastard…sorry, Maria…putting old Alex whole family away.’
He exhaled slowly, his voice now sombre.
‘Perhaps the strongest point we have on our side is the death of the mother and child. Public opinion is outraged. God, you’ve only got to see the morning headlines to realise what an effect this is having on the general public. Hopefully, by the time this gets to trial, it will still be fresh in people’s minds and by that I mean the jury. I hate to say it, but the best evidence we will have is the scene of crime photographs showing those two poor souls in the car.’
He drummed his fingers on the desktop then came to a decision, slapping both hands down on the desk.
‘Right now, Kevin; I want you and Maria to trace the Shogun’s history since manufacture. Obtain a statement if you can that the owner who sold the car to the car market, did so with the two sets of keys. Pursue a line of inquiry through the market and

try to establish the keys going from the market with the vehicle to Delaney's Car Sales. I want to establish a line of continuity for the Shogun and hopefully, the keys. We might consider charging Mary Crowden with being an accomplice and colluding with her brothers to steal the Shogun; particularly if we can prove she worked there when the vehicle, with two sets of keys, passed through the place and the current owner only got one set with the car. If not, then we can at least sow a seed of doubt in the mind of the jury as to her involvement and that,' he grimly smiled, 'should help to at least get these two sods convicted.'
Tapping the pencil against his teeth, he continued.
'If the PF won't accept a charge against Mary of aiding and abetting her brothers, then it should prove interesting if we summon Delaney and her as witnesses and she turns up on the prosecution list against them, eh?'

He nodded to them in dismissal. Right now he had a telephone call to make and instinctively knew that no matter how he told it, Johnny Bryce would not, could not, accept that the killers of his family were now out and, at least for now, free.

*

Johnny's boss at Garvey's Superstore, a prematurely retired cop, had heard from an old colleague about the crash and called to offer both his condolences and any assistance that he could provide, making it clear that he valued Johnny both as an employee and friend. He gratefully declined the assistance but grudgingly accepted the offer to take off as much time as he needed. An awkward conversation became suddenly tense when his boss remarked bitterly about the two arrested brothers being bailed by the court.
'What does that mean?' he asked, a tightness grabbing at his chest, inwardly fuming that the police had reneged on their promise to keep him updated.
'You didn't know?'
'No, nobody told me. So, what exactly does it mean?'
His boss paused, fearing he had somehow let something slip; then explained that the accused were free till the time of the trial, provided they complied with the bail conditions.
'Conditions usually mean staying away from witnesses, living at their known address, compulsory attendance at an identification parade, providing forensic samples like blood, DNA, that sort of thing,' he finished lamely, his mouth suddenly dry. God, he thought, why should it be me having to explain this to Johnny?
'Look,' his boss stressed, 'it doesn't mean anything. It just means the police have further inquiries to make and by having them in the jail, it puts a time limit on the inquiry. They'll still get convicted, believe me.'
'But surely if they were caught at the scene, surely that means the evidence against them would be…' Johnny searched for the word, '…overwhelming.'
'In theory, yes, but courts can be fickle when it comes to evidence, son. In my time, I've seen guilty men walk free and don't forget here in Scotland we have a thing called Not Proven.'
'What's that?'
He listened as his boss blew noisily through the phone, trying to work out the easiest way to explain it.

‘In short, an accused can be found either guilty, not guilty or, if the jury can’t come to a decision about his guilt or innocence, there’s a third decision they can deliver. Not Proven. Simply put, it means there isn’t enough evidence to justify convicting an accused. This kind of decision has been the subject of a hell of lot of discussion through the years. It sometimes means an innocent man walks free, but the stigma of guilt hangs over him while a guilty man, who also walks free, is out laughing at the system. It’s a cop-out decision and lets an undecided jury off the hook; eases their conscience, so to speak.’

‘Can it be appealed? I mean if new evidence is found?’

‘No. Once a decision has been made at court, the accused can’t stand trial on the same charge again. Sorry, Johnny. I know this isn’t exactly what you need to hear at the moment, but if my mate is correct, these two bastards are done out of the park. They were caught in the stolen car after….’ he paused again, ‘after the accident. I don’t see them getting away with anything. And don’t forget, if you’ve been reading the papers or watching the TV, the media are out to crucify them.’

Numbly, Johnny nodded at the handset.

‘Anyway, boss. Thanks for phoning…and for your concern. I don’t know when I’ll be back…’

‘Don’t you worry yourself on that account, Johnny. Just get…. things dealt with, and get your head together, son. This place will still be standing when you and I are long gone. One more thing, just before I go. It won’t be too long before the reporters will have your name, Johnny. Prepare yourself for a knock on the door. Some of these parasites think they have a God given right to intrude on people’s grief. If I were you, if you have somewhere else to go, even for a few days maybe, then think about it eh?’

Johnny replaced the handset and stared at the TV. Reaching for the control, he switched to the twenty-four hour news channel and waited for the local news summary. He didn’t have long to wait.

The reporter, her face solemn, confirmed what his boss had told him. The two men who had killed Karen and Laura were free, bailed at the Paisley Sheriff Court earlier that morning.

Savagely, he grabbed a warm winter jacket from the hallway cupboard and stormed out of the house.

A hundred yards down the street was too far for Johnny to hear the urgent ringing of the telephone call from DI Ronnie Sutherland.

*

Annie Hall was unusually nervous at the budget meeting, sure that the dozen or so others in attendance must be watching her, studying her and assessing her as a likely candidate for the job. They must know, she thought biting her lower lip. Nervously, she fidgeted with her notepad, dropping her pen that then decided to roll under the large polished desk and beneath the feet of Miss Brogan, whose sole responsibility for the previous twenty years had been the preservation of historical council documents.

‘Well, really!’ she complained as Annie scrambled between the older woman’s legs to recover the errant pen, choking back a snorting laugh when she saw Brogan’s spindly legs encased in thick woollen tights darned with odd colour threads.

When you’re quite ready, Miss Hall,’ boomed the voice of the Director.

'Sorry,' apologised Annie, pulling herself to her feet and somehow managing to noisily bang her head on the edge of the table. 'Sorry,' she repeated to the collective sighs that impatiently waited while she resumed her seat.
The meeting droned on for almost an hour, but only one thing occupied Annie's mind. Promotion.
Her fingers danced across the notepad and, as she later explained to her boss Sadie, she tried to listen intently, but hardly heard a thing; her mind racing with the news that Sadie had imparted earlier. She had not given it any previous thought, but now that the possibility had been raised, realised that her latent ambition was stronger than even she had believed.
Of course, she knew she could do the job. Hadn't she stood in or deputised for Sadie on numerous occasions? No, that wasn't a problem. Her ability and knowledge of the department and its contents was unquestionable and the equal if not slightly superior, she reluctantly admitted, to that of her boss.
No, the problem was her lack of confidence in her own ability.

Returning to the privacy of what now suddenly seemed to be a small and cramped office, she heaved a sigh. Her problem, she knew, was that her ability had *always* overtaken her ambition.
Only now, and particularly with Sadie's recommendation, there was a real likelihood she could achieve what previously she had only dreamed of.
Head of her own department. The opportunity to make positive change, structure the department to her own system, a system that she knew would be both cost effective and more productive. Not that Sadie wasn't doing a good job she thought, not wishing to seem disloyal to her friend.
Perhaps I should start putting things down on paper, prior to an interview she mused?
'How did the budget meeting go?'
Startled, she turned and saw Sadie smiling at her from the doorway.
Annie reached anxiously for her notepad. What the hell was discussed, she frantically tried to recall?
'Same old, same old,' she grinned back to cover her confusion, a red flush spreading across her cheeks.
'Old McGonagall still boring the knickers off everyone and moaning about wastage and electricity bills, then?'
Annie sighed and her shoulders slumped.
'To be honest, Sadie, I was only half listening. When you dropped that wee bombshell on me this morning, everything else just seemed to take a back seat.'
Sadie laughed loudly.
'If that's the case then Annie, you're obviously well suited to this job. I don't think I've ever fully taken in anything that was said at one of their meetings. They'd bore the paint off the walls, so they would, particularly that old goat McGonagall.'
It didn't help any when Annie recounted the episode of trying to recover her pen and joined with Sadie's hysterical laughter when they both agreed that it was likely that Annie had been the first thing between the prim Miss Brogan's legs for a very long time.
Sadie turned to leave then stopped.
'I hope you do apply for the job, but give it some thought. There's more to running the

department than me popping in and out, offering coffee to my staff. Some of the administration can be a real headache and though we get on well, there's some among us that I have to deal with that, outwith this department, I normally wouldn't speak to, let alone anything else. But you,' she grinned again, 'you're just the sort to get on with everyone. If you do go for it, I'll get hold of an application form for you, okay?'
Annie nodded, her face lighting up with pleasure; thrilled with confidence that Sadie believed she was capable of running her beloved department.
Alone again and smiling to herself, she turned back to her desk and began the laborious process of dealing with the correspondence in her in-tray.

*

The Black Bear Grill and Restaurant, associated with the large chain of pub and restaurants throughout the United Kingdom, lay situated on the high ground that bordered the entrance to the former Calderpark Zoo at the eastern approach to Glasgow City and adjacent to the start of the M74 motorway. Its location is a handy meeting place; a venue easily found and much visited by weary travellers en route to Glasgow. A place where they can relax and refresh prior to business meetings or be accommodated if business overtakes their timetable.
The bar and restaurant was almost empty of customers when Pat Delaney arrived; just a few weary souls celebrating or commiserating on the day's commerce and one or two regulars from the nearby housing estate.
The young, smiling waitress offered to show him to a tale, but he brusquely declined, preferring to first visit the bar where a double Bells whisky brought a warm glow to his stomach and quelled the uneasy apprehension that had begun when he arrived.
A huge paw like hand descended on his shoulder, startling him.
'Good evening, Pat. Long time no see, eh?'
Alex Crowden, smiling broadly, wearing a tight fitting grey suit that barely fitted his barrel chest, his bald pate reflecting the overhead lights, stood behind Delaney with his right hand proffered.
Crowden's daughter Mary, the Ice Queen, as Delaney now thought of her, stood to one side, a curious but patronising smile on her face.
Ice Queen or not, with her blonde hair piled high on her head and wearing a smart, two piece skirted business suit, even Delaney couldn't deny that she looked stunning; cold fish that she might be, he thought bitterly.
He shook Alex hand, inwardly wincing at the older man's strong grip.
The waitress, attending to Alex Crowden's raised hand, appeared and smilingly announced their table was ready.
Mary led the way; her svelte figure manoeuvring between the tables in a willowy way and attracting the attention of the few males' present, attention that abruptly ceased when the dour faced Alex caught their eye.
Both men stood courteously waiting by their chairs till she sat down.
Without preamble, Alex ordered steak for everyone and, smiling paternally at the waitress, instructed her to bring a good bottle of red. As she walked off, his attention turned to Delaney.
'Let's get down to it, Pat. I want to be your business partner.'
With a sinking feeling in his stomach, Delaney had already guessed as much, but the statement still took him by surprise.

'I'm not ready…. not really wanting or needing a partner Alex,' he stammered.
'Course you do,' replied Crowden with a soothing smile that Delaney thought was about as genuine as a shark inviting him for a swim. 'Think of the opportunities that your wee business's affiliation with me would bring. For a start your…. frankly I hope you don't mind me saying this… your two-bit company would get a real injection of cash; help out with your VAT problems too. Maybe let you do up that hovel of a place you're using as an office. Think of it. A real purpose built office and showroom. Concreted display area for your stock rather than the ploughed field you have at the moment,' he laughed with gusto. 'Jesus, Pat, I could sow potatoes in that forecourt, the amount of dirt you've got there the now. And lets face it; that Portacabin! My God! How do you manage in the winter? My wee girl here,' he reached across to stroke Mary's unresisting and beautifully manicured hand, 'tells me she was always having to wear her winter knickers, it was that cold.'
He stared hard at Delaney, who saw immediately an ominous and fearful change in his demeanour.
'But maybe you know all about my Mary's knickers,' Alex whispered savagely, his tone now threatening. 'She tells me that you've been trying to slide your hand down there for some time now, eh? And you a married, family man!' he scoffed.
Delaney swallowed hard. It had all been a set-up, he realised now. The bitch had led him on all that time. It was all a game to her, a con to trap him into submission before this big, evil bastard!
Across the table, Mary stared at him, her eyes wide and glassy; willing him to argue or protest so that she could watch her father hit him, hurt him bad. Make the little shit weep and moan!
Her heart was beating a little faster, her breathing more pronounced as she imagined her father beating the skinny bastard to a pulp. With a start, she realised that right now, here in this public place, she wanted nothing more than to watch Pat Delaney be viciously beaten. The idea amused her and she squirmed slightly in her seat, surprising even herself at how much the thought had excited her.
Delaney leaned slightly forward; the throbbing in his head had now become a jackhammer pounding at his temple. His throat was dry and his chest ached. He clenched his hands tightly together under the table, to stop them shaking. He knew he had been stymied; there was no way out. Refusal would mean more trouble, both personal and professional, than he could possibly handle and Pat Delaney had nobody to turn to. Nobody who would even consider going up against Alex Crowden and his mob. He was beaten and the best he could hope for was getting out of this situation with as much of his capital as he could protect.
The waitress returned with the opened bottle of red wine.
As though nothing was amiss, Alex chatted to the young girl, delighting her with his attention, helping her sort out the three short-stemmed glasses and consoling her when she accidentally spilled a few drops of wine on the pristine tablecloth. He watched her stride away with a smile and thoughts that were definitely not paternal.
He turned his attention back to Delaney, his steely eyes boring into the beaten man.
'So Pat, what I propose is a merger between our two companies, as it were. I've caused some background valuations to be done on your place and, with stock and land, estimated the value at four hundred grand.'

Delaney baulked.
'I'd have said nearer half a mill, Alex!'
Alex inwardly smiled. One pence or one pound, the hard part was done. The little bugger had capitulated. All it needed now was some shrewd negotiation and the ball was most definitely in Alex Crowden's court; his ball, his game.
'Lets say,' he paused, pretending he was considering a better offer, 'that I inject two hundred grand into Delaney's Car Sales as the… how shall we put it? The silent partner; and then slide another twenty-five grand under the table that the taxman won't see. Plus I wouldn't object to the company retaining your name with you managing it on a day-to-day basis and my interest being purely financial. How does that sound to you?'
Delaney thought it sounded like shit, but he was over a barrel. Mary knew far more about his business and VAT scams than was healthy and his wandering hand about her body was more than enough excuse for Crowden to assault him or worse! And, God forbid, if his wife found out, particularly after that last time with the previous sales assistant, then the divorce court would likely take away his business altogether.
Christ, he inwardly moaned, shrinking into his padded seat, what a bloody choice.
He sighed heavily and reached across the table to offer his hand to Crowden.
'Okay Alex, it's a deal. Two hundred grand for a partnership and twenty-five under the table. I'll speak to my accountant tomorrow.'
Crowden, a broad grin on his face, shook Delaney's hand and winked conspiratorially at Mary.
'Great,' he said, 'here come the steaks.'

She waited till they'd been on the road nearly ten minutes, but her curiosity finally overcame her.
'I know the land behind his place is important to you, but you've never told me why; never took me into your confidence.'
She didn't mean for her voice to sound bitter and it wasn't her intention to provoke an argument with her Pop, but after having put up with that old fart Delaney for all these months, she believed she was entitled to some kind of explanation.
He nodded his head and turned to smile at her, a smile of deep satisfaction for a job well done.
'You're right of course, sweetheart. The car sales place is just a front for what I really intend. The money I'm paying Delaney is just what I'd call a wee investment.'
'Isn't two hundred grand and the extra twenty-five more than you were prepared to pay, I mean for a half share of that shit-hole?'
'Not really,' he replied grimacing at her language. But he accepted she had a right to be annoyed. He should have told her earlier, he realised but he feared she'd let it slip and confront Delaney, bait him before Alex was ready to reveal his plans. He slowed the car, his attention concentrating on avoiding a group of teenagers that danced drunkenly across London Road in front of the evening traffic. Two of the lads, no more than sixteen or seventeen, stared hard at him, daring him to be provoked and looking for any excuse to exercise their toughness by attacking anyone that faced them down. Alex ignored them and sighed heavily. The days of the Glasgow hard man were long gone. Now it was teenage junkies and drunks hunting in packs. He turned to face Mary as he drove past the jeering youths.

'Because what I'm really paying for is the whole company. Our Mister Delaney believes that my cash is purchasing a half partnership. What he can't possibly know and won't learn until I'm ready is that within three months, he'll be eased out of the business and I'll have the whole company. As far as Delaney's Car Sales is concerned, it's a two-bit concern of junk. No, my dear, it's the land I want, that's where the real value is.'
He tapped a stubby forefinger against the side of his nose to indicate his association was of the utmost secrecy.
'I happen to know from my contacts within the council that a large private housing company is paying a lot of interest in the plot behind Delaney's and are closing a deal to purchase it, as we speak. They're keen to begin developing the land for construction and I know they'll need vehicular access for their heavy machinery and suchlike.'
He glanced with indifference in the rear-view mirror at the sneering, two-fingered salute from the pock-faced youth; but he wouldn't forget his face. Just in case. Smirking, he watched with pleasure as the youth fell heavily, narrowly avoiding being struck by the van travelling behind Alex.
'Now,' he explained patiently, 'to get to that land behind Delaney's, they need the access through the ground where the Car Sales sits and Delaney's plot will eventually become the main access road into the new housing estate. My contacts in the council tell me that the builders *might* be prepared to go as high as one and a half million for the land that Delaney's currently occupies,' he finished with a wide grin.
He stopped at a red traffic light at the intersection of London Road and Springfield Road, applied the hand brake and turned to face his daughter.
'So you see my dear, my little pay out to Pat Delaney isn't so much a good deal for him as a probable fortune for me.'

*

The Force Support Officer behind the wooden and glass counter at Paisley police office suspected the angry looking man with the white face, tight mouth and pinched nostrils might be trouble. Standing with her back to him, she shielded the telephone as she whispered her suspicions to the detective who answered her call. He told her he would inform Mister Sutherland and suggested she have Mister Bryce take a seat and inform him the DI would be right down.
Johnny stood impatiently staring at the notice board with its posters of smiling cops, patting school kids on the head and urging the public to turn in wrongdoers. He'd seen these types of advertisements before, but more usually with the free terrorist hotline emblazoned beneath in large, black type. A sudden flash of memories crossed his mind.
'Ah, Mister Bryce,' Sutherland greeted him, stepping from the lift with one hand holding open the metal door and waving him forward with the other.
Johnny scowled at him, nodded in greeting and strode through and stopped, waiting to be led to wherever the DI took him.
The FSO had heard his name being called and, with sudden understanding, now realised who the angry man was. No wonder he looked pissed off she thought, though not unkindly.
Exiting at the first floor, Sutherland led Johnny in silence along a corridor where uniform and plain-clothes officers shuffled between rooms, some carrying paperwork and all with their heads bowed low, making it easier to avoid looking at the pale-faced man. They

knew who he was and guessed why he'd come. He couldn't know that, to a slightly lesser degree, they sympathised with him and also felt his anger.
Sutherland pushed open a door and walking behind his desk, beckoned Johnny to have a seat in front of it. Johnny closed the door behind him and sat down.
'Can I get you anything? Coffee, tea perhaps?'
'An explanation would be preferable,' he curtly replied. He'd already decided a shouting match with the police would be useless. The courts had released the two bastards, not the cops. But that didn't excuse them from informing him, giving him forewarning and in no uncertain terms, he told Sutherland so and reminded him of his promise to keep Johnny informed.
'I did phone, but there was no reply. Maybe you were already on your way here,' the detective suggested. Sutherland had dreaded breaking the bad news to Johnny, but this was worse. At least by phone, he wouldn't have had to see his face and that last thing he wanted was to be provoked into an argument with this guy that he privately agreed, had every right to be angry.
Johnny's rage abated as suddenly as it had risen. Instinctively, he believed Sutherland had called. He slouched forward on the hard wooden seat, his hands clasped in front of him.
'So, what happens now?'
He glanced uneasily at Johnny, wondering just how much he could say without the younger man exploding here in his office. He decided to be straight. God knows, the man deserved at least some explanation, some truth out of this murky business.
'Cards on the table?'
Johnny nodded warily. He knew he wasn't going to like this.
'It's a waiting game. We prepare a more in-depth case for the PF and the defence go all out to rubbish what we put forward,' he told him.
'You'll know of course that the two accused belong to…. frankly, a successful criminal family. Their father Alex Crowden has been giving us the run-around for years, but always evaded conviction, usually with some other patsy taking the blame It's the same old story, Mister Bryce….'
'Johnny. I'd prefer Johnny.'
Sutherland smiled grimly.
'Then I'm Ronnie. And Johnny, you have to understand this. I'm on your side.'
'Anyway, to continue,' he clasped his hands together and narrowed his eyes, preparing himself to recount a long and difficult story.
'What I'm about to divulge could get me into serious trouble with my gaffers, so I'm trusting you to take this on board in confidence. Do we understand each other?'
Johnny nodded. He'd heard this kind of warning many times before, but not for a very, very long time.
'The witness who owns the Shogun that was involved in the incident. He's retracted his statement. Now claims that he won't be able to identify the two men that stole his vehicle.'
'But why would he do that? Surely he must know what the consequences of the theft were; the death of my family.'
'Course he does,' replied Sutherland with a deep sigh, 'but we think that the father, Alex Crowden has had someone put the frighteners into the man. Either threatened him or his

family. Despite that, however, we believe that in the end he'll come round. Tell the truth as it were. He's a good man, we feel sure. But the Crowden family are way out of his league. They're a menacing bunch right enough and to someone who has no experience of that type of violence, it must be terrifying to have them approach you, let alone threaten you.'
'So, you feel confident that the witness will tell the truth at court?'
'Yes, I do,' replied Sutherland with more conviction than he actually believed.
'But why were they released from court in the first place?'
'That, I'm afraid is a more difficult question to answer. We, the police that is, had requested a remand on the grounds we had further inquiry to make. The Depute Fiscal,' he glanced at his papers as if to again confirm the name that he already knew, 'Mister Richard Smythe has not opposed bail on the same grounds; that is we have further inquiries to make.'
Johnny was puzzled.
'Okay, I accept I have a layman's knowledge of the law, but that seems to be at cross-purpose to me. You both agree the police have further inquiries to pursue; yet he goes against your recommendation for bail? Is that not a contradiction of you working together on the same case?'
'I can't explain it Johnny. I've no idea what was going through his mind.'
'Don't you people speak to each other?'
Then a sudden suspicion crossed his mind.
'Or could he have been got at as well? As the witness was, I mean?'
Sutherland's face remained blank. The same doubt had crossed his mind, but a PF Depute being nobbled? Not unheard of, but still….
'Unlikely,' he slowly replied with less conviction than he felt, 'but for what it's worth, my boss is making an official complaint to the PF's department as we speak.'
'But in the meantime these two murdering sods are out an about?'
'That's the sad fact of it, I'm afraid.'
Johnny let his shaking head drop slowly, his mind reeling at the thought the Crowden brothers were free. Free to laugh, enjoy their life while his wife and daughter….
'Is there anything more you need from me?' he asked, rising from the seat.
Sutherland quickly got to his feet.
'There's the matter of formal identification.' He swallowed hard, trying to remember the phrases that he had been practising all morning, yet the lump in his throat betrayed his anxiety.
'You must understand that your wife and daughter… the fire was all consuming, I'd strongly suggest that you….'
'I'd still like to see them,' Johnny raised a hand and interrupted him. 'I've had experience of this type of injury before…. Ronnie. And besides, I need closure. I have to convince myself that they're really gone.'
Sutherland nodded, unwilling to look Johnny in the eye. He reached down and lifted some papers from his desk, mechanically shuffling them as he cleared his throat.
'I'll contact you, probably tomorrow morning and have one of my lads collect you from your home. Take you to the mortuary for the official ID. If that's all right?'
'I'll await your call,' replied Johnny and, to Sutherland's surprise, held out his hand.
'Thanks for what you and your people have done, so far. I know it can't be easy for you

either. I'm sure you must have families as well.'
Sutherland shook his hand firmly, then watched him leave.
He vowed silently that if he didn't convict those bastard Crowden brothers, it wouldn't be for the want of trying. By God it wouldn't!

*

The cafe discreetly tucked away within the small shopping precinct off Broomfield Road in Glasgow's west end was known locally for its fine coffee and hushed conversation. The surrounding residential area was a bastion of decorum and civility and the nearby shops, unusually for Glasgow, had no need to armour their windows at night with the obligatory steel shutters favoured by their city centre neighbours.
The waitress approached the two well-dressed gentlemen sitting within the rear both and asked if they required anything further?
Alex Crowden gave her a mischievous wink and requested two further coffees and a cake for his guest, turning to his companion with questioning eyes.
Gospel Gordon patted his stomach and raised his hands in mock surrender.
'No more for me, Betty,' he said with a satisfied smile, 'I'm supposed to be watching my weight. Another coffee will be just fine.'
Once again left alone, the two men resumed their conversation.
'So, given that the car owner is unlikely to testify to identifying my boys, what are their chances?'
Gospel sighed heavily and sat back, removing his hands from the table as Betty laid the coffee before them. When she departed, he stared straight at Alex.
'I've had a quiet word with Smyth, the PF Depute who'll likely be prosecuting the case and though he hasn't had the full report from the police laboratory, it seems that there is sufficient blood and fingerprint evidence to place both Davie and Sammy in the vehicle. The two arresting cops will undoubtedly speak to dragging them both from the wreck and that will tie up with them being in the car at the material time of the crash. I hesitate to say it, but the Shogun's owners statement is hardly the lynch pin to convict them; there is sufficient evidence otherwise.'
'So it comes down to the forensic evidence and they two cops saying it was my boys in the motor then?'
'Basically, yes. Provided of course that they don't do anything silly, like admitting the charges or getting caught interfering with witnesses.'
'And if the forensic evidence was…. unavailable?'
'Then it's down to the eye witness credibility of the cops,' Gospel slowly replied, his eyes narrowing with suspicion, a slight chill overtaking him as his mind envisioned the lengths that Alex Crowden was prepared to go to defend his family. Gospel couldn't imagine what Alex was conceiving in that devious head of his, but whatever it was, he wanted no part of it. Nonetheless, he felt obliged to counsel him.
'I have to warn you, Alex. You hinder the case and the polis will be all over you and your family like a bad rash. You know how they get when they think witnesses or their inquiries are being interfered with!' he hissed.
The caution was clear. If there are underhanded dealings, he was warning Alex in clear and unequivocal terms; don't get caught.
Alex nodded in understanding. Gospel was a good brief, but there was a limit to what he was prepared to know about his clients' involvement in the cases in which he represented

them and a definite limit in what Alex was prepared to reveal; not even his hold on Smyth, the PF depute.
'There's a further problem, one that you don't yet know about,' whispered Alex, leaning conspiratorially forward. 'Our Mary provided those stupid buggers with the key and the police will probably have found it in the ignition.'
Gospel tilted his head backwards, stared for a few seconds at the smoke stained ceiling and slowly exhaled. This then, he realised, is the real reason why Alex had called the meeting at such short notice and more to the point, away from Gospel's chambers where none of his staff could later speak to seeing them meeting together. The crafty old bugger! Of course, he had always known or at least ha his suspicions that Mary was the apple of her father's eye and this proved it. Alex would sacrifice a lot to get his boys off, but everything to protect Mary.
He sat forward, his hands clasped together on the table.
'Now that, old friend, is a real problem. If they can tie her in with providing the key, they'll no doubt charge her with conspiring to steal the Shogun. The subsequent crash and the deaths will result in a hefty sentence for them both and, if she is convicted of being 'art and part', Mary will also catch a few years in the fall out.'
He saw the normally relaxed Alex pale at the thought of his daughter being sentenced to prison and hastily leaned forward.
'There is another option, however. If the cops come knocking at your door for her, we might be able to arrange a deal; have her turn Queens Evidence against your boys to bolster their case against Davie and Sammy. I know it's not ideal, but surely its better two go down rather than three?' he suggested, his hands now apart and open as though in plea.
Alex's mind was racing. He had already considered the possibility that his daughter might be seriously implicated and had decided beforehand that if it came down to it, Davie and Sammy would be sacrificed in favour of Mary. They two clowns could handle prison. His daughter wouldn't cope so well. He slowly nodded his head. His mind raced as another idea thrust forward, one that he had better mull over in private before discussing it with Davie and Sammy. But for now, he'd enjoy the coffee and pass the remaining time with Gospel in idle chatter.
'Right, we'll go by your decision Gospel. You're the man with the knowledge of how their minds work. If that's what the police try on, we'll be ready for them.'
Gospel sipped at his coffee, delicately wiping his lips with the starched cotton napkin. You can't buy good old-fashioned style, he thought to himself, as he smelled the lemon-scented cleanliness of the material.
'I'm curious Alex. Why do you think the PF didn't oppose bail?'
Alex tapped the side of his nose and winked.
'What you don't know you can't repeat,' he replied, tapping his nose, as was his habit. 'Right, time for me to go,' he said, downing the dregs from the cup and rising from his chair. He fetched his wallet from his inner jacket pocket and withdrew a twenty-pound note that he left on the table. Then, almost as an afterthought, he also withdrew a small hand printed business card from the wallet that he placed in front of Gospel.
'I'd forgotten to say. That's the address of a new stable of mine. I've spoken with the,' he hesitated as he searched for the word, 'caretaker and she'll be expecting you. Just present that card when you arrive. Anytime that suits you, night or day. There's a new girl I've

acquired, just got her into the country through one of the English ports. Seventeen, but can look a whole lot younger if you want. Willing to do anything and that includes wearing a school uniform; just the type you prefer. Enjoy yourself,' he said with a backward wave.
Gospel watched him leave the café and reached for the card. Glancing at his watch, he involuntarily licked his lips. His wife, torn faced bitch that she was these days, wasn't expecting him home any time soon and the office wasn't expecting him back today. Now might be a good time to take up Alex's offer. With a polite nod to the elderly Betty, he shrugged into his heavy overcoat and walked quickly to his car.
Such a nice pair of gentlemen she smiled as she cleared and wiped the table clean. So mannerly and courteous.

*

The small garden at the rear of 39 Cotton Close, a rough grassed area that was really more ragged turf than lawn, led to a wooden gate that gave access to a common lane that backed onto all the houses in the terraced row. Across the narrow lane, identical terraced houses similarly backed onto the lane and all overlooked each other, preventing privacy within the rear rooms of the houses unless the curtains were tightly drawn.
Up and down the narrow terraced homes, the house occupants, mostly first time buyers, had tried to uniquely vary the rear of their properties; some with wooden decking, others with sheds or garden huts of all size and descriptions, while still others boasted small extensions or tight, double glazed conservatories; all designed to increase the living space in the cramped dwellings but adding little more than an extra seating area. A line of plastic bins, some crudely painted in various colours and denoting their owners' house number, stood at irregular intervals in the lane, roughly indicating the rear gateway to each residence.
At number 39, the Bryce's purchase of their home had included a plain, wooden windowless shed that Johnny had attempted to liven up with a coat of bright green paint and into which was stuffed garden and work tools, a spare car tyre, a dismantled child's plastic chute and swing combination; Laura's tricycle and sundry household debris completed the crush. The padlocked door was sheathed in a spider's web that glistened with dewdrops, a visible indication of the shed's lack of use through the winter months.
Returning from the police office, Johnny alighted from the bus and head down, walked slowly home through the narrow streets. Turning into Cotton Close, he spotted a car parked a few yards from his door, its exhaust billowing out a cloud of vapour and rightly guessed some enterprising reporter had by now discovered his address.
The two occupants seemed engaged in reading newspapers. Without a backward glance, he retraced his steps and made his way towards the entrance to the rear lane. He wasn't to know the guile of the tabloid press. Passing the rear kitchen window at number 35, the young mother at the kitchen sink saw her neighbour and quickly removing her rubber gloves, phoned the number on the card the nice man had given her along with the two five-pound notes.

He had just slipped off his outer jacket when the letterbox rattled at the front door. Making his way into the front room, he tugged the curtain aside and saw two men standing outside, the younger of the two carrying an expensive looking camera slung about his neck. The car he'd seen earlier was now empty and he knew he had correctly

guessed who they were.
Shit! he thought, but determined there was no way he was opening his door, let alone give an interview.
'Mister Bryce?' the voice called from the hallway. 'Mister Bryce? John? I know you're in there. My names Ally McGregor. I'm the chief crime reporter with the *Glasgow News*. Just a few words John about the dreadful circumstances of your wife and daughters death, eh?'
Outside, McGregor spoke from the side of his mouth and whispered that the photographer should get ready, just in case it was a straight forward open the door and push off sort of response. 'Try and get at least one shot in this time, okay?' he urged the younger man, irritably shaking his head as he watched him fumble with the lens cap.
'All I need is one photo. I'll fill the rest of the storyline in,' he promised, already forming a by-line in his head.
He bent down again, feeling the familiar twinge in his back that warned of the onset of yet another visit to his chiropractor, a constant reminder of the dangers when arguing with a punter at the top of a flight of stairs.
'Mister Bryce, come on, eh? You'll have to speak to someone eventually, eh?'
'Why not offer him some dough?' ventured the snapper.
McGregor glared up at him, the stupid dickhead.
'Aye, right. A guy just lost his wife and wean and you want me to offer him a couple of bob for the story? Are you stupid or what?'
Suitably chastened, the snapper looked away, again regretting his assignment with the well-known but acerbic reporter and wishing he had taken the job with his uncle; easy money, going around in a wee van and doing the school classroom photos.
McGregor pushed the letterbox open and shouted through his offer of an interview, 'With no strings attached,' he added. He wheezed heavily and stood painfully upright, his back killing him.
'This is getting nowhere,' he finally announced.
'Right, this is how we'll work it. Husband too sedated to express his grief,' he decided, framing the subheading in his mind, 'so get me a shot of the front of the house and then we'll get a description of the dead woman and her kid from the neighbours. You work that side for a couple of doors', he pointed left, 'and I'll knock on a few doors this side,' he pointed to the right.
'But I've never interviewed anybody before. What will I ask them?'
'Don't worry about taking notes, sonny; just get some neighbours names. I'll fill in the blanks when we get back to the office,' he assured the stricken snapper, patting him on the arm to restore his confidence that the professional reporter was always on top of the situation.
As an afterthought, McGregor scribbled his name and contact phone number onto a piece of notepaper and pushed it through the letterbox.

Through a crack in the upstairs curtain, Johnny watched them separate and move along the terraced houses, stopping at the nearest doors where they sometimes obtained a response. He guessed they'd be interviewing the neighbours, but knew they would discover little. Karen hadn't exactly encouraged contact with their neighbours and barely acknowledged them Yet again another indication of her inherited snobbery, believing that

those who lived about them were beneath her social circle. He felt sad when he thought of it. Her aloofness denied her any friendship and in turn prevented Laura from mixing with toddlers her own age. Even the local playgroup was deemed by Karen to be too common for *her* daughter.
He shrank back as the younger man stood on the roadway, aiming his camera at the house. Apparently satisfied, the photographer made his way to the drivers' door of the car and awaited the other man; McGregor he had called himself.
The letterbox rattled one more time, another plea by McGregor for him to come to the door, then a final cry that if Johnny read the *Glasgow News* tomorrow morning, he would find a sympathetic article about his wife and daughter. Then, McGregor finally shouted, maybe he might decide to phone.
He watched as McGregor strode to the passenger door and saw the car drive slowly away. An hour later, a film crew from one of the local news stations arrived, but receiving no response to their knock at his door, merely used the house as a backdrop to the reporter's broadcast and then drove off.
Restlessly, he paced about the house, finally settling in his bedroom. He glanced at the unmade bed and a sudden weariness overtook him, a desperate need for numbing sleep. He half walked, half stumbled into the small bathroom to use the toilet before he lay down to nap.
The white-netted bag that was attached by suckers to the tiled wall above the bath and contained Laura's bath toys caught his attention and involuntarily, he smiled. He became conscious of the pleasant fragrance in the air from the lotions and toiletries that Karen insisted were necessary for her skin, even when money was tight. With a sudden realisation, he knew there would come a time when he would have to clear out their things, perhaps even sell the house and move on. A rush of guilt overtook him.
Christ. How do people cope with that sort of thing, he wondered? How can I possibly decide what clothes or possessions that belonged to Karen and Laura have no value? What do I do with my daughter's toys, the dolls and teddy bears she loved and caressed? Do I keep them as reminders of her or get rid of them.
And Karen's clothes and things. How do I choose what is to be kept or disposed of? He felt that what he was considering was like an act of disloyalty, a betrayal to their memory.
He ran his hand wearily through his thick brown hair, deciding that right now what he really needed was sleep. Tomorrow, when it came, was difficult enough to face without making it worse.

*

Annie Hall didn't always have time to purchase a newspaper on her way home, it usually being dependent on whether she was running breathlessly for the five thirty train or sauntering along with time to spare. Tonight, she'd ten minutes before it departed and treated herself to the early evening edition of the *Glasgow News*. Settling into a corner seat, she pushed the bright yellow woolly hat back from her forehead and folded the paper in half to make it easier to read in the cramped space. The portly man sitting beside her had obviously had a hard day she assumed, if the overwhelming smell of body odour he gave off was anything to go by. She figured the concept of personal hygiene had escaped his attention and presumed he didn't have a 'best friend'. It was also evident that at least one of the two young women who sat facing Annie had over indulged in a lunch that was heavily smothered in garlic. Probably the one that keeps burping, she thought unkindly. Shouldn't be allowed in a commuter packed carriage like this. Ought to have been breath tested before she got on amongst the rest of us, she thought unkindly and decided that if she was promoted and did run her own department, then anyone caught having garlic breath at work will be immediately suspended; and underarm sprays will be compulsory, she inwardly grinned.

Nauseated, but happier now that she'd made her first managerial decision, she forced herself to focus on the paper. Predictably, the headline carried the story about the poor mother and child killed by the car thieves. She barely glanced at the report, having already discussed it sympathetically over lunch with colleagues at work. With an effort that involved her fellow passenger leaning to one side to ease her movement, she turned the pages to the crossword, fetched a pen from her bag and concentrated on defeating the resident compiler's love of anagrams.

The miles drifted by and her eyes felt heavy in the warm, claustrophobic atmosphere that conspired with the rhythmic motion of the carriage to cause the weary traveller to nap. With a start, she saw they had arrived at Gilmore Street station and jerked upright from her seat, upsetting the portly man who quickly dragged his legs in beneath him to prevent them being trampled upon by the mad young woman in the bright yellow hat.

'Sorry,' gasped Annie, pushing her way through the throng and making the platform just as the doors hissed closed behind her.

The leather backpack bounced against her shoulder as she made her way through the evening crowds and across the busy High Street to the bus stop on Causeyside Street. A light rain had begun to fall as she stood in line; heartening slightly when after just a few moments, she saw her bus approach. Unusually, she found a seat without difficulty and opened the paper to complete the crossword.

'Aye, they lived up in that new wee estate that was built just off the Glenburn Road up by Foxbar. Poor souls.... and the wee girl only three.'

Annie held her breath and listened, realising the elderly woman and her companion must be discussing the awful deaths of the mother and child. Her curiosity aroused, she opened the paper at the front page and scanned the story. No pictures of the deceased, but there it was, the address on the second paragraph.

My God, she thought, 39 Cotton Close! That's the road that runs parallel with mine. Suddenly, the tragedy had taken on a new meaning. She felt a pang of guilt that without knowing the full details, she had previously dismissed the deaths as just another in a catalogue of crime, but now that she could identify where the mother and daughter had lived, it seemed that much closer to home, something that she could now identify with.

The bus arrived at her stop and automatically, she got off; her thoughts filled with newspaper report. The short walk home in the drizzling rain passed in contemplation, a sense of guilt engulfing her at her previous indifference to the poor victims.

Fumbling in her backpack, she fished out her door key and let herself into the warmth of the hallway, stooping to recover the few items of mail that lay upon the mat. Glancing at them, they seemed to be mostly junk mail with at least one official looking letter, likely from the bank she thought with a grimace. As she took off and hung her coat in the small cupboard, she thought about the bank letter and guessed it was another warning about her overdraft. Maybe this chance at promotion is heaven sent, she sighed, reaming of the day when she might be debt free.

Bursting for a bladder relief and with the remaining mail in her hand, she made her way to the toilet at the top of the stairs. When she'd washed her hands a thought occurred to her. The newspaper had reported the woman and child had resided at number 39 Cotton Close. Annie made her way into the small bedroom at the rear and leaving the light off, glanced through the window towards the back of the houses across the lane. Since moving to the house just over a month previously, she hadn't really gotten to know many neighbours, other than old Missus Campbell next door who was constantly suggesting she buy a cat for company. As if sharing a confidence, she'd told her that Annie would have preferred a man but the joke was lost on the old soul.
Peering quizzically through the rain stained window, she presumed that number 39 could be any one of the tight little houses facing her. Better be careful, she mused and not stand too close to the window lest anyone watching think she was being nosey.
Which I am, she wryly grinned.
Aye, anyone of them she repeated to herself. Even that one across the way with the brightly painted green shed.

*

As Johnny Bryce napped fully clothed on top of his bed, his wife and child's killers sat with their father and sister devouring the remains of a take-away Indian meal that lay scattered about the large dining table in the back room of the family home.
'Well kids,' quipped Alex Crowden, 'I think we've done full justice to that, eh?'
Mary picked delicately at the small portion that remained on her plate. Her brother Sammy smacked his lips together as he drained a can of lager, while Davie watched with hooded eyes as his father practised the false bonhomie. He couldn't quite decide what his father was up to, buying them dinner and insisting they sat together to eat it like a normal family, but knew that whatever Pop was planning he'd learn about it in the next few minutes. He might have been interested to know that even his sister was surprised by their father's insistence they eat together. His body wracked into a rasping cough and morsels of food splattered from his mouth onto his plate.
Mary stared at him, her lips curling with disgust; she didn't fail to notice either that when he thought she wasn't looking, he had cast the odd furtive glance towards her bosom that threatened to explode from her tight, black coloured top.
'That was smashing Pop,' Sammy gushed. 'Do you want another can?' he asked, rising from his seat.
Alex waved him to sit back down.
'Not just now, son. There's something I want to discuss with you all. Like a family, eh?'
Sammy slowly lowered the now empty can and stared at his father. This was something out of his scope, a new experience; his Pop being civil to him.
'Now,' began Alex, leaning forward and placing his hands palm down on the table, 'I had a wee meeting today with Gospel Gordon and there's one or two things came to light. It seems that the cops have the second key that you two,' he nodded in turn to Davie and Sammy, 'got from Mary. That's unfortunate in that the CID has already visited Pat Delaney's trying to tie the key down. It won't take them long, if they haven't already done so, to realise Mary is your sister and it doesn't take a genius to work out how you got the key.'
Sammy turned pale and snapped his head round to stare at Mary.
'Does that mean….'

He didn't finish. Alex raised one powerful hand to silence him.
'It means nothing. Yet. Shut up and let me finish,' he growled.
Sammy swallowed hard. Pop's civility hadn't lasted long.
'The owner of the Shogun won't testify against you. All his evidence will consist of is owning the vehicle and seeing it being driven off. He's been warned and knows that he'll get more than a smacking if he speaks out against you. The coppers will likely try to have him attend an identification parade, but even if they do get him to attend it'll be a waste of their time. He'll not ID you. Not if he wants to keep….certain parts of his private anatomy,' he smirked, declining to use the word *testicles* in front of his demure daughter.
'What about the fingerprints and blood in the car that Gospel told us about?' inquired Davie.
'I'm getting to that,' replied Alex, his eyes flashing a warning that he didn't want to be interrupted again.
'I'm not finished with our Dickie. I don't care how he does it but he's to make sure that he gets assigned your case to prosecute. Once that's done, he instructs all the hard evidence against you to be taken to his room for his examination. When we know it's all collected together, we deal with it. Don't ask,' he again raised his hand to silence Davie. 'I'll tell you what'll happen at the appropriate time.'
'The key, Pop,' asked Mary, her impatience fuelled by her dread of being arrested. 'What about the bloody key!'
He smiled benignly at her. He'd need to speak to her about her language, but privately; not in front of these two reprobates.
'That's where your brothers come to your rescue, sweetheart.'

*

DI Ronnie Sutherland replaced the handset and swore softly. His wife enjoyed the benefits of his generous salary, but couldn't seem to grasp that to earn his money sometimes meant working that little bit over the normal shift hours. He sighed heavily and rubbed his tired eyes with the knuckles of his hands.
Maria Lavery appeared at the door with a china mug in her fist.
'Tea, boss?'
Sutherland grinned at her.
'Mark yourself down for four hours overtime…no, make that a day off, DC Lavery,' he joked, licking his parched lips in appreciative anticipation of the brew.
'Trouble at home?' she asked and then in answer to his questioning look, 'I could hear you pleading from along the corridor.'
'Ach,' he shook his head, 'you know what wives are like.'
'Well, actually I don't,' she laughed, 'but if it's any consolation, boyfriends who are not in the job aren't that much different. Anyway, I understand you want to see me?'
'I've a real shitty job for tomorrow morning and like it or not, I think you are probably the best person to deal with it. Mister Bryce, the husband is to be taken to the city mortuary for the formal identification of his wife and daughter.'
'But I thought that…after the fire, you know…'
'Aye lass, there's not a lot to identify, but the man's insisted and we *are* obliged to carry out his wishes. I just thought that maybe….'
He waved for her to sit down.
'A female shoulder to cry on, you mean?'

‘Actually, I thought that you might be more sensitive rather than some of the Neanderthals that I’ve got working here for me.’
Her face screwed up and she bit at her lower lip.
‘I’ve never actually did this sort of thing before. Taken someone to the mortuary I mean. Do you want a statement or anything after it?’
‘No, that’ll not be necessary. Just take him along and if he says ‘yes’, we’ll add it on when eventually we get round to sitting down with him and getting something on paper. I’d rather not push it too much at this time. I think that guy’s on the edge, if you know what I mean and to be frank, so far we haven’t really impressed him with our investigative skills,’ he said moodily.
What Sutherland didn’t say and what he privately thought was that Bryce worried him. The man was clearly upset, there was no denying that; but there was also something else, something Sutherland just couldn’t put his finger on.
‘Any time arranged to collect him?’ asked Lavery, breaking into his thoughts.
‘Eh, nothing formally arranged. Might be prudent to give him a phone call. Thanks Maria.’

CHAPTER 6

The following morning dawned bright and clear with the blossoming daffodils pushing their way upward through the winter, then autumn compacted earth and hinting at the advance of summer.
Johnny was showered and dressed in a sober dark blue suit, a navy blue tie stark against the crisp white shirt. Checking his reflection in the mirrored door of the wardrobe, he reminded himself he should purchase a black tie later in the day.
The doorbell sounded and, with a final pat at his hair, made his way down the narrow stairs.
DC Maria Lavery stood holding a thick, leather bound folder, the edges of paperwork peeking out from it, her bag slung over her shoulder and police warrant card in her hand.
‘Don’t want to be mistaken for a reporter,’ she smiled; reminding him of his complaint to her when she’d phoned the previous evening.
‘The neighbours seem to have heard,’ she continued, nodding with her head to his front wall.
To his surprise, he discovered at least a dozen separate bunch of flowers neatly laid against the wall under the front window, most of which seemed to have a card attached. One bunch was held firmly in place by an elastic band that was wrapped round a brown, teddy bear, still bearing the label with the purchase price.
Lavery stood to one side as, the beginning of a lump in his throat, he stepped out of the doorway and bent down to examine the card attached to the nearest bunch. Discreetly, the detective looked away.
The unsigned handwritten note expressed deep sorrow at the deaths of Karen and Laura and wished him to know they were now safe in God’s hands. A second card said much the same and was simply signed, ‘All at number 47’.
He stood upright, swallowing hard and blinking back the unexpected tears.
‘I’ve not had any breakfast this morning,’ she said, her eyes searching his face, ‘maybe we could have a cup of tea before we go?’
He suspected she was being kind, wanted to give him time to compose himself.

He took a deep breath and exhaled slowly.
'No, if you don't mind. Perhaps when we return. I'd like to go now please.'

The start of the journey towards the city was made in silence.
Lavery had already decided that anything she said might seem trite and superfluous to this mans' suffering. If he wished to speak, she'd listen. Travelling on the motorway, she reached down and switched on the car radio, turning the sound down low and hoping the music from the local station might lessen the tense atmosphere in the car.
Arriving at the mortuary, she carefully parked the CID car in the rear yard and fetched her folder from the back seat.
'Can you wait a moment, Mister Bryce? I just want to ensure that they're ready to receive us, that everything is in order.'
He watched as she walked across the cobbled yard, pushing her way through the large rear doors. She returned a few minutes later and opened the passenger door.
'They're ready for us now,' she smiled at him. 'I'll take you through to the family room and Missus Cosgrove, the attending official will speak with you.
The handsome and smartly dressed woman wearing a two-piece black-skirted suit and crisp white blouse, her greying hair tied in a neat bun, took his outstretched hand in both of hers, holding them as she spoke. Strangely, it didn't occur to him that he should pull his hand away from her.
'Good morning, Mister Bryce, I'm Julia Cosgrove. I'm sure that not many people can begin to believe the hurt and pain you must be feeling at this sorrowful time and it's my job to ease you through the ache of seeing your loved ones, here in this place.'
He stared numbly at her and though he knew she was being kind, intuitively believed that she meant what she said. He mumbled some sort of response and, still holding his hand in a childlike way, Cosgrove led him to a bench seat where she sat beside him. Lavery quietly closed the door and stood respectfully against the wall, saying nothing yet impressed by the manner in which the mortuary official had so easily taken charge of John Bryce.
'What will happen,' Cosgrove explained, her voice soft and hypnotic, 'is that we will walk from this reception area to a room just along the corridor where, within an adjoining room, will be a curtain across a glass wall. When you're ready, I'll open the curtain and you will see your wife and daughter upon tables in that room.'
Johnny felt her squeeze his hand just a little tighter as he stared at her, bewitched by her pale, blue eyes.
'I regret, Mister Bryce, that your wife Karen and little Laura were terribly burned at the time of the accident. You may wish to reconsider seeing them as they now are, perhaps preferring to remember them as they were when you last saw them?'
He stared at her. How could she know that his final glimpse of his wife was her eyes blazing, a tirade of abuse levelled at him as she stormed from their home; his daughter leaning across his wife's shoulder, her little arms outstretched as she cried and wailed, reaching desperately for her daddy.
'Thank you,' he took a deep breath. 'I know you're being kind. I'd…. I'd like to see them now. Please.'
With the briefest of nods, Cosgrove released his hand, stood up and slowly led them both to the viewing room.

He hadn't expected they would be so appallingly disfigured. He blanched and leaned sideways, using his hand to support himself as he leaned against of the wall. Instinctively, both Lavery and Cosgrove moved to steady him, but he shrugged them off and staggered from the room into the corridor. Lavery followed, maintaining a discreet distance, her face pale and her eyes full of concern, while Cosgrove closed the curtains, then led the way back to the family room.
The detective had seen there was no need for a formal identification. Bryce's very actions had decreed his recognition of his wife ad child.
Once seated in the reception room, he drew breath and spoke for the first time.
'What happens now? Arrangements I mean?'
Cosgrove glanced quickly at Lavery then replied.
'I'm sure you must have been told there will be a need for a post mortem. Once that…. examination…. has been completed, arrangements can be made to have your wife and daughter moved to a funeral parlour. I'll provide you with some written information, undertakers and suchlike who will make all the necessary arrangements. Again, Mister Bryce, I'm so very sorry that this has happened.'
Her kindness was genuine, of that he was certain.
Nodding quickly, he stood and glanced at Lavery, who rose and led the way into the corridor. Johnny turned back and stepped towards Cosgrove. He nodded and gently shook her hand.
'I'm grateful for what you have done.' His voice choked as he turned hurriedly away to follow Lavery into the bright daylight and towards the car.
Within the vehicle, Lavery tossed her folder into the rear of the car, scattering documents from the unzipped wallet onto the back seat, and was about to turn on the ignition when she recalled Cosgrove had forgotten to give Mister Bryce the pamphlets containing the information he needed to make the funeral arrangements.
'Damn! Sorry', she apologised to Johnny with a flustered smile, 'won't be a moment,' she told him and without explanation, left the car.
He watched as she quickly made her way back through the mortuary door.
Sitting in the comfort of the CID car, he had difficulty getting the image from his mind, the sight of Karen and Laura, or what remained of them, stretched out beneath the white sheets. He shook his head violently as if to remove the sight then sighed deeply.
Turning, he saw the scattered papers lying with the folder on the rear seat and with natural consideration, leaned over to neatly gather them together for the detective.
Shuffling the half dozen or so papers that were stapled together, his eyes narrowed as he realised the top page was a Photostat copy of a court charge sheet. There he read, in black and white, were the full details of the two men who had been charged with killing his family. The names seemed to leap out at him. David Mathew Crowden and Samuel Jason Crowden, complete with their birth dates and more interestingly, their home address; 129 Tweedsmuir Path, Cardonald, Glasgow. He glanced at the mortuary door, but there was still no sign of the detective. Hastily, he read through the remaining sheets of paper that was a report to the Procurator Fiscal at Paisley; learning about the circumstances of the theft of the Shogun, the subsequent crash and finally the intention of the investigating officer to continue the inquiry. The last page, he swiftly scanned through it, seemed to be what the police called an Action Report that related a visit Lavery and her colleague

Detective Sergeant Wilson, made to a place called Pat Delaney's Car Sales, where they learned that the Crowden's sister Mary worked and whom, in their opinion, had probably supplied the key to steal the Shogun.
He glanced at the mortuary door and saw the detective pushing her way through it.
With haste, he lowered the papers to his lap and flicked them backwards onto the rear seat, keeping his face towards the windscreen.
The unsuspecting Lavery smiled as she opened the driver's door.
'Sorry, again,' she said, handing him the pamphlets. 'How are you?'
He turned towards her, his thoughts racing with the information he had just learned.
'Oh, feeling a lot better now, thank you.'

*

Traffic Constable Archie Crichton, at home off duty and dressed in his old and worn gardening overalls, pushed the swing even higher, grinning at the yell of delight emitting from his four year old grandson, young Archie. His daughter Tricia, a mug of coffee in hand, stood smiling from the patio doors at their antics as she watched her father and son at play.
'Right you two,' she finally shouted, 'lunch is ready.'
Crichton's wife busied herself in the kitchen, laying the table and humming gently as the radio played an old melody in the background.
Her husband kicked off his muddy boots at the back door step and tickled his grandson through the door, laughing as the boy squealed with glee.
Hands washed, the two men of the family joined their womenfolk at the table and tucked into the prepared meal.
Outside the modest house, the former police officer sitting within the nondescript van and now earning his living as a private inquiry agent, chewed at his sandwich as he jotted down details of the type, colour and registration numbers of the two vehicles closely parked in Crichton's driveway.

*

Mary Crowden parked her car in its usual spot within Delaney's yard and sauntered into the office with more than a little pleasure. The meeting that occurred between Pop and Pat Delaney had, in her mind, firmed up her relationship with Delaney and set out the new rules; she was no longer the office skirt to be fondled and groped at will, but more the daughter of the man Delaney now obviously feared and who now was, albeit unwittingly, a suspect and likely due to receive a visit from the cops in the very near future.
He had seen her car arrive and rushed into the small toilet, scrambling at the plastic cistern with shaking hands.
Just the one wee pull, he thought, too ashamed to admit even to himself that he needed some vodka-induced courage to face her. He uncorked the new bottle and raised the neck to his lips. A sudden pounding on the door startled him, causing him to spill some of the liquid onto his collar and tie. Hastily he wiped himself with the back of his hand and took a deep breath, glanced at his pasty face in the chipped mirror and returned the bottle to the toilet cistern.
He licked his dry lips and forcing himself to remain calm, adopted a smile and opened the door into the main office.
'Morning Mary,' he greeted her, 'just freshening up a wee bit. Looking forward to a good

day now the sun's out, eh?'
'Pop said you've to phone him,' she said, ignoring his greeting. 'About that bit of business the other night.'
She turned away and busied herself at her desk, preferring that he didn't see the smirk that crossed her face.
'Oh, and I'll be needing the rest of the day off,' she added with a blank smile. 'Got a bit of shopping to do in the city, okay Pat?'
Delaney feebly nodded; too cowed by her new found confidence to refuse her. He experienced a strange sensation in his groin. It felt like his balls were shrivelling.

*

DI Ronnie Sutherland received Maria Lavery's report with stoicism, unable to comprehend why a man would wish to see his family after they had received such horrific injures, yet understanding that as Bryce had said; he needed closure.
The phone rang and he dismissed Lavery with an eyebrow-raised nod. The switchboard operator announced his caller.
'Good morning Mister Gordon, what can I do for you?'
'I understand Mister Sutherland that you are the officer in charge of my client's case?'
'If you're referring to the Crowden's, that's correct, sir.'
'Indeed. My purpose in phoning is simply to firm up on the details for the ID parade. I presume you have already set the date?'
Sutherland hesitated.
'Does Thursday afternoon suit you Mister Gordon?'
'Paisley office?'
'Yes, shall we say two thirty?'
'Two thirty it is. Oh, and one other thing, Mister Sutherland…'
Here it is, thought the detective, the real reason for the call.
'My clients are obviously keen to comply with the court instruction regarding their full and total cooperation, a fact of which I'm sure you will take cognisance. I have been instructed to make you aware that in the matter of the key discovered in the ignition of the Shogun, you may consider interviewing one Patrick Delaney, a motor trader dealer who operates from premises in the east end of Glasgow; some side street off the Shettleston Road, I believe. My clients have learned that it was he who provided the real thieves with the key.'
Sutherland's eyes widened in disbelief.
'Am to understand from that statement, Mister Gordon that your clients intend disputing their innocence in the charge?'
'That is their intention and their privilege as I'm sure you are aware,' he answered smoothly, condescension oozing from his voice. 'Now, do you propose doing anything about this man Delaney?'
'You can trust sir, that the matter will be fully investigated,' he did say; but thinking 'you slimy fucking bastard', which he didn't say.

Following the conversation, Sutherland took a moment to calm himself then, calling Kevin Wilson and Maria Lavery into his office, related the telephone discussion with Gospel Gordon. He added cynically that he was in no doubt that it was the father, Alex Crowden, who had instigated the contact. He instructed Wilson to follow up the

allegation regarding the key by interviewing Patrick Delaney, while Lavery was set to organise the ID parade for the following afternoon.
'And Kevin,' he beckoned the DS to wait, then when both were alone, told him, 'don't be charging Delaney on the word of that crooked bugger Gospel. If anything, obtain a negative statement in that Delaney denies giving the key to the Crowden's. If he alleges or even suggests that Mary gave her brothers the key, so much the better. But no matter what, obtain a *negative* statement regarding Delaney's supposed involvement. Got that?'
'You don't think he was perhaps involved with her then, the sister I mean?'
Sutherland sat back in his chair and rubbed his nose with an ink stained forefinger.
'Unlikely. Alex Crowden wouldn't have Gospel phoning us and firing Delaney in if he was one of the team. He'd worry that Delaney would roll over and tell us more than old Alex would want us to know. No, my guess is that Delaney is the sacrificial patsy; probably being delivered bound and gagged in lieu of Alex's daughter, Mary. He'll know we've no direct link other than suspecting Mary's involvement and by contacting us with the name of another suspect, he's trying to both deflect heat from Mary and can truthfully tell the court at a subsequent hearing that his clients are cooperating with the police, to their full ability. Shite!'
'Got you boss,' replied Wilson in understanding, keen to be gone before the normally placid Sutherland exploded and obviously still seething at Gordon's telephone call.
Now, wondered Sutherland, what exactly did Alex Crowden have against Partick Delaney and was there some ulterior motive for getting him out of Crowden's way or is he simply looking for a scapegoat?
A thought occurred to him. He reached for the phone and dialled the switchboard.
'Hi there. Can you get me the number for DS Danny McBride at Criminal Intelligence, Headquarters please?'

*

Annie Hall worked away at her desk, her eyes drifting from the paperwork in front of her as her mind drifted again to the shocking news that the dead woman and her daughter had lived just a few doors, away in a nearby street. She couldn't think what had possessed her last night, to walk the short distance to her local superstore and buy the flowers; and her heart had been in her mouth, lest anyone had opened the door, when she'd quietly laid them outside number 39. Strangely, walking briskly home she felt uplifted, that she had in some small way acknowledged the tragedy; showed a compassion for the family of the deceased. Hers, she saw, were not the only flowers placed there and as she had moved away, a young woman and small boy had laid more yet flowers against the wall of the house, with a teddy bear attached to them; the boy protesting and reaching for the bear while his mother, hushed him and held him close as though realising once more how precious he really was.
'Penny for them,' came the soft voice through the open door.
Sadie Parker smiled in at her young protégé and then frowned.
'Something on your mind young missy?'
Annie stood and moved a pile of books from the only other chair in the small room and bade Sadie sit down. The next few minutes she spent relating her discovery that the tragic accident victims lived practically round the corner and trying to make sense of the feelings she was experiencing; her sense of outrage and horror, her extraordinary feeling

of hate for the perpetrators of this monstrous crime. Even more so when she realised that number 39 was indeed the house opposite her back garden; the house with the brightly painted green shed.
Sadie listened quietly and to her surprise, realising for the first time just how lonely and private a life her young friend led.
'Really, my girl, you should get out more,' she suggested with genuine concern. She liked Annie. After all, who didn't?
She smiled tolerantly at Sadie. Finding a man wasn't *that* easy, she knew, particularly one who was willing to put up with quiet nights at home, candle lit dinners, long walks, classical music and a passion for the novels of the Bronte sisters. Ah well, that's me she thought with a self-depreciating sigh; your typical shy, retiring romanticist.
'About that little matter we discussed,' Sadie began slowly, interrupting her thoughts.
Annie's eyes opened wide and she held her breath, dreading bad news.
'I've spoken with the Director,' Sadie continued, 'and he's agreed that though the District Council regulations maintain that the post must be advertised both internally and externally, he will sympathetically receive your application due to your current knowledge of the post and my support; but you have to understand that he can't be seen to show any kind of favouritism.'
'Of course not,' replied Annie, 'I fully understand that Sadie and I'm grateful for your help.'
Nevertheless, her heart beat that little bit faster and already she was mentally composing her written application.
'If you need any help with the form, you know where to come,' Sadie reminded her as with a backward wave, she strode off towards her own office.
When she'd gone, Annie felt strangely depressed. Her comfort zone, once seemingly so secure, was about to be disrupted. She glanced dourly round her office at the aging desk, the wooden visitors' chair, its varnish chipped and scratched; the fading wallpaper and the old-fashioned plaster cornice that bore the dust of a dozen years.
With no little excitement, she figured maybe that wasn't such a bad thing after all.

*

He had just parked the car at the bottom of the block of flats in Wilson Street and prepared himself to pay an unannounced visit to the madam of his new brothel when the mobile phone activated in his trouser pocket. Flipping open the lid, he recognised the number with a smile.
'Morning Gospel, how we doing?'
'Greetings old friend,' inquired a surprisingly cheerful Gospel. 'You alone?'
With years of instinctive caution, Alex glanced about to ensure he would not be overheard.
'Yes?' he replied.
'As you instructed, I contacted the copper in charge of the case and fired in our Mister Delaney. Whether or not they follow up, we'll need to wait and see. However, if nothing else, it draws the main thrust away from our little Mary. On the matter of the second item, our associate has identified two cars that belong to one of the…. other the main witnesses and interestingly enough, saw that there is a young child in the family. From what he has discovered it seems the unmarried daughter and her son lives with her parents; the boys' about three or four years of age apparently.'

‘And the second witness?’
‘Alas,’ Gospel sighed through the phone, ‘our associate has learned of her home address, but it seems he’s also found out that she spends most of her time living with a boyfriend. Unfortunately we don’t yet have the details of this guy so it might be prudent if you wish to consider concentrating on witness number one, in the meantime? I’m concerned,’ he added with heavy emphasis, ‘that time is short and if we’re going to get it done, now might be the time.’
Alex chewed at his lower lip, contemplating his reply. Finally, he answered.
‘You’re right; we’ll lean on the one for now. Leave that with me. Anything else?’
It was obvious that Gospel was pleased Alex was agreeing with his suggestion. It would make things so much easier.
‘The ID parade has been set for the afternoon on Thursday, so that will give you all of tomorrow to work something out. Oh, and I’ve spoken with Davie and Sammy, told them to make themselves available.’
‘You haven’t mentioned to them our associate or what I’ve got in mind?’
‘Not at all,’ Gospel hastily replied. ‘Some matters, I’m sure as we’ve previously agreed, are best left unsaid.’
‘To be sure Gospel, to be sure. Now, anything else to tell me?’
‘Nothing else meantime, Alex. I’ll be in touch.’
Alex ended the call and with a further glance about him, scrolled through the phone’s directory, stopping at a recently inserted number. He pressed the send button and waited patiently.
The voicemail answer facility of the called number activated and Alex left the curtest of messages.
‘Shooter. Phone me.’

*

The subscriber of the phone that recorded Alex Crowden’s message heard the single beep of his mobile phone but ignored it, concentrating instead on the heavy weights that he held in both knuckle strained fists as he raised them above his head. A thin sheen of perspiration covered his shaven head and equally clean-shaven face. The faded tee shirt and football shorts he wore were sodden with sweat. At five feet ten inches tall, his muscular arms and thighs seemed to extend like branches from his barrel chested torso, particularly when dressed in the casual, baggy trousers and black coloured bomber jacket that he habitually wore. On each well-developed arm he sported colourful tattoo’s while across his brawny chest a Union Flag was surmounted by the scrolled words: *For God and Ulster.* Unusually, what contradicted this bold and proud statement was that Martin was Glasgow born and bred and had never visited the Northern Irish Province.
To the casual observer Tommy Martin’s physical appearance belied his forty-five years and the hard life he had led. An amateur boxer in his youth, his most recent employer Alex Crowden, utilised his unique physical talents in a variety of ways, most if not all involved him hurting people. His facial appearance, that he carefully cultivated, didn’t do his job prospectus any harm either; with shaven eyebrows, a blue coloured star tattooed on the lobe of each ear, much-broken nose and a vivid three inch scar running from his left lip towards his ear, giving him a lopsided face that chilled most punters when he smiled, which wasn’t often.
He had earned the nickname ‘Shooter’, by which he was more commonly known and

secretly delighted in, because of his inclination to carrying a cut-down, single barrelled shotgun that he infrequently carried on jobs in a specially sewn pocket, within his trouser leg. Twice the police had managed to bring him before the court on firearm charges and on both occasions his lawyer, the prominent Gospel Gordon, was successful in having him acquitted; more usually because either the witnesses disappeared or shortly before trial, suffered severe and total memory loss of the incident.
Shooters job description varied on Crowden's whim; invariably committing serious assault by any means, that included simple beatings, breaking bone, tearing flesh with a knife or, in extreme cases, pressing his shotgun against the rear of his victim's knee and pulling the trigger. Suspected of at least two unsolved murders, he was feared by all who crossed his path.
But Shooter's unique kneecapping talent wasn't called upon that often; his main pastime keeping Crowden's stable of girls in line or slapping around the occasional troublesome punter and of whom none would even consider reporting the assault to the police.
Most of all, the job that he really enjoyed, the task that gave him most satisfaction was when Shooter could give vent to his true feelings for women. Crowden merely referred to it as keeping the girls in line; the law called it rape. True to form, none of his terrified victims ever complained.
The sweat dripping from his body, he carefully laid the weights into their racks and proceeded to rub his neck and face with a clean, cotton towel. Leaning against the rough brick of the converted garage, he cast a proud glance around his brightly lit, homemade gym before reaching for the mobile phone. Brief though the message was, it was all he needed to know and decided to phone Crowden straight away.
The short conversation ended with Alex instructing Shooter to visit their mutual associate at his office in Warrick Street. Shooter didn't need a name.
He already knew where the former cop's office was located.

Thirty minutes later, a refreshed Shooter climbed into his modest Renault estate car and drove from his home in Glasgow's sprawling Easterhouse council estate to the north side of the River Clyde at the Broomielaw. The once thriving dock area now lay deserted of merchant ships; their passing glory remembered by the lonely vessel that now plied its trade as a floating casino. The nearby tenement buildings that formerly housed the merchant trader's premises lay mostly derelict, awaiting their destruction by developers; some for now inhabited by small businesses, many of which simply lasted till either the VAT man or the second rent month arrived.
In one such office on the first floor, a preferred location due to the top and second storey's being subject to water damage from the leaking roof, was situated the man Shooter had come to visit. The tarnished brass plate identified it to be the office of "Eddie Rawlings – Private Investigations".
Shooter didn't bother knocking at the front door but strode into the two roomed office, ignoring the protesting teenage secretary who mistakenly tried to bar his way, roughly seizing her by the arms and glaring into her frightened face.
'Sit on your arse, girlie and I'll no be hurting you,' he sneered at her through gritted teeth as he pushed her backwards.
The girl, her eyes wide in fear, sat heavily down at her desk and watched as Shooter pushed open the door to the inner office.

The fat man who sat behind the single desk with the two chairs arranged in front, half rose from his padded seat in wary expectation when Shooter strolled into his inner sanctum.
'Morning Eddie,' said Shooter, greeted the private detective with sarcastic politeness. 'Mister Crowden said you have something for me?'
He stood in front of the desk waiting; his hands clasped together in front of him, knowing his presence had caused the former copper to break out in a nervous sweat. He watched as Rawlings fumbled in a desk drawer and withdrew a plain manila envelope that he tossed onto the desk.
He stared hard at Rawlings who got the message. Rawlings reached across the desk, lifted the envelope and with shaking fingers handed it, to Shooter.
'Usual fee?' asked Shooter, concentrating on withdrawing the single sheet of close typed paper from the sealed envelope.
'Aye, a ton,' replied Rawlings, nervously licking his lips.
Shooter reached into his hip pocket and withdrew a thick wad of banknotes, peeling off four twenties; then with a tight smile, added a further twenty-pound note and tossed them across the desk, watching them fluttering around Rawlings head. The empty envelope he threw back on the desk, folding the paper and slipping it into an inner jacket pocket. He didn't need to read the report to know that all the information he required would be included. The fat shit was, if nothing else, at least meticulous in his investigations. Turning on his heel, he walked through the open door towards the exit, ignoring the open-mouthed secretary.
'Who the *fuck* was that!' she stormed into Rawlings office, her eyes blazing and fighting back the angry tears.
'That,' he replied as he fought to stop his hands shaking, 'is somebody else's problem for today.'

*

Later that afternoon, Tricia Crichton drove her small Corsa motorcar through the open gates and into yard behind the council run nursery. Checking her watch she breathed a sigh of relief. For once, probably for the first time in weeks she grimaced, she was early picking up young Archie. Not that the nursery staff had complained or said anything. But still, the odd glance and casual look at the large wall clock when she rushed in, intended to subtly remind her that she was or at least seemed to be always the last to pick up her child. They knew she was a single parent and, she had to admit, there was a bit of give and take by the nursery staff. Realistically, she liked her well paid job at the call centre and if a last minute customer inquiry was passed through to her switchboard, she couldn't just hand it over; no, it had to be dealt with by her and the commission she earned couldn't be ignored it the call resulted in a sale. Nonetheless, try telling that to someone who has their own domestic priorities.
She grinned again when she thought of the half-hearted chat up line her boss had made earlier that morning, smiling as she recalled his red faced embarrassment when she innocently asked if his wife would also be dining with them.
She hadn't seen him approach, was shocked when the passenger door was snatched open and a bald headed man quickly got in, slamming the door behind him. He placed a strong, restraining hand on her left arm.
'Don't make a sound, girlie,' he hissed at her, 'if you know what's good for your wee

boy.'
Her shocked scream immediately died in her throat at the mention of young Archie.
'What do you want?' she stammered at him, her eyes unable to tear away from the vivid scar on his cheek, the blue stars tattooed on his ears and his piercing dark brown eyes.
'Just a wee chat, girlie,' he leered at her, 'so don't be doing anything silly now, hear me?'
She nodded her head, aware of the curious glances of the mothers around her as they parked their cars to pick up their children from the nursery building.
Somehow, she instinctively knew he wasn't going to abduct her, not in broad daylight with people watching. No, he wanted something else.
'Your old man's a copper isn't he?'
She nodded her head, unable to breathe, not trusting her voice to reply.
'Well, tomorrow he's going to be attending an identification parade at the Paisley polis station, so here's what you are going to tell him he's going to do. Identify nobody. Got that? Because if he does,' he raised a forefinger to his scar, his eyes wide open and staring cruelly into Tricia's eyes, 'tomorrow, or maybe the next day; next week or next month, your wean is going to get one of these,' and slowly drew his finger along the line of his scar.
'Understand, girlie?'
Terrified, unable to move, Tricia swallowed hard and slowly nodded her head; aware her bladder had suddenly loosened, feeling the warm dampness beneath her.
As suddenly as he had come, the man opened the door and was gone. She sat stunned, her hands gripping the steering wheel, staring at where he had sat and unable to comprehend what had just occurred.
The side door of the nursery opened and there stood young Archie, smiling as he tightly grasped the hand of a young nursery nurse who pointed him with a smile towards the Corsa. As he ran excitedly to the car, Tricia whipped her head around and stared behind her wide-eyed at the entrance gate, but there was no sign of the man.

A mile down the road, Shooter stopped his car and reached into the inner jacket pocket for the sheet of paper. Meticulously, he tore the paper into dozens of little pieces and, glancing around to make sure there was no coppers about, tossed the scraps into the roadway.

*

CHAPTER 7

The dream was always the same. The top of the double decker bus, smooth and slippery as he lay flat, trying to reach Laura who screamed at him in fear; the unseen driver racing through the packed streets, twisting and turning round corners and forcing Johnny's prostrate body to swing back and forth as he sought to hold on, seeing his daughter slide helplessly to the side, just out of his reach. He crawled towards her, calling her name and watched in horror as she slid further and further away, nearing the edge and the fatal drop, her small hands desperately reaching but unable to grasp a handhold on the polished surface.
He cried out her name, one final time as he watched her slip over the side, a fingertip from the safety of his hand, her eyes pleading to him, her cry echoing in his ear.

'Daddy!'
He woke with a start, his body covered in sweat, muttering her name. Daylight streamed though a crack in the curtain, casting a dagger of light on the bed.
The digital clock told him it was almost six-thirty. He hit the button to prevent the alarm activating and swung his legs over the side of the bed, feeling the cold laminate flooring beneath his feet. He wrung his head in his hands and rubbed hard at his face. A thought occurred to him.
His nightmares always featured Laura.
He had yet to dream of Karen.

Johnny showered and run the hot water till he felt relaxed and calm. Not since the accident had he experienced a full night's sleep. He knew that he would have to discipline himself, get some pattern back into his life. He'd even thought about getting straight back to work, though his boss had assured him there would be no pressure; that he could choose his hours and filter back into full time but only when he was ready.
The funeral service and internment had been arranged for Saturday morning. There had been no contact from Karen's parents since he'd informed them of the details, other than an apologetic letter of sympathy signed by Hector. Pointedly, there had been neither a signature from his mother-in-law, Mavis nor any reference to her or mention of condolence either. Other cards, from the few friends he'd made at work, also arrived, as well as proposals from solicitors who obviously attracted by the high profile case, were keen to arrange civil law suits on his behalf. One cheaply printed, mock sympathy card even offered to dispose of Karen and Laura's clothes and possessions, suggesting the company could send a representative who would be happy to discuss a fair price. These ghoulish letters he tore to pieces in a frustrated anger.
His first task he decided, was tidying the house, beginning with the washing basket. Emptying the contents, the first items that tumbled out were Laura's play clothes, stained with food and other childish marks. He choked back a sob and, with an effort, began to sort through the various items, deciding that now wasn't the time to even consider making a decision about their things.
He recalled a handbill that had been posted through the door and that he had discarded the previous day and ransacked the bin till he found it. The circular requested contributions for old, clean clothing for a women's shelter in the Glasgow area. Donations of clothes and toys were sought for the victims of domestic abuse. A free phone number and the District Council logo seemed to legitimise the appeal. Ironic, he thought with a tight smile. Karen had sneered at these distressed women, believing them victims of their own making.
He read the leaflet and made up his mind. If he was going to contact them and send anything, at least he would send them clean. That decided he set about tackling the washing basket with renewed vigour, pleased that in some small way he had begun to take control again.
Maybe later, he'd give his boss a call and come to some arrangement about getting back into work.

*

Archie Crichton, dressed in civilian clothing, sat in the bleak witness room pondering over the previous night's drama that had unexpectedly unfolded in his home.

Julia Morton, similarly dressed in civilian clothing and sitting opposite and beside the Shogun's owner, stared hard at her partner, but it was obvious his mind was elsewhere. The little he had said that morning had been no more than a brief, but courteous greeting. She shrugged and turned again to her magazine. Must be the male menopause, she decided, dismissing his crankiness as normal for his age.
But what occupied Crichton's thoughts was a lot more serious than his age or his health. He'd been in the garden yesterday evening, digging at his vegetable patch when his distressed daughter had arrived home. His wife had difficulty getting any sense out of the girl and what had made it worse was that she had seemed to wet herself. The poor wee lad was astounded at his mother's behaviour and his concern soon turned to tears that needed consoling from his grandfather.
At last, when his wife had cleaned her up, Tricia had come downstairs in a bathrobe; embarrassed, still tearful and obviously shocked.
He'd manoeuvred her into the kitchen while his wife attended to young Archie and, through her sobbing and shaking, he'd at last got it out of her.
Who the man was, he had no idea. Who he was acting for, there was little doubt. It had to be the Crowden's and Archie Crichton had been police officer long enough to know the history of the family. It wouldn't be the sons that had threatened his daughter; the description Tricia gave him was too far removed from the two buggers he had arrested that night. No, this was obviously someone employed by the Crowden's and likely it was their father, Alex Crowden who had arranged the frightening warning.
Crichton had no personal dealings with the crime lord, but like most experienced police officers, knew who he was and what he was capable of. A shudder passed through him. That this type of violence should threaten his family appalled him. Yet he was in no doubt that if he refused to comply, if past stories were true, then Crowden was a man who was clearly capable of carrying out this threat.
Having settled the little fellow in front of the cartoon channel, his wife had come through to the kitchen and listened intently to the whole story. She gently massaged her daughter's shoulders and comforted her, sending her through to the lounge to sit with her son, before she turned to her husband.
'You'll need to do what he says, Archie,' she told him in a strangled voice.
'What, you don't think we should be reporting this?' he replied, stunned at her suggestion.
Her look of scorn silenced him.
'How many time you have told me Archie Crichton, that the polis couldn't protect themselves, let alone any other bugger,' she reminded him. 'This isn't a witness we're talking about here,' she hissed at him, keeping her voice low to avoid their daughter hearing. 'This is our grandson, wee Archie! Do you honestly think that your superiors are going to be more interested in protecting a four year old child than putting away a couple of car thieves, no matter who they are?'
She held up her hand to stifle his protest.
'I know what they did to that poor woman and her wee girl,' she said. 'I'm not without sympathy, dear God you know I'm not. But they're dead and gone! Let the police and the courts convict those two animals some other way, but not at the price of our lovely wee grandson!'
He hung his head in helplessness, for the first time in his life unsure what to do or how to

protect his family.
His wife reached across and held his hand as their pale-faced daughter returned to the kitchen and looked on. Her mother smiled reassuringly at her.
'Look love, I know your instinct is to report this, what happened to Tricia. But face facts. Even if you did tell your bosses and even if those two men go to court and are convicted. It isn't their father who'll be going to jail. He'll still be out and about. And if he's free to threaten us, how long can the police protect wee Archie? Days? Months? Years? How long before some new man in the police gets promoted and decides that the cost of looking after our grandson's safety isn't in keeping with his yearly budget?'
She stared harshly at him, knew that she was winning. It broke her heart to speak to him like this, to bully him; but she knew she must be strong.
'You've said it yourself often enough, you're only a statistic and that's all our wee Archie will be; just a statistic that the police have to look after, for a while. Until someone decides that the threat no longer exists. But who'll tell these…' she struggled to find the word, 'animals… that it's finished? Nobody. We'll never know when or even if they ever lose interest in our wee lad. It'll be him and us that's living their sentence!'
Crichton stared thoughtfully at his wife. How well she had grasped the economics of the police service, he thought; but then again, while he'd served, she'd been a cop's wife for nigh on thirty years, so it shouldn't really have come as a surprise to him.
'There'll be flak when I don't identify them, defiantly some kind of condemnation. Maybe even an inquiry,' he softly told her, his voice betraying his acceptance.
She knew then she'd won. That her husband was putting wee Archie's safety first. She sighed deeply and walked to stand beside Crichton, placing her arms about his head and drawing him to her full bosom. Their daughter standing in the doorway tearfully smiled for the first time since the threat had occurred, at her mother's genuine display of affection.
'You're a good man, Archie Crichton. A good husband, a good father and a good grandfather. And you're a good policeman too; so don't worry about the flak. We know the truth ad that's all that really matters. Besides, it will all be over in three months anyway.'

'First witness please.'
The detective nodded to the Shogun owner and escorted him from the room.
Crichton knew that as the senior cop, he would be next. They sat in silence for a few moments.
'You alright Archie?'
He nodded tight-lipped at Julia Morton, unable to face her.
'Fine. Don't be worrying about me. And no matter what happens….'
'Next witness please,' requested the grim-faced detective.
His limbs felt unduly heavy as he rose and followed the escort through to the parade room.
A plate glass window that was in reality a two-way mirror, was set in the wall behind which stood the two suspects and six stand-ins in a line, all facing their side of the mirrored wall and staring at their reflections. One stand-in was idly picking at his nose with nicotine-stained fingers; two more whispered to each other. A uniformed Inspector approached Crichton and read from a clipboard. The case officer, Ronnie Sutherland and

an expensively suited man, whom Crichton knew to be the lawyer Gospel Gordon, stood to one side.
As the Inspector followed the obligatory process lad out in his forms, droning on endlessly as he explained the parade procedure and reassuring the witness Archibald Crichton about security of the two-way mirror, Crichton stared at Davie and Sammy Crowden, standing at position two and seven respectively in the parade. He watched as Davie Crowden had a coughing fit, plucking a handkerchief from his pocket and dabbing at his mouth. The Inspector finished his dialogue and instructed the parade line to be quiet, then quietly invited Crichton to view the line of men through the mirrored glass. With sinking heart, Crichton made a brief pretence at looking at the parade and lowered his head.
'I don't see anyone I recognise,' he mumbled, his voice almost inaudible in the quiet space.
A shocked silence descended upon the room.
'Well, I think that's all…' began Gossip, his face opening wide in a huge grin.
'Do you mind, sir?' snapped the Inspector to the lawyer, silencing him with a frown.
'I'll ask you one more time, constable,' the Inspector stared hard at Crichton, all pretence at witness formality gone. 'Do you see *any* person to whom you referred to in your previous statement?'
Again Crichton shook his head and stared grey faced at the Inspector. 'No one,' he lied. He didn't have the courage to look at Ronnie Sutherland, a man he'd known for many years. Eyes bright with shame, he was escorted from the parade room as the Inspector abruptly called for the next witness.
Crichton stumbled listlessly into the small anteroom where the owner of the Shogun sat. Coolly, they ignored each other.
A few minutes later Julia Morton smiled at Crichton as she bounced into the room to join them.
'Easy-Peasy,' she joked, baffled by his grey pallor and blissfully unaware of what had occurred prior to her entrance into the parade room.
'Are you okay, Archie?'
Before he could reply, a white-faced Ronnie Sutherland opened the door.
'Got a minute, Archie,' he asked, in a voice that made it clear it was more of an instruction than a request.
Together they walked the short distance to Sutherland's room where once they were in, the door was angrily slammed behind Crichton.
'What the fuck was that!' demanded the enraged detective.
'I didn't see anyone….'
'Don't give me that old bullshit! This is me you're talking to now! What the fuck is going on?'
Crichton turned his watery eyes towards him, his shame compounded by having again to lie.
'Like I said in the parade, I can't…'
'Have you taken a backhander, Archie? Is this what it's all about, eh?'
The taunt worked. Crichton started towards Sutherland, his hands balling into fists, the anger evident in his snarl.
'I've never, *ever* accepted anything from anyone,' he angrily retorted 'and you should

know that better than anyone!'
Sutherland stood his ground, watching as the heavy set man calmed as quickly as he rose to anger. He turned to sit down at his desk, beckoning with one hand for Crichton to take a seat while running the other wearily through his hair.
'I've known you a long time, Archie Crichton. You're a good, hardworking honest cop. And I also know you're scared of nobody. So I'm guessing it's a bit more than that; somehow Crowden has got through to you. Some threat that you can't deal with yourself. Can you at least talk about it?'
Crichton shook his head. Of the few men he had met in his lengthy service that he believed he could fully trust, Sutherland rated highly; but even he couldn't protect wee Archie. No, this was something that he would have to bear alone.
'You know, of course, that when this gets to trial, you'll be expected to stand in the witness box and under oath, might I remind you, testify that you can't identify the two scumbags that you and your partner pulled from the Shogun? You do realise that, don't you?'
He nearly gave in then; almost exploded with the urge to explain, seek the help he so badly needed. But his grandsons smiling face swam before him. He raised his head and stared weary-eyed at the detective for a full twenty seconds, before replying.
'Is there anything else, sir?'
Sutherland returned his stare, then looked away in helplessness.
'Nothing else constable. See yourself out.'

*

Later that evening, DS Kevin Wilson held the door open while Maria Lavery edged past him into the DI's room carrying the tray with the three full mugs and an opened packet of biscuits.
Ronnie Sutherland, having again incurred the wrath of his increasingly quarrelsome wife, cleared some paperwork from his desk to allow her to set the tray down.
Once settled with their ea and biscuits, the three began their discussion.
'So,' opened Sutherland, spilling crumbs down his shirt front, 'what we've got so far. We can prove the two Crowden boys were in the car; that's down to fingerprints and forensic. We've got one eye witness taking them from the car at the time of the crash, our fair maiden constable Morton and precious little else.'
'No likelihood that Archie Crichton will change his mind then, boss?' inquired Lavery as she sipped at her coffee.
'Nothing to indicate he will, Maria. I don't know what his reason is, but I've known him for over twenty years. Something has got him running scared and it's definitely not like him. Unfortunately, the ID parade sheet has now been entered in evidence and we can't force them to appear in another parade for the same witness. So even if he does change his mind, it won't look good in court and would cast doubt on his reliability as a witness. No, he'd have to come up with a pretty good excuse for telling porky pies and from the short chat I had with him, I don't think he'll budge from the stance he's taken.'
'You know what's being bandied about,' interrupted Wilson, 'that Crichton's taken a bung?'
Sutherland ruefully shook his head.
'I don't for one second believe that,' he replied, the scorn evident in his voice, then added a warning, his eyebrows knitting together. 'And I don't want to hear it either.'

He nibbled at another biscuit, his face thoughtful.
'What I do think though, is that Alex Crowden has in some way had Archie threatened. Problem is that if he won't tell us, how do we find out?'
He chewed thoughtfully at the biscuit, idly tapping his fingers against the desk.
'What about this allegation that Pat Delaney provided the Crowden's with the key?'
'Well,' replied Lavery, 'therein lies a tale. It seems that our Miss Mary Crowden started *work*,' she held up two fingers of both hands that she wiggled, 'with Delaney after her father made a personal request to him and, according to Delaney, she has worked diligently for the six months she's been there. Seems that she has bookkeeping experience, a certificate or something she obtained at college he thinks. However, when we put pressure on Delaney, he confessed that Alex Crowden has offered him a partnership in the car business, one of those *or else* type offers, if you know what I mean. He wouldn't elaborate on what the *or else* was though but if his nervousness was any indication on how he felt about the offer, I don't think he had any option in the matter.'
She stopped to again to sip from her mug.
'Anyway, there's no way he would tell us this officially and insisted we didn't put anything down on paper, but he's as certain as he can be that there were two keys for the Shogun when it passed through his place and assumes that Mary must have given one to her brothers. He's also convinced that Alex wants him out of there, though he can't figure why. When we put a bit of pressure on him,' though Sutherland noted she was careful not to explain what she meant by pressure, 'he owned up the business turns over more than he admits to the taxman, but he's not stupid. He doesn't think that the car market is profitable enough to excite Alex Crowden and is unsure where Crowden's interest really lies. He's convinced there's got to be more to the takeover than simply securing Mary Crowden's job.'
'Okay, good work.' Sutherland finished his coffee and reached behind him for his jacket, aware that if he didn't get home in thirty minutes his dinner would be in the dog.
'Right, I'm off home. One more thing and it's up to yourselves. I'll be attending the funeral service on Saturday morning. I know you're both off duty this weekend, but if you can make it….'
Wilson pre-empted his request and glanced at the nodding Lavery.
'No problem boss. We'll see you there.'

*

The arrival of the detectives at the Car Sales Portacabin for the second time had panicked Mary Crowden, until that is they had politely inquired of her as to the whereabouts of Delaney. Mustering as much of her demureness as she could to recover from her initial shock, she flashed a wide smile at the Detective Sergeant while pointedly ignoring his female colleague, informing him that Delaney could be found having his usual liquid lunch at *The Eastender* across the road. It surprised and annoyed her that the detective thanked her with hardly a trace of acknowledgment. After the two left and her feminine vanity aroused, she checked her make-up in the wall mirror, but could see nothing amiss. That's when it occurred to her that maybe Gossip Gordon's information to the police wasn't so believable to them, after all. She wrapped her arms about her as a sudden chill enveloped her and decided then to phone Pop.

Alex Crowden snapped his mobile phone closed and sat back in the driver's seat,

contemplating his next move. It seemed then, from what Mary had told him, that the cops were keen to interview Delaney and he was anxious to know what the skinny bastard would tell them. Of course he would deny having given the key to Davie and Sammy, as was expected, but what else would he tell them? For the first time, Alex considered that maybe he had been too cunning and aware that the cops weren't that stupid.
He thought about the parade that had taken place and Gospels delighted phone call. At least that old fat filth bastard had got the message and didn't pick his boys out. The Shogun owner he never gave a thought, knowing full well that when he'd received his visit from Shooter, there would have been no need for the shaven headed man to go back and ask twice.
Now there was only one witness to worry about, the other filth, the female cop; but whether she was worth considering…he wasn't sure. According to Gospel, the Scottish legal system required two eyewitnesses or one eyewitness and corroborating evidence. Forensic evidence could suffice alone, Gospel had patiently explained.
But that, he grimly smiled at his lawyer, wasn't worrying him, at least not for the moment.
He thought again about Mary's phone call. He'd tied up a few quid in that little enterprise and it would be a pity if Delaney learned of his plan and spoiled it at the last moment. Maybe, he scanned his phone directory for the number, it might be prudent to let Shooter have a wee word with Pat Delaney. The type of conversation that Shooter excelled in.

*

Sitting alone in the canteen of the Traffic Department station in Govan, nursing a tepid mug of tea, Archie Crichton assumed that word had got round. The silent stares and cold attitude of his fellow officers was hard to ignore.
A shadow loomed over the table. Julia Morton, her face visibly hostile, stared at him. 'The Chief Inspector would like a word,' she informed him then without a backward glance, turned away to join a group of female officers sitting nearby.
The old cop pushed the chair away and strode from the canteen, staring straight ahead and pretending to ignore the furtive whispering that followed him out.
The Chief Inspector sat waiting for him. It was evident the man was uncomfortable, nervously rolling a pen back and forth across the pad on his desk. He didn't invite Crichton to sit down.
'I'll get straight to the point, Archie. There's been some talk about the parade yesterday and I've received a telephone complaint from the Detective Inspector in charge of the case. It seems that he is unhappy with your conduct and was curious if you had confided in me. Frankly, I didn't have a clue as to what he was talking about, but if there is anything that you wish to discuss?'
The opportunity was there. All he had to do was seize the opening, tell someone. He stared above his bosses head at the photograph on the wall; the laughing group of Traffic officers standing beside the old wrecked police car, seeing himself third from the left in the front row. In happier times.
'Nothing to say?' the Chief Inspector interrupted his thoughts, the resignation evident in his voice.
'Okay, Archie, well then, while what happened at the parade in no way detracts from your previous service here with us at Traffic…'
Here it comes, thought Crichton, the sucker punch.

'...however, I have to inform you that none of your colleagues are keen to partner you on duty.'
The Chief Inspector paused for breath and stared at his constable.
'I really don't know what got into you or what your reasons are for...doing what you did. But you must appreciate that in the best interests of the department, I intend assigning you to indoor duties as gateman for the duration of your time left with us.'
Gateman, Crichton inwardly seethed. The lame, sick and lazy post. The arse end job. Sitting in a wee hut by the yard entrance, giving out petrol and diesel pump keys for refuelling the cars, receiving and dishing out internal mail. Keeping the storage area tidy. Christ, what have I become?
'Yes sir,' he replied quietly, 'very good sir.'

*

The persistent ringing of his phone caught DI Ronnie Sutherland just about to depart his office in time to beat the Friday evening rush hour traffic. Reluctantly and against his better instinct he took the call, but his frustration turned to delight when he spoke with his old friend.
'Hello, Danny boy,' he greeted his former CID colleague with a smile, 'good to hear from you.'
McBride didn't waste any time, but got straight to the point.
'Sorry I've been late getting back to you, Ronnie, but I had some other things on the go. We've a real problem with this batch of killer heroin that's been going round and that's taking up most of our inquiry time. Anyway, about your man Pat Delaney. I've checked back through the archived files and of course, as you rightly suspected, we know him. Small time really, hasn't been in recent trouble and any conviction he has accrued is all vehicle related offences. Interesting thing though is that a source has been in touch with the Fraud Squad about,' he paused as he checked the date on his notes, 'four months ago.'
McBride then reminded Sutherland that all intelligence received by any police department, including the Fraud Squad, comes either directly or is copied to the Criminal Intelligence Department. Sutherland patiently waited, already knowing this, but thought it better not to interrupt and let the DS explain in his own, indomitable style.
McBride asked him, 'I assume you will have heard of a project called GEAR?'
Sutherland hadn't and asked him to explain it.
'You might recall reading a headquarters information bulletin, one of these monthly things the media department send out now and again about local initiatives and the effect they will have on modern policing. Well, it's all about a plan known as the Glasgow East Area Rejuvenation. In simple terms the District Council intended to level the poor quality and uneconomical housing in the east end of Glasgow and replace it with a mixture of modern council and low priced private dwellings. They're also determined to introduce a new work ethos into the area that has previously suffered social decline and industrial deprivation. The money for the project,' he continued, 'is being invested by both the Scottish Office and local enterprise who hope to entice foreign business to invest in the area by offering low rates, tax benefits and custom built factory premises. The high incidence of local unemployment also virtually guarantees a ready and willing workforce. Needless to say that our interest as the police was peaked simply because it's a well-documented statistic that unemployment directly relates to crime figures, hence the

bulletin that I'm sure you read,' he finished; knowing full well that the Ronnie Sutherland he remembered wouldn't have bothered reading the bloody thing.
The DI chewed at his lower lip and his excitement increased as he realised that maybe McBride was onto something.
'Anyway,' said McBride, 'the source has informed the Fraud Squad that a large building company is quietly buying up most of the small properties and derelict sites in the area that also includes the waste ground behind Delaney's premises. Our interest lies in that some of the private purchasers are serving councillors. Whether Delaney himself has been approached or not, I can't tell you. What *we've* assessed in the Intelligence Department is that it is some sort of large development that is being considered for the substantial piece of waste ground that lies there; either housing or commercial constructions, we don't know yet; but when the project becomes public knowledge then land in that particular part of the city will be worth a small fortune. What I *can* say in confidence is that I've got one of my people discreetly looking into it with some contacts in the Planning Department, but you know what that lot are like; promise to get back to you etcetera, etcetera.'
'The builder, do you know which company?'
'I'm afraid not, but if it's any help, the only companies being considered are those who are legitimate. This is a Scottish Government backed scheme using public money, so in the wake of the Scottish Parliament fiasco, there won't be any cowboys involved in this.'
'Look,' said McBride, his voice indicating he was obviously keen to get away, 'I'm kind of tied up with this other problem at the moment, but I'll have somebody get back to you, probably either Monday or Tuesdays if that's okay?'
'Thanks Danny that's been a terrific help. I owe you one.'
'No problem,' replied McBride, 'but if you are on to something, whether or not it ties in with your own inquiry, I'd be keen to know.'
When he'd finished the call, Sutherland sat back and smiled to himself, wondering if Pat Delaney was aware that maybe Alex Crowden's interest in the car business, as Delaney had rightly guessed, was instead associated with the proposed development. Using the desk to lever himself to his feet, he knew that until Danny McBride got back to him, he would have an anxious wait over the weekend, already planning in his mind to have Wilson and Lavery bring the car salesman into the office for a formal interview.
As chance would have it, and unknown to Sutherland, Alex Crowden had already made his own plans for Patrick Delaney.

*

CHAPTER 8

The passing of spring heralded the summer months, predicted by long-range weather forecasters to be the hottest for a decade.
The Saturday morning of the funeral arrived without fuss and the service had gone off quietly. With uncommon courtesy, the media respected the privacy urged by the police and remained an appropriate distance from the mourners. To Johnny Bryce's surprise, the crowd numbered several hundred. *A Community United in Tragedy* as headlined by the *Glasgow News*. Predictably, his mother-in-law Mavis ignored him throughout the church service and the moving burial ceremony.

It didn't escape his notice either that her coat and hat appeared to be new or that when exiting the small church, she pushed her way through the few members of Karen's related family; her head constantly turning to glance at the camera crews, ensuring she positioned herself to the maximum advantage to allow the snappers to obtain the best shots. Lifting the black veil, she dabbed lightly at her eyes in the full knowledge, Johnny suspected, that their cameras would capture her contrived and splendid dignity.
In complete contrast, her husband Hector seemed pale and genuinely distraught, ignoring his wife's sullen stare as he first solemnly shook Johnny's hand and give him a warm and compassionate embrace. No words were exchanged, but Johnny could see the man was deeply distressed.
To Johnny's further surprise, a number of colleagues from the Corps and their wives attended the service; the marines formally dressed in uniform, some having travelled from their base in Devon, to personally sympathise with the man that they all liked and admired. Their presence and simple sentiment brought a lump to his throat and he found it difficult to speak with them. They respected his dignified silence and with promises to keep in touch, in the main let him be with his grief.
The single photograph of Johnny, alone bearing the small, white coffin of his daughter from the church and closely followed by the undertakers carrying Karen's body, made national headlines and rekindled the public outrage about the incident.

Within a few weeks of the service, Johnny thought he was going stir crazy and almost pleaded his way back to work. His co-workers at Garvey's, believing they were being kind, persistently approached him and offered their condolence; so much so that, with his boss's permission, he volunteered for a week's unpopular duty manning the CCTV system, virtually locking himself in the small, compact room merely to avoid their sympathy.
As a diversion he had volunteered for a computer study course at the local college, two of his evenings now occupied applying himself to the intricacies of Information Technology, a subject in which he had previously demonstrated little interest.
But nothing prevented the re-occurring dream that and nightly wakened him, crying out his daughter's name.

*

Other newsworthy issues quickly overcame the media outcry over the deaths of Karen and Laura Bryce; most notably the scandal that ensued when a prominent Member of the Scottish Parliament, whose open-secret dalliance with an opposition Member's wife, had had resulted in a public punch-up within the Debating Chamber. It didn't help the situation that the resulting fight was televised live and involved further Members, who supported either the philanderer or the cuckolded man. The ensuing battle effectively closed the debating session for that week and predictably led to calls for disbanding the Parliament. To Johnny's quiet relief, public interest in his wife and daughter's deaths soon waned.
The matter of the Bryce deaths was resurrected some months later when in reference to such incidents, it was reported that a drunken youth stole a high powered vehicle and raced it through a Cornish town before mounting a pavement and flying through the air. The heavy car finally came to a sudden and spectacular halt outside a sweet shop, crushing to death an eight-year-old girl innocently standing there. The tragedy was

paralleled with the deaths of Karen and Laura and a number of other victims who had died in similar circumstances.

*

As promised, Danny McBride caused the inquiry to be made on Sutherland's behalf and the following Tuesday morning, his colleague Brenda Paterson contacted the DI to inform him that planning permission for a large and exclusive private housing estate had been secretly granted for the waste ground directly behind Pat Delaney's property. It seemed from her reading of the plans, reported Paterson that an access road to the proposed site would require to be cut through the property at the *exact* position where Pat Delaney's car showroom was currently located. This was necessary she added, to avoid causing further congestion to the already overstretched road network and would link the proposed construction with the nearby Shettleston Road. In short, this ensured Delaney's small but important piece of ground to be a lucrative asset.

Armed with this new information, Sutherland happily dispatched his detectives Wilson and Lavery to fetch Delaney into Paisley police office; the plan being to induce him to speak formally against Mary Crowden by providing the police with a written statement, in exchange for this profitable news. To the Sutherland's consternation, not only did Wilson and Lavery fail to locate Delaney, but it seemed that no one, his wife included, had seen or heard of him since the preceding Saturday.

In the weeks that followed, Delaney remained out of touch with everyone and when the readily available cash in their joint account had been exhausted, his livid and admittedly mystified wife attended at her local police station where she formally registered her husband as missing. The officer noting the report shrewdly included a confidential postscript that Missus Delaney did not seem to be over-anxious about her husband's mysterious vanishing. As standard procedure, the police visited all known haunts and hangouts of the missing man and close and casual acquaintances spoken with, but none could provide any clue as to the whereabouts of Patrick Delaney.

The local media become aware of the search for the missing man. During a period when there was a deficit of newsworthy items, Ally McGregor of the *Glasgow News,* for the clear purpose of beefing up his story, slyly speculated that the missing man might have somehow been involved with local gangsters.

Alex Crowden read the article, but on the advice of his lawyer Gospel Gordon, dismissed the claim as a piece as crap.

However, now that Delaney's disappearance had become public and armed with McGregor's fabricated information, Gospel Gordon again contacted DI Sutherland and reiterated his clients David and Samuel Crowden previous statement, alleging Delaney's complicity with the real but unnamed criminals.

'Delaney has provided the true thieves with the Shogun's key and now apparently absconded to avoid prosecution,' persisted the haughty Gordon. 'In light of this I wish you to convey to the Procurator Fiscal that at the forthcoming proceedings, it is my intention to present Delaney's disappearance as a defence alibi in bar of trial.'

'Perhaps you might be willing to identify this mysterious source, this alleged informant who knows so much, so that I might interview him or her?' suggested the cynical Sutherland.

Gordon smiled at the phone, knowing full well that having made his allegation, Sutherland was duty bound to carry out his request and promptly refused to divulge anything further.

Sutherland seethed at Gospel's obvious ploy but without Delaney to formally refute the allegation, he knew it left a hole in the persecutions case and caused the hunt for the missing man to be stepped up.
But all to no avail. Patrick Delaney remained missing.
Sutherland later leaned that Delaney's wife, now revealed by her lawyer to be a previously unknown silent partner in the car business and panicking as the mortgage and other sundry debts mounted up, struck a business deal with Alex Crowden and accepted the sum of one hundred thousand pounds for the company that included all associated stock and land. Missus Delaney thought Crowden to be a gracious man, particularly when holding her hand in sympathy for her financial predicament, he suggested that the Inland Revenue needn't know about the twenty thousand pounds cash he privately handed over.
Mary Crowden, now Chief Executive of the newly acquired Pat Delaney's Car Sales, immediately on paper hired her brothers Davie and Sammy as sales representatives, thus providing them with legitimate employment records when finally their case was called at Paisley Sheriff Court. At their father's firm insistence, both Davie and Sammy dutifully attended daily at the premises where to their annoyance, Mary employed them assisting the teenage worker in menial tasks; washing and valetting the vehicles.
As far as she was concerned and now that Delaney could not be found, the matter of the Shogun key no longer worried Mary. Keeping her brother's around was of little consequence now that she had her first foot on the rung of her father's property ladder. Besides, she privately smirked; she enjoyed the power she wielded over them both and in particular Davie, who used every available excuse to visit the Portacabin office where he would sneak a sly and proprietorial glance at his blonde and shapely sister.
Six weeks after Alex Crowden's purchase of the company, he warned his daughter that a council contact had been in touch and she was to expect a formal approach any time.
Two days later, Mary fluttered her eyes and pressing a well manicured hand to her lovely throat, pretended surprise when visited by two business suited men who informed her they represented a building corporation keen to negotiate the sale of her company and the land attached thereto. Regretfully, they were not at liberty to discuss why their corporation wished to acquire the company or the land. With suitable charm and demureness, she dazzled the two men with her disarming beauty, referring them to her father's lawyer Mister Gordon, who represented her family in all legal matters.

*

Like Johnny Bryce, Annie Hall had also been studying hard but in her case for her forthcoming promotion interview. At the appointed time and suitably attired in newly purchased bottle green coloured business suit with flared skirt, pale green blouse, matching shoes and handbag, her hair professionally cut and styled, Annie nervously presented herself at the Director's office and smiled at one of the departing candidates for the position. Sitting in the foyer awaiting her call to the interview, she pointedly ignored the surprised glances she drew from her male co-workers. It didn't occur to Annie that none of her colleagues had suspected that beneath her usual dress of garish clothes and frazzled hair was an extremely attractive young woman.
Under Sadie's tuition, she had practised her entrance, how she would sit, her listening skills and the responses to likely questions she'd be asked.

Her head felt like exploding; full of details about budget restrictions, staff issues, racial diversity and equal opportunities and she experienced a slight panic when her name was at last called. Her legs felt sluggish and heavy as she rose from the seat in the waiting room. True to form, she dropped her open handbag and spent an anxious thirty seconds recovering the spilled items, finally walking to the door and shaking her head, praying her hair was again falling neatly into place.
With an effort, she forced a smile and underwent the forty-five minute interview; later returning to her office where Sadie discovered her with her head in her hands, hair now in disarray, suit jacket carelessly slung across a chair and a dismal creature from the smartly dressed young woman who had entered the building an hour previously.
'I was bloody rotten,' she wailed, close to tears. 'I'm sure they must think me an idiot.'
'Don't be silly,' her friend tried to comfort her. 'So, what do you think went wrong?'
'Every-bloody-thing!' she snapped back with uncharacteristic fury. 'I'm just not ready for this promotion. Oh hell, why did I put myself through this?'
'Right,' decided Sadie, 'let's get out of here and head across to the pub. I always feel that if I'm going to be miserable, I'm better being miserable with a packet of crisps and a vodka and orange in my hand.'

Later that night lying in bed, Annie was grateful for the older woman's friendship. The downside of the vacancy for the position of Department Head was that Sadie would be leaving. With that sad thought, she turned over and closed her eyes, but the consoling and inordinate amount of alcohol she had consumed denied her sleep. Her throat felt as though an army of ants wearing sandpaper boots had marched down to her stomach. Sliding her legs out of bed, she reached up to open the hopper window and glanced across to the light burning brightly in the opposite bedroom.
She knew now who her mystery jogger was, having now seen him several times using the back door of his house and recognised him; and again when the sad photograph had appeared in the newspaper. A wave of sympathy passed through her. She couldn't imagine what he was feeling, how he was coping.
Her previous imagined thoughts of becoming acquainted with the man she now knew as John Bryce returned to haunt her and with pangs of guilt, closed her curtains tightly and went to fetch a glass of water.

Two weeks later the plain buff envelope bearing the logo of the Glasgow District Council dropped through her letterbox. With shaking fingers, she burst open the envelope and withdrew the single sheet of paper that formally informed Ms Ann Matilda Hall she was a successful candidate and that effective as of 1 September, she was to assume the position as Head of Department, Archived Records at the Mitchell Library, Glasgow.

*

Working in almost total isolation from his colleagues, Archie Crichton settled down to serve his remaining few weeks within the police service as gatekeeper at the Traffic Department station. His daily routine consisted of filling in vehicle log sheets and issuing the keys to the fuel pumps to poker faced colleagues. With hardly a glance, the officers attending the small gatehouse seldom exchanged little more than a curt word and made it clear their opinion of the old cop was that of a betrayer. Association in any form with Archie Crichton, it seemed, was frowned upon.

He didn't complain, knowing that any explanation would simply be accepted as an excuse, an acknowledgment that he had succumbed to threat. His previous record was now of little value and once where junior officers sought his counsel, they now turned away; his expertise and standing among the Department was no longer needed.
His exile he bore with fatalistic acceptance.
One wet afternoon, as the rain splattered against the walls of the small office, he sat at the small workstation and using his password, logged onto the Police National Computer, watching as the screen flashed out its obligatory DATA protection warning while the system booted up. He smoothed out the scrap of paper that he carried, slipping on his glasses as again he read the scribbled details, noted when his weeping and distraught daughter had stuttered the description of the man who had threatened his grandson. He tentatively pressed the button that projected the search field and with uncertain fingers, hesitantly typed in the details.
He didn't have long to wait. The information that flashed back at him confirmed his worst fears.
Thomas Aloysius Martin; nicknamed Shooter, with a propensity for violence that included the use of weapons. The screen flashed a warning sign, designed to alert officers that Martin was often in possession of a sawn off shotgun that he would secrete in a pocket of his trouser leg. Crichton read the antecedent history, of his association with Alex Crowden on whose behalf he was suspected of committing two murders, both unsolved. He scrolled down through thc screen pages, aghast at the degree of violence used by Martin and saw the record included his home address, description and vehicles used; updated Crichton saw, as recently as two weeks previously by a locally based Easterhouse officer who witnessed Martin driving a Renault estate car and who prudently noted the registration number. The photograph attached to the record portrayed a man who glared at the camera with eyes blazing, his teeth bared in defiance. Crichton felt chilled and unaccountably enraged that this animal had threatened his daughter and grandchild; in essence, his wife and he also.

At home, he didn't discuss his work situation, simply telling his wife that he no longer was assigned operational duties; a lie she rightly guessed, but likewise accepted as the price her husband had paid for the well-being and safety of their grandson. They smiled and assured Tricia that all was well and never once hinted at the anguish they both felt. They had come to terms with the closure of his career and knew that uncommonly, there would be no large party with well-wishers seeing him off the station, bearing gifts that indicated their like of him and admiration of his thirty years of service. They faced his retirement as they had faced other difficulties, throughout their marriage. Together.
The trial he knew would condone his colleague's and likely also the public's scorn, but that he would deal with, when the time arose.
For now, they had agreed that either he or his wife would always accompany their daughter on each occasion that wee Archie had to be collected from the nursery. Their daughter and the wee lad would never be left alone.
Just in case.

*

Working studiously within his ground level corner office at the Procurator Fiscal's Department in Inchinnan Road, the warmth of the sun magnified by the double glazed

window that refused to open, PF Depute Richard Smyth persevered with the aching pain from his recently diagnosed duodenal ulcer; a condition he presumed exacerbated by his dread of the day that he knew would undoubtedly come. When once again Alex Crowden would remind him of the debt he owed to the crime lord, a debt he suspected would never be fully paid.
Again he cursed his ill luck on that fateful night, wishing by all that he held to be sacred that he had not given way to temptation; but the blonde haired youth, he recalled with stark clarity, had been so, so beautiful, with skin as clear as that of a new born baby. His pain diminished slightly as the memory of the young man took over, aware that he was becoming physically aroused at the memory of what the youth, whose name he fought to recall, was prepared to do for and to him. If only he hadn't taken the coke.
He swallowed hard and clutched at the police report in his hand, mouth suddenly dry and unaware the paper now lay crumpled in his fist.
Not since that time had he succumbed to his basic instinct, apprehensive that he might yet be discovered, his secret made public and his private life open to investigation. Crowden had never revealed to him what had become of the boy's body and daily Smyth feared its resurrection in some field or wood.
He broke into a sweat as he recalled again the night, wondering how it had all gone so horribly wrong, the belt about the boy's neck, leading him about on all fours and then finally….
He shuddered and gave a slight, involuntary cry.
'All right Dickie?'
He almost jumped from his chair as the inquiring voice cut through his thoughts. Wide eyed and dry mouthed, he saw his colleague standing at the open door of his office, a bemused smile playing about her mouth.
'Yes, fine,' he replied and then, as she walked away, shouted angrily after her, 'and don't call me Dickie!'

*

Gospel Gordon stood with both hands placed firmly on each side of the carved pulpit, his strong voice echoing across the wide expanse of the cathedral. The majority of the congregation watched him with admiring eyes, attentive to hear what this well-known figure, this prominent and reputable man had to say. Not so his wife, sitting in the fourth pew who stared impassively at him; the righteous man that they all liked and admired, she inwardly sneered. If they only knew him for the philanderer he really was. She smirked at her knowledge of his private perversions and considered again her good fortune; for what her husband didn't know was her new discovery of his great secret; the details she had learned of his off shore account numbers, information she would soon put to her own, personal use.
He slipped on his gold-rimmed spectacles and glanced down at the prepared text.
The Sunday sermon gave him the opportunity to practise his public speaking, an art form he had painstakingly perfected through his years as a defence counsel and after dinner speaker at many of the high profile public ceremonies to which he was often invited.
With a theatrical glance at the gathering before him, he informed them that the Lesson for the day was taken from the Romans; Chapter Twelve: The Duties of Christians and then proceeded to recite the passage.
Knowing full well his love of quoting Scripture throughout his criminal cases, they

listened intently. The irony of the last sentence: *Be not overcome by evil, but overcome evil with good* was completely lost on the egotistical lawyer.

*

While Gospel Gordon intoned his Lesson in the Catholic splendour of the Glasgow church, the body of a man floated gently, face down on the rising waves in the Irish Sea, almost two miles to the west of the coastal resort of Largs. A closer examination would have revealed that the left side of his head seemed to be missing, as though torn asunder by some brutal force. The man's cheap clothes were completely sodden, his whitened flesh peeling and ripped by the sharp beaks of marauding seagulls. A bird flew towards the corpse and landed with a great flapping of wings on his back. The action caused the corpse to roll over and the bird flew off, squawking irritably, its food source denied as the late and unlamented Patrick Delaney, slipped once more beneath the water.

CHAPTER 9

Johnny Bryce returned home and let himself in through the front door, stepping over the half dozen or so items of mail that lay upon the mat. Stooping, he collected the envelopes and saw most were leaflets or flyers that he immediately dismissed, but two attracted his attention.
In the kitchen, he filled the kettle and sat at the small table where he carefully opened the large, white A4 sized envelope. He smiled with pleasure at the certificate inside with his name printed on it, confirming his successful achievement in passing the computer course. The hand written letter from his tutor congratulated him and encouragingly suggested he complete and submit the accompanying application form that offered further instruction in computing skills. He'd already made his mind up, amazing himself with his competence and aptitude at IT.
The second letter in the buff envelope had the return address of the Procurator Fiscal stamped upon the reverse side. Inside he discovered a summons, citing him to attend court on Monday 1 August at the Paisley Sheriff Court in the trial against David Crowden and Samuel Crowden. A typed note attached to the summons further instructed that as the first day of trial would be spent selecting a jury, his presence would not be required till ten o'clock the following morning.
Johnny read and reread the summons with a curious detachment, not quite believing that at last, the day had finally arrived. The kettle boiled and clicked off in the background ignored, his thoughts reluctantly once again turning to the fateful night when the Crowden brothers had robbed him of his daughter. And of course his wife, he thought guiltily.
The phone rang and he stood and lifted the receiver.
DI Ronnie Sutherland greeted him and offered an apology for not phoning earlier, explaining he had preferred to wait for Johnny's return home, rather than call him at his work.
'I assume you will have received your court citation today?'
'Found it when I got home,' he replied. 'I've not to attend till Tuesday morning.'
'That's standard practise, allows the court to select a jury rather than have the witnesses waste a day sitting about.'
An awkward pause lay between them, broken by Sutherland who said:

‘I thought the service went well. Sorry I haven’t been in touch since then, but I didn’t think you’d need a heavy flatfoot calling you every other day, just to tell you there was nothing new.’
‘I read in the papers about the guy Delaney going missing. The reporter tied him in with the theft of the Shogun. Is that right?’
He didn’t miss the heavy sigh that came through the phone. Sutherland obviously wasn’t comfortable talking about it.
‘Yes and no; Delaney is still missing and the Shogun *did* pass through his Car Sales. But we don’t think he’d anything to do with the theft. Between you and me Johnny, the defence lawyer Gospel Gordon is using Delaney’s disappearance in an attempt to deflect blame away from the Crowden’s. He’s a real slippery bastard is Gordon; it’s not beyond reason that it was him who fed the reporter that load of shite.’
‘So, do you think that the Crowden’s had anything to do with Delaney going missing? I mean, do you think he’s been warned off or something? Maybe killed him?’
Johnny could hear a tapping noise through the phone, unaware that Sutherland was rattling his pen against his desk as he considered the question. More than anything, he wanted to be able to take the younger man into his confidence, believing that he deserved the truth. At last he replied.
‘There’s no body turned up or any reason to believe that Delaney might be dead and our inquiries which, believe me have been really extensive, have failed to turn up anything new. If you were to ask my opinion and I stress, this is just my gut talking, I think Mister Delaney is permanently out of the scene. His wife has since sold up his business and you’ll never guess who the new owners are?’
He heard a sharp intake of breath.
‘You’re not talking about the Crowden’s?’
‘Got it in one. Alex Crowden has his daughter Mary running the show, but he’s the brain behind the business. Coincidentally, I hear that’s where the brothers are employed, though if my source is correct, washing motors and doing the odd job isn’t what I’d call employment. I figure they’re there until the trial is finished, sort of keeping them out of harm’s way, as it were.’
‘So there’s a daughter too?’ Johnny wasn’t about to reveal that in the car outside the mortuary, he’d read the female detectives report; that he knew about the car sales place and that the police suspected the Crowden’s sister of supplying the key.
Sutherland drew a sharp intake of breath. He didn’t intend telling Bryce too much and decided to close his loose mouth right there. No need for Bryce to know about his suspicions regarding the Shogun key.
‘Aye, a looker by all account and probably well aware of her old man’s businesses, but nothing that we can pin on her at this time. Look, the trial’s over a week away, so if there’s anything else that develops, I’ll let you know, okay?’
‘I appreciate the call and about the funeral. I’m grateful that you came. Thanks again.’

Later that night, nursing a bottle of beer, Johnny again read the letter from his attractive tutor and smiled. He wasn’t that naïve and was aware her interest in him was not *totally* devoted to his budding computer skills. Still, he knew that did show promise and was loosely attracted by the possibilities of a career in that industry. Anything, he sighed to avoid the mind-numbing job of guarding ladies lingerie, gents’ clothing and garden accessories, he mused.

*

After he'd hung up, Sutherland placed his hands behind his head and thought about the case. The evidence now solely consisted of the female cop Julia Morton's eyewitness account and the forensic evidence. Which reminds me, he thought glancing down at the slip of paper on his desk. Picking up his phone he dialled the extension for the Divisional Productions officer.

'Graham? DI Sutherland here. I've a request from the PF's office that all forensic and fingerprint productions and written statements be delivered to their office for examination by the prosecuting counsel prior to trial and they've to be there for, wait a minute,' he read the slip again, 'the twenty-fifth of July. See to it for me, will you?'

'Have they to be delivered to anyone in particular?' inquired the Productions officer.

Sutherland glanced at the slip again, as if confirming to himself the identity of the recipient.

'Mister Smyth,' he shook a weary head. 'Our very own devious Dickie.'

*

Archie Crichton stared hard at the witness summons. It was fate he decided, that the court case should begin on the very day he finished as a working police officer. Granted, he'd still theoretically be a serving cop for a few weeks thereafter, but with annual leave entitlement and days that he'd accrued through his service, that few weeks would have seen him through to his final day of service; but now this.

With a resigned sigh, he showed his wife the summons and she too realised the irony of the situation.

'Never mind, dear,' she stood behind him and gently ruffled his thick mop of snowy white hair. 'The note says that you'll not need to attend till the next day and if you like, I'll come with you.'

'They'll put me into the witness box,' his voice faltered slightly, 'and I'll have to stand there and look at that pair of…that pair of….'

His voice broke as he struggled to contain his anger and his rage, 'and again I'll have to deny that I can identify them. Judas!' he shook his head in misery, 'that's who I am! Judas!'

She wrapped her arms about his neck, holding him close against her breast and almost choking him in her eagerness to contain his hurt.

'But we know the truth, Archie and surely that's what counts?'

The shriek of their grandson hurtling through the front door and the screaming of his mother as she pursued him seemed to act like a switch, both straightening up and adopting a cheery expression.

'Granddad!' screamed the giggling boy as he threw himself at Crichton in an effort to avoid the tickling fingers of his mother.

'What?' asked the smiling Tricia, suddenly aware that maybe all was not right with her parents.

Her mother, smile frozen on her face but her eyes betraying her, lifted the summons and passed it to her daughter.

Tricia's expression changed. She gulped hard, suddenly aware of what this meant.

'Then it will be over soon?'

Crichton gently took the paper from her trembling fingers.

'It's already over, sweetheart,' he told her, his deep voice more reassuring than he felt. Without waiting for a reply, he turned his attention to the laughing child. 'And you, young man, are a wee scamp!'

*

Following the confirmation of her appointment, Annie Hall spent the next few weeks shadowing Sadie Parker, listening and learning the intricacies of being a department head, watching as Sadie dealt with the minutiae of the job, knowing full well she probably would never refer to the notes she laboriously scribbled frantically.
At the end of each day, she felt more exhausted than she'd ever been before and at her lowest ebb, the self-doubt raised its ugly head.
'I mean,' she whined to Sadie, 'when that girl from research complained about flexi time working regulations and quoted the union's stance, how did you know that she was trying to wangle a week off?'
'Human nature, my dear Watson,' Sadie quipped. 'In general, nobody does anything for anyone else. She wasn't really interested in fighting the corner on behalf of her section. If she was, her union rep would have accompanied her and he would have been the mouthpiece, not her. No, I guessed there was something else she wanted and that is why I asked her straight out. I find that if you are honest with people and tell them to lay their cards on the table, so to speak, you usually get the right response. If she had come to me without blustering about her *'right to work flexi time,'* she parodied the woman's high pitched voice, 'and simply asked for a week off to deal with her domestic problem, do you believe I'd have said no? Course not. A happy staff is a productive staff and if you follow that simple philosophy, you will always get the best from your people. Just so long as you don't let them walk all over you, of course,' she finished with a warning note, wagging a finger at Annie, her eyebrows knitting together to stress the point.
Annie stared dejectedly at her.
'I don't think I'll ever get the hang of your job,' she muttered miserably.
'Course you will,' smiled Sadie. 'It's just a question of practise. You'll be fine, she said encouragingly.
'So tell me Annie. How is this promotion and the extra dosh going to affect your life? New house? New car? New man in your life? What?'
Annie sighed. If only.
'First things first,' she decided, 'will be a new look. Out with the post-hippie oblique beatnik style and in with the Dior business suits, or at least Marks and Sparks anyway. House? No, I'm quite happy living where I am, thank you very much. Car? No way will I spend an hour each day trying to get parked in *this* city'.
'New man?' She smiled at Sadie, hoping to appear mysterious. 'Let's wait and see what the future holds on that score.'

*

Following DI Ronnie Sutherland's instruction, Graham the Divisional Productions officer duly attended at the Procurator Fiscal's Office in Inchinnan Road where, crammed into a large cardboard box, he jovially handed over all the required items to the custodian in charge of the strong room.
She like Graham, always had a joke ready and in turn, duly noted the contents; itemising in an old fashioned thickly bound ledger the various items that included blood and DNA samples obtained from the Shogun vehicle; books of photographs that depicted views

from the scene of the crash; mortuary pictures that showed the horrific injuries suffered by the fire ravaged victims as well as photographs of the sullen faced accused, taken directly after they were imprisoned at Paisley police office.

The reams of statements that accompanied the forensic productions included that grudgingly provided by the witness who, despite pressure from his strongly Christian wife, remained adamant that he was unable to identify the men that stole his Shogun vehicle. Unbeknown to his wife, he had taken to doubly checking that his doors and windows were secured before retiring for the night, the memory of the rough spoken shaven headed man still fresh in his mind. The statements of the police witnesses Julia Morton and Archibald Crichton and of other officers who assisted throughout the inquiry were also included and lastly, the report of the identification parade.

The reports of the professional witnesses, those who had examined the blood and DNA and confirmed the origin to be from one or the other accused, as well as statements from those persons who had participated in the post mortem examination of the deceased, were bound in a separate file.

Other sundry items of evidence were each labelled, itemised and everything returned to the cardboard box.

When finished, the custodian presented Graham with a receipt and assured him that Mister Smyth would soon be delivered of his court productions.

The overweight custodian, puffing at the uncommon exertion of transporting the oblong and surprisingly heavy cardboard box, regretted her decision not to use the small wheeled trolley and finally arrived at Smyth's partially open office door. Balancing the box on one knee as she leaned against the wall, she quickly knocked on the doorframe and grabbed at the corner of the box to prevent it tipping its contents onto the floor.

'Come!' was the shouted response.

'Your productions Mister Smyth,' she wheezed, 'case against David Crowden plus one.'

'Ah yes,' he acknowledged, barely raising his head, 'place the box on the table against the window please. Oh, and do be careful. I don't want anything damaged,' he added unnecessarily, continuing to examine the document in his hand.

The red faced custodian limped across the room, mentally wishing the lazy sod would get out of his chair and give her a hand when it was patently obvious she was struggling. With a gasp, she gave one final heave and noisily deposited the box on the wooden table with a thump.

'Careful I said!' he glanced sharply, then dismissed her with a wave of his hand declaring, 'that will be all.'

Without a backward glance the custodian, relieved of her burden, strode from his office, ensuring that she slammed the door in a bad-tempered and noisy protest to the smug bastard.

He glanced curiously over at the cardboard box. The brief phone call two weeks previously from Alex Crowden had insisted that Crowden be told when the case productions were delivered to his office, though for the life of him he couldn't imagine why Alex would want to know. Nevertheless, it didn't pay to upset or annoy the man who literally held his balls in his pugilistic hand. Rising from his desk, he reached for his jacket and told his disinterested secretary that he was off out for ten minutes.

*

Upon receipt of Smyth's call, Alex Crowden scrolled through the telephone directory in his electronic diary and found the business number for the secretary that worked at the Paisley Procurator Fiscal's office. He didn't want to tell Smyth too much, he decided. The guy couldn't handle stress and if anything should occur that Alex hadn't planned for, Smyth might unwind and burst completely to the rotten mob and the last thing he needed was coppers crawling all over him, particularly now that the business with the building contractors about to develop into a done deal.

The pleasant voiced secretary hadn't expected another phone call from him so soon. Her blood literally ran cold when she heard his gravelly voice and, to Alex's amusement, brightly pretended the caller was her mother.

'Okay,' he accepted with a smile, understanding that there must be someone else near by who might overhear, 'I'll be your mother. One question and that will be your debt paid in full. Understand?'

'Yes Mum,' she replied breezily, her stomach in turmoil while she smiled at her colleague, who flashed her a toothy, but sympathetic grin.

'Where in your office is Richard Smyth's office?'

He could hear her hesitate and realised that if she were supposed to be speaking to her mother, it would have to be a yes or no answer, that she wouldn't give out such information to her mother.

'Wait,' he told her, recognising her confusion, 'answer yes or no only. Is it on the ground floor?'

'Yes mum,' she replied.

'Bingo, first time my dear. That's good. Now is it facing onto Inchinnan Road?'

'No, the back of the house.'

'Good,' he replied, realising that the office must be located somewhere on the ground floor of the three storey building and at the rear. 'Is it in the centre of the building?'

'No, I prefer it in the corner, right in the corner,' she replied.

Bright girl, he thought to himself, unconsciously nodding his head in appreciation of her quick thinking. Maybe I should have reconsidered letting her go, he wondered.

'Is it the corner that faces towards the airport?'

'Got it in one, Mum,' she smiled at the other girl, turning her eyes upwards as though exercising considerable patience with her parent.

From his knowledge of passing by the building, he knew then that Smyth's office was located on the north side at the rear corner. Easily found and the security fence wouldn't present much of a problem, at least not to someone with Shooter Martin's capabilities.

'Right, forget you've received this call, my dear and if you should consider perhaps renewing our acquaintance?'

On the other end of the line, the girl involuntarily gave a shudder, a fleeting memory of his cold clammy hands upon her. Never in a million years, you slimy, horrible bastard she thought. But, still mindful of Alex Crowden's reach, knew she had to be careful.

'Thanks anyway Mum, but I'm okay here. Bye now,' and replaced the phone. As she stared at the telephone, she saw her colleague had lost interest and was now concentrating on typing a Dictaphone translation. The secretary regretted the loss of her job. She'd enjoyed her time at the Fiscal's office. But now that Crowden had found her and used her again, she realised her usefulness to him would mean more telephone calls.

She gave a low sigh; it was time to move on.

*

Using the vague promise of a backhander as his excuse, the court usher made use of by Ally McGregor of the *Glasgow News* tipped him off about the trial date. Armed with this information, McGregor decided to petition his editor for his consent to do a feature on the case, believing it would be newsworthy when the trial began and thus steal a march on their competitors. The editor, an old hand, recognised the sentimental impact and public emotion the trial might again evoke and mindful of the possibility of increased sales, grudgingly gave his permission. 'But do not,' he wagged a finger at his chief reporter, 'incur the wrath of the police. You know as well as I do Ally, that if they buggers decide to freeze you out when the next big story breaks - and this being Glasgow could be anytime - then your arse will be sliding along the pavement trying to catch up with the horoscope columnist of *Farmer's Weekly* before they give you another chance'.
McGregor knew only too well his own reputation among the cops that served the Greater Glasgow area. Too often he had delivered a storyline that vilified the police or accredited his account to that well-known informant, *a police source,* otherwise known as Freddie Fiction. And the cops, he grinned cynically, have long memories.
'And don't forget Ally, that this story isn't to take precedence. You're still chief reporter, so if anything else breaks meantime….'
'I'll not let you down, boss,' he nodded at the editor.
'See you don't,' was the harsh response.

*

He'd been told that the barbwire topped chain link security fence that protected the one hundred year old, three storey high Procurator Fiscal's building in Inchinnan Road was in poor condition, originally erected to encompass a small visitor's car park to the front and large staff car park at the rear. The unmanned main entrance comprised of gates that were locked by the nightshift janitorial staff and only when the building was closed.
Several outbuildings, sheds really, lay neglected and disused to the rear and the security fence, rusted and rotted in several places, had fallen unseen and ignored, behind the sheds. The token security lighting was inadequate to cover the area of the grounds and several high mounted wall lamps were either inoperable or their broken bulbs had not been replaced. All this led him to believe getting in wouldn't be a problem.
Parking his car in the early hours of the morning and just over a quarter of mile away in one of the streets surrounding the St. Mirren football team's Love Street stadium, Shooter Martin had walked the short distance without meeting or even seeing another person. Dressed in his customary dark coloured baggy trousers and black bomber style jacket, he'd donned a navy coloured baseball cap to complete his disguise. In his hand he carried a small, dark red sports bag. He glanced at his watch. The luminous face reflected the time, almost two o'clock in the morning.
His long stride quickly found him at Inchinnan Road and he walked past the building, never giving it a second glance and pleased to see that the adjacent buildings were closed business premises, not dwellings that overlooked the location. A taxi speedily passed him by, the only occupant the driver, ignoring Shooter as he laughed into a hand held mobile phone and concentrated on the poorly lit road.
Satisfied, or as best he could, that there was no cops parked nearby waiting to surprise him or having a sneaky shut-eye, Shooter sprinted across the road and ducked down into

the waist high grass of the rough ground that lay beside the building.
He controlled his breathing, listening intently for any sound that was out of the ordinary, but heard nothing. He smiled, enjoying the moment and imagining himself to be a soldier on a mission.
Body bent low, he clutched the sports bag to his chest as he cautiously made his way through the shrubbery on a parallel course with the fence, cursing softly as he realised the grassy area had through the years been used to dump all sorts of debris, mostly it seemed, bottles and cans. With sudden revulsion, he stepped in fresh dog shit and had to physically work at containing his rage, vowing to kill the next bastard he saw who let his dog freely shit and didn't clean the mess up. Hurriedly, he wiped his boot on the grass and then gagged, nauseated at the fetid smell that emanated from the ground, before continuing towards the rear, spitting as he walked as though trying to remove the taste from his mouth.
At last he came to where the fence turned towards the rear of the building and soon discovered a fallen concrete post that without difficulty allowed him to clamber over the wire and enter the back yard behind a shed.
He stopped and listened. Alex Crowden had told him that the building did not employ a security guard and the only protection was an antiquated alarm system. He hadn't asked how Alex had come by this information, trusting his employer to be correct.
Listening intently, he could hear nothing other than a distant aircraft landing at Glasgow Airport, over a mile away.
The darkened window that he'd been told was Smyth's office lay directly beneath a blacked out security light, one of the many that was unlit. He grinned again. This was too fucking easy.
Unzipping the sports bag, he donned a pair of dark coloured plastic kitchen gloves and then removed the two bottles from the bubble wrap, putting one in each of the large pockets of the bomber jacket. Lastly, he lifted out the two half-bricks and carried them, one in each hand, towards the corner of the building.
The windows of Smyth's room were modern replacement uPVC, double glazed and draught proof. But not brick proof.
He shook the bricks as though weighing their suitability for the job, then drawing back his arm, heaved the one in his right hand. The first brick crashed through the left window, shattering it instantly and causing Shooter to flinch at the loud noise. Quickly he transferred the second brick to his right hand and also heaved it through the adjoining window. To his unexpected relief, the alarm did not activate. It then occurred to him that perhaps the system was a silent intruder alarm and was now alerting the police to the break-in.
Acting with haste, he pulled the bottle from his left pocket and withdrew a small lighter from his trouser pocket. Lighting the rag stuffed into the neck of the bottle, he drew back his arm and threw the petrol bomb through the first hole, watching with widening eyes then stepping hurriedly back as with a loud whooshing noise, the bottle broke and spread its fiery liquid about the interior of the room. He hesitated; undecided if the second bottle was necessary then made his decision. Again he threw the lighted bottle through the second broken window and stepped back in alarm as a sudden flash occurred when the petrol ignited. Grinning hugely, he watched entranced as the fire took hold, the flames sweeping out of the broken windows and upwards, the brightness momentarily blinding

him.
Then, as if realising the danger of remaining, he sprinted towards the fence, altering his course to collect the dropped sports bag and plunging through the hole in the fence, eager to make as much ground between him and the flaming building.
A moment later, as Shooter emerged from the waste ground into the dimly lit carriageway, he saw a car stopped askew in the middle of the road, the occupant standing by the driver's door, a mobile phone in his hand and staring at the flames that could now be seen spreading about the rear of the building and lighting up the darkened sky.
With a start, the man saw him and shouted something, taking a few steps towards Shooter, one hand reaching out and still speaking on the phone.
Shooter's natural aggression urged him to go for the bastard, have him right there and then, but caution overtook him as he heard the wail of a siren in the distance. He ran for the safety of the darkened buildings across the road and disappeared from the man's sight through a narrow lane, running fast towards his vehicle. Curiously, as he jogged through the night he wondered why the building's alarm still had not activated.

The attending police vehicles knew that a man wearing dark clothes had been seen running from the rear of the Procurator Fiscal's office that was now well ablaze. Fire engines racing to the scene joined the cacophony of sound that filled the night.
But the suspect was gone. He'd outwitted the bright blue lights and sirens of the coppers and vanished.

Windows completely open and gagging slightly, Shooter drove his Renault on the motorway towards Easterhouse, vowing to get rid of his boots that had obviously retained some shit between the grooves in the sole.

*

CHAPTER 10

The fire that occurred within the east wing of the Procurator Fiscal's office destroyed vital evidence in a host of criminal cases. Police forensic experts and fire investigation officers later crawled all over the scene and bin loads of debris was removed for further examination. What became quickly apparent was that the fire had been set in the ground floor corner office occupied by PF Depute Richard Smyth and the accelerant used had clearly been petrol. Two half bricks and glass from two broken pop bottles discovered among the rubble seemed to suggest the windows were smashed, presumably prior to the bottles containing the petrol being cast into the room.
A passing motorist, a baggage handler finishing duty at the nearby airport, had initially reported the incident and his frantic call, recorded and listened to several times over, revealed that he saw a male figure emerge from the waste ground directly adjacent to the premises and run across the road and into a nearby lane, before being lost to sight.
A few of the younger and scornful detectives, full of their own bravado, opined the baggage handler might have pursued the suspect, but DI Ronnie Sutherland dismissed this idea as foolhardy and decided the man did the right thing; remaining on the phone and directing the emergency services to the scene.
The identity of the suspect remained a mystery. What seemed apparent was that the fire

was not a random work of mischief or vandalism, but a clear and calculated act to destroy whatever evidence was located within that part of the building.
It didn't escape Sutherland's attention that once again PF Depute Richard Smyth, having already inexplicably argued that the Crowden's be bailed prior to trial, seemed to once more be curiously concerned in their future when his office was targeted and resulting in the destruction of all the case productions in the suspicious fire.

*

A meeting held two days later within the conference room at Paisley police office and attended by representatives of the Procurator Fiscal Department and the police was a tense affair. The trolley with coffee, cups and saucers and plate of dry biscuits stood ignored in the corner.
Richard Smyth, accompanied by his senior PF Assistant Roderick MacFarlane, met with the Assistant Chief Constable (Crime) John Moredun, Detective Superintendent Frankie Johnson and the locally based CID Inspector, Ronnie Sutherland.
'Right, gentlemen,' began Moredun in his clipped English voice, 'to business. The report that I have received from Mister Sutherland,' inclining his head towards the DI, 'implies that the fire has likely been started to destroy evidence, the court productions in fact, in the case against David and Samuel Crowden. These items were lodged within your office, Mister Smythe that was proven to be the seat of the fire. I presume this is correct?'
Smythe nodded, his face sullen and was about to speak when MacFarlane butted in.
'As you will be aware Mister Moredun,' he smoothly began, 'my department has fully assisted in this inquiry and I also have received a copy of Mister Sutherland's report. And yes, you are correct. Regrettably, it seems the culprit has unfortunately identified the very time that the productions were being examined by Richard…eh, Mister Smythe, and chosen the very night that they lay within his office. Regrettable indeed.'
Frankie Johnson glanced at Smythe and while he expected the Depute to be uncomfortable, to his surprise he thought the man looked positively…. no, Johnson couldn't quite put his finger on it.
'Now, I realise that our procedure normally dictates that all productions be returned to the strong room at night for safekeeping,' continued MacFarlane, 'and in this case that has not happened. But I'm sure that you will agree with me that we are not met today to attribute any fault, simply to try and decide the next course of action in the case.'
Sutherland stared at the Assistant PF as MacFarlane tugged at the crisp white cuffs of his shirt showing beneath the sleeves of the expensively tailored suit. Very smooth, he decided, very smooth indeed. It was evident then why he had accompanied Smyth; clearly he neither intended nor would accept that any censure be directed against his department.
Moredun raised his eyebrows and pressed his fingertips against each other to create an arch with his hands. He stared hard at MacFarlane then spoke.
'What will become apparent to the general public on the date of the trial, Mister MacFarlane is that having delivered all evidence to your department, the police no longer has a case against the Crowden brothers. It is inconceivable that any jury will convict these two men on the word alone of a single arresting officer, now that all the corroborating productions in the case have been destroyed.'
For the first time, MacFarlane squirmed uncomfortably in his seat, for the first time regretting his decision not to send Smyth alone to face these pompous bastards.

‘I take it that the other arresting officer, Constable…’ he hesitated.
‘Constable Crichton,’ volunteered Sutherland, enjoying the sight of the PF’s department being in the hot seat for a change.
‘Indeed. Constable Crichton. I take it this officer has not changed his evidence, that he continues to deny identifying either accused?’
Moredun wasn’t liked among his colleagues who generally thought of him as being a manipulating and conniving careerist. But his strength lay in recognising others like him and saw where the question was leading. MacFarlane was trying to deflect blame for the fuck-up in this case onto the police, inferring this constable Crichton was primarily responsible for the shortfall in solid eyewitness evidence.
‘I don’t see this officer’s evidence as being totally relevant to the matter under discussion,’ he smoothly replied. ‘As far as I am led to believe your department accepted the relevant evidence as sufficient to prosecute this case and thus the evidence was deposited with you prior to the trial date as requested,’ he glanced down at the papers in front of him, ‘by Mister Smythe here, to DI Sutherland.’
He passed the paper and receipt along the desk to MacFarlane, who deliberately ignored them.
‘All very well, but as I said before,’ countered MacFarlane, his nostrils flaring, ‘where do we go from here?’
Sutherland could see Moredun was enjoying this and suppressed a grin.
‘If I may,’ interjected Johnson, leaning forward and dominating the table. ‘There’s no likelihood that at the moment, we will obtain a conviction in this case. I don’t see that we have any option but to abandon the trial and leave the inquiry open so that, if at a later date further evidence does arise that might implicate the Crowden’s, then we proceed at that time.’
MacFarlane turned to look at Smyth, giving him time to contemplate the Superintendent’s suggestion. Then, as if coming to a decision, responded.
‘Agreed. On the morning of the trial, Mister Smyth will announce to the court that proceeding have been dropped due to unforeseen circumstances and we will retain the case till such times as Mister Johnson has so rightly suggested.’
‘There remains one vital question, though,’ butted in Sutherland, a heavy leaden feeling in the pit of his stomach. ‘What about the husband of the deceased, Mister Bryce I mean?’
MacFarlane ignored him and turned to Moredun.
‘We will face the wrath of the court and the media if you agree to deal with the family,’ he replied.
Moredun nodded his head and stared at Johnson.
‘See to it, Superintendent.’

The meeting broke up with a perfunctory handshake between Moredun and MacFarlane. Frankie Johnson watched Smyth and the PF Assistant being escorted downstairs by Sutherland when it hit him.
The feeling he had about Smyth, the feeling that something was wrong. He knew now what it was. His instinct told him that Smyth had something to hide. Some guilt that was pressing down on him.
A gut feeling that nagged at him and told him Richard Smyth was dirty.

CHAPTER 11

The morning of the first day of the trial dawned clear and bright. The *Glasgow News* chief crime reporter, Ally McGregor had proven to be correct. In response to his three short but concise articles the previous week about the incident and others similar to it, public interest had resumed in the proceedings and aside from the frenzy of media outside the court, an immoderate number of the nosy and the curious packed the public benches to observe the two men who had killed the woman and her child.

Both accused, by mutual agreement between their lawyer Gospel Gordon and the PF's Department, arrived in a large car with tinted windows and drove straight into the enclosed, secure back entry to the court, thereby denying the waiting photographers any opportunity to record their entrance.

Neither their father Alex nor their sister Mary attended to support them.

Similarly dressed in dark suits, white shirts and sober ties, their hair neatly trimmed and faces shaved almost raw, the two men seemed to all intent a pair of businessmen attending a formal meeting, rather than facing accusations of theft and murder.

The court proceeded with a hushed silence and both accused were again brought before Sheriff McInally.

The old man's face was drawn and waxy pale. He stared at the Crowden's and then crooked a finger to beckon forward Procurator Fiscal Depute Richard Smythe and defence Counsel Mathew Gordon.

Brandishing a piece of paper between his finger and thumb with apparent distaste and in a low voice, he began.

'Am I to understand from this motion Mister Fiscal that the Crown no longer wish to proceed with this case?'

Smythe wallowed hard and slowly nodded.

'Let me hear you say it,' commanded the Sheriff, his gravely voice and bleary eyes levelled hard at Smythe.

'The Crown do not wish to proceed against the accused at this time my Lord, but instead have decided to abandon the case *pro loco et tempore*,' he muttered.

The silence in the court was heavy with tension.

Gospel Gordon maintained a dignified silence, content to let the old Sheriff's fury fall upon poor Dickie.

The Sheriff made a notation in his diary and looked up, only once, at which time he snapped:

'You're free to go.'

Davie Crowden breathed a sigh of relief. By his side, Sammy punched at the air, but at a reproving glance from Gospel, stopped short of crying out loud.

The court usher moved forward and taking an arm of each, tried to pull them from the court. Sammy, flushed with the success of freedom, sneeringly objected and pushed hard at the man, who staggered against Davie.

The uproar from the public benches began at once. Cries of *'Shame!'* and *'Disgrace!'* echoed throughout the chamber.

The Sheriff banged his gavel several times hard on his desk, but to no avail. The melee continued in the central aisle as Sammy, now joined by Davie, celebrated their new found

liberty by screaming abuse at the crowded court, baring their teeth and gesticulating with two fingers as they challenged to fight all comers. Nobody took up their offer.
Gospel, realising the situation was getting out of hand, assisted the usher and attending police officers to physically restrain the pair and escort them from the court to the rear access corridor. In the rear yard, the brothers continued to gesticulate towards the watching media, mouthing their insults as they danced together and round their lawyer towards the waiting car. Settling his clients in the rear of the vehicle with quiet relief, Gospel Gordon watched it speed off and quickly returned to the front entrance of the court. There he stood on the top step and beamed a grin down to the group of assembled journalists.
'I have been instructed by Mister David Crowden and Mister Samuel Crowden to issue a statement on their joint behalf,' he began in his strong voice. 'Today, justice was not only done but seen to be done with the correct and righteous acquittal of my clients.'
He turned his head slightly to allow the young man operating the shoulder held BBC camera to catch his photogenic side, smiling paternally as though speaking to children.
'The scurrilous actions of the police and the Procurator Fiscal's Department in submitting my clients to several weeks of anguish has ended and it is my considered opinion that a public enquiry into their actions should be invoked by the Crown Office in Edinburgh.'
He paused, allowing the reporters a brief few seconds to note his words.
'But surely your clients have only been released temporarily Mister Gordon. Didn't the prosecution indicate they were simply deserting the case for now, until such times other evidence might be found?' inquired one sharp young reporter.
Gospel licked his lips and stared hard at the reporter.
'Of course, you're correct,' he replied, facing the reporter and surprised that any of these buffoons understood Latin. 'But please remember that if the Procurator Fiscal *did* have any evidence against my clients, they would have proceeded with the trial. It is my opinion that by deserting the case the prosecution are simply attempting to save face; being now aware that they have mistakenly brought a case against the wrong men.'
He turned to address the crowd.
'It must also be understood that the regrettable deaths of Missus Karen Bryce and her young daughter might have been avoided if the mother had been at home with her child and the question must be asked of her actions; why was she driving on a dark road at that time of night?'
Even the most hardened of those journalists present baulked at this vitriolic statement in what was a clear and deliberate ploy to deflect interest from the Crowden's.
'But your clients were caught in the stolen vehicle and it was them who crashed into Missus Bryce's car,' shouted one young female reporter.
Gospel wagged an admonishing finger at the woman.
'Must I remind you that my clients *might* have been charged by the police with this heinous crime, but no evidence was presented at court by the PF to substantiate this allegation. Be careful my dear, for you have made an unjustifiable allegation.'
Through the shouted questions Gospel seized upon one, pointing a forefinger at the well-known local television news correspondent.
'Your clients don't seem to be showing any kind of remorse, Mister Gordon.'
'Must I remind you again, there is no need for my clients to show remorse,' he loudly replied, 'because they are not guilty and the innocent have nothing to regret.'

He shrugged then, as though about to impart some great secret, his hands spread before him.
'I accept that because of their previous conduct, it is no secret that my clients are known to the police and therefore that makes them a target for accusation at the drop of a hat. They were an easy catch for our over-zealous guardians of the law on that fateful night, when the true thieves and those responsible for the tragedy seem to have easily evaded arrest. You might also wish to know that I have on two occasions, provided the police with the name of a well known car dealer from the east end of Glasgow who might have information on the real culprits.'
This comment provoked a flurry of questions, mostly wishing to know the identity of this car dealer, but Gospel refused to be drawn, smiling as he suggested they refer that question to the local CID.
He raised his hands and loudly apologised, but the interview he said, was over and turned to make his way back into court. Gospel was well satisfied that he'd achieved exactly what he had intended; steered the thrust of the questions from Davie and Sammy and hinted at the involvement of another person, Pat Delaney.

*

Later that afternoon, Ally McGregor whistled tunelessly and pulled the sheet of paper from the printer. He scanned through the text, stopping once to score out a few words and substituting another in their place. Satisfied, he rose from the swivel chair and strode across to his editor.
'Thought that this might be worthy of catching the evening edition, boss,' he said, handing over the paper.
The editor scratched at his head and began to read.
'Agreed,' he replied, handing the paper back, 'and I'll be happy to have this part and maybe this,' he highlighted two paragraphs with a bright yellow highlight pen, 'run as the editorial, so get that down to Charlie at printing.

The evening edition of the *Glasgow News* featured a full-page headline above a photograph whose caption read: David and Samuel Crowden accompanied by their lawyer, Mathew Gordon, departing the court.
The photograph, apparently taken with a telephoto lens from a nearby building that overlooked the courtyard, clearly showed all three grinning together with Gordon hugging the two younger men close to him, as they walked towards the dark coloured saloon car. Sammy Crowden, nearest the camera, was caught in the act of thrusting a middle finger upwards towards nearby bystanders.
Underneath the photograph in the early evening edition, Ally McGregor's main story began with a reminder of the circumstances that led to both accused appearing at court.
The editorial that ran as a by-line continued the theme on page two:
The town of Paisley is today in shock and disbelief, appalled that the two accused should be released without further censure. The question that must be asked of the police and prosecution service is: 'What exactly is going on?' Following the collapse of this ludicrous trial, inquiries by this newspaper to both Paisley police office and the Procurator Fiscal's office at Inchinnan Road were met with: 'No comment', hardly an appropriate response demanded by an outraged public who have suffered the loss of two of its citizen's; a young mother and her three year old daughter.

Once more this newspaper must ask; is the patience and fortitude of we, the general public, to be trifled with? Are we to meekly accept that there was no failing by those sworn to keep us safe against the criminality that abounds in the Greater Glasgow area? Must we endure more young lives lost before the law finally protects us and exacts some form of retribution upon the wrongdoers? Just how secure are we from the shadowy figures that stalk our streets at night, stealing and killing at will?
This newspaper has learned from highly placed sources within the police service that not only have the Crowden brother's been set free from further accusation, but not one person has been censured for what is certainly a calamitous failure on the part of our so-called guardians of the law; particularly as it has later emerged, since the police have been provided with the name of a strong suspect in the case.

*

'I'm grateful that you've taken the time to come with me, sir,' said Sutherland.
'Least I could do, Ronnie,' replied Frankie Johnson. Privately, he believed that it was more the responsibility of John Moredun, but the ACC was known to be a slimy bugger and more than capable of designating any duty that might reflect badly upon him. And this, he inwardly sighed, was the sort of thing that might just lead to a critical press if Mister Bryce so deemed.
Sutherland knocked on the door and waited patiently, unaccountably dreading the reaction.
Johnny opened the door, his face reflecting his puzzlement.
'Hello there,' he half smiled, 'I didn't think I was due to attend court till tomorrow.'
'It's not about that Johnny,' replied Sutherland. 'May we come in?'
After introductions, Johnny invited both men to sit down. Curiously, they sat pressed together on the neat little couch as though seeking support from each other's close presence.
Slowly and patiently, Sutherland related the circumstances of the fire at the Procurator Fiscal's office and the resulting loss of the evidence. As though speaking with a child, he tolerantly explained the outcome that this had on the trial; the circumstantial evidence now lost that had been vital to a successful prosecution.
Johnny didn't utter a word, his eyes narrowing and his face pale with incredulity.
'So, in short terms, what you're telling me is that you are abandoning the trial? These two guys will be set free?'
Sutherland nodded, reluctant to continue speaking and drive the wound deeper.
'Mister Bryce,' began Johnson, 'there's nothing I can say or do that will make this any easier. It has been a complete and utter failure on our part. The incredible incompetence of the police and the PF's Department has united in failing you.... and your family,' he lamely added.
'But...is there no way that you can pursue these two guys? For Christ's sake, after all, they murdered my wife and daughter!' he rose to his feet, his anger obvious
Shamefacedly, Johnson shook his head.
'I'd like to be able to give you assurances that we would get them somehow, but right now we've no evidence to work with. Everything was lost in the fire. I'm so very, very sorry.'
Johnny turned away, his face distraught. He could feel the bitter helplessness and tears of rage welling up inside him and his throat felt constricted.

‘What about the eye witnesses, the two police officers who arrested the Crowden’s?’
Sutherland knew it was coming and had prepared his response. He licked his unaccountably dry lips before he spoke.
‘One of the officers, a constable Crichton, attended at the identification parade we held and refused point blank to identify the Crowden’s as the men he had taken from the Shogun.’
Johnny turned and stared him, thinking he had misunderstood.
‘How can he refuse to identify them? Surely as a cop he’s obliged to…’
Johnson raised his hand to stifle any further question.
‘We don’t know what his reasons are, Mister Bryce. DI Sutherland applied as much pressure to Crichton as the law allows, but he’s adamant that he can’t,’ he glanced quickly at Sutherland, ‘rather, won’t identify the Crowden’s. We are of the opinion that in some way pressure has been exerted on him to prevent him making the ID, presumably by the Crowden’s. I’m sorry.’
Sutherland run his tongue round the inside of his suddenly dry mouth and extended his hands, palms upward as though in plea.
‘If you want a personal view, I’ve known Archie Crichton for over twenty years. He’s always been a good, hardworking cop and in my mind it’s inconceivable that he would have taken a bribe or anything like that. I’m privately of the opinion that there must be an underlying reason for his non-cooperation and you may recall that I warned you; the Crowden family have a long each. They are not above having witnesses of their families threatened.’
Johnny’s brown furrowed. It wasn’t that he disbelieved the two detectives, but he couldn’t accept that a police officer in today’s day and age would succumb to personal threats. But then just as quickly, he remembered another time, not so long ago. Another young family, killed when the bomb went off under their car just as the mother prepared to take the kids to school.
But this wasn’t Belfast.
‘I’d like you to go now, if you don’t mind,’ he said quietly, turning his back and staring through the window, watching the children laugh as they played in the street outside.
Behind him, the two detectives glanced at each other and as one, rose to their feet.
Nothing they could say would ease the hurt. Sutherland lifted his hand to pat Johnny on the back, then thought better of it and let his arm fall to his side. The detectives let themselves out.

They walked to their car in silence and drove off. Once clear of the small housing estate, Sutherland slapped his hand hard against the steering wheel.
‘Well, that was really shitty, if I do say so!’ he cried out, the frustration obvious in his voice.
Johnson didn’t reply, but stared ahead through the windscreen. Despite almost twenty-eight years of police service, that short visit he reckoned had to count among the three worst things he had ever done.
That’s when he remembered.
‘Ronnie, what can you tell me about the PF Depute, Richard Smyth?’

*

Within the house at 39 Cotton Close, Johnny Bryce sat dumbfounded, still unable to fully

grasp that the two men were to be, no had been, set free. It had all been for nothing. Karen and Laura's life had been worthless, simply two people being in the wrong place at the wrong time. And these two bastards were living their life as they pleased, slaughtering innocents and getting away with it!
He had always been a fair-minded man, always observed the rules and regulations and never considered being anything other than being honest or straight. And all for nothing. He recalled a saying, a quote from the bible; a book he had never read. *The meek shall inherit the earth.* But that wasn't correct, he unconsciously shook his head; it was so wrong. The meek inherited nothing. It was the parasites, the criminals, those without conscience who invariably triumphed, who always won.
He clenched his fists as the rage slowly built up inside him and he felt an overwhelming need to scream out loud, destroy something – hurt someone!
His shoulders slumped and his breathing slowed, the anger and pain dissipating as quickly as it had arisen.
It didn't occur to him then, not knowingly anyway.
But Johnny Bryce had become a changed man.
A change that would soon involve and affect more than just his own life.

*

The civilian citations officer who knocked on the door and delivered Archie Crichton's court countermand was simply delivering a message and unaware of the circumstances of Crichton's involvement in the case. Cheerfully he informed the soon to be retired officer that the trial had been abandoned and Crichton was no longer required to attend court the following morning. With a wave, the citations officer returned to his vehicle, thinking that the older man's face had been vaguely familiar; the thought passing as he flipped through his paperwork, looking for the address of his next port of call.
Behind him, Crichton stood in the doorway, stunned. His wife called to him and receiving no reply, found him half-slumped against the wall, the cancellation slip clutched tightly in his hand. With difficulty and soothing words, she helped him into the kitchen, sat him down at the table and busied herself putting on the kettle, smiling with trembling lips as she fought to hold back the tears. The elation that her husband was no longer required to attend court and demean himself in the witness box overwhelmed her and with a sob, her resolve broke and the tears coursed their way down her checks. She leaned across her man, holding his head in her arms and squeezed him with loving affection, mumbling soothing words to the top of his white head.
He stared blankly ahead with sorrowful eyes, his complexion a waxy grey and stumbled to his feet, telling her that he intended lying down for a little while.
She watched him go and wrung her hands together, unable to find the words that would comfort him; nonetheless a strange feeling of relief swept through her.
In the bedroom, Crichton sat upon the edge of the bed and stared at the wall. The cancellation should have been welcomed, but it meant nothing to him.
He lowered his head into his hands and tried to remember when he had been a man.

*

The BBC (Scotland) early evening news began with a heart-rending story of the murder of a teenage boy in Stirling whose body had been discovered near to the world famous castle. The item ended and Johnny reached to hit the record button on his video machine, sitting tensely on the edge of his seat. The anchorwoman switched to the murder trial that

began that day at Paisley Sheriff Court and the dramatic scenes that followed the astonishing acquittal of David Crowden and his brother Samuel. An earlier recorded scene closely followed and he watched intently as their lawyer escorted the Crowden's to a waiting car. The scene again switched to where a young female reporter indicated the man standing on the steps behind her was the Crowden's lawyer, Mathew Gordon.
Johnny turned the volume up slightly as the cameraman panned from the correspondent to snap Gordon, who appeared full-face on the full screen.
As he listened, his eyes widened in surprise, slowly shaking his head as Gordon easily parried the shouted questions then his eyes opened wide in shock as the lawyer suggested that in some way Karen was responsible for not only her own death, but that of Laura's also. The lawyer continue to rebut questions, other than one he chose to answer and inferred another person called Delaney might be responsible for the killing.
Johnny wasn't fooled and recognised the cheap stunt for what it was. An excuse to dismiss the Crowden's culpability for Karen and Laura's death.
As Gordon turned away from the journalists, Johnny rewound the tape a short distance and watched the interview again, pausing the flickering tape to stare at Gordon's face on the screen.
A face that he would easily recognise again; even in the darkest night.

CHAPTER 12

The private party that took place that evening within the top floor lounge at *Jakey's Bar*, one of the many pies into which Alex Crowden had dipped his stubby finger, was to celebrate the acquittal of Davie and Sammy and attended by more than sixty people, most of those men present whose movements were constantly or casually monitored by the police. The majority of those attending deliberately neglected to bring their wives and current girlfriends, knowing full well that good old Alex would provide female entertainment and companionship from his many brothels and lap-dancing clubs. The free drink from the bar and abundant food supplied by a city caterer had all been pre-arranged, so certain was Alex that his sons would be freed, if not totally exonerated from all charges. None of those attending, other than the immediate Crowden family, their lawyer Gospel Gordon and Alex's henchman Shooter Martin, would ever be privy to the full circumstances of the courts decision, but whispered rumours abounded that the fire at the Procurator Fiscal's office went far to secure Davie and Sammy's freedom.

Mary Crowden, the low cut scarlet dress hugging her figure and accentuating her bosom, nursed her soft drink and stared at the semi-naked woman cavorting about the stage, slowly disrobing till at last she wore nothing but a gold coloured thong and a thin, black lace knotted round her neck. She was curiously aroused by the lewd display and swallowed hard, her throat tightening as the cropped haired brunette, stage named Annabelle, curled one leg about the vertical silver pole. Mary watched spellbound as the dancer bent her lithe, oiled body almost backwards and then to wild applause, succeeded in slowly and provocatively licking the toes of her foot.
Five, ten and twenty-pound crumpled notes rained down on the stage. With a huge grin, Annabelle acknowledged the crowd with a wave, collected her clothes in a bundle and began gathering up the cash, her large breasts swinging freely as she skipped towards the

rear kitchen that doubled as a dressing room, the loose money clasped in both fists.
Glancing about her, Mary slid easily between the crowd and their female companions, slowly making her way towards the kitchen, smiling automatically and nodding to her father's cronies; some of whom she recognised as drinking partners, others she guessed would be debtors or acquaintances with whom Pop would have some or other business with. None of those present overtly considered Mary Crowden as sexually available, conscious that they'd forfeit more than their kneecaps should they in any manner offend the stunning looking blonde. But it didn't prevent the sly, lustful glances.
Gospel Gordon, whisky in one hand and the other arm languidly hung about the shoulder of a teenage Chinese girl, his hand beneath her silk gown as he idly caressed her breast, winked at Mary as she passed.
She reached the kitchen door and licked her lips; her breathing shallow, her desire for Annabelle overtaking her usual self-assuredness. Strangely, she was uncertain how she would introduce herself to the supple dancer. That Mary could have her and use the dancer if she so wanted was not in doubt. As Alex Crowden's daughter, any of his possessions and that included his female stock, was at her disposal.
Tossing her loose blonde hair, she undid the top button of her dress in readiness and pushed open the door, unprepared for the sight that greeted her.
Annabelle stood against the far wall; her head thrown back, eyes half-closed and mouth slightly open, the gold coloured thong now lying discarded on the floor. Her right leg was raised, the ankle pulling against the rear thigh of the man thrusting at her, one hand behind his neck and her other pulling his shirt upwards, his trousers in a heap around his ankles. Mary saw the mans right hand firmly gripping Annabelle's left breast, his left hand hidden behind her, clutching at her backside. Their panting was loud and hurried.
She stood stock-still, glassy eyed and unable to breathe. Annabelle's eyes opened slightly wider and she slowly smiled at Mary. The man turned his head to see what had distracted the brunette and saw her standing by the door.
His frown turned to a grin, his eyes slowly widening with understanding, realising why she had come.
'Hello, little sister,' said Davie.

*

Predictably, the acquittal of the Crowden brothers caused friction between the police and prosecution service and all communication between the two agencies was for a time abrupt and petulant. But DI Ronnie Sutherland had other matters to concern him.
While the Crowden's celebrated, Sutherland attended the call to appear before his Divisional Commander, where he was officially, but firmly berated for his inability to produce more eyewitnesses and thereby strengthen the police case. It was pointless Sutherland had decided, defending himself against the accusation of failing to persuade the Shogun owner and the errant constable Crichton to identify the accused. The subject of the destroyed evidence was not raised.
That done the Chief Superintendent then unofficially sat the detective down and offered him coffee. While they sat awkwardly together, his boss explained that as a former CID officer himself, he knew what Sutherland had been up against; that he had no choice but to comply with the instruction of ACC Moredun whose memo dictated the DI be counselled for his part in the fiasco. It didn't help that Moredun had instructed the rebuke be placed on his file, effectively scuppering any opportunity for immediate promotion.

Making his way back to his office, Sutherland couldn't decide if he'd been shafted or consoled, feeling as if he'd been punched with a velvet lined glove. He closed the door of his office, threw off his suit jacket and sat down and then pushing back his chair, placed both hands behind his head and lifted his feet to sit them crossed at the ankles, upon his desk.
The brief meeting with Johnny Bryce had affected him profoundly, more than he was prepared to admit. Upset though the man had been, Sutherland had still been taken aback at how calmly Bryce had received the news of the abandonment of the trial.
And that he puzzled, though not knowing why, concerned him more than anything.

*

The man in Ronnie Sutherland's thoughts had considered long and hard his next move. The unexpected news that the killers of his wife and child were released without punishment had totally changed his perception of right and wrong, of fairness and of justice.
A small amount of insurance cash accompanied the letter of sympathy from the insurance broker who had dealt with and settled the claim for the burnt-out Ford Escort. The money had served as a down payment for the aging but serviceable four door Nissan Micra that he now drove along Paisley Road West. On the passenger seat lay an A to Z street map of the Greater Glasgow area; the page open at the Cardonald suburb of Glasgow and where he had discovered the shortest route towards Tweedsmuir Path, the address he recalled reading in detective Lavery's paperwork.
His mind made up, Johnny had decided to take that first step towards revenge. He would make a reconnaissance mission, a journey to determine where exactly where the men who had killed his family, lived. What he would do when he arrived? He exhaled deeply, thinking about that next step as he drove eastwards. That he had yet to decide.
In the fading light he discovered Tweedsmuir Path. Turning into the long, straight but poorly lit road with its high hedges and overhanging trees that bordered the homes set back from the road, he realised that in the darkness he might have some difficulty establishing where the Crowden's resided. Driving slowly along the narrow road, his concentration centred on the few house numbers attached to front gates, he was considered leaving the Micra and reconnoitring on foot but was startled when the bright lights of a vehicle overtook him at speed and stopped with a tyre screeching halt, almost one hundred yards down the road. As he slowly coasted past the red coloured Mini, his headlights framed a stunning blonde in a figure hugging dress emerging from the driver's side. She ignored the passing Micra as she pushed open a green coloured wooden gate and even with his engine running, Johnny heard the gate slam behind her. Though she hadn't turned to look at him, in the car's dipped beam he'd thought she seemed angry or upset.
He watched in his rear view mirror as the figure of the woman strode quickly down the path to the darkened building, and then saw a brilliant light illuminate the front of the house. A porch light, he rightly guessed, mentally noting the fact for future reference; a long and tried training to detail kicking in.
He turned the Micra at a junction further down the street where Tweedsmuir Path ended and slowly cruised back towards the lighted house he had seen the blonde entering, hoping that if he could establish the house number, he'd be able to work out which was the Crowden's residence. As he passed the woman's front gate, he saw it clearly and a

thin smile played about his mouth. A brass plate affixed to the brick wall beside the door, displayed in large numerals the number 129. He thanked his good fortune, his first piece of luck. He continued driving and stopped almost one hundred and fifty yards further along the road at a spot where the overhead light was poorest, unconsciously aware that his fingers were shaking from gripping the steering wheel so tightly, still surprised it had been so easy identifying the address. As he watched in his rear view mirror, the porch light slowly dimmed. He guessed it must operate on a sensor system, switching on at movement and off after a preset period, allowing the occupants or visitors to reach the door with plenty of time to prevent them falling from or tripping on the path.
Sitting in the darkness, idly chewing his lower lip, he thought again about the blonde woman from the Mini. It occurred to him that she could be their sister Mary, the woman mentioned in the police report he'd read while attending the mortuary, and who had supposedly provided the ignition key to steal the vehicle. And if so then that that, he grimly decided, made her just another target.

*

Within the front sitting room of number 129, Mary Crowden seethed, her fury directed not only at her own stupidity for allowing herself to be compromised so easily, but also at her brother Davie. Her face coloured with unbridled shame as she thought again of his grinning realisation that she had visited the kitchen for the same purpose as he; the seduction of the brunette lap dancer. But he had got there first and, she angrily admitted, that was what had enraged and also worried her; if not certain then he must surely suspect his sister's secret; her suppressed homosexuality.
Mary had no doubt she understood Davie, how his mind worked and he disgusted her. She had decided long ago they were brother and sister in name only. For years she had avoided his furtive groping at her beasts, his whispered lewd comments and suggestive remarks. She knew that he wanted her, would bed her if she gave him half a chance. But now after tonight she realised with a shiver she was vulnerable, that he would use every means available to exploit his new found knowledge.
Her face white with fury and delayed embarrassment at the memory of their sniggers, she angrily poured a glass of straight vodka and gulped the drink down, gasping as the fiery liquid burned her throat and caused her to retch.
Refilling her glass, she sat down heavily on the thick padded couch, kicking off her high-heeled shoes and sliding her bare, tanned legs beneath her as she curled into a corner of the couch and contemplated her next move.
Her father loved her, she was his favourite and of that she was certain. But if he were to discover that his daughter preferred her own kind? He had heard him speak of "that type of women". She swallowed hard and gulped at the vodka. Women like her. There was no tolerance where Pop was concerned; no acceptance to the diversity of society; his vulgar jokes of poofs, dykes and lesbians still fresh in her memory. She shivered as she thought what his reaction to Davie's news would mean. Pop wouldn't care that her experiences were limited to just a few brief, liaisons and of course he would never understand the aching after her own kind that she had suppressed all these years. Except, she sighed in self-admittance, on those few occasions when she had succumbed to temptation and daringly visited her father's more discreet brothel. Her name and his reputation had opened the bedroom doors and the smooth thighs of those girls she had chosen and used - then left with a ruthless warning should they even think of revealing her secret.

But now that warning seemed ludicrous and she knew if he asked it of them, none of them would dare deny to Alex Crowden anything he wanted to know; or what his daughter did to them. Her heart seemed to miss a beat. If Davie talked, Pop would easily discover her secret.
There had been men, two in the early years; an experiment almost. But both experiences had been brief, leaving her feeling numb and slightly revolted, but most of all, unfulfilled. She thought again of her father's reaction should he become aware of her secret and knew that his first thought would be for his reputation among his friends and associates; *a man's man*, as he liked to say *and women in their place*.
Except where his wee Mary was concerned. She involuntarily shivered as she recalled Pop's paternal plans for her future betrothal, his urging of her to find herself a husband, joking the man must be one that he would approve of. He'd promised her the ultimate in white weddings, already planning his speech and the jokes he would relate.
She felt trapped and alone. A tear escaped and trickled down her cheek., but Mary cried not for her father, but for herself.
Her shoulders slumped as she realised that all was hopeless, her efforts to maintain an advantage over her brothers now wasted because of one, lustful recklessness; an indiscretion that hadn't even come off, she groaned miserably. Davie, she knew, didn't need to have proof. The right word, the slightest hint, an innuendo. All he needed was to sow the seed of doubt, cast a shadow over her life and the old man would soon pick up on it. She'd committed the unforgivable crime, the one indiscretion Pop wouldn't excuse her; she'd embarrassed her straight father by being gay.
Unless…a sudden and dangerous thought sneaked into her mind like an uninvited guest; unless something happened to Davie before he could open his mouth?
The seed of the idea germinated into a full-blown scheme. What Mary needed was somehow to shut her dear brother's mouth. Permanently.

*

The taxi arrived in the early hours of the morning, slowing to a halt as it passed by the darkened Micra and then stopping outside number 129. Its bright fluorescent livery displayed it's phone number and the lit roof sign made it clearly visible from the fifty yards Johnny sat slouched in the driver's seat. He'd decided earlier to edge that little bit closer, parking under a blacked out street lamp and banking on the locals being sound asleep. He guessed that any patrolling police would be within a vehicle and as long as he kept sharp and monitored the front street and his rear view mirrors, he'd have time to slide down the seat and duck out of sight.
He watched with bated breath as the front passenger door opened and a large, bald man wearing a long dark coat exited from the taxi, seeing him pull his coat closed, as he stood upright on the pavement.
The rear doors then opened and a man got out from each side, one stumbling onto the pavement and against the bald man in what seemed to be a drunken stupor. The darkness wasn't total and with the help of the dull overhead street lighting, he could clearly make out the faces of the two rear door passengers. He almost stopped breathing as wide-eyed, he recognised their faces from the front-page photograph in the late edition of the *Glasgow Times*.
David and Samuel Crowden.
In the stillness of the night Johnny could hear the one called Samuel loudly singing *The*

Sash, a song he and every other inhabitant of the west of Scotland knew to be the anthem of the supporters of the Orange Lodge. The bald man, the Crowden's father, he presumed, grabbed the slightly built Samuel by the scruff of his coat collar and forcibly propelled him towards the garden gate, his deep voice growling for him to shut up. David Crowden stood by the drivers' door and seemed to be handing money over. That done, the taxi drove off as David, swaying slightly, followed the other two along the path towards the house. The porch light illuminated and through gaps in the foliage within the large garden, Johnny could just make out the three figures at the front door that opened and closed immediately behind them.
He sat still, breathing softly, trying to come to terms with what he had seen; his first sight of the two men who had killed Karen and Laura. He felt powerless and his hands were shaking, but with rage or shame at his helplessness, he wasn't quite sure.
He watched as the porch light slowly dimmed, then turned the key of the ignition and drove past the house, switching on the car headlights when he was further down the road. He made his mind up, coldly determined that once he'd had a good nights sleep, he would settle on a plan of action.

*

CHAPTER 13

The following day Johnny Bryce decided to put into action the first stage of his plan. He set himself a routine, rigidly sticking to a pattern that saw him rise early each morning and regardless of weather conditions, conduct stretching exercises in his rear garden before setting off on a run, favouring a route that led him through all of the adjoining streets in the local neighbourhood. Not only did he maintain a regime of fitness, but the regular risers making their way to work, walking their dog or travelling by car become accustomed to seeing him at their chosen time each day. More than one, recognising him as the local man who had recently lost his family, waved or smiled in a sympathetic greeting that he always returned. Similarly, on his chosen route, Johnny noted the faces of all those he saw and expected to meet, constantly watching for and observing changes in routines or strange faces. Gradually, the houses and the regularly parked vehicles became familiar sights to him.
Among these early morning well-wishers was Annie Hall, standing each morning at her usual bus stop. Since his misfortune, Annie's feeling towards Johnny had changed considerably, seeing him now as a tragic figure and herself as sympathetic neighbour rather than of an attracted female with a vivid imagination.
Regularly jogging by the bus stop, he never forgot to smile broadly as he passed the smartly dressed young woman with the smiling eyes, her shiny new leather briefcase hung by a thick strap over her shoulder.
When driving his Micra, Johnny practised long forgotten skills that he had been taught by his Security Service instructors; using his mirrors more often, making unexpected turns in the road and often stopping suddenly and without reason. On occasion he would hurriedly leave his vehicle and make his way quickly through nearby streets, all the while constantly watching about him.
In the evenings, he increasingly took to parking the vehicle a little further from the house each time, until at last it became the norm for him to leave the Micra among many others within a common car park at the end of the street. When leaving the car, he habitually

noted and remembered what other vehicles were parked nearby.
He remembered devices that could be attached magnetically to the underside of cars that would aid tracking them in heavy traffic. As though inspecting the tyres, he would balance a matchstick the front drivers tyre under the mudguard and out of sight of passers-by, discreetly checking each time he returned to the Micra that the matchstick was still in place. Now the vehicle could not be disturbed without the matchstick falling from its place.
At work Johnny adopted a philosophical attitude to the court's decision and to his co-workers surprise, apparently accepting the judgement with sorrow and misery; shrugging his shoulders and seemingly resigned to the loss of his family. Some of his colleagues could not understand this attitude and a few of the more belligerent believed he should appeal the decision, at the very least employ a lawyer to fight the decision through the courts.
Johnny smiled sadly, kept his own counsel and became the timid wimp they become to believe he was.
His boss however, was overly sympathetic and through time, gently steered him back into full employment.
The days turned to weeks.

Johnny continued with his computing course, applying himself rigidly to the studies and surprisingly discovered he looked forward to being with and enjoying the developing acquaintance with his tutor. To his relief, the bright and attractive woman did not press him for more than friendship and outwith the classroom, their intimate time amounted to nothing more than a coffee together in the college canteen. Unbeknown to Johnny, her feminine instinct had alerted her that should she pursue a more aggressive seduction of the handsome widower, his recent loss and fragility of mind might easily lose her the man she was slowly coming to respect and have feelings for. She decided that for the time being, it was enough to see and be with Johnny Bryce, if only for a few short hours a week.

*

When considering his arrangements at home, working within Garvey's or driving in his car, he put nothing down on paper, relying on his experience and active imagination to devise a plan in his head. With each idea came a counter-plan as he scathingly picked holes in his preparations till at last he created the scheme that he believed would best serve his purpose.
The few items that he needed he purchased over a period of time, confident that no matter what transpired, his procurement would not be traced back to him. From the small loft room of his home, he brought down a dusty and long forgotten military kitbag, filled with clothing and bits and pieces from his previous life.
Instinctively, Johnny Bryce was once more slipping back into the role of the trained marine that he had been, his old abilities coming again to the fore.
Tonight, it would begin.

*

Alex Crowden's long-term plans for the premises in Shettleston Road were slowly coming to fruition and accompanied by his lawyer Gospel Gordon, his luncheon meeting that afternoon with the builders had pleased him tremendously. So much so that in

celebration he extended an invitation and he and Gospel now sweated together, the only members present in the sauna of the exclusively select and expensive Gentlemen's Health Spa Club in Crow Road.
'This will get the old pores opened, eh Gospel? Get rid of some of that shite that you poured into yourself today.'
Gospel sighed audibly. Self made man he might be, but Alex Crowden knew sod all about the finer benefits of a good glass of vintage Port.
'Perhaps if you were to relax more often, you old bald headed bugger,' he smirked as he patted his rotund midriff, 'and a little less of throwing lumps of iron about your head, you'd be more of a gentleman. In fact, a bit like me.'
Alex grinned hugely at the references to his baldness and weight lifting. Gospel Gordon was the only man of his acquaintance who had the audacity to ridicule Alex's hair loss, an issue that privately still caused him regret, but not that he'd admit that to another living soul. If anything Gospel, he conceded, was probably the only man with whom he felt anything akin to true friendship.
A relaxed quiet descended upon them both as they perspired freely in the steaming heat.
'The little matter of my lads defence, Gospel. The fee was to your satisfaction, I presume?'
'Indeed,' replied the lawyer, his eyes closed and head laid back, resting upon the pinewood wall. He sighed lazily, the thought of the money in the secret account bringing a soft smile to his face. Money that at long last would set him free from the grip of this squalid city and the poker-faced cow he shared his life with. 'I received confirmation from my accountant only yesterday that the cash had gone through. Very generous of you, I might say,' he wearily opened his eyes to slowly wink at Crowden.
Alex waved away the thanks.
'You did my boy's a big favour and I'm not one to quibble over something as petty as cash. Besides, when this building deal is tied up and we've off-loaded that piece of Delaney's ground, you'll have more than earned your commission.'
Naked, he arose from the wooden seat and pressed the button on the wall. A minute later in response to his call, a young teenage and fresh faced blonde girl, her hair swept back in a tight ponytail and wearing a short, white linen toga, opened the outer door and noiselessly padded barefooted across the tiled floor, bringing with her two large fresh white cotton towels that she handed to them both.
Alex took his and immediately began roughly drying his face, arms and barrel chest while the girl stood silently, her face expressionless and her hands neatly clasped together in front of her as she watched him. Handing her the towel, he turned without speaking and raised his arms above his head as she massaged the sweat from his back, then knelt down and rubbed hard at the rear of his legs. He turned round and she began rubbing the front of his legs and more gently, dabbing the towel round his groin. Staring over her head, Alex grinned at Gospel.
The lawyer, lying naked on the on the bench seat, one hand propping his head, a thin line of sweat beading his upper lip, felt himself become erect as he watched the kneeling girl working. As she continued to rub at the front of Crowden's legs, the skimpy toga had slipped loose from her thin shoulder, exposing one neat pubescent breast that she made no attempt to cover.
At last, Alex told her, 'That's enough,' and taking her hand to help her rise to her feet,

took the towel from the girl and twisted it round his waist. He turned to Gospel.
'I'm jumping in for a short swim in the pool before go up the road. Join me?'
Gospel sat up and shook his head, unable to prevent the leering grin.
'Not right now, I've something else to attend to, so I'll maybe phone you tomorrow.'
Alex grinned knowingly and crossed to the door, closing it behind him.
Gospel reached a sweaty hand out towards the blank faced teenager, beckoning her to him.
'Now my dear,' he whispered in a breathless voice, 'maybe you can rub me all over?'

*

Night had fallen by the time Gospel left the club. He stood in the doorway and glanced at the sky, seeing the dark clouds that threatened rain, but they didn't trouble him; his happy mood brought on by the success of his day. Turning up the collar of his Burberry coat against the expected shower, he tucked his briefcase under his left arm and walked the short distance to his car, reflecting on the meeting with the building company's lawyers. It had proven most satisfactory and the offer for the piece of scrubland currently occupied by the car sales showroom that was now managed by Alex's daughter, was the first paltry sum in what he knew would eventually be a capitulation by the company who would finally agree to his demands. Yes, the day had rounded off nicely, first with the expensive lunch, followed by the relaxing sauna and finally the sweet little blonde for dessert. And all at Alex Crowden's expense, he sighed contentedly. Yes, he thought as head down he plodded through the first faltering drops of rain, life couldn't get any better.
Had Gospel been more attentive to his surroundings, perhaps a little less tired from his recent sexual encounter and remembering he was walking in the City of Glasgow, he might have taken more care upon entering the poorly lit street. The waste ground that bordered the street and served as a makeshift car park was deserted when he arrived, less than a moment later. As he stepped from the smoothly paved street into the uneven land of the car park and his eyes adjusted to the darkness, he slowed his pace and picked his way carefully across the broken ground, head down and mouthing silent oaths at the damage he must surely be doing to his hand stitched leather shoes.
Reaching the driver's door of his Mercedes coupe, he breathed a silent sigh of relief and with his right hand, scrambled in his coat pocket for the keys. That's when he noticed the front tyre, completely flat.
With a groan, he automatically bent down and stared frustrated at the wheel, momentarily distracted and failing to hear the soft footsteps behind him.
The first indication that Gospel knew he was not alone was when a hand seized his brow and pulled his head up and backwards, causing his neck to jerk painfully. Almost immediately, an excruciating pain shot through his mouth. What he couldn't know in the few seconds he had left to live was that as his assailant pulled back his head he simultaneously and with tremendous force thrust a sharpened screwdriver upwards through the underside of Gospel's throat. The steel shaft pierced his gullet and tongue and continued up into the rear of the left eye socket, the metal implement finally coming to rest in Gospel's brain where the sharpened tip scraped the bone inside his upper skull. The damage to his brain was in itself significant and would ultimately likely have proven fatal. But this injury alone simply contributed to his demise. As the blood from his wounded mouth coursed backwards down his throat and effectively restricted his air passage, he fell to the rough ground gulping like a beached fish in his effort to breathe.

His last conscious thought was of a pair of dark coloured trousers and black boots standing over him.
Though death was not instantaneous, the few seconds of his life that remained were insufficient for him to cry out, particularly as the screwdriver had effectively skewered his tongue.

Johnny Bryce quickly made his way back through the darkened street to the parked Micra and settled himself into the driver's seat. As far as he could tell, no one had seen him park, leave or return to the car; a nondescript man and a nondescript small car.
He drove away, surprised that having killed the lawyer, he felt nothing.
It had begun.

CHAPTER 14

The report of the death of the eminent and popular defence lawyer Mathew Gordon, known as Gospel to his clientele and the media alike, made headline news for almost three days, however, the public's appetite for salacious stories regarding their television heroes overtook even world events when the tabloids revealed a well-known local soap actor was cheating on his wife with his co-star.
The police intelligence bulletin about the murder that was circulated throughout the force area described in detail the *modus operandi* employed to murder Mathew Gordon, adding that any information that might lead to the identity of the killer or killers should be immediately forwarded to the investigation team that was operating from Partick police office on the north side of the city.
Some members of the press, invariably quoting the unnamed police source, suggested a number of reasons for the brutal murder; the most notable being a conspiracy by rogue police officers who, embarrassed by their numerous failures in court to convict clients defended by the redoubtable Mister Gordon, had decided on a more radical approach to curb his success.
Ally McGregor of the *Glasgow News*, not one to miss an opportunity to hint at his knowledgeable underworld contacts, put forward his own theory; inferring that a gangland feud between clients whose interests the lawyer represented had led to the demise of the unfortunate Mister Gordon at the hands of his clients brutal opponents.
Hoping to impress his editor by alluding to these fictitious underworld contacts, McGregor implied the murder might be linked to the disappearance of the car dealer, Patrick Delaney and in doing so unwittingly attracted the attention of Alex Crowden.
Reading the article over breakfast, Crowden almost choked on his cereal. He seethed at the reporters deliberate misinterpretation of the situation and spent an hour weighing his options that included, in the extreme having Shooter Martin deal with McGregor, to simply ignoring the reporters' story.
Unbeknown to the journalist, McGregor's reputation among the criminal fraternity was as much mocked for his inaccurate reporting as it was among the police and so, on this occasion, Crowden wisely decided to ignore the report.

Nevertheless, the hunt for the lawyer's killer continued, but though several hundred persons were interviewed and dozens of suspects grilled, the case continued to stump the

investigating detectives.
As the enquiry progressed, it was inevitable that details of Gordon's twilight life and frequent use of prostitutes would emerge and once again he posthumously made the headlines. His grieving widow's photograph, snapped as she exited a male friends house and with a handkerchief to her face, featured on the front page of the *Glasgow News* under the banner headline: *Grieving Widow: The Last To Know*
Daily she faced newspapers that uncovered increasingly younger women, mostly depicted in provocative poses and all of whom were prepared to sell for public consumption, details of their intimate liaisons with Gospel Gordon.
Four weeks after his murder, the lawyer's funeral ceremony attracted a massive crowd, though it didn't fail to attract the media's attention that following the revelations surrounding his personal life, many prominent members of the Scottish judiciary stayed away. Not so the criminal figures that he had spent his life defending; the congregation reading like a *Who's Who* of the underworld. Renowned among these, reported many of the tabloids, was Alex Crowden, his sons David and Samuel and his daughter Mary. The Crowden's occupied a pew two from the front of the altar that indicated both their importance in their relationship with Gordon as well as their position in the hierarchy of the Glasgow underworld.
The anguished widow sat with her family in the front bench. She had practised this moment, knowing full well that many eyes would be upon her. Hidden behind her white, linen handkerchief, as the minister droned on, she silently thanked the killer that had released her from the loveless marriage; her thoughts turning to the fortune secreted in the foreign bank accounts and was already making plans for her happy future.
To the rear of the congregation sat the two senior detectives involved in the murder investigation. As the pallbearers carried the coffin down the aisle, Chief Inspector Barry Thomas watched the sullen faces of the mourners pass him by, he recognising most of the criminals among them and they all recognising him and his Detective Inspector for what they were; the rotten mob.
The detectives watched with expressionless faces as the Crowden's, heads slightly bowed, slowly passed by; both men admiring the strikingly good-looking Mary.
It was then it occurred to Chief Inspector Barry Thomas that the sons had recently been acquitted for a case at the Paisley Sheriff Court, a case in which Gospel Gordon had figured prominently. Might not do any harm, he considered, speaking to the officer in charge of the inquiry and getting his views on it. Idly, he watched the procession go by and vowed when he returned to the office, that was to be his first aim.

*

Since killing the lawyer, Johnny Bryce had continued his routine, constantly alert and paying particular attention to his movements and those of his neighbours, but had been unable to detect any strange faces or vehicles in the vicinity of his home or his workplace. For now, he was satisfied that he was not under any police surveillance.
He had surprised himself by his own indifference to the death of Gordon and more than once considered himself to be immune to human emotions. But he knew this was not so. Nightly, the horrible dream continued; he clinging to the roof of the speeding bus, watching as his daughter Laura slipped from his grasp and plunged screaming over the edge.
Whisky didn't help and a selection of over the counter sleeping draughts had proven

useless. It briefly occurred to him that maybe he should seek medical help, explain his sleeplessness and perhaps be prescribed medication, but he feared that anything that caused him to be drowsy might affect his sharpness, his judgement, and so this was out of the question.

When not at work, he took to napping during daylight hours or going to bed early; all calculated to allow him the required sleep time and keep him sharp. So far, it seemed to be working.

Early one Saturday morning, the post delivered another computing certificate and a card from his tutor that invited him to an after-course cocktail evening within the college, all above board, the attached handwritten note teasingly assured him. He decided it would be churlish to refuse and besides, thought it sensible to give the impression he was trying to rebuild his life.

He wasn't to know his tutor had an anxious three days, awaiting the RSVP that accepted her invitation.

Finishing work late one Friday night, coincidentally the same day as Gospel Gordon's funeral, Johnny saw the sky was overcast and, unusually for that time of the year, threatening a heavy thunderstorm. He glanced at the overhead clouds and decided that tonight was as good a time as any to continue with the next stage of his plan.

He drove home, dressed and checked his equipment. Glancing through the curtained window, he saw the darkening sky and the sudden deluge begin. While the rain continued, nobody would be noticing him, he decided. Any pedestrians he encountered would be more concerned with keeping their head down and avoiding the deluge. Throwing the small rucksack over his shoulder, he extinguished the back light and slipped from the darkness of the rear door towards the Micra.

*

Ronnie Sutherland sighed, replaced the handset and swore softly. The enquiry for the post office raid that afternoon had landed on his desk and by the time he had organised the arrest teams and organised the search of the suspect's homes, he had completely forgotten his wife's warning about being on time to accompany her to her sister's house for dinner. Her angry phone call left him in no doubt where he was sleeping tonight and finished abruptly with the sarcastic suggestion, if he wanted something to eat, bring himself home a fish supper.

The phone rang again almost immediately.

'Ronnie? Barry Thomas here. Sorry to bother you; I hear you're busy, caught up with an armed raid. Just wonder if I could have a few minutes of your time?'

'No problem Barry,' Sutherland replied with more bonhomie than he felt, 'what can I do for you?'

'You'll have heard I'm dealing with the Gospel Gordon murder. I know that he represented those Crowden thugs when they killed that woman and her child and I'm told that you were the reporting officer. I understand the inquiry went apeshit. What I'm wondering is, could there be anything remotely connected with your inquiry, any kind of circumstances that resulted in his death?'

'You mean some sort of revenge killing for his defence of the accused? Something like that?'

'Yeah, well, to be frank, Ronnie, I'm grasping at straws. His murder was very slick, professional most likely. The way that he died suggested it wasn't a random killing and

there was nothing to suggest robbery. Whoever topped our Mister Gordon knew exactly what he was doing. According to pathology, the wound that was inflicted caused death within a minute, possibly even less than that; maybe just a few seconds.'
'I read the circular you put out. A screwdriver, wasn't it?'
'That's right. A sharpened Philips headed screwdriver, ten inches long with a moulded green coloured plastic handle, square chrome metal shaft; the cheaper type that can be bought in sets of five from any of the discount stores on the high street, but nevertheless, quite a strong tool. Nothing distinctive in the weapon and no forensic evidence to work with either and, needless to add, no eyewitnesses. Whoever stuck him with it knew exactly what he or she was doing and it wasn't a kid either. There had to have been a certain amount of strength behind the thrust.'
Sutherland's eyes narrowed as he listened, remembering a photograph on a wall. But no, he dismissed the thought. Johnny Bryce didn't deserve that type of attention, not after the police had already failed him. And after all, it wasn't Gordon that had killed his family.
'Nothing comes immediately to mind,' he slowly replied, 'but I thought that you were looking at the suggestion it was some sort of gangland hit?'
'That's the newspapers getting their tuppence worth out of the case,' Thomas sighed, 'and I can tell you it's led us a merry bloody dance, following up a load of useless tips. So far, I've nothing and Frankie Johnson is doing his best to help, but he's having a hard time keeping that plonker John Moredun off my back. That sod phones me at least twice a day, looking for updates,' he complained.
Sutherland chuckled. It seemed that it wasn't just he who was having a hard time from the ACC (Crime).
'To be honest,' Thomas continued, 'I personally don't think that Gordon was any loss to society, but him being a member of the Bar has got the rest of these highly paid windbags running scared; happy to shaft and ridicule us when we're standing in the witness box, but when they need our help? I've heard that a number of judges and lawyers have inundated Moredun for police protection, all protesting that they might be next to get the chop. Bunch of shitbags!' he spat, then added with a chuckle, 'we can only keep our fingers crossed that maybe Gordon was the first, eh? Maybe cull some of these buggers off the public purse.'
'Sorry I can't be of more help,' Sutherland sympathised, 'but I'll keep in mind what you've told me and put the word out to my lads. If anything crops up,' he added, 'I'll give you a bell.'
When he had replaced the handset, he thought again about the photograph. Johnny Bryce and his wife, Bryce in the uniform of a Royal Marine sergeant. He hated to even consider the notion, but there was no getting away from it. If anyone knew how to kill a man, quickly and quietly, then it had to be someone with Johnny Bryce's training.

*

The subject of Ronnie Sutherland's thoughts was at that time steering his Micra through the dark and rain drenched streets of Cardonald in the south side of the city, intent on carrying out the second phase of his plan. He realised that much depended on his next victim being out of the house and gambled that being Friday night and human nature as it was, it was Johnny's experience that two young men such as David and Samuel Crowden would likely be out socialising; more so if they had money in their pocket.
He parked the car in a quiet street, several hundred yards from the house in Tweedsmuir

Path and sat waiting. After sitting in the darkness for a short time he was satisfied that neither the presence of the vehicle nor he had attracted the attention of any of the houses overlooking the street. The foul weather added to the darkness and at last, he slipped from the Micra, gently closing the door behind him with a soft click. Quickly he made his way along the pavement, using the cloaking shadows to aid his movement.

Two houses from the Crowden's he stopped and held his breath as he listened. The sound of an engine approaching caused him to turn into a driveway, the gate squeaking and his heart almost stopping at the metallic noise as he pushed it open and crouched down in the shadow. But the vehicle, a hackney cab he saw, passed by apparently with neither the driver nor the two young female passengers seeing him. He glanced behind him. Three cars were tightly parked in the drive where he stood and a party was in full swing within the house; the sound of *ABBA* being played loudly and people laughing and singing along to the music.

He quickly crossed the dividing fence into the next garden; pleased to see the house was in darkness. He knew from his previous visits to the street that within this house was a Labrador dog, but he didn't worry too much. Johnny had seen plenty of cats running about the area and presumed that the surrounding occupants who owned dogs, would be well used to their pets becoming anxious when they sensed a cat within the garden and would likely ignore the yapping. His experience had taught him that unless the dogs were trained to detect intruders, most owners were too lazy to follow up their pets' fretfulness and usually silenced them with a yell. On this occasion he listened closely as he passed slowly past the window, but the Labrador did not react to his presence.

Silently, he made his way cautiously across the well-tended lawn and arrived at the hedge that separated the lawn from the Crowden property. The hedge presented no problem as he squeezed through, his thick, camouflaged jacket resisting the plants effort to snag the heavy material. Conscious of the porch light sensor, he stayed just outside the beams radius and settled himself in a squatting position beneath a large, oak tree. Removing the black coloured balaclava that completely covered his head, he began to apply an army issue face paint that blackened most of his pale features.

A downstairs light was on in the Crowden's house, a lounge he presumed, but he couldn't hear any sound from within. A red coloured Mini Cabriolet was parked in the driveway. He recalled that it was the same car he'd seen the blonde exit when he'd first visited the street, the young woman he believed to be their sister Mary. A light was switched on in an upstairs bedroom, the curtains closed and he guessed that whoever occupied the room was preparing to retire for the night.

A few droplets preceded further rain and he remained squatting in position. He glanced at his wrist, peeling back the leather cover of his watch. The luminous dial indicated eleven minutes to midnight.

Johnny had come prepared, but if it didn't happen tonight, then there would be another time. But, he decided, he'd set up the equipment anyway, just in case he got lucky. Carefully he made his way towards the side of the house to the patio area and collected a green plastic chair, then returned to crouch by the thick trunk of the oak tree.

All he had to do now was wait.

*

Sammy enjoyed the status brought him by being Alex Crowden's son, particularly when he visited *Jakey's Bar* on Paisley Road West. He liked to hold court in the public bar,

revelling in the way that the punters would fall over themselves to buy him a drink, keen to curry favour with the son of one of the most powerful men in the city. He also liked the fact that he never had to put his hand in his pocket, let alone buy them a drink in return. It never occurred to him that the very same drinkers who smiled with him and laughed uproariously at his corny jokes thought of him as a wee, tight fisted bastard.
The bar staff were equally wary of Sammy Crowden. The more he drank, the more loathsome he became. Any other young guy who shouted his mouth off as he did would have been unceremoniously tossed out on his ear long ago, but not Alex Crowden's son, for the simple reason that Alex Crowden owned the pub, though not on paper; so refusing his drunken son more drink was not an option that was recommended. Not if you wanted to keep your job.
It wasn't the first time that an unsuspecting stranger had innocently wandered into the bar for a quiet drink, only to be verbally abused, then bullied by Sammy and challenged to fight; and woe betide any stranger who got the better of Sammy. For Sammy was no fighter, nothing like his father. At the point it became obvious Sammy would be overcome, his opponent would discover that two or three others would come to Sammy's assistance and hand out a severe beating. Not because Sammy was such a popular fellow, but for the simple purpose of currying favour with him and through him, with old Alex, whose spies would in due course whisper what had taken place.
And of course no one ever complained to the police, no matter how serious their injuries. While never publicly discussed for fear of reprisal from the young bully, it was commonly agreed among the older clientele who frequented *Jakey's* that Sammy Crowden would never be the man his father was and he would always live in old Alex's shadow.
That Friday night the young love struck Englishman and his student girlfriend had stopped by *Jakey's* for just the one drink, a quickie to settle his nerves before he met with her parents for the first time. While she found a table, he attended at the bar and ordered their drinks; unaware that his Surrey accent had for some unaccountable reason riled the inebriated Sammy.
'Where you from?' slurred Sammy, one hand clutching his glass of whisky, his glazed eyes trying to focus on the smartly dressed man.
'London,' the Englishman briefly smiled in response, rather than trying to explain regional differences to the drunken Jock and concentrating more on attracting the barmaids' attention.
The bouncer by the door could not hear what was being said, but previous experience had taught him that in his present state, the intoxicated Sammy was well worth the watching. Slowly, he began to make his way towards the pair, pushing through the crowd who were now becoming quiet and turning to watch with interest the developing scene at the bar.
'Fuckin' English bastard,' spat Sammy loudly, full of liquid courage and turning aggressively towards the young man.
The Englishman sensibly decided to ignore the lout and half turned away, but that was his undoing. Believing he had intimidated him, Sammy swung the hand holding the glass, smashing it across the nose of his unsuspecting victim, the liquid spilling onto both of them. As the Englishman fell to the floor, Sammy stamped at his face, striking the helpless young man on the cheek with the heel of his heavy shoe and fracturing the bone as his downward strike savagely tore the skin from beneath the eye. The young man's

girlfriend screamed and panic-stricken shoved through the crowd towards her boyfriend. But by now the bouncer had reached Sammy and pinioned his arms to his side, forcefully dragging him away and attempting to calm him with soft words as he pulled him towards the doorway.

'Right that's enough wee man,' he firmly told Sammy, 'you've done for him, you've won.'

Privately he thought the skinny wee bastard deserved a right good bleaching, but the bouncer needed this job and the last thing he wanted was to piss off Alex Crowden by giving his son the hammering he so definitely deserved.

'See me? See what I did to him? English bastard!' boasted Sammy, full of drunken bravado and shrugging off the bouncer's hold. By now though they were standing outside the pub, passers-by walking warily around the drunken man and the sober bouncer.

Sammy made to re-enter the door, but the bouncer stood blocking his path, his hands raised before him.

'Better not,' he cautioned Sammy, 'I think that lassie called the coppers on her mobile phone, Sammy,' he lied. 'Might be better getting yourself down the road before they arrive, eh?'

The warning cut through Sammy's alcohol induced thoughts and he blinked rapidly, suddenly remembering his father's warning about getting in trouble with the law, particularly so soon after the problem with the woman and her kid. He stared glassy-eyed at the bouncer.

'You're right, big man,' he slurred. 'Be a pal, get me a taxi, eh?'

The bouncer sighed quietly and placed two fingers of his right hand in his mouth, issuing a sharp whistle and beckoning with his left hand to the next cab from the taxi rank nearby. The vehicle moved twenty yards forward and the bouncer pulled open the rear door. As Sammy drunkenly climbed in the back, the bouncer leaned in to the driver.

'Get the wee man down the road, eh? Number 129 Tweedsmuir Path,' as he threw him a ten pound note. 'That should cover the fare and your tip, pal.'

*

Annie Hall couldn't believe it. The middle of bloody September and here she was, victim of a sodding, bloody summer cold! It could only happen to her, she sighed gloomily. The first party she'd been invited to for months and she'd had to cry off. She dabbed at her runny nose with a scented tissue and swallowed painfully, her throat raw from coughing and spluttering throughout the day. She pressed the remote control and changed the television channel, seeking something that didn't involve murder and mayhem or late night adult cartoons, all which seemed to have a sexual theme and reminding her once more she didn't have a boyfriend!

Channel Five, she saw with relief, was showing a re-run of the Merchant Ivory series and she smiled as Mister Darcy rode his horse across the wild, Yorkshire moor. She glanced at the clock and promised herself she'd watch for just half an hour, then get to bed and try to sleep again, half sitting propped up with her pillows around her, trying to breath through her stuffed nose and failing miserably.

Savagely, she punched at the cushions behind her head and tried to concentrate on Darcy, his high boots and his tight trousers.

*

Johnny heard the throaty sound of the diesel engine as the taxi arrived, searching for

number 129. Through the breaks in the front hedge, he could see it stop opposite the gate and a figure climbed wearily from the rear seat. He heard the taxi radio broadcasting and the controller seeking a call sign. The taxi driver was also speaking; patiently telling the passenger something about the fare having already been settled. The taxi then drove off, the driver noisily changing gear as it disappeared along the road.
The gate swung open and bounced against the small wooden post set in the ground, swung back and was again violently pushed open. The passenger stumbled through, banging the gate shut behind him. In the darkness Johnny couldn't make out his features, but from his slow, deliberate walk it was obvious he was male and drunk.

Sammy Crowden staggered a few yards along the garden path and into the arc covered by the porch light sensor. The bright light immediately illuminated and he blinked repeatedly as his eyes tried to adjust to the harsh glare, raising one hand to fend of the dazzling light. He took a deep breath then heard his name being softly called. He stopped, unsure if he'd heard correctly. Again, his name was softly being called, but more insistently this time.
'Who's there?' he asked, but there was no reply.
'Saaaammmmy,' the low voice drawled a third time.
Puzzled, he stepped off the path and stubbed his toe against the kerb edging. Cursing, he almost fell, but regained his balance.
'Okay, who the fuck's there?' he called again, this time more threateningly. But still there was no reply.
'Saaaammmmy,' said the low whisper tauntingly.
He bunched his fists and advanced towards the darkness, intent on punching the shite out of whoever was playing this trick on him.
'That you, Davie?' he asked hesitatingly, peering into the darkness.
In the distance, the party music was playing Dexy's Midnight Runner's *'Come on Eileen'*.
'Over here,' urged the low, soft whisper.
Convinced now that his brother was playing a trick on him, he relaxed slightly and stumbled into the dark towards the large oak tree. He thought he could see something white, a shapeless thing on the ground. Behind him, the porch sensor no longer detected his movement and the light slowly dimmed.
Sammy stopped, fearing he might trip and fall and squinted his eyes as he tried to make out the shape, but all that he could see was the large dark trunk of the tree. Yes. The shape looked like a chair, a garden chair.
Behind him, Johnny approached unobserved and in one swift movement, slipped the circle of nylon rope around his neck.

Sammy didn't have time to turn round before the circle of rope became a tightening noose, choking him and cutting off his air. Panicking, he grabbed with both hands at the noose, but no matter how he twisted and turned, couldn't get his fingers in between the thin rope and his neck. In his terror his fingernails clawed at his skin, scratching the surface and causing it to bleed, but this he didn't notice, too intent on loosing the grip of the noose. All the time he was trying to breath, but no air was getting through. He knew he was choking to death. It didn't help that while he was trying to ease the pressure on his

throat, he was gradually being pulled upwards, first his heels then his toes lifting from the ground and his head being forced to one side by the vertical incline of the unresisting rope. He strained his body to keep his feet on the ground, but that didn't work. At last he dangled off the ground and slowly spun round, still trying to gain purchase with his fingers inside the circle of rope and still desperately trying to breath.
Now he become aware of the figure of a man pulling at the other end of the rope that was looped round the branch above Sammy's head; a man dressed in a camouflaged army uniform, his face streaked with black and brown paint, his teeth clenched and showing white in the darkness as he strained to heave on the rope, lifting Sammy a few inches further from the ground. Sammy didn't give the man's dress too much thought; he was too concerned with trying to get some precious air.
'Oh, God! No! No! No!' he wanted to scream, but the rope was getting tighter and his chest felt as though it were about to explode. Eventually the stars dancing before his eyes merged into one bright light then suddenly blanked out into darkness as his brain was starved of oxygen. His arms become too heavy to hold up and he had to let them dangle by his side.
His last conscious thought was that he was floating in the night.

*

He returned the way he had come, through the adjoining gardens; moving swiftly but still conscious that he might yet be observed. At the least suspected noise or movement, he would stand stock still, his training kicking in and remembering that nothing attracted the peripheral vision of the human eye as quickly as faint movement.
But nobody saw Johnny Bryce return to his vehicle. Within the Micra, he snatched off the balaclava and used a moisturised baby wipe to clean most of the camouflage paint from his face, shrugged off the army jacket, then donned a dark coloured anorak. His balaclava, jacket and the used wipe he stuffed into a black plastic bag that lined the inside of the rucksack.

The return journey to Paisley was completed without incident, he simply being another driver in a small nondescript car among the many vehicles travelling the late night roads. As it was now into the early hours of Saturday morning, the majority of the traffic was taxis or party goers, coming from or going to parties, the driver's intent on avoiding the occasional drunk who either wandered across the busy main roads or even perhaps sitting behind the wheel.
Johnny didn't know how he felt as he drove home. He knew from experience that his body was still in the throes of the adrenalin burst that action brought and only later, when he relaxed, would reaction and emotion set in.
Parking the Micra in the common car park close to his home, he sat for a few minutes to ensure no late night dog-walker would see him emerge from the darkened vehicle and later be able to recount his presence. Before departing the vehicle, he balanced a matchstick on the front nearside tyre and made his way quietly towards the lane that would lead to his back door.

*

Annie Hall awoke bleary eyed, sniffed miserably and decided that Mister Darcy's tight trousers obviously weren't tight enough to prevent her having fallen asleep on the couch. The channel now blared loudly as an American sports presenter tried to explain the rules

of baseball.
Her neck cricked from the awkward position she'd lain in. Switching off the television and turning out the lights, she decided to try sleep one more time. Coughing and sniffing and dabbing at her runny nose, she wearily climbed the short flight of stairs. Tutting to herself at her forgetfulness, she remembered she had forgotten to turn off the central heating radiator and the room was now far too hot for her to sleep within. Grabbing her pillows, she made her way into the cold, spare bedroom. Moonlight streamed into the room through the open curtains. She reached out to close them and stopped. To her surprise, her neighbour from across the lane, Mister Bryce, was returning home, a small bag of sorts bumping against his shoulder as he strode towards his gate. Curiously, she saw that beneath his dark jacket he seemed to be wearing a strange pair of multi coloured trousers; like the type the army wore, she guessed.
She stepped behind the curtain, suddenly aware that if he'd glanced up he couldn't fail to see her standing framed in the window. From behind the drape she watched as he cast glances about him before pushing open his gate and slowly closing it. It occurred to her that he was being very furtive, creeping slowly and seemingly not wishing to make a noise. Not daring to breath, she saw him unlock and enter his back door.
During the few minutes that followed, she was mystified that no lights were switched on in the house.
Her eyebrows narrowed in puzzlement. Whatever he was up to, he certainly seemed to be taking pains that no one was to see him.
It didn't occur to her till later that night that she hadn't coughed once since she'd first spotted Johnny Bryce in the lane.

CHAPTER 15

It was the fifteen-year-old milk boy who discovered the hanging body of Sammy Crowden. Banging repeatedly on the front door of the house, he incurred the wrath of Alex who arrived in his dressing gown, cursing the youth and about to clout him on the ear before he realised that the speechless and wild-eyed lad was shaking uncontrollably and pointing towards the garden. Stepping out into the porch Alex saw his son hanging limply from the old oak tree, but unlike the popular song, with not a single yellow ribbon in evidence.
His frantic scream brought a dishevelled Davie downstairs to the front door, cursing as he stepped in the glass and spilled milk from the broken bottle that had been dropped in the boy's panic, more intent on his gashed foot than what was going on abut him. A dazed and puzzled Mary, coming downstairs behind Davie, pushed by her brother and head down, stepped around the glass and spilled milk into the early morning sun. That's when she saw her father in the garden, his dressing gown flapping around him as he screamed for her to come and help him. Her jaw dropped and her eyes opened wide with disbelief when she saw her father supporting the legs of the limp body of Sammy, who dangled from a rope at an awkward angle as he hung from a stout bough of the tree. She rushed towards Alex, shouting for Davie to fetch a knife to cut Sammy down. Davie hesitated with uncertainty, then turned about and ran to the kitchen, fetching a large serrated bread knife that he brought out to Alex.
Mary threw aside a green coloured plastic garden chair that impeded them and watched

as between them, her father and Davie managed to lift the dead man and ease the tension of the blue coloured rope. The rope shuddered then awkwardly, Alex cut through it in a sawing motion. When the rope parted, they caught Sammy and laid him on the dew-covered lawn. It was obvious he was dead; his body cold and clothes sodden from early morning rain. His face was chalk white, the blood having graduated by gravity to his lower body region. His eyes and mouth were bulging open, staring at them, his tongue swollen and extended as he'd fought for his last breath. The rope was deeply embedded into his neck as through the night, his body weight had pulled down on the noose, tightening it and causing an even deeper groove in his skin.
Shocked, Alex stumbled a few steps back. Mary held the plastic chair steady, taking his arm and assisting him to sit down as wide-eyed, he stared at his sons' body. Davie, his knees wet from kneeling the wet grass, stared helplessly up at his father.
Mary backed away shivering and fled to the house, pushing roughly past the youth who remained standing in the porch. With trembling fingers she dialled the emergency number for an ambulance and the police.

*

The attending police arrived within a few minutes, their blue light flashing as they approached. The two young uniformed officers recognised the address and glancing at each other, immediately called for their Inspector as well suggesting the CID be informed and recommending they also attend the scene. An ambulance arrived shortly after and the two paramedics examined the body of Samuel Crowden before pronouncing life extinct. Ignoring Mary's angry protest they explained they were unable to offer any assistance and then apologised and told her it was a matter for the police casualty surgeon and that they were leaving. There was nothing they could do to assist the victim.
Alex Crowden remained seated on the plastic garden seat, oblivious to the ongoing argument, his eyes never leaving the dead face of his son. Mary stood beside him, a comforting hand on his shoulder, shivering in the early chill of the morning; her silk dressing gown and fluffy slippers offering little protection against the cold.
Davie, unsure how he felt, had shrewdly gone back indoors and changed into jeans and jumper before bringing out a tray on which he'd placed three milked mugs and a pot of tea. The police officers he simply ignored.
The teenage milk boy sat on the porch step, casually warned by Davie that if he didn't remain where he was until the coppers had spoken with him, he'd get his legs broken.

The arrival of the Inspector almost provoked a volatile situation when suggesting the family move back indoors, he was overheard by Alex instructing his constables that he needed to preserve the scene of the suicide.
Alex leapt to his feet, the plastic chair bouncing back against the ground in his fury.
'What the fuck do you mean? Suicide?' he snarled at the Inspector. 'My laddie has been murdered! Are you blind, you fucking moron?'
The Inspector shook his head, determined not to be provoked by the large and furious father.
'Sir, I can understand that you must be extremely upset,' he began, 'but the circumstances as I see them…'
He didn't get the opportunity to finish. Alex advanced towards him, his fists raised to pummel the smarmy faced idiot to pulp, when Davie and Mary grabbed at him, hanging

onto his arms. The two young cps nervously moved their hands towards their metal batons, one also reaching for the canister of CS spray attached to his belt. The situation they both later agreed was turning ugly.
Alex, still trying to tear free of his son and daughter's restraint, roared at the Inspector. 'Get me someone from your lot who knows what they're doing, you dickhead! Get me a fucking detective!' he screamed as they both dragged him still cursing, towards the house.
The constables stood silently watching, for once relived that there had been no need to resort to wielding their batons.
The Inspector, struggling to maintain his dignity in front of his officers, exhaled slowly and ordered them to fetch the blue and white plastic tape from their vehicle and seal off the general area. Taking advantage of their temporary absence, he swallowed hard and wiping the sweat from his brow, thrust his hands in his pockets to prevent them shaking. Alex Crowden was a large and vicious man and he dreaded to think what kind of situation might have developed if his son and daughter hadn't pulled him away.
'That's all I need,' he thought to himself, 'bloody headlines saying that we set about a grief stricken father with batons!'
The arrival of the two detectives in the unmarked car came as a welcome relief. As far as he was concerned, it was down to them now, making his way towards their car to brief them.
'They can speak to the mad old sod; that's what they get paid for', he thought ungraciously.

*

Johnny Bryce woke with a lightheaded feeling, and then recalled the previous nights work. He rolled his legs out of bed and shook his head; the memory of Sammy Crowden swinging from the tree came flooding back, his eyes staring wildly at Johnny as he gasped his dying breath.
After killing the lawyer, Mathew Gordon, he had thought long and hard about a possible police search of his home and at that time decided on a plan of action. Now he intended carrying out the same procedure before he set out for work.
Wearing just his running shorts, he went down stairs and into the kitchen where he opened the front door of the washing machine. All the clothing he'd worn the previous night, including his boots minus their laces, were crumpled together. He fetched the clothing and boots out of the machine, separated each damp, wrung item and replaced them back into the machine. From the bottom of the machine he unscrewed the plastic filter and emptied the fluff and thread contents into the kitchen sink, then replaced the filter in the washing machine. The filters contents he carefully placed in a small plastic food bag alongside the boots laces and tied the bag at the neck.
Once again he set the controls for a hot wash and poured in the required amount of strong detergent and small drop of bleach. Switching the machine on he returned back upstairs and set the shower controls to a temperature that he could just bear. Showering vigorously for the third time since he'd arrived home, he ensured that no trace of the camouflage paint remained on his face and scrubbed under his fingernails with a small brush. Satisfied with his ablutions, he unscrewed the drain and lifted the round wire mesh that he'd previously inserted. The hair contents from the mesh and the nailbrush he emptied into a second food bag, likewise tying the neck. Both bags he would later

dispose of in a public refuse bin.
Finally, he poured the remaining half of a bottle of strong disinfectant down the plughole before satisfying himself that any forensic evidence that might have adhered to him was now disposed of.
That done, he dried and finished dressing for his early morning run.

*

Detective Superintendent Frankie Johnson had been looking forward to his Saturday morning. An hour spent sitting in the quiet of his conservatory with his wife; she knitting and he reflecting on the week's business over the morning papers and a cup of quality coffee. The phone call from the newly promoted Detective Inspector that alerted him to the death of Sammy Crowden had come as more than a little surprise.
The journey from Johnson's home in Inverkip to Glasgow was punctuated by two further telephone calls; first Govan CID suggesting Johnson drive straight to the scene in Tweedsmuir Path where he'd meet with the DI and followed by ACC (Crime) John Moredun wondering why Johnson had not yet arrived at the scene and demanding an immediate update, when he finally did.
'And for God's sake, Superintendent.' Moredun added impatiently, 'please see that this incident is properly handled. I don't want the press reporting that this…' he faltered as he tried to recall the name, 'Crowden's death is in anyway connected with his release from court. I've enough trouble at the moment trying to deny these bloody newspaper reports linking the lawyers death to a police hit squad!' he whined.
With that, he hung up.
Johnson sighed heavily and threw the mobile phone onto the passenger seat beside him.
'Hope this doesn't interfere with your sodding golf today, sir,' he muttered sourly.

Upon his arrival at 129 Tweedsmuir Path, Johnson was obliged to park almost fifty yards from the house. Blue and white tape was stretched across the road and a young uniformed officer stood manning the tape and barring any further entry. A 'Police Incident' diversion sign needlessly positioned at the tape, warned driver's to take an alternative route.
Flashing his identity card at the cop, he was directed towards a parked CID car where he found the young, overweight Detective Inspector sitting in the front passenger seat, writing in his notebook.
'Ah, boss,' the DI greeted him with a smile as he climbed heavily from the car and stood respectfully, 'glad to see you could make it.'
In short, sharp sentences, the DI proceeded to relate the circumstances surrounding the discovery of the body.
'So, let me get this straight. He was found suspended by the neck, swinging from a blue nylon rope tied to a tree, a plastic chair lying overturned by his feet?'
'Correct; well, mostly anyway. The rope that was round his neck was hung over the top of a thick branch and led down to a small branch about two feet off the ground. That's what the end of the rope was tied to. It seems to me that he's looped the rope over the branch, tied the end to the small branch then finally tied it round his neck. That's when he's stepped off the chair, kicking it away from him.' He stopped speaking, slightly breathless and awaited Johnson's response to this theory.
The Superintendent nodded slowly then simply said, 'Continue.'

'The body's away to the mortuary now, but the casualty surgeon had a quick inspection and as far as he can tell at this time, there is nothing to indicate any injury other than to the neck; rope burn, I mean. Oh, and he had been drinking, if his breath and clothes are anything to go by. No trace of a note by the way. Suicide note, I mean'
'Any indication as to the time of death?'
The DI made a perfunctory glance to his notes.
'Doctor reckons body temperature indicates that, giving the conditions last night, it was sometime between midnight and 3pm.'
'Have you called forensics?'
The slight hesitation didn't escape Johnson's attention.
'I've called them to make them aware sir, but it seems pretty clear cut to me. There's no evidence of another party being involved and everything seems to indicate suicide.'
'Seems to indicate suicide,' parodied Johnson, one eyebrow raised and again nodding his head; then aware of the DI's relative inexperience at his rank, not unkindly suggested, 'Let's get them here anyway, eh? Just to be certain.'
Leaving the DI to use his car radio to request the attendance of the forensics, Johnson strolled across to the oak tree, nodding to the two detectives and uniformed Inspector who stood quietly speaking among themselves. He glanced at the tray with the three china mugs that sat on the grass nearby, annoyed that the crime scene was contaminated by their presence.
The ground beneath the large branch was heavily disturbed and he realised it would now be impossible to ascertain what type or size of footwear had trod there.
The plastic chair still lay upon its side, though now some slight distance from where it had been discovered; having since been kicked over by Alex Crowden.
As he stared up at the tree, Johnson could see the blue nylon rope still hung limply over the thick bough, the fresh cut raggedly clear where it was sawn through to release Samuel Crowden's body into the arms of his father and brother.
The knot tying the rope to the lower branch appeared to his untrained eye to be a simple granny knot, tied without any particular skill. As he looked up, he immediately became curious. Where the rope had looped over the branch, he could see what looked like a fine bluish colour showing against the bark.
Calling a detective to him, he sent him to fetch a second plastic chair from the nearby patio area and then upon the detectives return, steadied himself against the man's shoulder while he climbed on the chair to inspect his findings.
It was as he thought. The bluish tinge was the same colour as the rope and it seemed as if the rope had been forcefully dragged across the top of the branch, causing the friction to break the bark and rub the colour from the rope into the bare wood beneath. He heaved a sigh. It could only mean one thing.
A dead weight, likely Sammy Crowden, had been pulled upwards from the ground.
And more than likely, that meant another person being present and therefore probably murder.

*

During their routine interception of the police radio broadcasts, it wasn't long before the local media noted the request for Forensics to attend the suspicious death that had occurred at 129 Tweedsmuir Road.
Ally McGregor of the *Glasgow News* knew the address meant something, but couldn't

quite put his finger on it. It took just a few minutes scrolling through his Rolodex for him to make the connection; the address belonged to the Crowden family. Grabbing a photographer, he excitedly made his way there.
By the time that McGregor and the rest of the journalistic circus descended on the quiet suburban street, the police were heavily in evidence and diverting all questions to their media representative at headquarters. Nonetheless, they couldn't prevent the reporters knocking on neighbours doors and eliciting all sorts of tales about the notorious criminal family in their midst; some almost true and others downright lies.
To McGregor's mind, it didn't take a genius to work out that there must be some connection between the demise of Sammy Crowden and his recent acquittal at court. If there weren't, that wouldn't stop him writing about it. Smiling inwardly, he called his snapper to him.
'Right, I've seen enough. Get me back to the office and double quick. I've a story to deliver.'

*

Mary Crowden watched detachedly from her bedroom window, curious as to why the detective had called for another chair and not used the one that lay by the tree. Dressed now, she idly brushed her long blonde hair, wondering why Sammy would kill himself. And no note either. Her father, though grief-stricken, had loudly protested at the Inspector's suicide comment and if she and Davie hadn't managed to get Pop into the house, chances are that he would have went for the tosser.
She'd made the old man go for a shower, taken aback by his sudden outburst of love for his dead son; trying to get him to control himself and knowing that the police would want to come into the house. It went against her natural instinct to invite the filth into their home, but in the present circumstances she could see no other option.
But she couldn't have them seeing him like that. He was Alex Crowden, for God's sake!
Davie was in his own room, sulking that she'd taken charge of the old man. She knew he was also on a short fuse. His hatred for and deep mistrust of the police overcoming his shock at Sammy's death. For now at least, his baiting of Mary would stop, but she hadn't forgotten the previous week since that night at *Jakey's Bar*; the sly grins and mocking gestures when Pop's back was turned.
Even Sammy had wondered and grown suspicious by Davie's taunting of their sister, though she'd guessed Davie would keep her secret all to himself. He wouldn't want to share his knowledge, not even with his brother; not if it meant that Davie would I some way benefit from the secret.
She stopped brushing her hair, watching now as the detective stepped down from the plastic chair and ambled across the lawn towards their front door. She knew he was coming to the house and dropping her brush, sped through her door.
She was on the hallway stairs when he rang the bell.
'Miss Crowden? Detective Superintendent Johnson,' he announced. 'Is your father up to seeing me do you think?'
Behind her, Pop's voice bellowed from the top of the stairs. She was relieved that he sounded his usual, strong self.
'Let him come in, sweetheart. Show him into the lounge.'
Mary led Johnson into the comfortable front room, inviting him to take a seat. She'd already decided she wouldn't offer him any tea or coffee.

Blank faced, they sat quietly facing each other.
'I'm sorry that your brother has died,' he began softly, 'please accept my condolence.'
Before she could reply, her father entered the room, showered now and wrapped in a clean towelling robe, his shiny bald head reflecting off the glass in the ornate door as he stood with his back against the massive drinks cabinet.
'Are you here to tell me that my son committed suicide too?' he asked, the scorn evident in his voice. 'Well, let me tell you that is a load of shite! That boy had everything to live for and I….'
He didn't get any further. Johnson stood and faced him at eye level. He wasn't going to be dictated to, regardless of the anguish this prick might be going through.
'Hold on a minute,' he began, his authoritive voice cutting through the older man's anger. 'I don't know what you might have been told, but I have my own suspicions.'
Alex stopped and stared at Johnson, his eyes narrowing slightly as though in recognition. 'I know you, don't I?'
'Our paths have crossed, Mister Crowden. Frankie Johnson,' he introduced himself. 'I used to serve as a Detective Inspector with the Serious Crime Squad.'
'That's right. Your mob tried to fit me up a few years back. During my problems with the licensing board,' he slowly replied, his head bobbing in recognition.
'You mean when you got caught out running your brothels?' suggested Johnson, his face stern. 'But that's not the issue right now. May I?' he asked, indicating the seat behind him.
Alex nodded and watched as Johnson sat back down again. It was clear this detective was no fool and he recalled what his old boxing trainer had taught him; *careful in what I say and careful in what I do*.
'I've examined the rope that was used to…' Johnson hesitated, '…that was tied to the tree. I'm not satisfied that it was suicide and I have arranged for the scene to be examined by forensic experts. They should be on their way now.'
He watched as Alex Crowden's shoulders slumped slightly, recognising the relief that statement had brought the man.
'I know that you and,' he glanced briefly at Mary, 'certain other members of your family have a history with us. However, if we are to do our job fully we will need full cooperation from you all. In turn, I promise that I *personally* will keep you fully apprised of everything that we do and any progress that we might or might not make; anything in fact that could affect the outcome of our investigation. Is it a deal?'
Alex stared hard at him. Making deals with cops went against his creed, but this was an extraordinary circumstance, even he had to admit that.
'When will you know, confirm I mean, if he was…. murdered?'
Johnson rubbed his chin.
'Once the Forensics give me their findings and I receive the post mortem examination report, I'm thinking I should know by Monday. If it's before then, I'll personally phone you. If there's a delay, I'll let you know. Is that okay by you?'
Alex slowly nodded.
Mary stood and stroked her father's arm as she passed him. She held the lounge door open.
'I'll see you out,' she told Johnson in a flat voice.

*

As he walked to his car Frankie Johnson beckoned to the young Detective Inspector to join him. Without disclosing his findings at the oak tree branch, he issued him with instruction that in the absence of any evidence to indicate otherwise, this was now a suspicious death and would be treated with the same diligence as any other similar inquiry.
The DI, crestfallen and worried that he might have missed something obvious, readily agreed to the instruction, anything to demonstrate to his boss his eagerness to please.
Johnson understood the younger mans apprehension and clapped him on the shoulder.
'Get your lads to start tracking back on our victims whereabouts last night. It might also be a good idea to speak to the family, but do that yourself. Try and establish a pattern of Sammy's day-to-day movements; particularly if he's pissed off anyone in the last wee while. And don't forget to get that plastic chair printed either. Another thing; as soon as forensic have a verbal report of their examination, phone me right away with their findings. The paperwork can be dealt with later, but I want to be kept apprised of any update, anything at all. Okay, is that clear then?'
'What about suspects, sir?'
Johnson climbed into his car.
'For suspects, son,' he smiled wryly, 'try the Glasgow telephone directory.'

Driving away from the scene, Johnson again questioned if he had done the right thing. The young Detective Inspector had so obviously missed the rope burn on the branch and by not having forensic attend, showed an appalling lack of experience. The death could so easily have been written off as the suicide the DI had originally assessed. That would have wrapped the whole affair up in a neat and tidy bundle; no suspect, no need for an investigation and natural justice satisfied.
His brow furrowed and eyebrows knitted together as a thought suddenly came to him, an thought that seemed at first unbelievable.
Natural justice.
The two words haunted him as he turned onto the M8 motorway.
He hated himself for even considering the idea, but being the good and tenacious detective that Johnson was, once he had a suspicion had taken root, he wouldn't let it go till he had satisfied himself that he was either right or wrong; and in this case he hoped and prayed to God that he was wrong.
Reaching for his mobile phone from the passenger seat, one wary eye on the road, he scrolled through the directory till he found the home number of the man he was thinking of.
The phone rang several times before it was answered.
'Ronnie? Frankie Jackson,' he smiled. 'Look, I know you're at home on your day off, but something has come up. Put the kettle on, there's a good man. I'll be popping by for a cuppa.'

*

Alex Crowden shouted loudly for Davie to come down and join him and Mary in the lounge. When all three were seated, he glanced at them in turn.
'The cops will be coming in and they will want statements. We *will* speak to them,' he directed this to Davie, 'and tell them what they want to know. But within reason. They don't get the names of anyone that we suspect. Clear?'

Both his son and daughter nodded, but their eyes showed their confusion.
'Do we suspect anyone, Pop?' Mary asked.
'I don't know Mary and I don't know what the fuck is going on - pardon me - but Sammy was killed for a reason. Gospel's death was no ordinary killing either. He was targeted. By who, I don't know yet, but I mean to find out. I figure that he and Sammy,' he choked, his voice braking and his hands shaking uncontrollably at the mention of his sons name.
They both made towards him, but he shrugged them off, waving them back to their seats and noisily cleared his throat, taking a handkerchief from his robe pocket and wiping his eyes.
'Gospel and Sammy,' he began again slowly, 'were killed for a reason and it has something to do with us as a family.'
Davie and Mary glanced at each other; Davie silently urging her to speak first.
'Do you think it's got something to do with Delaney's business, Pop?' she asked at last.
Davie's eyes narrowed in suspicion, He knew there was something more to the takeover of Delaney's than the old man and the two-faced, scheming lesbian bitch were telling.
'What about the business?' he finally asked. He watched as Alex and Mary glanced sharply at each other.
'I've been keeping it tight, son,' began his father, 'but Gospel was working a deal for me. A building company need Delaney's yard as access to a housing estate they're constructing behind the car show room. That's why I had Mary working there; getting to know the books and figure out how Delaney was running the place.'
And likely getting her feet under the table as well, thought Davie, angry that his younger sister was entrusted with this information while he, the oldest son, had been kept in the dark. He turned to stare darkly at her.
'It's not her fault that you weren't told, Davie,' said his father, guessing at his sons' disappointment. 'That was my decision. I wanted the whole thing kept as tight as possible till the deal was settled.'
'And is it settled then?'
'Sweet as a nut, or it was till Gospel got bumped off. Now I'll have to find a new brief to negotiate from where Gospel left off,' he sighed.
'Anyway, that doesn't help any. What we'll have to figure out is who might gain from ruining us or trying to frighten us off from the deal?'
Mary chewed on her lower lip, broadcasting her doubt and catching her father's eye.
'What?' he asked.
'Maybe it's nothing to do with the property thing. What if it's something to do with that crash that Davie and Sammy had; some kind of revenge thing for killing that woman and her child?'
A silence descended across the room.
A slow grin spread across Davie's face as he turned sideways to stare at his sister. Then he laughed out loud, his laugh turning to a cough that he stifled behind his hand.
'You're trying to pin all this on Sammy and me, aren't you? You've been reading the papers. You think there's some kind of vigilante mob out there, knocking off guys that get away from court; get acquitted you mean? Ridiculous!'
Alex slowly nodded his head.
'Mary might not be too far from the truth, son. After all, we really don't have a clue as to

who might have murdered Gospel and your brother and their deaths are too closely linked to be coincidental. No, it's something we'll have to consider, another option. Maybe a cop or cops that don't like the law getting beat, losing their cases.'
'Shite,' ridiculed Davie, 'I mean, Gospel wasn't in the motor, was he? He had nothing to do with the crash.'
'No,' agreed Mary, 'but he did represent you at court and you know the old saying; if you fly with the crows you get shot with the crows.'
The doorbell rang and Mary left the room to answer it.
'They're here', she dryly announced.

*

Elsewhere that Saturday, life continued.
The general public, concerned more with the televised gladiatorial action of the two main Scottish football rivals, Celtic and Rangers, were indifferent to other items of news. The suspicious death of Samuel Crowden, found hanging within his garden in the Cardonald area of Glasgow didn't attract much attention till it featured on the front page of the Sunday tabloids.
Mid-morning at Garvey's Store in the Braehead Shopping Centre, Johnny Bryce and his security colleagues succeeded in deterring six members of a notorious Manchester based shoplifting team from stealing almost three thousand pounds worth of designer label gents suits. The ensuing chase through the packed shopping mall resulted in the recovery of the property, but the suspects made off.
The same afternoon, Chief Inspector Barry Thomas was having a much needed rest day from the Mathew Gordon murder inquiry. To his frustration his irate wife, angrily holding the phone, summoned him from his garden. Thomas's duty Detective Inspector, calling from the Gordon murder incident room, thoughtfully informed him that an all divisions bulletin had been issued regarding the suspicious death of Samuel Crowden and requesting any information relative thereto. As he hung up, he pondered the possible and highly likely connection with his own inquiry, but like the fictitious Scarlet O'Hara, decided tomorrow was another day and returned to pruning his prize-winning roses.

That evening, Annie Hall resigned herself to attend another family party where once again her fussing mother had invited yet another eligible man whom, she would later confide to Annie, had his own house, a good job and whose divorce was imminent. The former wife, she whispered, was *bound* to get custody of the four children, though she couldn't be sure who would get the marital home.
'But then,' she smiled at her stunned daughter, 'you already have a house, don't you?'

Sitting quietly within her lounge in the neat detached house in the Simshill area of Glasgow, Archie Crichton's wife worried desperately about him. Since receiving the court cancellation, he had settled into a deep depression, refusing all contact with family and the few friends who remained loyal; shutting himself in the bedroom and brooding constantly or taking himself off alone at all hours of the day. Sometimes even in the night, for hours on end in his car; not saying where he was going or when he would be back. She had given up asking him; simply accepting his need to be on his own.
It was, she thought, as if he was waiting to explode. More than once she had considered contacting their family GP, but if Archie discovered she'd went behind his back, he

would see it not as concern, but as a betrayal of trust. No, whether she liked it or not, she'd have to play the waiting game.
But how long, she nervously wrung her hands, can I wait?

Pounding away at his keyboard, Ally McGregor licked his lips as his imaginative writing skills come to the fore, preparing his piece for the Sunday edition. His eyes danced across the text, substituting a word here or there, a hint or innuendo that reinforced his suggestion that the deaths of Samuel Crowden and the lawyer, Mathew 'Gospel' Gordon might in some way be connected. Then, with a smile and for good measure, he decided to include the missing Patrick Delaney as a possible link in the crimes currently being investigated.
He was not to know just how closely his imaginative report would ultimately influence the ongoing police inquiry.

CHAPTER 16

Annie Hall woke early on Sunday morning and immediately grimaced. The few glasses of red wine she had drunk at her mother's party had left her with a parched throat. She shuddered at the memory of the man who had been invited as a potential suitor. My God! she grinned inanely. Where did her Mum find these people?
She stretched and puffed the pillow beneath her head to a more comfortable shape and then smiled as she recalled her reaction when she'd been introduced to Arthur. Almost two full inches shorter than Annie, she guessed his shape was the result of the oversized helpings he'd consumed, if his attack on the buffet was anything to go by. Annie was surprised he hadn't brought along a plastic bag to fill from the leftovers, the way he eyed the table behind her as he tried to engage her in conversation. It didn't help that every time he spoke with her, he sprayed food matter onto her new top, which reminded her; get it dry cleaned as a matter of urgency!
She closed her eyes and tried to sleep, but knew that without a drink of water, her thirst and now aching bladder would keep her awake, tossing and turning till she drunk for one and drained the other.
With a grunt, she tore herself from the cosy bed and stumbled to the window, throwing open the curtains and letting the summer morning's sunshine flood the room.
At least my head cold's gone; she thought gratefully, idly rubbing a forefinger across her itchy nose.
Glancing through the window, she made a decision. Fifteen minutes later found her dressed in her new tracksuit, hair tied back in a ponytail, arms flailing and power walking towards the newsagents shop, almost a mile distant in Glenburn Road.
Great idea, she coughed throatily while still only halfway there, but if I don't slow down I think I might have a heart attack.
Now walking at a more sedate pace, she reached the shop and collected her regular Sunday morning newspapers; the quality paper for world events and the tabloid for local gossip and the weekly TV magazine that accompanied it. Added to these she purchased a bottle of sparkling water to slate her now raging thirst. Papers tucked under her arm and drink firmly clasped in her hand, she breathed deeply and set off for home. By the time she had reached halfway, she was struggling slightly, now contributing her condition to

the effects of her summer cold rather than admitting it might be the wine she had consumed the previous evening. A nearby bench by a bus stop, much scarred and vandalised, offered a temporary refuge and she sat down to catch her breath, taking a deep mouthful of the bottled water.
While she sat, she unfolded the smaller paged tabloid and stared at the headline.
Revenge Death of Car Killer Suspect.
Quickly she read that one of the accused in the Karen and Laura Bryce death crash had been found hanged in the early hours on Saturday morning. According to the reporter, Samuel Crowden had been drinking within a Glasgow pub prior to his death then caught a taxi home. A few hours later a milk boy discovered his body. Police were refusing to comment, but the reporter linked the death to that of the Crowden family lawyer, Mathew Gordon and also tentatively linked both deaths to the earlier and mysterious disappearance of Patrick Delaney, a businessman from the east end of Glasgow. The reporter finished the piece by quoting his source as an underworld contact.
Annie's eyes returned to the start of the sentence in the first paragraph.
One of the accused in the Karen and Laura Bryce death crash...
Discovered on Saturday morning! She shook her head as though trying to clear it, her thoughts returning to the recent memory of her neighbour John Bryce arriving home in the darkness, dressed in army trousers and wearing a dark coloured jacket. Whatever he had been doing or wherever he had been, she knew as she had suspected then; he was hiding something.
For the first time in her young life, Annie Hall was experiencing a serious crisis of conscience, balancing her sympathy for the polite man who had lost his family at the hands of car thieves against the knowledge that she now possessed. She read again what the reporter had written, but there was no mention of the police naming or having a description of any suspect; simply stating, as they usually did, that they were refusing to comment.
She decided right there and then. There was no question of her getting involved. Without any other information to go on, she was probably putting two and two together and coming up with five. Besides, she was no detective. If the police had any suspicion that Mister Bryce was involved in this man's death, then it was their job to pursue it, not hers.

*

While Annie Hall sat upon the wooden bench reading the newspaper report regarding the demise of Samuel Crowden, five miles away in her own bedroom, Mary Crowden was also thinking about the police suspicion's surrounding her brother's death and with a slightly similar concern.
Lying in her palatial bedroom, Mary considered how she might turn poor Sammy's death to her advantage. She listened intently for a moment, but could hear no movement within the house, guessing that her father and Davie would still be fast asleep in their beds, no doubt sleeping off the effect of the whisky they had jointly consumed the previous night in their unofficial wake for the dead Sammy. Lazily, she stretched over and reached to the underside of the bedside table where she had taped her small tin. The low adhesive tape gave way easily and she lay back on the bed, examining the tin. Within was the three home made cannabis cigarettes and cheap plastic lighter. Selecting a cigarette, she lit it and closed the tin, returning it to its hiding place.
She inhaled deeply, feeling the hot smoke run its course through her lungs and thought

again of Sammy. Of course, she was sorry he was dead and given the choice would rather have him alive. But if truth be told, he didn't really figure too greatly in her day to day life; simply a brother who said hello in the morning and goodnight in the evening, such was the difference in their existence. Her detachment wasn't lack of interest; it was just that Sammy had never presented much of a challenge to her in Pop's affection and likely would have gone through his dull life living off his father's reputation and always at the beck and call of his older brother, Davie.
Now Davie, she grimaced slightly; he was a completely different kettle of fish. She knew that he saw himself as the rightful heir to Pop's empire; the natural successor to the businesses and the hidden bank accounts.
But he had done little to prove his worth; his criminal record proved that for he was always getting caught. But right now he had something of value that he could use, something that he could exert which might tip the scales and obtain Pop's favour over her.
The secret of her sexuality.
With a well-manicured fingertip, she removed a loose strand of tobacco from her lip and puffed deeply at the joint. Her problem now lay in what she could do to combat the menace that Davie presented. She was sure that he hadn't yet revealed her secret, knowing that if he had, Pop would have demanded from her an immediate explanation and refusal of his lies!
She clenched her fists in frustration, knowing that all she had worked and schemed towards might easily be gone with those few, whispered words.
Pity it was Sammy and not Davie that had been killed, she fumed.
Sammy, not Davie, she repeated in her mind.
The idea that presented itself was so scary, so frightening that at first she ignored it as stupid. But it persisted, then nagged mercilessly at her to consider its merits, the advantages of having Davie out of the way, gone from her life; no more worry that he might expose her.
But how, she thought, could she accomplish such a dangerous idea?
It all depended on one thing; that she knew. It must be proved by the police that Sammy had been murdered. If that *were* the case then Pop would have to accept that there was a killer who had murdered his son. *If* Sammy was murdered, why then could Davie not suffer the same fate, she wondered, her eyes bright and her breathing a little faster as she contemplated it.
And if Davie dies, then that killer, whoever he or she might be, would almost certainly also be blamed for his death.

*

Just three detectives attended the unofficial meeting that took place that afternoon within Paisley police office. Chaired by Detective Superintendent Frankie Johnson, Detective Chief Inspector Barry Thomas and Detective Inspector Ronnie Sutherland sat behind the large table upon which lay three short glasses and a carafe of water and all agreed that no record of the meeting would be kept. In short, none of the men felt comfortable in what they were about to discuss.
'Now, gentlemen,' began Johnson, 'before we begin I can confirm that the findings of the forensics seem to indicate that Sammy Crowden was indeed murdered; their examination of the locus has suggested that he was somehow taken or lured to the tree, the rope

slipped around his neck then dragged from his feet and suspended till he choked to death. The post mortem will no doubt bear out their findings. The killing was made to look like suicide, a plastic chair left nearby as though the victim had stepped off it. Why it was made to look like suicide, I'm not sure. My guess is that the killer wanted us to disregard murder and maybe let him get on with *another* killing, without worrying about being hunted while he planned his next victim. His *next* victim, gentlemen,' he stared at each of them in turn, 'so we must presume that it's likely there could be more killings. Regarding the scene at Tweedsmuir Path, I'm told there is nothing of evidential value at the locus so the killer has been very, very careful.
I've informed the Crowden family, so they are in no doubt we've a murder investigation on the go. What kind of cooperation we'll get from them, well,' he sighed heavily, 'it's old Alex's family, so I'll leave it to your imagination. I'll be in overall charge and also liasing with you guys. Right,' he slapped his hands down on the table top, 'let's consider first the facts that we have.'
'We know that Sammy Crowden, accompanied by his brother Davie, stole the Shogun that killed Missus Bryce and her daughter. We know that Gospel Gordon defended them both. We strongly suspect the Shogun owner and the arresting cop,' he glanced at his notes, 'constable Crichton were somehow threatened or warned off, but they're not telling; we know that the forensic evidence in the case was deliberately destroyed at the Fiscal's office and finally, we are now investigating the murder of two of the primary characters in the whole story. Ronnie, since you were the first man involved, anything to add?'
'I'm sure that you'll have read the *Glasgow Sunday News* tabloid story this morning put out by Ally McGregor that he's connecting the disappearance of Patrick Delaney with the murders. Well, by sheer ill luck he's hit the nail on the head. Delaney's property was slap bang in the middle of the access road to a new housing estate. Since his disappearance, Delaney's widow has sold the property and it is now owned by Alex Crowden.'
Sutherland saw Johnson's eyebrows raised and pre-empted his question.
'Danny McBride at Criminal Intelligence did a bit of background for me. Seems the Fraud Squad have now set their sights on a couple of District Councillors for corruption and I don't think it is coincidence, these same councillors are recorded as close associates of Alex Crowden.' He glanced down at his notes.
'To continue and digress slightly, while I don't suspect that the murders of Sammy and Gospel are connected to Delaney's disappearance, I do believe that Crowden's daughter Mary, who worked for Delaney, provided her brother's with the Shogun key and was probably also keeping tabs on Delaney while her father was negotiating the property deal behind Delaney's back.'
'You think then it's likely that Alex Crowden is behind Delaney's disappearance? Get him out of the way, so to speak?' asked Thomas.
'More than likely,' replied Sutherland, 'but at this time, without a body to investigate, we're stuck with a missing person inquiry only. And that's turned up nothing so far.'
Thomas stared at them both in turn.
'I get the feeling that you two know or suspect something about who killed Sammy and Gospel, but you're not keen to go with the idea.'
Reluctant though he was, he knew he had to ask.
'Are we talking about a police officer or officers, here?'

The tension in the room was a tight as a drum. Johnson glanced at Sutherland then spoke.
'Tell him,' he said quietly.
Sutherland drummed his fingertips on the table and then as though reluctantly coming to a decision, began.
'You're right, Barry. Frankie and I had a long discussion yesterday about a possible suspect. We think it's possible…and I stress *possible…* that the dead woman's husband, John Bryce might be the killer.'
Thomas sat back, his face blank.
'Tell me about him.'
'His wife and daughter, his family, were all he had, so he's not only widowed, but childless as well. He's currently working as a security guard at Garvey's in the Braehead Shopping Centre and has been for the last couple of years, but prior to that he was a member of the armed forces, the Royal Marines. He's a fit and athletic type of bloke, not known to us other than the usual police vetting check that was carried out by his employer due to the fact that he sometimes oversees large amounts of cash. In short, a hardworking, decent man.'
'But he was a marine, you say,' interrupted Thomas. 'Aren't those types trained in all sorts of unarmed combat, that kind of thing? Remember, my victim was stabbed and it was professionally done, according to the pathology report. The piercing wound caused death almost instantly, which suggests the killer knew *exactly* what he was doing.'
'That's why I had Ronnie make a little visit, late last night,' said Johnson, leaning forward and pouring water into the three glasses, two of which he then pushed towards his colleagues, 'and apologies again to your wife, Ronnie,' he added.
Sutherland inclined his head slightly in acknowledgment, trying to forget the outburst and tongue lashing Johnson's instruction had provoked.
'We considered Bryce might be violently upset over the acquittal of the Crowden's and decided to inquire into his background. Seems from what Ronnie found out that our Mister Bryce has a bit of a past.'
He nodded for Sutherland to continue.
'After a discussion with Frankie, I travelled yesterday afternoon to Edinburgh where I visited the Castle and met with an army guy, a Captain; one of the Military Intelligence unit that is stationed there as part of the Anti-Terrorist wing. Frankie had already spoken with our own Special Branch to make the arrangements, so I was expected. Anyway, to cut a long story boring, this Captain had in turn been instructed by his boss in London to assist me. After warning me in no uncertain terms that if I wrote anything down, he'd have my balls…then use the Official Secrets Act against me…he sat me down at a computer terminal in this cupboard of a room, logged me in and allowed me to read the file pertaining to one Sergeant John Bryce, Corp of Royal Marines. And what a bloody experience that was. Oh, and the bugger never left the room, simply sat in a corner and watched me like a hawk. Quite disconcerting, I can tell you.'
He paused for breath, aware that both men were leaning forward, anxious for him to continue.
'Bryce's career started like any other young guy; enlisted at seventeen, passed his Green Beret commando course and was posted to Seaton Barracks at Plymouth. At eighteen, he served on his first tour of Belfast and during a street gunfight, hotly pursued then faced down and shot dead a notorious PIRA gunman, for which he was later commended. At

twenty, he was identified as NCO material and promoted to Lance Corporal. Served abroad in various countries, returning to the UK where he was again promoted and posted as an instructor corporal to the Commando Training Centre, where he excelled and was deemed worthy of further promotion.' He stopped and sipped at his glass of cold water.
'It seems that on the domestic front, that's where things began to go slightly awry for Bryce. He met his future wife Karen, who was visiting the area on holiday from Glasgow, and after a whirlwind romance they married. According to the highly confidential reports that I read, Missus Bryce was not the faithful and loving wife he supposed, but continuously phoning complaints to his senior officers about his frequent absences, which of course were wholly due to the training schedules he was bound to follow. It also seems that she was not averse to throwing herself at other marines and one unofficial report indicated that without Bryce's knowledge, the units' padre attempted to speak to her about her behaviour, but apparently was told in no uncertain terms, to fuck off.
Pretty damned straight those reports were,' he grinned.
'Anyway, it might be that Bryce *was* aware of his wife's conduct, but if he was he chose to ignore it. Anyway, following promotion to sergeant, he was selected for eighteen months undercover work in Northern Ireland; operating with a clandestine unit and I quote, *to identify and neutralise terrorist cells,*' and you can guess what that meant,' he laughed mirthlessly. 'To continue; during this time it seems that the padre and families welfare officer visited his wife on more than one occasion, as there are a number of confidential complaints about her…. behaviour… registered on his file.'
Sutherland chose his words carefully, in some small but decent way still acutely sensitive about speaking ill of the dead.
'But it's Bryce's training and his experiences during his eighteen months in the Province, where the real interest lies. Prior to his deployment, he spent at least six weeks being trained by the Security Service in London in all types of surveillance; that includes pedestrian and mobile surveillance and remember; he was already a trained man who himself was an instructor. Once deployed, he used these skills daily and took part in several deep cover operations and though there were too many for me to recall in total, two stick out.'
'Shortly after he arrived in Northern Ireland, he and another member of his team were staking out a farm close to the Irish border in South Armagh, what they call bandit country. Apparently they were unwittingly compromised by a local farmer who shopped them to the IRA. A heavily armed Active Service Unit, an ASU they call them, then challenged the men and in the ensuing shoot-out, Bryce's partner was killed. By the time the army back-up people arrived, Bryce had accounted for two of the ASU and one more was captured by the soldiers, trying to crawl away with a leg wound. He got a Mention in Dispatches for that little episode.
The second incident I thought was interesting occurred shortly before Bryce completed his tour of duty. It seems that a planned ambush of an ASU who were en-route to assassinate a high-ranking police officer, went badly wrong. The ambushed vehicle, with the IRA guys aboard, crashed into a line of parked cars and burst into flames. One of the IRA men was still alive and Bryce ran to help the injured man. Even though his team tried to restrain him, he broke free and attempted the rescue. Turned out the guy was only sixteen years old, on his first turn with the ASU. The rescues didn't work and the teenager died. There were a couple of photographs in the file. Horrible mess it was,' he

grimaced at the memory.
'Bryce was later reported as being moody and withdrawn. A doctor's evaluation, a shrink I think if you read between the lines, afterwards described him as clinically depressed. Shortly after that occurrence, he was returned to his unit and, against his commanding officers advice, decided to terminate his enlistment. A brief handwritten note from his CO suggests his wife was the primary cause for him leaving the marines.'
Again he took another drink of water, his throat uncommonly dry.
'The one thing that is worthy of mentioning and in my mind stands out in the report is Bryce's service record of skills and achievements; it had what you'd expect to find; skill with firearms, leadership qualities, etcetera, but his real speciality, the field in which he excelled and taught to commando recruits? Unarmed combat, silent killing and the use of the commando dagger.'
His lengthy report ended, Sutherland sat back and allowed both men to digest what he had told them.
Thomas spoke first.
'So,' he quietly began, his eyes staring at Sutherland as he spoke, 'if we consider the method used to murder Mathew Gordon, the technique used to kill him. It's conceivable that he was approached and taken from behind in some kind of unarmed combat hold and the sharpened screwdriver, a substitute for a commando dagger? Jesus Christ! Who is this guy? Rambo?'
Johnson nodded his head slowly.
'There's no doubt Barry, that Bryce not only has the training to have murdered Gordon, but having met the man, I don't doubt he also has the strength to have hung Sammy Crowden from that tree. If we look at him as a reasonable suspect for Crowden first, he has the motive, the ability, and the opportunity for planning the murder and again his training will have provided him with the necessary preparatory skills.'
He paused.
'But why kill Gospel Gordon? Simply because of his representation of the Crowden's at court?'
'I think I can answer that boss,' replied Sutherland. 'It's my belief that Bryce watched the television report, the BBC news item following their acquittal, where Gordon more or less ridiculed both us and the Fiscal's for the failure to commit them two sods to trial.'
'I know the item,' said Johnson, 'I watched it myself that night.'
'Well, I think that Bryce has seen Gordon accuse Bryce's wife of more or less being responsible for their daughter's death. I know if I had been him, I'd have been baying for Gospel's blood after that. It was shocking, what he said.'
'I agree with Ronnie,' interjected Thomas. 'I think that our Mister Bryce possibly saw their lawyer as a valid target after that broadcast and our Gospel had unwittingly signed his own death warrant. Certainly taught him not to run off at the mouth again, anyway,' he dryly observed, then with a sardonic grin, 'no pun intended.'.
'Well,' he continued, 'if our suspicions are correct then there seems little doubt that Bryce won't be satisfied till he's completed his task. And that means that his next target will be the surviving brother, Davie Crowden. How do you propose to deal with it, Frankie? Warn off Bryce or let him run and hope he does us all a favour?' he smirked.
'I know you're kidding Barry,' replied Johnson, 'or at least I hope you're kidding. Duty of care to the public and all that bollocks, even if they are the lowest of the low.'

He rubbed his face between his hands.
'Having briefly met with Bryce and aware of what tragedy the man has been through, it gives me no pleasure in listing him as our primary suspect in the murders of Gordon and Crowden. For obvious reasons, our suspicions must remain confidential and a *'need to know'* policy operates from this time onwards. I myself will update ACC Moredun in the morning. Only involve those officers from your inquiries that you trust to keep their mouths shut. If the media or John Bryce himself should ever learn of our suspicions about him, I suspect he'll simply fade away until we lose interest, then strike again. By that time, we'll have little chance of catching him.'
'Gentlemen,' said Johnson, 'I propose that our next plan of action is to involve our surveillance boys from headquarters, have them attend here at Paisley, perhaps tomorrow morning, and brief them on what's required. Can you attend to that Ronnie?' he asked, but in such a polite way that the instruction was disguised as a question.
'Of course, boss. Will you be present?'
'No, I'll travel to headquarters for the meeting with the ACC. Barry, please continue with your own investigation and liase with that young DI at Govan; sorry, I've forgotten his name, regarding Sammy Crowden's inquiry. Right,' he rose to his feet to indicate the meeting was concluded, 'please keep me informed of any developments.'

*

Shooter Martin pushed back the metal garage door on its springs to aid the ventilation and continued with his workout regime, the sweat pouring from his naked torso as he pulled at the heavy weights, determined to exceed his previous best.
The news of the murder had come as a surprise, but if he was honest, he was completely indifferent about the death of Sammy Crowden. The wee guy had been a weasel, always picking on punters that either couldn't or wouldn't fight back, too scared of Alex's reputation. Shooter despised that type of coward. If a man didn't have the courage to pick a fight that he might lose, then he wasn't a man as far as Shooter was concerned. It never occurred to Shooter's twisted logic that bullying and intimidating those weaker than he, was in itself the ultimate cowardice.
As he jerked at the heavy weights, he thought again of the anguished telephone call from Alex. He could almost hear the pain in the older man's voice, his distress at losing a son. It was all that Shooter could do to tell Alex he was better off without the little shit and concentrate on Davie, for at least Davie could handle himself. But he bit his tongue and allowed his old friend to vehemently curse away, listening as Alex vowed to find whoever did this to his boy and the revenge he would take, in return.
Tomorrow, Alex instructed as he listened intently, Shooter was to get in touch with their mutual associate whose office was in Warrick Street and have him make contact with any former colleagues; anyone who could tell Alex if the cops had an interest in a particular suspect for his sons' death.
Money was no object, he reminded Shooter. Find me an informant, a tout, a grass, he hissed through the phone at Shooter. Pay any price.
'Just get me the name of the man that killed my Sammy'.

Across the street, the man sat patiently in the dark coloured car, watching as Shooter went through his punishing routine; studying the bald headed man through narrowed eyes and watching as he pumped iron, his muscles glistening with sweat.

The moment wasn't now, too much activity in the busy street.
He experienced a shiver, a sensation that crawled across his body.
Glancing at the dashboard clock, he decided that enough was enough for today.
Time, after all, was on his side.

CHAPTER 17

The casually dressed eight men and four women comprising the surveillance team that sat around the conference table that Monday morning, chatted quietly among themselves, speculating on why at such short notice they had been pulled from their on-going drugs operation and diverted to Paisley police office.
The door opened to admit Ronnie Sutherland who accompanied by his Detective Sergeant Kevin Wilson and DC Maria Lavery, entered the room. The hubbub died away as Sutherland greeted them; some he knew by name, others by sight while the remainder were strangers to him.
The team leader, Detective Sergeant Andy Dawson, rose from his seat and greeted Sutherland with a handshake.
'Nice to see you again, boss,' he grinned broadly. 'Hear you might have something for us to do?'
At five foot eleven, broad shouldered with wiry black hair and a permanent seven o'clock shadow that gave him an almost Mediterranean look, Andy was usually a popular man with the ladies, but his passion for rugby and real ale in the end tended to sidetrack him from his love life. His lack of success with women was a standing joke among his colleagues, who ribbed him mercilessly and laughingly reckoned that Andy couldn't catch his fingers in a door, let alone hang onto a woman.
Sutherland knew the big man, having used his team for previous surveillance operations and was pleased that his squad had been selected for the job.
Waving Andy back to his seat, he began the briefing by introducing his detectives and reminding all those present of the need for complete confidentiality.
As he spoke, Wilson and Lavery circled the table, handing out briefing sheets and a diagrammatic map of the area around surrounding 139 Cotton Close.
'The target I am about to identify to you is not your average thug. John Bryce is the man whose family was killed by David and Samuel Crowden. I have no doubt you will all be familiar with the case and I must remind you that no matter what your personal opinion is or where your sympathies might lie, we have a duty of care to the public and, ladies and gentlemen, that includes the opposition – even the Crowden's. Do I make myself totally and unequivocally clear on this point?'
He stared meaningfully at them all in turn, noting the curious faces, the nod of heads and the occasional grunted 'Sir'.
'Right, now that we are all agreed on that, let me continue. John Bryce is the primary suspect in the murder of the Crowden's lawyer, Mathew Gordon and of Sammy Crowden, found hanged last Saturday morning.'
A stunned silence descended on the room, the officers not surprisingly taken aback by this revelation.
'Some of the information I am about to reveal is not common knowledge, so again I insist that you please treat everything you hear as highly confidential. I'll take questions when I've finished.'

Sutherland's concise briefing followed and detailed the background to the case, the circumstances that led to the failure of the trial to commence and subsequent acquittal of the accused. When describing the discovery of both bodies, he had Wilson and Lavery pass round the scene of crime photographs.
He paused and helped himself to a glass of water.
'We don't have a photograph of Bryce, but we can provide you with all other details and he isn't hard to identify. Ideally, the purpose of your surveillance, ladies and gentlemen, would be to gather evidence for the two murders currently under investigation, however, Detective Superintendent Johnson has agreed with DCI Thomas and myself that there is little likelihood at this point in the investigations that we will discover anything incriminating against Bryce. No, your primary task is to possibly *prevent* another murder.'
He stopped, aware that he ha the teams full and undivided attention.
'It is our considered opinion that Bryce believes our failure to convict his family's killer's has prompted him to seek his own revenge and this has for some reason known only to Bryce, included the lawyer, Mathew Gordon. There now remains the second brother, David Crowden. It is our considered opinion he will be targeted next.'
He shuffled some notes on the table in front of him and continued.
'Your collective experience will be paramount in this operation for Bryce is no ordinary target. He's a former Royal Marine who has worked undercover in Northern Ireland and is familiar with most of your surveillance techniques. I won't presume to tell you how to go about your job, but I must stress that his knowledge of your procedures could be a deciding factor as to whether or not we will be successful in preventing him carrying out his task. Regretfully, I'm bound by the Official Secrets Act not to divulge details of his past life, but please take this on board – I want you all to exercise the utmost care when dealing with this man. The loss of his family has obviously caused him such grief that he is capable of killing and because of - certain incidents – he was involved in, in the Province, I can say he has an expertise in that field.'
Sutherland didn't miss the worried glances that particular statement evoked. Two hands were raised and he pointed to the female officer first.
'Are you suggesting, sir that if Bryce should compromise us, he might resort to violence and if that is the case, are we to be authorised to carry?'
Sutherland shook his head.
'You know the rules as well as I do, Sheila. Firearms will only be issued by order of an ACC and only then if there is a suspected threat to life. If I've read your surveillance policy correctly, should you feel compromised or threatened, you simply back off and get away from your target. Isn't that right?'
The detective slowly nodded her head, but Sutherland could see that she wasn't totally satisfied with his answer.
'Look,' he continued, addressing the whole room, 'I don't want to hinder how you work as a team and I'm sure that Andy here will have his own ideas of how you'll go about surveying Bryce, but this operation is an extremely low key, tip-toe affair. All we need is for you to present us with evidence that he is targeting David Crowden and we'll move in on Bryce, before he gets to David Crowden. Once we have sufficient evidence, we'll deal with him as we would in the normal course of any investigation. We aren't keen on having you compromise yourselves by becoming involved in an arrest situation; if

nothing else, we don't want to have to present you in open court and have you publicly reveal you were watching the victim's husband, who took his revenge because of our failings.'
He leaned forward and steadied himself with both hands on the back of a chair.
'This is as much about protecting him from the Crowden's as anything else. You all know them, or at least you will know of their capability. If they should discover that we suspect Bryce, he will be as much a target to them as Davie is to him. He's not interested in hurting anyone else, as far as we can assess; just seeking to get back at the ones that he believes responsible for the death of his wife and daughter.'
That said, he pointed to the second detective who had raised his hand.
'I realise you've assessed Davie Crowden as the likely target for Bryce, but I've had dealings with these people before and I know there's a daughter, Mary. Earlier in your briefing you also mentioned she's suspected of providing the key to her brothers. Don't you therefore consider her a target? Or even the old man, Alex Crowden?'
'Okay Gerry point taken, ' replied Sutherland. 'First let's discuss Mary. Bryce was never told of her suspected involvement, so there's no reason or him to go after her. As for Alex Crowden? Well, just how wide does Bryce intend casting his net, we have to ask ourselves?
We know there's no evidence or witnesses to implicate him in Gordon's death, which was blatantly murder and we've assessed that he reasoned we wouldn't connect Gordon's murder with him seeking revenge on the Crowden's.
But then he tried to make Sammy's death look like suicide. Now, again we asked ourselves, was it Bryce's intention to make Sammy's death seem like suicide to remove suspicion from himself and allow him the freedom to go after Davie, without hindrance from the police?'
Sutherland puckered his lips as he nodded his head.
'We concluded he made Sammy's murder look like suicide so we'd not suspect anyone was targeting the Crowden boys, thereby allowing him the time to arrange and execute,' he grinned widely, 'forgive the pun - execute his plan.'
He stood upright and stretched himself; finally admitting his back had been bothering him since that night on his couch, then exhaled loudly.
'However, saying that I have to admit what I've told you is our *considered* assessment of the situation. If you have any other ideas or questions, now or later, feel free to speak to either Andy or myself. Frankly, folks, I know this is a real shitty assignment and that privately, you might believe Gordon and Crowden had it coming to them. I can only reiterate, our *duty of care* extends to even those that we dislike. We can't choose the good guys or the bad guys; we simply work with the hand that's dealt us. Any further questions?' He glanced around the table. 'No?'
He turned to Dawson.
'Right, I'll leave you to get on with it, Andy. Mister Johnson has instructed me to be your liaison, so feel free to phone me at any time. If you can't contact me, either Kevin or Maria here,' he indicated his detectives, 'will assist you.'

Once Sutherland and his staff had left the room, Andy sat back down and stared at his team.
'I know we've been handed a rotten job,' he began, 'but in a way it's a back handed

compliment. The sensitivity of the task requires the best team,' he grinned slowly, 'but they weren't available so we got the job.'
The good-natured growls and abuse that followed was silenced by him raising his hand.
'Right,' he smiled softly, 'down to business. So here's what we do.'

*

Shooter Martin parked his Renault car on wasteland near to Warrick Street and climbed the stairs of the old building to Eddie Rawlings office. Pushing open the squeaking door, the young secretary was about to rise to greet the visitor, but closed her mouth tight in fearful recognition, the memory of his last visit fresh in her mind. Shooter ignored her wide-eyed stare as he strode into Rawlings inner sanctum.
'Got a wee job for you,' he snarled at the fat man, eyes staring wide as he leaned across the desk, his breath warm on Rawlings sweaty face. 'Mister Crowden has suffered a bereavement and would like you to find out if the coppers have anyone in mind for his sons death. Pronto like,' he added unnecessarily for in the scheme of things, any inquiries that Rawlings worked on always took second place to Alex Crowden's requirements.
'I've…one or two… people I can…. speak to at police headquarters,' he stammered in reply, clearing his throat in a fruitless effort to give the impression Shooter didn't *really* frighten him.
'Then get it done, eh?'
With that, the shaven headed man turned on his heel and left the office, stopping briefly at the door from where he turned to the young secretary, leered at her and winked.
'Alright, girlie?'
The secretary swallowed hard and shuddered, watching as he shut the door behind him. She could hear his laughter echoing down the stairs.

Still laughing at his own humour, he walked swiftly to the Renault and climbed in, blissfully unaware that the man in the dark coloured car was watching his every move.

*

Across the city, Mary Crowden sat working behind the desk formerly occupied by Pat Delaney and glanced through the window of the portacabin. She could see her brother Davie, arms folded and lounging against the door of a Mercedes car, idly watching the young teenage boy Mary kept on when she had taken over the business, as he furiously polished the car bonnet.
Since Davie discovered her secret, he had been insufferable; refusing all her instruction when at work, often skipping off without telling her and generally ignoring her during the working day and at home; and always with the sneer pasted to his face. She inwardly fumed. He had power over her and by God was he letting her know it!
She had come to hate him.
At home, he acted out the role of sympathetic son to Pop's grief, but in her heart she knew that the police confirmation of Sammy's murder had affected him even less than it had upset her. In Davie's mind, Sammy had just been another sibling, a third member to share Pop's inheritance and now with him gone, there was only Mary to contend with and he believed he had her by the short and curlies.
He glanced up and grinned as he caught her staring at him. She quickly looked away, a flush spreading from her neck. She waited a moment, and then slowly glanced back, but again his attention was taken; directing the youth polishing the car.

A man and woman, arm's entwined, strode slowly through the front gate and Davie sauntered towards them; customers she presumed. She watched as he pointed them towards a Volvo estate car and opened the driver's door, inviting the man to sit in the driver's seat.
Placing her pencil down on the file, she sat back and imagined again what life without Davie would mean to her; for one thing, all of Pop's empire would be hers and her secret, safe.
The more thought she gave it, the more it occurred to her that maybe Sammy's killer wasn't a stranger after all; she narrowed her eyes in the suspicion that maybe Davie had decided to get rid of his own brother and thereby cut the inheritance to a fifty-fifty split with her, rather than a three way division of everything. Then why, she wondered, would the killer have gone to such pains to make Sammy's death seem like suicide? The only reason that seemed plausible to Mary was to ensure Pop believed that nobody else was involved and that way, no suspicion could ever fall on Davie. Yes, she involuntarily nodded her head in agreement with her own assessment; that would work.
The idea that Davie might be Sammy's killer caused her to shiver slightly. If Davie were prepared to kill his own brother to inherit a larger part of the old man's businesses and money, to what lengths would he go to inherit *everything*? To do that, she shivered again as a cold hand seized at her chest; he would have to get rid of me!
She swallowed hard, the thought horrifying her; convinced now in her own mind that her brother might be plotting to kill her. She quickly glanced through the window, seeing Davie and the couple standing by the open door of the Volvo, engaged in conversation. He caught her eye and grinningly nodded his head, confidently assured of a sale and warning her he'd be bringing the couple into the portacabin to discuss and complete the paperwork.
Nobody would blame me if I acted first, she thought. After all, why would he keep my secret if he had other plans for me? Why not just go straight to Pop and tell him outright? The more she thought of it, the less likely it was that he'd divulge her secret if he was planning to kill her.
No, Davie was too smart for that and that was why, when they were around Pop, he did nothing to alert the old man to their bitterness towards each other. He'd want to be thought of as the loving brother, upset by her death; all the while acting to fool Pop.
She saw him walk with the couple towards the portacabin.
Standing, she smoothed flat her skirt, readying a smile to greet them as they came through the door, but in her mind she had already made her decision.
Before he could act, she would somehow find a way to deal with Davie.
Permanently.

*

Eddie Rawlings stood alone at the bar of the popular Elmbank Street pub and feigned interest in the Channel Four horse racing programme on the television above the gantry. He sipped sparingly at the pint of lager, occasionally glancing towards the entrance and watching for Paddy the cleaning supervisor, hoping the old man hadn't changed his routine. He didn't have long to wait. The corner door shoved open and the bespectacled, grey haired man limped in, heading straight for his usual seat at the bar.
'Long time no see, Paddy' greeted Rawlings as he approached him, a broad smile on his face, his right hand extended.

The older man peered suspiciously at him before breaking into a toothless grin. He reached forward and shook Rawlings hand, knowing that his face was familiar, but having forgotten his name and too embarrassed to ask.
'You'll have a pint, Paddy? Lager?'
'Aye, eh…Lager will do me fine, eh…'
'Eddie. Eddie Rawlings. I used to work as a DC with the Serious Crime Squad, before I retired,' he explained, hoping the old man wouldn't recall the incident and just how quickly the police did retire him, or as it was said at the time; how Rawlings had escaped just ahead of the posse.
'Oh, aye, of course, Eddie,' Paddy replied, his memory still failing him but sure now he recognised the guy's face. He sipped at his pint to give him a few more seconds, trying to recall Rawlings.
'So, Eddie, what are you doing these days, eh? Still retired?'
Rawlings tapped a forefinger against the side of his nose and whispered:
'Working hard, Paddy. Got my own business, private detective agency. Doing very well too, if I do say so myself,' he boasted with more aplomb than he felt.
'Got a big case on at the moment,' he leaned across to Paddy, speaking softly and laying a reassuring hand on his shoulder. 'Not supposed to really discuss it outside headquarters, but I mean after all, you're in the job too, aren't you? Being police staff and all,' he confided to the older man, the unsaid implication that Rawlings still had access to headquarters.
He had known Paddy when he had worked at headquarters, known of the old man's pride working for the police, of his hobby collecting police memorabilia and occasionally spoken with him in the passing. He didn't add that Paddy's enthusiasm to be working in the Squad office among the detectives was something of a joke between a few of the younger officers; some of who had unkindly taken advantage of his willingness to be in their company, using him to run errands or do odd jobs. On the whole, he had been treated fairly, but today fairness was the last thing on Rawlings mind.
'So, how are things with you, these days? Still supervising the cleaning staff, running around after those scruffy detectives?' he warmly joked.
'Well, you know how it is Eddie, things get in a real mess if I'm not there,' he said with a hint of pride. 'Bins need emptying, carpets need cleaned, windows washed and the state they leave that kitchen,' he tittered as he shook his head, his shoulders heaving as he laughed.
'Another pint, Paddy,' Rawlings waved to the barmaid, 'and on me. I insist; after all the police are giving me a right good commission because of this job.' Again he tapped the side of his nose.
Paddy smiled. Eddie's face was definitely familiar, but something else was trying to nudge his memory.
'Anything interesting happening with the Squad, these days,' Rawlings inquired, sipping his pint and trying to sound casual.
'Not that they tell me,' replied Paddy, cautiously.
'Things must have changed then, eh? Weren't you always the first to know what was going on? Who was on what inquiry? Where the lads were heading out? That sort of thing?'
Rawlings worked at flattering the old man, knowing he'd be pleased he was thought of so

highly.
'Well, I do hear the odd thing now and again. But you know the score, Eddie. Tittle tattle and all that, eh?'
'Two halves of Glenfiddich, please, darling,' Rawlings waved a ten-pound note at the barmaid.
The busty redhead made it plain she didn't like being called darling by the way the glasses was slammed down on the bar.
'I shouldn't be drinking whisky in the afternoon,' complained Paddy, lifting the glass and draining its contents in one gulp.
'Nonsense,' replied Rawlings, 'it's been ages since we've had a drink together, Paddy and besides, you're off duty now. Here, you made short work of that one. Let me get you another,' he said waving again at the scowling barmaid. Rawlings own whisky lay untouched.
It took three more straight whiskies before Paddy, burping and glassy eyed, whispered in confidence to his new best friend Eddie about a message that he had overheard on the Squad radio in the general office. One of the surveillance teams being diverted from their operation to an urgent meeting at Paisley police office. No, he slurred, he didn't know what it was about but the word was it was pretty hush-hush. This time Paddy tapped the side of his nose, though missing at the first attempt.
'The team?' he stared at Rawlings, trying hard to focus on his flabby face. 'Oh, Andy Dawson's squad. Word is that they're the best,' he burped again.

*

The officer under discussion, Andy Dawson was at that time sat in the front passenger seat of the Ford Mondeo and studying the blown-up map of the area that surrounded John Bryce's house. He could see that the housing estate extended for some distance around Bryce's home and any attempt at situating manned surveillance cars within close proximity to the target address would he knew, inevitably attract attention and result in residents calling in the local police. No, he decided, he would have to position his people somewhere along the routes that Bryce's vehicle was likely to depart from the estate. That left him with a headache. How could he monitor Bryce's activities within the area of the estate? If he decided to leave on foot, what warning would they have?
He glanced again at the location of Bryce's mid-terraced house. The lane running behind it, he saw, was the ideal exit from the house; particularly during dark hours and if he guessed correctly, it was unlikely a back lane would be well lit, if indeed lit at all. Bryce was less likely to be spotted leaving the house from there than from the more exposed front door where presumably, there will be street lighting. For that he already had the idea to borrow a couple of experienced van men, a task that required a particular patience and tolerance.
What the team needed at the rear of the house was some kind of observation point; somewhere that overlooked the lane; somewhere to place a spotter and perhaps use as a command post.
He turned to his dozing driver.
'Gerry, me old son,' he said to the team's second in command, an experienced detective though junior to Andy, 'drive me back to Paisley office. I'll need to have a look at the Voter's Roll for the area. I think we'll have to find us a hidey-hole to set up an OP.'

*

Davie Crowden returned home that evening to find his father still dressed in his bathrobe and sat in the front room, a glass and an empty bottle of whisky lying on its side by his chair.
But the old man wasn't drunk, that was patently clear.
'You okay Pop?' he asked uneasily. He stayed out of his father's reach. The last few days had seen some violent mood swings and Davie feared the old man was losing it and if he got into one of his rages; well, Davie didn't intend being within swinging distance of those scarred and brutal fists.
'Don't worry, laddie. I'm not going out of my mind.' He waved nonchalantly at the empty bottle. 'Just a wee refreshment during the day, my own private wake, so to speak.' He drew himself up from the chair and staggered slightly. Davie moved forward to help him, but he shrugged off his hand and wrapped his robe about his huge frame, tightening the belt.
'Your sister not with you?'
'No Pop, she stayed on behind to do a wee bit more paperwork. She said to tell you that if she can fix the books to show a more regular turn-over of the stock, it might impress the buyers and maybe even push the purchase price of the business up slightly.'
Alex gave the briefest of smiles, unaware that his son was inwardly raging at the old man's pleasure with his daughter's diligence.
'Smart girl your sister. You can learn quite a bit from her, Davie. You're not daft yourself, son. I know that if you apply that brain of yours, you can do well for yourself.'
Davie bristled as he watched his father stumble past him and towards the kitchen at the rear of the house, his fists clenching as he thought of her. His shoulders heaved as yet another coughing fit overtook him. Mary had always been the fucking favourite, he snarled. Even her shite likely smelled of roses, as far as their father was concerned.
He hadn't realised till now just how much he despised her. Keeping her secret had been difficult, but now wasn't the time to use it against her. No; that time still had to come.
He followed Alex into the kitchen. The savoury smell of mince simmering on the cooker reminded him how hungry he was.
'That copper phoned today, when you were out at work,' his father told him. 'That big 'tec, the guy that was in the Serious, eh…' His memory failed him. He reached into the cupboard for a bag of potatoes and emptied them noisily into the steel basin of the sink.
'Johnson?' prompted Davie.
'Aye him. Said that they couldn't release Sammy's body till the PF had authorised it and it might yet be several weeks. In case they arrested somebody,' he slammed his hand down hard on the metal daring board.
He drew a deep breath to calm his inward rage, turned on the tap water and begun peeling the potatoes with a sharp knife.
'Told me that if they catch anyone then the defence would be entitled to a post mortem examination as well. Do you want peas or turnip with your mince?'
'Turnip. Peas make me fart too much. Does that mean we won't have a funeral till the body's released then?'
Alex stopped peeling the potato and leaned with both hands on the sink, then slowly turned his head to stare curiously at Davie.
'How the fuck can we have a funeral with no body?'
'Aye, right enough. Sorry Pop, I wasn't thinking.'

His father stared out through the kitchen window at the thick oak tree, it's heavy branch now sawn off and removed by the police for further examination; the freshly cut stump staring back at Alex like an amputation, in the fading light.
'No, Davie,' his voice began to rise, 'you weren't thinking and you don't think, son. If you had been thinking that night when you and Sammy stole that bloody motor, we wouldn't be in this position now, would we?' he shouted at his son.
Davie stood stock still, his father's anger sweeping over him like an enraged storm. His farther had obviously decided then; Sammy and Gospel's murder had to do with whoever was taking revenge for the deaths of that woman and her kid and them both being released from court. But who?
Alex calmed as quickly as his temper had risen.
'Set the table,' he told him, peeling at the potato, 'for three.'

*

The electrically controlled steel shutters took forever to descend from their casing in the ceiling, but at least it meant no more customers when they were down, sighed Johnny.
'Hold it there,' said a voice behind him. He smiled at the two matronly checkout operators laughing together as they limbo danced beneath the shutter, their ribald comments intended to bring a blush to Johnny's face. It was generally agreed by all the staff at Garvey's that Johnny Bryce was a nice man, usually willing to help out or do the odd favour.
He grinned in appreciation of their antics as they theatrically wiggled away, shoving at each other like a couple of teenagers as they clowned around, pleased to be going home.
Overhead the tannoy system again announced the closure of the mall in five minutes.
He watched as the shutter continued to descend. That's when he saw her.
She was standing in the public side of the mall, her back to him, dark hair swept back and pinned by a silver coloured clasp, tight jeans, black boots and wearing a pale green blouse, the darker green sweater about her shoulders. Young, he thought, no more than thirty, staring intently at a lingerie display behind the plate glass window in the fashionable women's shop, opposite Garvey's. Her arms were folded over and her handbag hung from her left shoulder. He could just see her face reflected in the mirror image of the window.
Pretending to concentrate on the shutter, he deliberately slowed its speed as it approached the ground, watching her with his peripheral vision. Her head didn't turn at all.
The first time he had seen her was earlier that afternoon. Then she had been wearing the sweater and her hair was curled up on top of her head.
She'd been holding a dress on a hanger, displaying it in front of her before the lengthy portable mirror, as though measuring its size against her body. He had passed by and caught her eye in the mirror as she watched him. She had looked away sharply. Too sharply, he had thought at the time, then dismissed it from his mind. But not quite.
The shutter softly clanged against the tile flooring and he turned the key to lock it in place. The woman was walking away towards the far exit.
Well, he thought to himself, either you're a damned attractive man Johnny Bryce and you've got yourself a stalker; or more likely, it has begun.

*

Daylight was fading fast when Annie Hall, briefcase slung across a tired shoulder, fumbled in her handbag for her keys as she approached her front door.

'Bugger,' she mumbled as the briefcase slipped from her shoulder and the strap pulled round to her hand, knocking the handbag sideways and spilling its contents onto the path. She stooped awkwardly in the tight business skirt, her loose hair falling across her face and the briefcase landing with a thud on the ground.
'Can I help you, Miss Hall?'
She turned quickly, startled at the sound of the mans' voice behind her. Her first impression was of a large, bear like figure standing over her.
'Who…who are you?' she gaped at him.
'My names Andy, Andy Dawson,' he replied, a large smile splitting his face. He stood a respectable distance from her, his hands crossed neatly in front of him.
'I was wondering if I could have a wee word with you? When you're ready of course,' he grinned as he slowly approached, bending down to lift her purse from the ground.
Annie instinctively grabbed at it.
He stood back; suddenly aware that maybe he was frightening the lassie and raised his hands in mock surrender.
'Honest, I'm a good guy. I'm too frightened of women to even think about robbing them,' he joked.
Facing him, her hair in disarray, she backed away towards her door.
'Look,' he began speaking softly, 'I'm a policeman. I'm very carefully going to go into my back pocket and reach for my warrant card. Only when I show it to you, promise not to laugh? I had a beard when the photograph was taken and I never bothered getting it updated. Okay?'
She nodded dumbly. Large as he was, she couldn't help but notice that he was quite good looking, though in a rough sort of way.
'Okay, but no funny business right? My husband will be at home and he knows karate and all I have to do is scream. And I can scream really loud, let me tell you.'
Andy resisted a grin. This was getting out of hand. Husband? The Voter's Roll indicated just one occupant. Anne Matilda Hall, aged twenty-nine.
He held up the card and she peered at it.
'Maybe if you turn it the right way up,' she suggested, her eyes narrowing as he quickly turned the card.
'Oh, aye. Sorry. There. Tell me it's me and you're happy it's me,' he boyishly pleaded, assuming a stern look to mirror the photograph.
'It's you. But I've never seen a police thingy card before. How do I know it's real?'
'Ah, good question. I've never actually been asked that one before. Hold on,' he replied, fumbling in his jacket pocket for the details he had written down.
'Right, you're Anne Matilda Hall, born December the fourteenth and…' he smiled at her, 'unless you've just got married, you live here alone.'
She stated at him aghast.
'How do you know these things?'
'From the Voter's Roll,' he grinned.
'Anyone can get access to those details,' she replied, 'you can read them at any public library.'
This is getting ridiculous, he sighed.
'Got me there, Miss Hall. Look. If I give you my office phone number, I'll wait here while you go inside and call it and then once you're satisfied I'm a cop, maybe I could

have a word with you.'
'What about?'
'Wouldn't you rather confirm my identity first?'
'Sod that,' she said tiredly, her instinct telling her he was being truthful and it *had* been a long day. 'I'm dying on my feet here. If you're a mad axe man or something, you've a funny way of choosing your victims. Voter's Roll? Hmmm. Here,' she handed him her briefcase, 'hold that a minute.'

Once inside the house Annie dumped her briefcase in the lounge and shrugged off her coat.
'Cup of tea, officer?'
'Andy and yes please; milk, no sugar. Nice place you got here.'
He watched her as she filled the kettle, admiring her legs as the skirt tightened across her neat behind.
She turned to speak and found him in standing in the doorway, arms folded and leaning against the wall, a lopsided grin on his face. 'What you smiling at then?'
'Sorry, I was just waiting on this karate wielding husband of yours, with the black pyjama suit dropping out of a cupboard.'
'Don't mock,' she returned his grin with a tight smile, 'there might yet be violence. I'm not convinced you're a real policeman. You don't exactly fit the image of the smartly turned out cops that we see on the recruiting posters.'
'No, I'm plain clothes all the time,' he replied, 'hence the untamed, wiry hair, rugged good looks and seven o'clock shadow. But honestly, I'm the real thing. Sure you don't want that number?'
'No, I'll believe you this time.'
The kettle boiled and she prepared the teapot, milking two cups as the tea brewed.
'Right then, officer Andy, what exactly do the police want with me?'

It was a full thirty minutes before Andy returned to his vehicle. His driver Gerry was dozing, his second favourite pastime after golf.
'So,' he rubbed the sleep from his eyes, 'how did it go?'
'No problems,' replied Andy. 'Nice woman, gave me a cup of char. Good looker too,' he added thoughtfully. 'Told her the old cock and bull about a high incidence of break-ins in the vicinity and the thieves using the back lanes. Seemed to accept it and more than happy to have her house watched by the police when she's out working.
Her smaller bedroom faces right out into the lane and is almost directly opposite the target address. Told her that at least one officer would be in the house on a twenty-four hour basis, so we'll have to work a shift system and might mean raiding the other teams for bodies; said we'd be there no more than a week and I've told her that if we cause her any inconvenience, we'd be out without complaint.'
He held up a door key.
'Kindly gave us our own access and said we could use the kitchen. We start tomorrow and insert when we know that Bryce is at work.'
'Bloody charmer you are Andy Dawson.'
'Well Gerry,' he grinned mischievously, 'either you're hot or you're not.'
'Sheila was on the blower earlier on boss, when you were having tea with your new

friend. She watched Bryce closing up the store; saw him lowering the shutters. The team will follow him home and want to know what you intend once he's been housed?'
Andy absently scratched at his prickly chin and considered his options. If Bryce were to strike tonight, then it would be just bad luck. The team had been out since early morning and were tired. He had shift patterns to arrange and a dozen other things to sort out.
'Right,' he finally decided, 'we'll call it a day. Get on the blower and inform the team to house Bryce. Once that's done, we'll head back to headquarters and make arrangements for tomorrow.'

*

After he'd gone, Annie made herself another cup of tea that she took through to the small lounge, squirming comfortably in her favourite armchair and putting her feet up.
Of course he wouldn't tell her the real reason why he was there. But she wasn't stupid. It must be her neighbour across the back, Mister Bryce she guessed; likelihood was that for some reason he must now be the subject of a police inquiry.
She thought again of his early morning return home, when she'd seen him wearing the army trousers. Her brow furrowed as she reasoned they must suspect him of killing that man, the one who was found hanged and had got off with the driving charge that killed Bryce's wife and child.
She sipped carefully at the hot tea.
She had tried to ignore the memory of that night. After all, maybe she was imagining what she'd seen. How would she explain it now, after all this time, even if she did go to the police?
It was nothing to do with her, after all and secretly, she sympathised with Mister Bryce and his loss. Well, even if the police *were* now involved, rightly or wrongly she was going to stick to her original decision. Let them deal with it.

*

He waved good night to his co-workers and made his way quickly towards his car, as he normally did. The short walk to the staff area at the far end of the massive car park was across open ground, but with a furtive glance abut him, he could see nothing that made him suspicious. The real test would be on the drive home. He fumbled with the keys as he tried to insert them into the door lock and deliberately dropped them. Bending low to retrieve them, he snatched a glance and saw the matchstick was still balanced on top of the tyre.
Inside the car he took a deep breath and started the engine. Looking about him he unhurriedly drove across the deserted car park. Nothing else seemed to be moving.
The journey home through familiar roads was uneventful, his eyes constantly flitting back and forth from the rear view mirror, but he couldn't or was unable to spot any particular vehicle following him.
He parked in his usual place in the common car park and sat in the car, watching for any strange vehicle to follow him into the narrow street. A woman wearing a scarf over her head, one hand in the pocket of her shabby coat and the other holding a bulging, plastic shopping bag that banged against her leg as she walked, passed by on the other side of the road. He glanced over at her, but the scarf prevented him for seeing if she was a local person. Head down, she continued her journey towards the far end of the estate.
Johnny shrugged and picked a loose matchstick from the dashboard ashtray. Alighting from the car, he locked it and bent down quickly, balancing the matchstick on the front

tyre.
The woman in the scarf decided to cross the narrow street and looked both ways to ensure no traffic was coming. In the distance, she saw the target leaving his vehicle. The woman pressed the button in her coat pocket and spoke quietly into the microphone hidden in her lapel.
'Tango one out of vehicle and now towards his house, over.'
'Roger. We'll pick you up as arranged. To all stations from the boss, that's a stand down for tonight. Out'.

Later that evening, Johnny took the extra and unprecedented precaution of taking a leisurely evening walk, a stroll that led through the estate and back to his vehicle where he pretended to fetch a jacket he'd deliberately left in the boot for such an occasion. He saw no sign of anything that caused him concern, no vehicles or strange faces. But then remembered what his surveillance instructor had daily drummed into the students. Not seeing them didn't mean they weren't there.

Unknown to both Johnny and Andy Dawson, the Detective Sergeant's earlier decision to stand his squad down for the evening had unwittingly proven to be a sensible move for the surveillance team; sowing the seed of doubt in their target's mind as to whether or not he was being watched.

*

CHAPTER 18

The following day dawned bright and clear. Sitting in his car a mere sixty yards from police headquarters, Eddie Rawlings idly scratched at his unshaven face and yawned. Difficult as it had been he knew the early morning rise was necessary, since the surveillance units always liked to be plotted up around their target home address, prior to their targets departing for whatever mischief they were suspected of.
He sipped at the tepid coffee and remembered days like this; living out of a car, eating irregularly, a flask of hot tea or coffee and sandwiches to sustain him for the day. No wonder my bowels are in such a bloody mess, he sighed.
He reflected on his subtle interrogation of old Paddy. Not that he felt any pangs of guilt; he needed the information, after all. But whether the information he had gleaned was correct, he couldn't be sure. One thing was certain. The old man had been correct; if there were a hush-hush job to be done, it would likely be Dawson's team. He'd heard on the grapevine of their exploits against the drug dealing kingpin Maxie McLean, as had most of the Glasgow underworld. Dawson's team had become a victim of their own success; most of the druggies in the city were now routinely practising anti-surveillance procedures though, he smirked, probably getting most of their training from watching Hollywood action movies.
A car slowly rolled to a halt at the junction of West Regent Street and Pitt Street and then turned right and away from him into the one-way system. He relaxed, guessing it was a headquarters nightshift worker going home.
He figured parked as he was alongside the hotel building and behind the white Transit van that even with his limited view, he should be able to have enough time to identify the surveillance vehicle carrying Andy Dawson. As a backup, he had the high-tech Japanese

scanner on the passenger seat beside him that was capable of breaking into the encrypted wavelength. Providing of course, he mentally crossed his fingers, the surveillance teams still used the same frequencies.
During his service with the Serious Crime Squad, the short time he had been seconded to surveillance had provided him with the necessary language skills to interpret their coded speech.
'So let's hope that's enough for me to be able to tail you today, Andy my lad,' he mumbled to himself.
He knew the cost of failing Alex Crowden and with an unaccustomed queasiness in his stomach, considered again his decision to pin all his hopes on this one shot.

*

Eddie Rawlings wasn't the only early bird at work that morning. Sitting in her portacabin office, Mary Crowden had spent most of the previous evening in her room, feigning a headache and assuring her concerned father that a good night's sleep was all she needed. Unfortunately for Mary, sleep was the one thing denied her, her mind racing as again she thought about her brother Davie, now convinced that he meant her harm.
She couldn't express her fear to her father. To do so would simply provide Davie with the excuse he needed and he would defend himself by exposing her secret and apart from his disgust; Pop would simply believe she was making it up, to protect herself from Davie's allegation, that her brother would never harm her. Particularly when he had been making a show in front of Pop of being so considerate.
It had occurred to her to phone Shooter Martin, reveal her problem and seek his advice while persuading him to do the job for her; getting rid of Davie. But that was too risky. Shooter was too much Pop's man. Of course, she realised Shooter fancied her, knew of his reputation with Pop's stable of girls and was confident that she could use her body to persuade him; but the idea died almost as she thought of it. He would never take advantage while Pop was on the scene. Anyway, she grimaced, she would only be swapping Davie's hold on her for Shooter's and he was far more dangerous than her brother.
Most of the men she knew who were capable of doing what she asked were mostly through Pop's business; associates who either worked for or had interests with Alex and whose loyalty was first and foremost to him. To elicit their help in killing her brother? Well, that was tantamount to asking Pop himself to do it.
She put her elbows on the desk and lowered her head into her hands.
She felt trapped. No way to turn and no way out.
Trapped. No way out. The phrase kept repeating itself in her head. It was as if the very words were trying to tell her something.
She slowly glanced about her at the office, her eyes narrowing as if seeing for the first time the portacabin she was sitting in. The cheaply painted walls and grey coloured flat ceiling; the small, sliding windows with the strong metal grills bolted to the outside to prevent break-ins. She looked down at the sturdy flooring and, hesitantly, stamped her feet. Too solid to break through.
A feeling of desperate hope filled her. But to do what she had in mind, she'd have to devise a plan; some preparation that would cause her father to suspect Sammy's killer.
She stood and walked to the door. The aluminium handle was designed merely to open and close the door that opened outwards, the real security being the padlocked bolt

welded to the outside of the metal frame. Pushing the handle down Mary opened the door. She walked out onto the small raised step, then squatted down and examined the lock. It seemed firm enough; sufficiently strong to ensure that when the door was closed over, only the action of depressing the handle would release the catch. She closed the door and nudged it from the inside, with her shoulder. The door stayed firmly shut. She pushed harder, then harder still, but the door would not budge unless the handle was pushed down. But what if the handle wasn't in place, she wondered? What if the handle wasn't there or didn't work? The door would remain firmly closed and trap anyone in the portacabin, inside.
She closely inspected the six sliding windows; two either side wall, one at the far end and one in the small toilet. All had the metal grills bolted outside. The window could all be slid opened, but the grills prevented not only entry to the portacabin, but also exit through the windows.
The more she examined the portacabin, the more excited she became.
She sat down again to giver her time to think. Now, how do I bait the trap?

*

The early morning breakfast meeting between Alex Crowden and Shooter Martin took place at the café off Broomfield Road. The smiling waitress that removed their plates brought them each another coffee.
'Last time I was here was with poor old Gospel,' sighed Alex.
'Yeah, any word from the coppers about who might have done him, boss?'
Alex shook his head.
'Nothing, and to be honest I don't expect they will tell me anyway. They'll worry that I might try to get to the bastard before them, as if I would.'
Both men grinned.
'Besides,' Alex continued, 'it seems likely that whoever did for Gospel might be the same bastard that done my Sammy. I take it that you met with Rawlings?'
'He's on the case as we speak. I told him that it was urgent and to get his arse in gear. Can't stand the fat shit myself but to be fair, he does produce results, eh?'
'Aye, and he knows to keep his mouth shut too. What else has been happening? I've been kind of tied up, what with losing Gospel, then Sammy.'
'There's word the London boys might be able to provide us with some new girlies; some Ukrainian's that slipped the net at Folkestone. Seems they've got the women, eight of them I heard, stashed in a house in the east end of the city. They're prepared to sell us three of them provided we arrange transport, as of next month.'
Alex considered the offer. Two of his brothels could use fresh meat. He'd lost one of his girls to an overdose a fortnight previously, having her body dumped by Shooter through the night at the doors of the Glasgow Royal Infirmary casualty department and another had got herself knocked up.
'Okay, here's what we'll do. Ask if our Cockney friends will consider supplying us with four women and I don't want any of them to be older than, say twenty, maybe twenty-one; and I want them younger if possible. Looking younger anyway. Tell them I'm prepared to offer the usual fee and we'll arrange transport, but they have to obtain medical certificates showing the girls are clean and healthy. I don't want any poxed-up girls in my stables. Clear?'
'As a bell, boss. But why four girlies? We're only two down.'

'I know, but I'm thinking about two to replace those we've lost and two to begin a new house, somewhere in the Dennistoun area I'm thinking. There are always good quality tenement flats being punted over that way, the old Victorian ones with the large rooms and high ceilings. Besides, I think it's about time that my Davie got himself more involved in the business and a couple of these women should give him a good start. You could show him how to break them in, eh Shooter,' he sniggered at his accomplice. Shooter leered back at him, his mind already enjoying the pleasures the four girlies would bring.
'You want me to start collecting schedules for properties then?' he asked Alex.
'Good idea. Anything between a hundred and one-twenty grand with a minimum of three bedrooms. Make sure they're not ground or top floor though, eh? Don't want to be stuck with punters getting out of windows and doing a runner, or leaking roofs. I'll speak to Davie tonight and let him know his old man is looking after his interests. The thought of his own stable should keep him on the straight and narrow, at least for now.'
'I thought he was working with your Mary?'
'Yeah, well he does give her a hand at the car business. Strange, they didn't seem to be getting along too well recently. Mind you,' he exhaled slowly, 'this business with losing Sammy seems to have healed their rift. I don't know what the problem had been, but one minute they're avoiding each other like the plague and the next they're all smiles and touchy-touchy, know what I mean? Kids,' he grunted, 'who needs them?'
As if suddenly aware of what he had said, his face turned ashen.
In an unusual display of sympathy, Shooter reached over and patted Alex on his arm.
A heavy silence hung over them.
'Well,' said Alex, pushing himself to his feet from the table, 'that's me. Remember Shooter, keep me informed of anything Rawlings reports, anything at all that. Savvy?'

*

Eddie Rawlings had little difficulty identifying Andy Dawson as the front seat passenger in the Ford Mondeo and the five double manned vehicles that followed him in quick succession through the junction were, he suspected, further surveillance vehicles. Apart from two faces, a male passenger and a woman detective driving the last car, the other occupants of the cars were strangers to him.
As the last vehicle turned out of sight, he pulled out from his parking pace and gunned the engine to the corner, following the convoy round the police headquarters building and just in time to see the tail end of the woman's car turning right onto St Vincent Street. Reaching the junction, Rawlings forced his way across the road and enraged a van driver, who waved a fist at him. The surveillance vehicles were ahead of him, he saw with some relief, and turning onto the slip road that led westwards on the M8 motorway. He glanced at his dashboard clock and saw the time was now seven am. Whoever Dawson's team were targeting today, he reckoned, they obviously believed that they would be in time. His recollection of surveillance was usually a five or, at the very latest, six am start.
The convoy continued westwards at a steady pace. Rawlings held back, with just enough distance to keep the rear car in sight, guessing that wherever the female detective was going, Dawson was bound to be heading there also.
The convoy passed Glasgow Airport and then swept onto the off ramp that led to the Paisley cut-off.
A set of lights held up the two rearmost vehicles, with Rawlings vehicle directly behind

the female driver's car. He thought it unlikely she'd recognise him after nearly three years, but wore a dark coloured baseball cap pulled low over his eyes, just in case.
The lights turned to green. The scanner on the passenger seat activated, a voice inquiring if the two vehicles were still held at the lights, the sound of a car engine in the background.
The male who responded informed the caller that they were clear and proceeding to join the convoy. The traffic began to build up as the surveillance vehicles and their shadow continued to proceed through Paisley town centre, turning towards the High Street. Still, he felt confident the female driver had not seen nor recognised him in her rear view mirror.
After all he smiled, who in surveillance would believe themselves to be surveyed?
He closed up on the car in front, and then braked slightly to hang back and that was when his problems began.
As the female's officer's vehicle approached an amber traffic light, she took a chance and sped through. Rawlings cursed and braked hard, the red traffic light glaring at him. He slammed his hand against the steering wheel in frustration as he watched the detectives car disappear from sight.
The scanner on the seat beside him remained ominously silent.

*

He had routinely completed his early morning jog and again seen nothing amiss; or at least nothing to substantiate his initial suspicions from the previous evening. The regular faces and cheery waves greeted Johnny as he made his circuit and there was no sign of any strange cars or vans. The young businesswoman that he passed most mornings, standing at the bus stop, her briefcase hung on her shoulder, had once more shyly smiled as he passed by. He supposed she lived locally, certainly within the area covered by the bus stop. For a second as he returned her smile, he thought she was about to speak; but then she'd glanced away. Probably too shy, he reckoned.
Towelling himself dry in the bathroom, he knew this was a dangerous time. The police had reported on the television news the previous evening that the death of Samuel Crowden was being treated as suspicious. That could only mean one thing. His suicide ruse hadn't worked as he had hoped. They must know Crowden had been murdered and if that were true, then they would examine all likely motives and, in the worst-case scenario, revenge would be considered. That must mean he would top their list. And if that was the situation, then they must surely conclude he was likely to go after the brother, David Crowden. But what kind of protection would they offer him? How would they approach the problem? How hard would it be to get near him? He walked through to his bedroom and figured that his one advantage was time was on his side.
Johnny rubbed hard at his damp hair as he considered his dilemma. He surmised that if the cops suspected him to be responsible for Samuel Crowden's death, they wouldn't ignore him, no matter how bad they felt about their own incompetence. They'd come after him with everything in their arsenal, including surveillance. Yes, he decided. That's how they'd go about it first. Survey him and establish a pattern of his movements in the hope of trapping him as he made his play. If that failed, there would probably be a direct approach by detectives; a formal interview either trying to make him confess or to warn him off from any further action against the Crowden's.
The one thing he felt confident in was that he had left nothing behind; no evidence or

witnesses to the killings.
But he couldn't stop now, not when he still had his wife and daughter to revenge. Even if in the end it meant being caught, then that was that chance he would just have to take. After all, he grimly thought, if the Crowden's got away with it at court, then he had an equally good chance.

*

Travelling on the bus to the Gilmore Street railway station, Annie Hall experienced a haunting guilt at her behaviour that morning when Mister Bryce had passed by. For one fleeting moment, she had the irresistible urge to stop him, warn him the police intended using her rear bedroom to watch him; but the moment had passed as swiftly as it had come.
Still, the shame haunted her. She had lain awake for almost an hour, trying to come to terms with her agreement with the policeman, Andy. In a fit of self-confession, she had to admit that his charm and roguish good looks had initially swayed her more than she was prepared to admit; her eagerness to be charmed overtaking her compassion for her neighbour's loss.
She thought again of Bryce running past her, his soft smile of greeting and she felt a hot flush of shame rise from her neck. She had never been a deceitful person; far too honest for her own good, as her mother was fond of saying. But the die had now been cast and rightly or wrongly, Annie Hall was going to have to live with her decision.

*

Eddie Rawlings sat in the lay-by on the quiet of Potterhill Road, just off the busier Neilston Road, the scanner held low in his hand.
'Come on, you bugger,' he shook the radio-like device, but still it remained silent though obviously working if the red light was any indication. He threw it disgustedly down on the passenger seat, regretting his decision to leave the instruction manual at home and wondering just what the search radius of the bloody thing was.
'Sheila, any sign of life at the target address, over?' squeaked a male voice from the set. Rawlings stared down at it and held his breath.
The scanner activated again and he could clearly hear the sound of hurried breathing, as though someone walking quickly; a footman he thought, then two clicks replied to the question. He remembered that if a footman was unable to verbally respond, a series of clicks could be sent; the number of clicks relative to the reply. Two clicks he recalled meant 'no'.
'Right,' said the male voice, 'I'll pick you up at the south end of Cotton Path,' said the voice.
Three clicks in reply - 'Yes'.
Rawlings scrambled in his glove box for an A to Z map, pulling the box's contents out and scattering them on the floor.
'Cotton Path, Cotton Path, Cotton Path' he mumbled to himself as he flipped through the book to the index. Finding the correct page number, he used his finger to trace across the page till he found Cotton Path.
'Glenburn area,' he murmured with a relieved grin.
Starting the engine, he pulled out into the traffic and headed towards Glenburn, intent on tracking down the surveillance team.

*

The matchstick was still in place when Johnny Bryce got into his car. He glanced about him. No sign that the interior had been interfered with, either.
Driving through the estate, he used his mirrors to check his rear but, he was quietly relieved to see, nothing so far.
It wasn't till he reached the main Glenburn Road that he spotted what looked like a tail. The silver coloured Laguna with the woman driving and her male passenger had slipped behind him as he crossed the brow of a slight hill. He couldn't be sure at first, but the car maintained a steady distance between them, slowing as he did and speeding up ever so slightly when he accelerated. He maintained his speed within the limit. Two sets of traffic lights later, the Laguna took a left turn and was replaced by a dark coloured Audi, blue he thought, with a male driver wearing sunglasses. Odd, he grinned tightly as he glanced above him, considering it was pretty overcast. Still, he wasn't certain but mentally noted the registration number as he had done with the Laguna.
The Audi took him to the slip road for the eastbound M8 motorway then peeled off towards Renfrew. Johnny joined the busy Glasgow city bound traffic and remained in the nearside lane, seeing a green coloured Mondeo using the slip road behind him to enter the motorway. He couldn't see if the two occupants were male or female.

Approximately two miles away, Eddie Rawlings listened intently as the scanner picked up most, but not all the traffic. He realised the surveillance target was now mobile and as quickly as he could, without unduly breaking the speed limit, headed towards the tracking vehicles.
At the mention of the eastbound motorway, he frowned at the thought of trying to keep up with the surveillance vehicles in Glasgow's busy morning traffic.
'Taking the left hand lane towards Braehead,' intoned the scanner.
He breathed a sigh of relief. With some luck, the convoy wasn't going to Glasgow, but maybe somewhere more local and if it were a workplace, so much the better, knowing it would then be far easier to identify the surveillance target.

Johnny drove through the large roundabout, one eye on the road, the other in the rear-view mirror. The Mondeo passed his exit and continued around the roundabout, but from the angle of the sun shining on their side windows, he couldn't make out the occupants faces.
He slowed the Micra and deliberately took station in the inside lane behind a heavily laden delivery lorry that laboriously made its way towards the large shopping mall. Cars and vans also travelling to the mall overtook the slower vehicles. He watched in his mirror as the silver coloured Laguna arrived at the roundabout cut-off and then seemingly hesitated, before ignoring the junction and continuing round the roundabout and out of his sight. He couldn't possibly identify the registration number from that distance, but same inner instinct told him it was the same car he had earlier spotted.
'Got you,' he whispered, a slow smile creeping across his face.

'Target vehicle towards Braehead,' stuttered the scanner and then, 'that's the Micra into the staff car park and stopping, over'.
In his own vehicle, Rawlings' relaxed slightly, sighed with relief and took his foot from the pedal. It had been an unexpected bonus, hearing the target vehicle identified as a

Micra. He grinned as he remembered his own surveillance training; knowing that the officer would later be criticised for identifying the vehicle type on the radio. The shopping mall wouldn't be open to the public for at least another hour, so it was safe to presume the target being followed was a staff member, working somewhere within the massive complex. All he had to do now was get there, find a position in the large car park and wait.

*

CHAPTER 19

The mobile phone in Andy Dawson's pocket vibrated. He retrieved it, glanced at the small window and punched the button.
'Yes, Gerry.'
'That's the target at Braehead, Andy. The mall isn't open yet, so I'm keeping the footmen in their cars till we can send someone in with the shoppers and verify that he's at work. The target's car is in the staff car park and we've got the single exit covered, so if he's off on his toes it will be without his motor. Too many pedestrian exits from this area to cover with just half the team here so I'll need to trust that he's inside Garvey's. How you doing there? Found the choccy biscuits yet?'
'Still looking.' He grinned at the cheeky bugger's sarcasm. It wouldn't do to torture him that their host, Miss Hall had laid out a plate with caramel wafers and Swiss rolls, as well as coffee and tea and a small post-it note inviting him to help himself.
'How did the tail go?'
'Seemed to be straightforward. He took what is probably his regular route to Braehead, through Paisley onto the motorway and off at the Renfrew turning. Didn't do any naughties that we could identify so we're guessing he didn't suss us at all.'
'Okay, but keep the team on their toes, Gerry. We can't give this guy any rope. He's had the same training as we've had, if not more and his experience of surveillance was against the big boys over the water. If you need a change of vehicles, I'll release my back-up from here to come and support you. Any sign that he has spotted the team, pull off and we'll review the situation.'
'What if when we pull off he's heading towards the Crowden's house?'
Andy tightened his lips and narrowed his eyes as he thought about it.
'Better to pull out than show out. If we need to pull off him because we suspect he's rumbled us, equally *he* might believe he's being followed and more than likely will abort any plan he might have at that time, particularly if he can no longer see us. If that *does* happen, I'll get right onto Ronnie Sutherland and put him wise. He can make the decision whether or not to send a uniformed car to sit outside the Crowden's house as a visible deterrent. Okay, anything else?'
'Sweet so far, boss. I'll give you a phone on the hour with an update.'
After terminating the call, Andy sat on the edge of the single bed and stared through the narrow crack in the curtain at the house across the back lane. Bryce's rear bedroom window, an exact replica of the house in which Andy sat, had the curtain tightly closed. If he guessed correctly, the smaller bedroom would have been Bryce's daughter's room. Following Ronnie Sutherland's briefing, the team had discussed the prospective surveillance and the DI was correct; there was been a general agreement that the job

stunk. Never had any of his team expressed disquiet about their job, but then again they'd never had to follow a grieving father; a man whose family had been wiped out by two members of a well-known criminal family; in essence a decent, upright citizen who had, according to the powers that be, gone over the edge. Some of the team had expressed misgivings about their participation in the operation; so much so that Andy suspected their heart wasn't in it. Unusually, he had to firmly remind them that it wasn't their job to decide who was right or wrong, that the bosses would determine whether charges should be brought against Bryce and only if the surveillance evidence supported their suspicions. Equally, he'd argued, they might conceivably prove Bryce to be innocent.
He couldn't tell if he had convinced them. More to the point, he wasn't too sure he had convinced himself.

*

Mary Crowden unlocked the padlock that secured the door of the small lean to shed where the spare tyres, cleaning materials, water hoses, petrol cans and other sundry items connected with the car business were neatly stored. Since she'd hired the odd-job teenager, Davie had the lad working like a slave to get the place tidied up; anything he could do to lord it over the boy, she bitterly thought. His one opportunity to pretend he was some kind of manager in the business.
She stepped warily into the tight place, carefully avoiding the box of dirty oil stained rags that might stain her suit, her eyes becoming adjusted to the poor light. She stooped at the dozen or so plastic gallon containers that stood neatly in a row, rapping her knuckles against them each in turn; most seemed to be at least half full. When Delaney run the business, he'd boasted that he'd sell each car with enough fuel only for the new owner to get to the nearby petrol station, any extra in the tank he usually had siphoned off for his own vehicle. Funny that she had given Delaney a thought. Mary was now looking at the petrol Delaney never had the opportunity to use. She briefly wondered what had become of him? It once had occurred to her that she'd ask Pop, but then thought better of it. Likely, she shivered in the cool of the shed, Shooter Martin had something to do with Delaney's disappearance but what she didn't know, she learned many years ago, couldn't hurt her.
Lying on a waist high wooden shelf was an old metal toolbox with a creaky hinged lid, within which she discovered an assortment of rusting tools, screwdrivers, a hacksaw, a claw hammer and several different sized spanners and wrenches. Frowning at having to touch the dirty tools, she finally selected two items that she thought might be useful. Carrying her booty, she returned to the portacabin, her mind now made up. What she needed now to do was to devise some means to lure Davie to the premises, some means that he wouldn't or couldn't ignore.
With a sinking feeling in the pit of her stomach, she knew what would work, the one thing she could offer Davie that he wouldn't refuse. And that, she grimly thought, was her next objective.

*

He'd dressed in an old overcoat that he carried in the boot and still wearing the baseball cap, set out across the large car park. Rawlings knew what he was looking for, the lonely parked car, its occupants slouched in their seats; the customary position of the bored surveillance officer whose shift comprised usually of five per cent frantic action and the remainder sitting about, waiting on something occurring.

He didn't have far to travel. The first vehicle with its male and female occupants was located in the lower floor of the three-storey car park. He saw the car, a Laguna from a distance and had no need to approach to confirm its identity.
The second surveillance car, an Audi with the two men, heads back as though dozing, was parked in a lay-by outside the car park; covering the vehicular exit route. The Mondeo was a little more difficult to spot, having been situated some distance away in the car park of a large DIY store. Try as he might, Rawlings could find no further surveillance vehicles and his task was made that more difficult by the constant stream of cars arriving to shop at Braehead.
He returned to his vehicle, satisfied that he had at least confirmed his earlier suspicion, that the target was probably employed within Braehead. He retrieved the scanner from beneath the passenger seat and switched it on. The set automatically retuned to its previous wavelength, but there was only silence.
He sat back, unwittingly once again united with his former colleagues in the waiting game.

*

Johnny feigned a slight headache and asked permission of his boss to operate the CCTV cameras for the day, a request that was readily agreed to for his boss knew that unlike his other guards, Johnny Bryce could be relied upon to be totally observant and more likely than his lesser trained colleagues to spot potential thieves. What he didn't know was that using the cameras, Johnny would have better access covering the entire public area of the store in his search for a familiar face; a young woman who the previous day had worn a green coloured sweater. He was almost certain that he was being surveyed, but being almost certain wasn't the same as being positive.
He watched the monitors as his colleagues operated the electric shutters, seeing the first of the day's shoppers drifting into the store. The sixty-four high-tech cameras that he operated and could in turn, individually display upon his five screens covered virtually every aspect of the two floors to which the public had access; as well as half a dozen cameras mounted on the wall outside, covering the immediate vicinity of the car park. Two of the fixed cameras that scanned both mall entrances and the two cameras that covered the food hall and car park entrances, he displayed on four of the overhead screens; leaving the fifth and largest screen to display whatever roving camera that he chose to activate and controlled by use of a joystick.
Johnny guessed that the mobile surveillance would have brought him to the car park, but it was unlikely the occupants would follow him on foot towards the closed mall. He reasoned it was more likely they would send a footman into the store, probably a woman or a couple, as soon as it opened to confirm his presence there. He smiled to himself; knowing that by spending the day in the CCTV room, it would confuse the surveillance and guessed they would not wish to query his whereabouts with any of the shop staff in the likelihood word got back that someone was asking after him.
He didn't have long to wait.
He watched on the overhead screen as the woman he'd seen the previous day entered the store through the ground floor mall door and hurriedly walk towards a far wall, using the hanging rails of women's clothing as a screen from behind which she observed all about her. She had changed her clothing and appearance, her hair now in a pony tail and dressed in a light coloured blouse and short, dark skirt underneath a dark blue jacket; but

there was no doubt it was her. It seemed obvious to Johnny she was looking for him and her actions confirmed what he already strongly suspected. He was being surveyed.
He considered having a little fun with her, using his in-store radio to send a security guard to overtly watch her, a procedure he had instigated to deter would be thieves, but on reflection decided that it would suit his purpose for the police not to be aware he knew of their interest in him.
The policewoman stalked the store, occasionally stopping and purporting to examine some or other item, her eyes everywhere. She was good he saw, nodding his head in appreciation of her skill. The system he operated had a close zoom feature and he used this to maximum effect; closely monitoring her movements across both floors. The longer he observed her the more he had to grudgingly admit she was very professional and but for his advantage, would have had difficulty spotting her had he been on the shop floor. He watched as she smiled at an assistant and entered the public toilet area; the one place in the shop where cameras were not permitted. He guessed she was looking for somewhere secure to report her failure to locate him to her colleagues outside.

Rawlings scanner burped and the female voice, echoing slightly, reported her lack of success in finding the target. He guessed the echo suggested she was in a toilet cubicle or something similar; his suspicion proving correct when the male voice acknowledged the call and requested the female have a pee for her colleague.
'He could be here,' continued the female, ignoring the jibe, 'but Garvey's has two floors and I might be passing him by. Also, I've been in too long without purchasing anything so you should consider sending someone else in, over.' The sound of a door opening suggested the operative was no longer alone.
'Acknowledged,' replied her male counterpart. 'Bobby's on his way.'
The answering three clicks confirmed what Rawlings suspected. The female was no longer able to speak freely.
Garvey's Store, he thought. So that's where the target works and where the relief Bobby was heading. He made a snap decision. Knowing where the surveillance vehicles were parked, he reckoned he could get to Garvey's before Bobby arrived there and he might be able to identify him from one of the vehicles he had earlier seen while on his recce. He decided to drive closer and park his car outside the store and get to a door before the detective called Bobby. If he recognised Bobby, he might in turn be able to see who Bobby was looking for. Nothing to lose anyway he grinned to himself, a nervous excitement overtaking him as he pushed out of the car.

*

Meetings, more meetings and finally another meeting took up most of Annie Hall's day. It seemed to her that since assuming the departmental managerial position, she had done little but discuss budget's, expenditure, shift patterns and sort out the humdrum and trivial complaints of a dozen whining staff members.
Coffee in hand and pencil rattling against her teeth, the phone call from Sadie Parker came as a welcome relief.
'So, how are you settling in Annie?'
'Slowly,' she replied. 'Very slowly, if truth be told. I didn't realise half the petty problems you were dealing with on a day-to-day basis. No likelihood you want your old job back?' she teased.

‘Let me tell you young lady, I’m in the middle of packing for a very expensive three weeks Mediterranean cruise, so the answer is a firm and definite ‘No’. The job is all yours.’
‘Anything else to report,’ Sadie continued, ‘on the domestic front I mean?’
To her friends uproarious laughter, Annie recounted the recent disastrous family party and her mother’s vain attempt to introduce her to another ‘Mister Right’.’
‘God, Annie, you make him sound like something out of a Charles Dickens novel,’ Sadie guffawed.
‘Not too far from the truth,’ she replied. Her excitement took over.
‘There is another little thing happening,’ she slowly began. ‘Do you remember me telling you about that poor man who lives across the back from me? The man that lost his wife and child?’
Sadie did.
‘Well, I had this dishy detective type come to my door yesterday and ask if he could use my house to spy on him. Gave me a fairy tale story about break-ins in the houses around my area. Load of rubbish really. Must have thought I was some stupid and naïve young woman. Anyway, the point is that I think they, the police I mean, are really watching the guy across the way, this Mister Bryce.’
‘And did you give them permission to use your house?’
‘Well, yes,’ she slowly drawled. ‘Don’t you think that was the right thing to do?’
‘I don’t know really. I mean, they don’t intend using you as a kind of witness or anything. Do they?’
‘No. Well, not that he said. As far as I know they just want to use my back bedroom to watch the lane that runs behind my house.’ A doubt had now crossed her mind. ‘Tell me truthfully, Sadie. Do you think I’ve made a mistake?’
The short pause added to her uncertainty.
‘Not a mistake,’ Sadie slowly replied, ‘particularly as the police have told you they are looking for persons breaking into houses. As long as you continue to believe that, you can’t be accused of allowing them to spy on your neighbour. Just keep that in mind. You are only assisting them because *they* told you that it’s their aim to catch housebreakers. Okay?’
Annie knew her friend was being kind, but still the reservations persisted.
‘So,’ Sadie continued in a cheerier voice, ‘tell me about the dishy detective.’

*

Shooter Martin parked his Renault car in a bus bay on the busy Duke Street, ignored the sharp glances of the elderly couple waiting patiently by the bus stop and strolled into the nearby estate agents.
The young female assistant started to smile brightly, but then her face froze to a half smile when she saw the large, shaven headed man with the tattooed ears grinning at her. Her male colleague busied himself with the paperwork on his desk, deciding if he caught the mean looking guys eye he could end up dealing with him and that, commission or no commission, was one prospective customer he didn’t relish handling.
‘Any three bed roomed flats for sale hereabouts, girlie?’ inquired Shooter in a quiet voice, sitting down opposite her, his elbows on her desk and his eyes tracing a deliberate path from her face to her ample cleavage.
The young woman swallowed hard and tried to find her voice, watching him as she

reached nervously for the plastic file beside her.
Outside the shop and across the road, the man in the dark car easily manoeuvred his vehicle into a tight parking space and settled back to wait.

*

The detective called Bobby arrived at the Garvey's food hall entrance and leisurely strolled in. He'd missed breakfast and was pleased with the opportunity to purchase a sandwich and carton of juice and then, with the purchase in a Garvey's plastic bag as a prop, would wander through the store.
He paid no heed to the fat man wearing the baseball cap who walked through the swing door behind him, his concentration centred upon finding the security guard whose description was filed in his mind.
In the CCTV control room, the fixed camera above the doorway caught both men enter the shop, but Johnny Bryce had no reason to be suspicious of them as he continued to use the joystick to follow the female police officer through the wide doorway, watching as she exited into the mall. He had no way of knowing the voice in her ear had instructed her to depart and return to her vehicle, that her relief had now taken over the search. Satisfied that for the moment the surveillance had given up the search, he concentrated on his job, trawling the two floors for potential shoplifters. It was about fifteen minutes after the female had departed that he became suspicious of the actions of two men, one of whom seemed curiously to be shadowing the other. As he watched, he saw the younger man who was carrying a food hall bag, enter the public toilets. The older and heavier set man loitered outside, discreetly watching the toilet entrance as he idly fingered the price tags attached to the racks of children's pyjamas, yet his head bobbed about searching the faces around him. That was enough for Johnny.
Suspecting the men to be thieves engage in some ploy, he used his in-store radio to position the four guards on duty to stand within the men's vision and stare them out; make it plainly obvious they were being monitored.
The younger man exited the toilets and visibly startled when he saw a guard was watching him. As Johnny observed them on camera, he saw the younger man approach the guard and produce something from his pocket. The guard nodded and using his radio, informed Johnny the guy was a copper who had followed a known thief into the shop. Johnny grinned broadly. Good excuse, but not true. He suspected this must be another surveillance footman.
The heavier man rather than speak to the guard simply turned away and walked out of the store and retraced his steps, exiting from the food hall. Johnny switched cameras and watched as the he climbed into a beat up Volkswagen Passat and drove away. Idly he scribbled the registration number on a piece of notepaper.
He sat back and placed his hands behind his head, puzzled as to why the heavier man was watching the surveillance officer. That was one he would have to give that one some thought.

Outside the store, the detective called Bobby shamefacedly reported that he had been compromised by the store security; and worse, there was no trace of the target.

*

Gerry called Andy Dawson with the bad news.
'So, you took him to the shop, his cars still there, but there's no trace of him at all?'

'Correct, boss. If he's in there, he must be working behind the scenes. And there's more bad news,' he sighed. 'Wee Bobby got sussed by the security so he's out of it for now.'
Dawson acknowledged the call and sat back on the bed against the headboard, contemplating his next move. If he reported to Ronnie Sutherland a loss of the target, that could mean a whole new ball game. It would look bad for his team, losing Bryce so early on in the game, but for all they knew Bryce could be actively stalking David Crowden at this moment. But not to tell Sutherland was equally as dangerous, particularly if Bryce got to Crowden while they were supposed to be surveying him! Shit!
Reaching for his phone, he realised ho had no other option. His best move would be to declare a loss and let Sutherland make the decision regarding the next move.

*

Eddie Rawlings drove hastily away from Braehead, checking his rear view mirror to ensure the hunter had not become the hunted.
That had been a close call. He hadn't expected the security to close in on him like that, chuckling to himself as he remembered how fast he had shot from the store.
One thing was certain though. If Andy Dawson's team had been tasked to watch the suspect in the Sammy Crowden killing, then he had at least established the suspect worked within Garvey's and lived in the Glenburn area of Paisley and likely in or somewhere close to a street called Cotton Path.
His next stop would be the municipal library just off the high street in Paisley. Like most police trained detectives, he knew that the public Voter's Roll was always an excellent source of reference when searching for a particular name. Right now, he didn't know the name he was looking for, but sometimes chancing it made the effort worthwhile. Occasionally even he got lucky.

*

Davie Crowden was suspicious. Mary had recently hardly exchanged a civil word with him all morning, let alone offered to buy him and the kid their lunch. What the hell was she after, he wondered?
Sending the young lad to the local bakery with her twenty-pound note and their order, he wandered back into the portacabin, ignoring his sister as he coughed into his handkerchief and surprised when she delivered a huge smile at him.
'You're up to something sis, but I can't quite put my finger on it. What is it?'
'Nothing Davie. I just feel that maybe you and I should make some effort into getting along right now. There's an atmosphere between us and even Pop knows it. I don't think this is the time for us to be at odds with each other; not with Sammy's funeral coming up sometime in the near future. I think we should try to make our peace; at least for Pop's sake. What do you think, eh?'
He moved closer and leaned with both hands on her desk, glaring at her.
'Don't think that being nicey-nicey to me is going to change anything, Mary. I know what you are, a dyke. And if I have to use that, then I will. For too long you've been Pop's wee pet, his favourite. He's always fucking boasting about you being the brains of the family. Well, enough is enough.'
He jabbed at his chest with his left forefinger.
'I'm the oldest. If anything should happen to Pop, then it's me that will inherit everything. That's the way of it, the way it's supposed to be! And that's the way it *will* be!' he hissed at her, his outburst provoking another fit of coughing.

She hadn't sought confrontation, didn't want him riled. She needed him to trust her, at least just once and determined not be provoked, reached across and placed her hand on top of his hand that remained resting on her desk.
'I'm not quibbling with that, Davie,' she said quietly, her eyes opened wide and searching his. 'Don't be getting yourself upset now,' she continued, stroking his hand soothingly.
He stared back at her, his eyes narrowing as he searched for something in her eyes, some subterfuge behind the smile. He hadn't previously seen her quite like this. His eyes wandered slowly down, all of a sudden realising her top blouse button was undone. He could plainly see her bra, her milky white breasts spilling out over the lacy edge and the faint bulge of her slightly darker nipples, as they strained against the thin cotton material of her blouse.
With a start, he pulled his hand away, acutely embarrassed at the thoughts that were racing through his mind. He stood there, not quite knowing how to handle this unexpected and tensely electric situation.
Mary suppressed a grin, knowing that had she continued to offer herself, he would have reached out for her. The smile remained fixed on her lips. She had long ago accepted that her sexuality was a tool she would use for whatever purpose she considered necessary.
'Look Davie, there's no need for you and I to fight over this,' she told him, her voice deliberately husky. 'Of *course* I accept your position in the family; I mean I've always looked up to you. Pop's given me the business here and likely I'll get a cut of the profit when he sells this place on. I'm no threat to you, honestly. I know you think it's just women I like, that I've got my…. preferences. But if nothing else, I like to…. experiment and I have other needs as well, you know. So perhaps you and I one night, maybe even…. tonight…' she finished speaking, her eyes wide, running her pink tongue around her ruby red lips, daring him to look away, the sexual innuendo hanging between them.
He swallowed hard, his throat suddenly dry; aware he was becoming aroused as he continued to stare down into her milky white cleavage.
The door burst open and the teenage lad burst in.
'Two with cheese and tomato and one of roast beef and mustard,' he announced with a grin.

*

CHAPTER 20

The long summers day drew to a close.
At Braehead, the three surveillance cars concentrated their attention on watching the target's Micra car, parked beside the few that remained as the shopping centre staff escaped from the nearby stores and wearily headed home. In the Audi, the detective called Bobby continued to mope about his bad luck until his irate partner finally told him to shut the fuck up and give it a rest.

*

On the train home, Annie Hall had decided to take Sadie Parker's advice; if the police said they were trying to catch housebreakers, then so be it. Who was she to question their purpose?

*

Alex Crowden was bemused; when they had left for work that morning, his son and daughter had barely glanced at each other. Now here they were, full of cheer; Davie,

home early and helping him prepare the evening meal and offering the later arriving Mary a drink of wine from the cupboard. She patting Davie's shoulder and smilingly suggesting they fetch him and her father a can of beer from the fridge. Kids, he shook his head. You never know the next with them, yet pleased that somehow, in some way, they had resolved their differences.
Alex listened as Mary described the day's business, her annoyance that tomorrow she would have to be at work really early, that the new owners of the Volvo Davie had sold requested they uplift the vehicle as soon as possible as they planned to travel down south to Devon and wanted a good start on the rush hour traffic.
Davie coughed, politely turning his head away from the table and hiding his mouth behind his hand then offered to accompany her to work. After all, he reminded her, it had been his sale and good naturedly waving away her refusal; then Mary giving in and graciously accepting her brother's offer.
It was important to her that Pop would see she and Davie were on friendly terms.
She was right. It pleased Alex to know they were again a close-knit family.
But their father would not have been so pleased if he had become aware of Davie's plans that night for Mary and even less so if he had but known of her plans for Davie.

*

In the rear bedroom of Annie Hall's home, Andy Dawson manoeuvred the tripod into yet another position, attempting to obtain the maximum coverage for the video camera, cursing softly as the faulty leg again slide inside the telescopic tube.
'Bugger,' he mumbled, fumbling with the strong adhesive tape to try and stabilise the leg.
'Anyone home?' asked the voice behind him.
'Jesus Christ!' he jumped in fright as Annie giggled behind him, a mug of tea in each hand.
'You didn't hear me come in then?'
'Er, no. I was trying to get this thing sorted,' he replied, catching his breath and taking a mug from her and setting it down on the bedside table. 'Good day at the office, then?'
'Not really, but thanks for asking. How long will you be here, then?'
'Do you mean in total, or just this evening?'
'Well, lets begin with this evening.'
'Well, I'll likely be here till about ten or eleven o'clock. I've arranged to have a nightshift officer from another team maintain a vigil through the night. The officer who'll be coming in is from another team. Gracie Collins is her name. She'll operate the camera and I promise, she won't disturb your beauty sleep.'
'So, you think I need beauty sleep then?'
'Er, no that came out all wrong, Of course you don't need beauty sleep, Miss Hall,' he stammered, wondering how the hell she had manoeuvred him into this conversation.
'What I meant to say is….'
'I think you should quit while you're ahead, Andy. And it's Annie,' she smiled coyly at him, surprising herself at her own forwardness.
'I take it you haven't eaten then or are you going home to a midnight super with your wife?'
He glanced at her, taking his eyes from the window, the casual question catching him unawares.
'Wife? No, I'm not married,' he replied, wondering where this was going.

'Girlfriend then?' her eyes twinkled mischievously.
'Not at the moment,' he slowly replied, returning his gaze to the window and hoping she hadn't seen the half smile on his face.
'So if I rustle up some dinner for us both, I won't be getting irate phone calls?'
'Only from my manager. I play rugby on most Saturday's and he's forever trying to get me to diet, or at least eat healthier food.' He patted his stomach. 'Not that I think I've a paunch, but it seems that I'm in constant training these days,' he sighed, 'and you wouldn't believe the cravings I have for the occasional mince pie and chips.'
She smiled at his broad back; her eyes absorbed by the dark curls that fell over his shirt collar and resisting the overwhelming urge to run her fingers through the tangle.
'Leave it to me and I'll see what I can do, then.'

*

Eddie Rawlings was pleased with his day. He drove home to his flat in Maryhill, anxious to get rid of his information and be done with the whole business.
It was as he thought; the Voter's Roll had come up trumps yet again.
Cotton Path and the adjacent Cotton Quadrant had little to offer, no names he recognised. But it was when he'd searched the list of Cotton Close, seeing the names of the couple residing at number 39 that at last he made the connection. Like most of the news hungry public of Glasgow, he'd followed the Crowden boys' court case closely; happy to learn that at last the two shits were getting their just deserts. Killing the woman and her kid? Even he baulked at that kind of slaughter. He had been as surprised as anyone when they'd got away with it, conveniently forgetting that he had in part assisted in their acquittal.
Karen Bryce; that had been the woman's name. The kid didn't feature on the Voter's Roll, not having had the opportunity to reach her eighteenth birthday. Karen and John Bryce.
The rest had been simple. A phone call to Garvey's Store, asking to speak with John Bryce then when he had been put through to Bryce's extension, introduced himself as a reporter doing a feature on bereavement caused by criminal acts.
Bryce had swallowed it; told him he wasn't interested in any such article and requested he not be called again.
Rawlings offered a grovelling apology and hung up.

He wasn't to know that Johnny Bryce hadn't believed him, but in a curious coincidence, Johnny had thought the caller to be a surveillance cop who was simply making sure he was still within the store.

*

Shooter Martin replaced the handset and checked the scribbled information. The dead woman's husband! Well, well that was a right turn up. He realised that the information was far too important to keep till tomorrow.
He grabbed his bomber jacket and made for the door, punching in the number on his mobile.
'Alex? Shooter. I'm coming over to speak with you. Our fat boy has come up with something that I think you should know and right away. No, no,' he told his boss, 'I don't want to tell you over the phone. Look, I'll be there in half an hour, okay?'
He climbed into the Renault and started the engine, accelerating out of his driveway and

towards the city.
The dark coloured car drew away from its parking spot and lights now switched on, followed him through Easterhouse, towards the motorway.

*

In his large office at Govan police station, Frankie Johnson stretched his aching muscles and rolled his back in an attempt to ease the cramp. Too many hours at his desk poring over witness statements had taken their toll.
He flicked through the paperwork, reaching for the phone when it rung.
'Hello, Ronnie,' he greeted the Detective Inspector then listened to the plaintive tale of how surveillance had come to lose control of the target, John Bryce.
'But they think he's still in the store?'
'Last seen walking towards it this morning anyway, boss and his car's still in the staff car park. I was considering paying a visit to the Crowden's, speaking with the son David and issuing him with a general warning; you know, something like *'We suspect your life might be in danger so don't do anything silly'* that sort of thing. But I held off. Telling the Crowden's to be careful is as good as admitting we have someone in mind for the murder. No sense in letting Alex Crowden know we might have a suspect for his sons' murder. If he got wind of that, well…' he tailed off.
He didn't have to elaborate; both he and Johnson were aware that it was difficult enough keeping secrets in the police. Most murder inquiries usually leaked information like a sieve, with many officers keen to boast they knew more than they actually did and the two detectives suspected it was likely that Crowden had more than one copper on his payroll.
'I presume that surveillance will continue to monitor the vehicle?' asked Johnson.
'They'll stay on and hope he returns to fetch it. Likelihood is that he *is* in the store but they just haven't spotted him. One of their footmen got burned I hear. Not so much burned as toasted,' he chortled. 'Seems that he was approached by security in the store and quizzed, but came up with some excuse for being there.'
'Anything on the Crowden murder at your end?' he asked Johnson.
'Nothing much. We've learned that prior to his death, young Sammy was beating up some kid in *Jakey's Bar*, that den of iniquity Crowden owns on Paisley Road West. The victim, an English student, was taken to hospital and records confirm it so he's not in the frame. His girlfriend was able to provide a statement naming Sammy Crowden, whom she recognised as the assailant, but nobody else is talking. Needless to say the place was cleaned up by the time our lads visited it; though it would be difficult to tell the difference between the blood and guts and the filth in that squalid pit. Local CID also traced a private hire taxi that dropped him off at his house just after midnight, so everything ties in so far as chronological order goes. The post mortem confirmed that death was due to strangulation and Forensic state the rope used, a common variety purchased in any cheap goods store, was hauled across the tree branch to lift Sammy off his feet.'
'How heavy was young Sammy?'
Johnson glanced at the notes on his desk.
'Weight at death puts him about eleven and a half stone, so the murderer has been a relatively strong person, which leads me to conclude it's either a fit man or a weightlifting woman,' he smiled, then added, 'and of course our Mister Bryce is quite a

strong guy, isn't he?'
Sutherland absentmindedly nodded at the handset.
'Oh aye, if nothing else I'd say he's an extremely fit and strong individual. I remember speaking to one of the uniformed Inspectors here, a pal of mine who broke the news to Bryce on the night his family was killed. She'd stayed on from her nightshift to give me a complete rundown on the circumstances and happened to mention she knew Bryce from an incident she'd attended at Garvey's, where he works. Seems the staff had caught this violent shoplifter, an individual that the other security guards were a bit frightened of, and a druggie by all accounts. But not apparently Bryce. He had the guy pinned to the floor as easy as if he'd been holding a child, she said.'
'So in your mind, this only adds to what we already know and suspect? That Bryce is capable of dragging Sammy Crowden up by the neck?'
'Aye, Frankie, I'd say more than capable.'

Following his conversation with Ronnie Sutherland, Johnson decided that enough was enough and it was time to go home. He slung his coat over his shoulder and strode to the rear car park, nodding to the late shift CID as he passed.
All in all, it hadn't been a bad day and at least there was progress of sorts in the Sammy Crowden murder inquiry; even if that progress was identifying John Bryce as the prime suspect.
And that, he admitted, was probably why he felt like such a shit.

*

Archie Crichton's wife was now seriously considering making an appointment for her husband with their GP. He had again come home from one of his disappearances, his face haunted and pale, ignoring her pleas to talk.
They ate their supper in silence.
She watched as he pushed himself wearily from the table, making his way into their comfortable sitting room, reaching for the TV remote control.
This was not how she had envisaged their retirement. She had imagined evenings out together, whether at the theatre or simply walking in the nearby woods; at least they would have made up for all those years when Archie had been on shift and she had spent the evenings alone, sitting knitting as she waited on his return home.
She sat down heavily on the opposite chair.
The television presenter was explaining the hazards of dry rot; another mind numbing programme.

*

Johnny Bryce slowly made his way across the deserted car park to his car. He didn't look for the surveillance vehicles, giving the police the benefit of the doubt that they would be watching him from close by. He casually glanced down at his front tyre, seeing the matchstick lying on the ground. He smiled softly to himself. If nothing else, he realised they had at least inspected the car, perhaps tried the handle that caused the matchstick to dislodge.
The interior seemed to be undisturbed, but it was the underside he really needed to inspect. He switched on the engine and for the benefit of any observer, got out of the car and walked to the rear, bending down to the ground to seemingly check the exhaust. He had a quick glance underneath knowing the gadget he was searching for wasn't large and

usually held in place by a small but powerful magnet. He couldn't find or see anything out of the ordinary and got back into the drivers' seat.

Watching from three hundred yards away and from behind a parked delivery lorry, the detective called Gerry smiled. He'd recognised what Bryce was doing, searching for a tracking device.
'Mister Bryce,' he spoke softly with grudging admiration, 'you are a real smart man,' and then alerted the convoy and the waiting Andy Dawson that the target was preparing to travel in his car and possibly heading for home.

*

Later that evening the ringing of the doorbell surprised Annie, but then Andy reminded her it was likely his relief.
She skipped down the stairs and was met at the front door by a slim, fresh-faced woman of about her own age, her dyed blonde hair cut in a bob style and a cheery grin that lit up her blue eyes.
'Gracie Collins,' the woman held her hand out. 'You must be Annie?'
Introductions made, Annie led the way back upstairs and into the rear bedroom. While Andy greeted his colleague, Annie returned downstairs to fill the kettle, her hostess instinct rightly guessing that tea or coffee would be appreciated.
'Right, that's me,' said Andy, standing behind her and shrugging into his jacket. 'Gracie's fully briefed so I'll be, er.... off now.'
He stood awkwardly and she guessed he was reluctant to leave. Strangely, after their cosy evening chatting together, she didn't want him to leave either.
'You'll likely be gone to work by the time I relieve Gracie tomorrow morning, so I'll see you when you get in from work.'
He backed off towards the front door, a boyish grin on his face.
'Better be going,' he said again needlessly, banging his shoulder against the open door.
As Annie closed the door behind him, she felt the first stirrings of something that she hadn't experienced in some time; not quite affection and yet, something that she just couldn't put her finger on. What she did know was that she looked forward to seeing him again.

'Our Andy?' said Gracie, blowing at the hot coffee as she stared out of the darkened window. 'Good guy, but hopeless record with women,' she smiled.
Annie was pleased that she and Gracie had got on almost from the word go.
'How do you mean?' she asked the detective.
'Well, you know the type, typical macho male. Rugby and beer on a Saturday come hell or high water. But a good boss to his team, I hear. Good at his job, I mean.'
She saw the affected casualness on Annie's face and the penny dropped.
'You fancy him! My God,' she giggled, her shoulders heaving with surprised amusement.
Annie blushed.
'How can I? I've only just met him, for God's sake!'
'You lie like a cheap Chinese watch, Annie Hall,' Gracie giggled again, 'I can see it in your face. Well, you've no competition, at least none that I'm aware of and I hear *everything* that goes on in the surveillance department,' she winked. 'Except of course

you might have to compete with his fondness for rugby and beer.'
'So,' Annie decided to come clean, 'no mysterious wife or girlfriend in the wings then?'
'No, I have to give Andy his due in that. He's an honest guy where the ladies have been concerned, no ghosts in that particular cupboard as far as I know,' she sighed.
'That's his downfall actually,' she continued in a matter of fact manner, 'I hear the last woman he fell for, a detective called Mary Murdoch, gave him the run-around. She was all job, if you know what I mean. As I heard it, she dumped poor Andy for a lawyer. Married now and out of the job, last I heard,' she sipped at her coffee.
Their conversation continued till Annie saw that it was almost one in the morning and cried off complaining she had an early rise. Excusing herself, she went off to bed. Lying awake she thought of her conversations with both Andy and Gracie.
Yes, she had to admit, she was attracted to the big guy and Gracie had clearly made her aware there was no one hiding in the wings. But did he feel the same attraction, she wondered, or was she simply a convenient householder from where he and his team could observe the rear lane?
She turned over, punching her pillow as she writhed around and settled again, forcing her eyes shut and willing sleep to overtake her.
Maybe just once, she sighed, I might get lucky.

In the rear bedroom, Gracie Collins quietly acknowledged the fifteen-minute radio check and ensured for the umpteenth time that the video camera was still working.

*

The thick heavy curtains completely darkened the bedroom in the house across the city, where Mary Crowden lay naked and fully awake in her bed, her blonde hair spread about the pillow. She waited patiently; her senses attuned for the quiet knock on her door that she knew would come and preparing herself to pay the price for the devil's bargain she had made earlier that day.

CHAPTER 21

The following morning was yet another dazzling day and the smug forecasters on breakfast radio predicted more good weather was on its way.
Gracie Collins, her eyes gritty from her all night vigil, yawned and stretched her arms wide. She glanced at her wristwatch; the quarterly radio call was due in two minutes and she grinned; realising it was just another hour or so before her relief arrived, probably Andy Dawson, then home to her bed and her husband.
The back door of the target house opened and Johnny Bryce, dressed in running gear, exited, locking the door behind him before jogging down the path and turning right into the lane.
Gracie grabbed wildly at the hand held radio, all thought of sleep now gone.
'Target out,' she urgently whispered, still conscious of the sleeping Annie next door.
'Target out and right, right, right into the lane,' she continued, leaning forward to the curtained window as far as she could dare only to see Bryce disappear from sight.
Her colleagues acknowledged her call then inadvertently left the transmit button on and she could hear the frantic bustle as they tried to get themselves together to watch out for and follow the target.

They weren't to know their target's early morning punishing physical routine that doubled as his area search for strange and previously unidentified vehicles. One by one, the three back-up cars and their sleepy-eyed occupants saw the jogger pass close by; the target apparently ignoring them as he pounded the pavements past their vehicles.
The crew of the offending car finally realised their mistake and at last released the transmit button of their radio and clearing the airwave, before sending a plaintive message that the target had compromised them, a message that was unhappily repeated by the remaining two vehicles.
In the rear bedroom, Gracie had already guessed the target's purpose, the clothing being her first hint and patiently waited for Bryce returning home. Finally she conceded she might be mistaken and informed her back up that there was no trace of the target; in her log she angrily recorded yet another loss.
To the teams' further dismay, a subsequent check of the common car park revealed the Micra was gone.

*

Standing at the kitchen worktop, Davie Crowden concentrated on buttering his toast, an aura of guilt hanging over him, averting his eyes when his sister entered the kitchen. She sidled up behind him, her bare breasts pushing against his back and her hands reaching round to his groin.
'Morning, lover bruvver,' she jokingly whispered against the nape of his neck.
He pushed away from her, urging her to be quiet.
'Pop might hear you,' he hissed at her.
She smiled and stood back, sliding the silk dressing gown down from her shoulders to her waist, exposing her full and naked breasts.
'Jesus Christ!' he panicked, grabbing at the robe and pulling it up and about her. 'Do you want to get us murdered? If the old man saw us….'
She forced herself to smile mischievously at him. She could not allow him to suspect her loathing for him.
'Didn't you enjoy last night?' she asked him, her eyes opened wide, one forefinger tracing its way along her lower lip and playing her role as she knew she must.
'Yes of course I did,' he whispered fiercely at her. 'But we can't take chances.'
'You'd better get ready,' he mumbled, turning away t reach for his cough medicine bottle, 'if we're to beat the traffic across the city.'
She made her way back to her bedroom, tiptoeing along the upper hallway and suppressing a grin at the grunts and diesel engine like noises emitting from her father's bedroom.
While she dressed, she thought of the previous night. Davie's hands on her, what he had done to her, what he had made her do for him and again her stomach heaved.
But just another hour or so, she told herself; one more hour and then all my problems are solved.

*

Andy Dawson was not a happy man.
In the kitchen, Annie could hear the hushed but angry whispers from upstairs and knew something had gone wrong.
She remained where she was eating her cereal, not wishing to become involved in their argument.

She heard the sound of someone coming downstairs and saw Gracie, her face red, heading for the front door.
'See you,' she called after the detective.
Grace turned and waved, a tight smile on her pale face, before closing the door behind her.
Andy came downstairs a few minutes later.
'Sorry about that,' he said, ' a slight hiccup during the night or rather this morning.'
She didn't want him to explain, dreaded him revealing that the man they were really watching was her neighbour, Mister Bryce. She knew that she didn't want to hear that; didn't want to become part of the whole ruddy mess.
'Coffee?' she asked brightly, hoping to change the subject.
He acted on cue and nodded his acceptance.

Later, standing at the bus stop, she watched for the running man and her curiosity deepened when he didn't make his regular appearance.

*

Alex Crowden stretched himself and switched on the kettle. Early as it was, Davie and Mary had already left and again he smiled at their change in attitude to each other. He remembered he had meant to speak to Davie about opening his own stable of girls, but his unexpected visitor had caused him to forget his intention.
The wall clock showed it was almost eight o'clock and again he reflected on his late night meeting with Shooter. His next meeting with the hard man he reminded himself was at their usual café and in a little over an hour's time.
He had been as surprised as his henchman at the news the police was watching the dead woman's husband. Could he really be responsible for my Sammy's murder, he wondered? And what about Gospel? Could this man have killed him as well?
It didn't occur to him to question Eddie Rawlings information. The fat man had never let him down before. Still, he had a feeling in his gut, something he hadn't experienced in a long time; not since his days in the ring, he smiled at the distant memory. He wanted Rawlings information confirmed before he made a decision. If he was going to go after this man Bryce under the very noses of the coppers, then he had to be totally sure he was the right guy.
He sat down heavily on the kitchen seat, his dressing robe falling open to reveal his hard torso. His hands unaccountably shook with anger.
If that were so then nothing, he vowed, nothing on this earth would prevent him taking revenge.
But first, he needed to confirm Rawlings information and smiled at his own brightness. He had the phone number of the very man with the right contacts and who could determine exactly whom the police suspected of the brutal slaying of Gospel and his son. Now, he glanced at the wall clock, was as good a time as any to call him

*

Richard Smythe replaced the phone with a shaking hand. How the hell did Crowden get my home phone number, he wondered?
'Who was that dear?' asked his wife, her shrill voice calling him from the kitchen as she frantically tried to organise their children for school.
'Eh, no one in particular,' he called, 'just somebody from work. Look, I have to go in

early. Can you manage the kids to school, dear?'
Her whining protest followed him through the door. He ignored her, his thoughts jumbled together as his mind raced. He thought he was finished with this fucking case! Hadn't he done enough for Crowden? Wasn't the official reprimand on his personnel file adequate punishment?
Jesus! He slammed a hand against the steering wheel, his heart racing and oblivious to the fine bead of perspiration forming on his forehead.
With a sinking feeling he knew he had no choice and his shoulders slumped. He would have to comply with the demand, as Crowden had instructed; find out what the police were doing.
But to do so he would first need to get to his office.

*

Mary halted the Mini Cabriolet at the padlocked gate and glanced along the quiet side street, before placing her hand gently on Davie's right thigh.
'Be a sweetheart,' she smiled at him, stroking his leg affectionately and running her fingers lightly across his groin, 'and get the gate.'
She'd chosen carefully what blouse she wore, deliberately selecting low cut top and loose fitting bra, conscious that throughout the journey he had kept sneaking sideway glances at her breasts.
His mouth dry, Davie slipped off his seat belt and slowly moved his hand across to place it on the firm flesh of the bare leg that was revealed beneath her short skirt. She pushed her thigh against his caress and closed her legs, trapping his fingers. He watched wide-eyed as unbelievably, Mary placed her left hand inside her blouse, then under her bra and gently began to caress her right breast.
Eyes half closed, she intentionally uttered a sensual murmur of pleasure; she knew that she was arousing him.
Any doubts or misgivings that Davie might have had about what occurred in Mary's bed last night disappeared. She listened to his shallow wheezing as he tried to draw breath; then he spluttered, his body jerking to his rasping cough, the moment lost.
But still, she needed to make sure, make certain he would follow her plan. She squirmed in her seat, ignoring his coughing fit and allowing him to slowly remove his hand from between her thighs.
'Can you open the portacabin too,' she purred. Opening her purse, she handed him the key and stared into his eyes. 'And it's still early, so before the lad comes in, sit yourself down at my desk and get your zip undone. I think we'll have time for me to come in and say hello again to my new friend, but only if you're up for it,' she shamelessly simpered.
He swallowed hard, choking back his phlegmatic cough at the thought of the unexpected promise of sexual pleasure and grinned as he unlocked the padlock; pushing open wide the metal fenced gate to permit her to drive through. She parked her car at her usual spot.
Smiling tightly, she watched Davie half walk, half limp to the door of the portacabin.
She needed him inside the metal box.
Quickly she got out of her car and followed him to the office, reaching into her purse, her eyes fixed on him as she walked and slowing slightly to let him get the door open.
Davie fumbled with the padlock on the portacabin door, cursing slightly in his anxiety to get inside and be ready for Mary, her promise ringing in his ears. He was aware that she was walking behind him from the car. Breathing heavily, in his haste he dropped the

padlock onto the ground beside a discoloured blue scrap of rag, pulled open the door and stepped inside, fumbling with the shaking fingers of both hands at his trouser zip. Almost at once the overwhelming reek of petrol immediately assailed his nostrils. Eyes nipping, he turned to warn Mary. His face registered surprise, seeing her suddenly squat down as she placed half the discoloured blue rag onto the floor, jamming it in the door that she banged shut.
Still unaware of his predicament, he pulled down the inner door handle, his eyes widening in disbelief when the four screws fell from their retaining holes and he was left uselessly holding the handle in his hand. Puzzled, he pushed anxiously at the door, but the lock held firm and the door didn't budge.
The smell of petrol fumes was now almost overwhelming him and he began to cough as the acrid tang hit the back of his throat. Still unaccountably holding the handle, he walked further into the office, rubbing with his free hand at his eyes and seeing at once the overturned petrol cans.
His confusion turned to a sudden realisation of his predicament.

Outside the door, Mary fumbled with the cheap, plastic lighter; hastily flipping it once, twice and a third time with her thumb before the flint caught and ignited the small wisp of butane gas. She applied the flame to the blue rag and watched as the petrol soaked cloth ignited and shrivelled, the flame disappearing under the door. Turning, she walked quickly away, and then glancing behind her, her stride becoming a frantic run as she saw the flame had now seeped along the cloth and into the petrol filled portacabin.
Inside the portacabin, Davy watched horrified as the yellowy flame of the blue rag licked into the office beneath the door.
The petrol fumes ignited immediately and a tremendous flash that lit up the surrounding area was followed almost instantaneously by a booming noise, caused when the interior of the office exploded and the metal roof and walls buckled outwards. Burst of yellow coloured flames blew out the metal framed windows and sent the glass hurtling through the air.

His first impression of pain was when the very air ignited and the blinding, fiery light melted the corneal membrane of his eyes, ferociously cauterising the sockets. The suit he wore instantly burned away, exposing his skin that with his hair, at once seared and scorched like old, brittle wood. Unfortunately for him, the very act of trying to take a panicked breath also allowed the tremendous heat to coarse through his throat and down into his lungs, singeing them so badly that this alone would have proven fatal.
As it was, the combination of shock, horrendous burns and irreparable damage to his inner chest cavity all contributed to his death.
As far as he was concerned though, the whole thing was academic; for Davie was dead in the short time it took his corpse to fall down upon the burning floor.

Thirty yards from the building, Mary was bowled over and flung onto her face by the force of the blast, bruising her knees and the palms of her hands. The windows and door blown outwards landed with dull crashing noises in different parts of the yard.
She turned her head fearfully around, appalled at the devastation she had caused.
A cry from the gate caused her to whip her head back and she saw the young teenage lad

standing their, his eyes wide with fear. A sudden inspiration came to mind and loudly, so the youth would clearly hear, she cried out in a terrified voice, '*DAVIE!!*'

*

CHAPTER 22

Johnny Bryce allowed himself a smug chuckle at outwitting the surveillance. Leaving his car parked on the roadway, he entered the cemetery and climbed the gentle slope, walking on the narrow paths between the tracts of neatly trimmed grass. The headstones stood like silent sentries, reminding passers-by of those who lay resting, awaiting that time when, if the Christian faith were to be believed, the dead would arise and join their God in the kingdom of heaven.

At last he came to the recent burials, the ground nearby still showing signs of spoil where the gravediggers had plunged their mechanical bucket down into the soft earth; far deeper than the supposed six feet popularly held to be the true depth that had proven to be far too shallow to accommodate the mainly family lairs.

He stood in front of the barely visible mound, the three foot high white stone etched with the black lettering informing all that: *Here Lies Karen Bryce, Wife and Mother to Laura, aged three; Both now with God and at Peace.* The date of their birth and death was also recorded and carved into the base of the stone, two small hearts intertwined and surrounded by flowers.

He thought it odd that he felt nothing; no, not nothing, simply numb. He had never really been a religious man, brought up by his indifferent, but now deceased parents to believe in the goodness of man. In Johnny's own lifetime he had seen goodness, but also experienced the evil that men are capable of. Not that he would ever criticise anyone for believing in God; no, he had long ago decided, that was down to personal choice.

It occurred to him that maybe he should say something, voice some deep and meaningful words, but he felt silly and knew that anything he needed to say should have been said when Karen was alive. Regrets now she was gone were useless.

'Laura,' a little self-consciously, he half smiled to himself as he softly spoke, 'I miss you. I won't be seeing you grow up and you will be forever a little girl to me; full of life, laughs and cuddles for your daddy.'

He hadn't expected his eyes to fill up and shook his head, snorting at his foolishness and using the sleeve of his sweatshirt to rub at his face and wipe away the tear that threatened to escape him.

In his heart he knew that what lay beneath the earth was no longer his wife or his daughter. Their very life was the spark that made them what they were and the bodies were simply receptacles. He forced himself not to think what damage had been done to their bodies, trying instead to recall good times. With Laura it was easy, for every day with her was a joy, but a little more difficult trying to remember happier times where Karen was concerned.

He glanced at his watch; time to get home and showered before beginning his back shift that would coincide with the late closing of the store.

He walked slowly down the track, head down and wondering how long the police would follow him before he could make an attempt to get at the remaining Crowden.

He didn't see the old woman on her knees, tending her long dead daughter's grave as with interest, she watched him walk down the path. Nor could he know that her nosiness would get the better of her as she stumbled on weary, arthritic legs to see whom the tall man was visiting so early, on such a fine morning.

*

The scene of utter devastation that greeted Alex Crowden shocked even the hardened criminal. The pall of black smoke that continued to rise from the debris of what had once been the portacabin blanketed the area. Several of the sale vehicles, their bodywork and windows damaged or broken, remained where they lay in the yard; their value much decreased by the aftermath of the explosion. Three fire engines, an ambulance and assortment of police vehicles lay parked in the narrow street as though thrown carelessly down by an untidy child. Thick fire hoses snaked from the engines like canvas umbilical cords. Uniformed police, fire fighters and figures in white overalls, some carrying cameras, walked back and forth, seemingly without purpose. He stopped his car at the white and blue plastic tape stretched across the road and pushed through the excited throng of locals who had gathered on the roadway and pavement to watch.

'Sorry pal,' said a young, pimply faced policeman, one hand raised in restraint, 'nobody allowed through.'

'I'm the owner,' he growled in reply, 'Mister Crowden.'

The cops' eyes narrowed and he asked Alex to wait, calling to a plain-clothes officer whom Alex presumed was a detective. The detective led him past the fire engines; avoiding the river of water that cascaded from the car sales yard into a nearby drain that the fire fighters had opened to prevent a flood.

The rear doors of the ambulance were open and inside he could see a green clad paramedic attending to Mary, a blanket round her shoulders. She saw him approach and barging past the startled medic, rushed down the step, throwing herself into his arms and sobbing as though her heart was breaking.

Stunned, he held her tightly, glancing around him as he searched for Davie, desperate to know what the hell had happened. At last, he found his voice.

'Are you all right, sweetheart? You're not hurt pet, are you?' he asked her, his eyes full of concern.

Her face was smudged, her blonde hair matted with dirt and in disarray. The crisp, white blouse was grimy and her skirt soiled at the front where she had fell on an oil patch. He saw her palms were scratched and her knees scraped, one with a sticking plaster that had already begun to peel away. She smelled of smoke, tears running down her cheeks and her lips trembling.

'Where's Davie?' he asked.

'Oh, Pop,' she clung tighter to him, burying her face in his shoulder.

That's when Alex saw the stretcher lying on the ground beside the smoking shell of the portacabin, the outline of a body beneath the white sheet. Stunned, he gently prised himself from Mary's grasp and slowly walked alone towards the stretcher. A scene of crime officer stood in his way, attempting to block his path, but she was slightly built and he roughly pushed the woman aside. It seemed to him that he couldn't take his eyes from the outline beneath the white sheet, that it drew him like a magnet. Nobody else seemed to notice him approach the stretcher.

The scene of crime woman stood beside him and he was aware that she had one hand on his arm, trying to pull him away and calling for assistance, urging him not to look. He heard everything through dulled ears and fascinated, he couldn't help himself as he raised

a corner of the sheet.
The claw like hand and face that he exposed, burned beyond recognition, revolted him and a wave of nausea engulfed him at the smell. The woman grabbed the sheet from his fist but by doing so inadvertently pulled the sheet further off the stretcher and exposed the corpse in its entirety.
Alex Crowden's strangled cry was heard across the yard and beyond.

He saw the detective called Johnson approaching him, a second man by his side.
'Mister Crowden,' he heard Johnson call out, but he ignored him, instead steering Mary towards his car parked outside the police perimeter line.
Johnson and his colleague quickly followed, but he hustled his daughter away, too angry and upset to listen to their excuses.
He was settling Mary in the front passenger seat when Johnson arrived.
'Mister Crowden,' he began, 'Alex. Wait a minute. We have to speak…'
He rounded on Johnson, one threatening fist raised, his face red and his eyes blazing.
'Speak? Speak? I've fuck all to say to you!' he screamed at the detective.
The crowd standing nearby turned to stare at this unexpected development that was far more interesting than watching fire fighters roll up hoses.
'My boy, my Davie is dead! Another of my…. my only son… dead! And I almost lost my daughter too….'
His voice failed him, his eyes bright with unshed tears. He pushed past Johnson and pulled open the drivers' door, settling himself inside.
Johnson held the door, preventing it being slammed shut.
'Alex, I'll need to speak to you and soon,' Johnson tried again; yet knowing he was wasting his breath. The big man was far too overwrought to listen. He removed his hand before Alex jammed it against the doorpost.
In the passenger seat, Mary listened intently, her physical shock at the unexpected result of her handiwork settled, but knowing that at least for now, she must continue to play the part of the victim.
Alex reversed at speed, almost knocking down a group of jeering teenagers, attracted to the scene like carrion by the news of a death.

Johnson watched Alex Crowden right the vehicle and drive away and then exhaled slowly.
'Well, that wasn't much of a result, Barry' he remarked to his Detective Chief Inspector.
The jeering youths began catcalling to the fire fighters.
Johnson turned to the young pimple faced cop and angrily pointed to the teenagers.
'Get these scum moved or jailed, I don't care which,' he instructed him through clenched teeth.
Striding towards the yard, the two detectives were joined by a senior fire officer.
'Long time no see,' grinned the grey haired man, his five feet six inches belying his enormous strength. Fire helmet held under his left arm, his uniform reeked of smoke.
'DCI Barry Thomas, meet Divisional Officer Martin Ferguson, Fire Investigation Unit. Fergie to his friends, all two of them I mean,' he grinned wickedly at the fire fighter.
Johnson watched as the both men shook hands.
'So, what you got for me Fergie?'

'Preliminary findings only at the moment, Frankie and it might be a wee while before I get the paperwork done,' he added a note of caution. He knew what the police inquiries were like, always wanting his results yesterday. 'You any idea the number of fatal fires I've been to in the recent past?'
'Nothing's changed then, you miserable sod,' Johnson smiled, 'you obviously still enjoy a good whine.'
'If I wanted to be happy, I'd never had got married again,' complained Ferguson.
'Right, back to this,' he crooked a thumb over his shoulder at the remains of the portacabin.
'The place, as you can smell, was literally doused in petrol. All the windows and the door were probably closed over, hence the reason they all blew out. A partially ajar window or door would have been damaged likely, but retained its place in the metal frame. That suggests to me that whoever set the petrol wanted a sealed compartment, allowing the fuel vapour to build up. I should add we've discovered several petrol cans or similar containers lying among the debris. As far as I can gather from him,' he pointed to the pale faced teenage odd job lad who was speaking with a detective, 'the petrol is normally stored within that lean to shed over there, so whoever has caused this must have moved them into the office.'
'Got a seat of the fire yet?' asked Thomas.
'Too early to say and I haven't yet found anything that suggests a timing device or suchlike. There is the likelihood,' he stared at the detectives, 'that the deceased might have himself inadvertently triggered the petrol vapour explosion by lighting up when he entered the portacabin; a cigarette maybe or even switching on a light.' He sighed and shook his head. 'It's a bright day, so I'm less inclined to believe that the dead guy needed to switch on a light. Agree?'
Johnson nodded his head.
'The vapour explosion will, though post mortem should confirm it, likely have killed your victim outright. The damage to the body has resulted when the petrol ignited and burned everything inside. What I'm investigating at the moment is how the petrol vapour was ignited and to be honest, I'm not too sure I might get a cause. I would suggest your scene of crime people concentrate on the metal door lying over there,' he pointed towards a corner of the yard. 'Curiously, when my guys discovered the victim, he had the door handle clutched in his hand. So I reckon one of two things; that either the force of the explosion ripped the handle off…and that's not likely…. or what seems more likely is that someone tampered with the handle and he couldn't get the closed door open, once he was inside the portacabin.'

*

In her office at the Mitchell Library, Annie Hall found it difficult to concentrate on her paperwork. Something was nagging at her and mental pictures of her neighbour John Bryce kept interrupting her thoughts and it didn't help that the detective, Andy Dawson kept running through her mind either; but in a nice way, she had to admit with a smile. This morning while travelling on the train, she had realised to her surprise that today was the first occasion for months that she had stood at the bus stop and not seen Mister Bryce running by. Out of his routine, she idly thought, then stopped, amazing herself with her own perception.
His routine. Of course. That's what he did every day; running the same route or at least

that's what she suspected, remembering that he passed her by at roughly the same time each working day.
When Andy and Gracie had their argument, it must have been because Bryce hadn't stuck to his routine.
Her imagination took over. If as Annie suspected they *were* watching Mister Bryce, they must have somehow lost track of him this morning. That's why he hadn't passed her by at the bus stop. He had somehow disappeared. Which caused her to wonder, her brow furrowed. Where then, was he now?

*

Right then, Andy Dawson was asking himself that very same, frustrating question. The curt phone call from Ronnie Sutherland informing him that David Crowden had been burned to death in his office over on Shettleston Road had sent a shiver down Andy's back. Sutherland wanted him to attend immediately at Paisley police office for a hurried conference. And yes, Sutherland added, Detective Superintendent Frankie Johnson and DCI Barry Thomas would also be there.
Instructing half his team to maintain a vigil in the surrounding area, Andy was about to deploy a car to Bryce's workplace when he received a radio message.
'Boss, that's the target pulling up in the car park now. Yes, it's him all right. Still dressed in his running gear. Looks like he's walking towards his house. What do you want done?'
Swiftly, Andy issued his instructions and waited on his temporary relief before he departed for Paisley office. Halfway to the station, he listened on his car radio as his relief observed the target exiting his house and then followed the commentary as his team tailed Bryce in his Micra, to Braehead Shopping Centre. The shopping mall was open and two footmen confirmed Bryce's entry into Garvey's where almost immediately he assumed his security duties on the shop floor.
'At least I've something positive to report,' mumbled a disgruntled Andy.

*

Frankie Johnson, chairing the emergency meeting that was held within the conference suite, began with a brief summary of known facts on the suspicious death of David Crowden and concluded with the initial deductions of the Divisional Officer, Martin Ferguson. Johnson also made it clear from the outset that he was not about to apportion blame for the balls-up that had occurred that morning by the surveillance team's loss of Bryce. That said, however, he then proceeded to recount the previous days loss and wondered if the surveillance team could have handled the matter differently?
Andy Dawson took a deep breath and shook his head.
'Mister Sutherland did warn me that this guy was trained, sir. I won't try to offer any excuses nor will I say we've been complacent. He's good, there's little doubt about that; little things that we've clocked, like leaving tell tale signs on his vehicle tyres.
My primary concern is that during the time this morning when we had no control over him, he might have had time to travel to the car sales place in Shettleston and set the trap that killed Crowden.'
He sat forward, an inquisitive expression on his face as he faced Johnson.
'You've spoken with him; do you believe he's capable of carrying out such an act now that he's now aware he is being watched by us, boss? What I mean is, no matter how good Bryce is at anti-surveillance tactics, he must always assume that we're there watching him, even if he can't see us; so therefore if he did visit that car sales place, he's

taken one hell of a chance.'
'Anything's possible, Andy. It all depends when he managed to exit his house. According to your nightshift log, he was seen departing first thing this morning. Could he have left his house from the front door or even the back door before that time without being observed? I'm thinking that perhaps he set the trap for Crowden through the night.'
Johnson sat back, watching the younger detective's brow furrow as he considered his theory.
Andy puckered his lips and shook his head.
'The front door was covered by a van with two guys inside who spell each other on watch. Lighting in the street is pretty good and those two are old sweats that I borrowed from Special Branch. Even if Bryce had managed to slip out of the door, he had to travel the length of the street and, walking at a fast pace, that would take him about thirty to forty seconds. The houses are all mid terraced, so he couldn't slip between the buildings because of the high retaining walls that join the buildings, which means he would be visible for all of that period of time. No, I'm satisfied that he didn't get out from the front door.
As for the back door, he has to exit and come down a garden path. I had Gracie Collins watching the back door and she is one of the most conscientious officers that we have in the department. I can state with utter confidence, in answer to your question boss, that when Gracie spotted Bryce leaving his house this morning, that was the first time he had left via that door.'
Johnson stared at Andy without comment. He knew the guy by reputation as an honest and forthright detective; highly respected by his own headquarters bosses and had heard confidentially that the big guy was marked for further promotion.
'Right, that's good enough for me, then,' he said at last, to Andy's quiet relief.
'Personally, I believe that if the time on the log is correct,' he glanced over at Andy and smiled tightly , 'and I've no reason to doubt it, then it seems to me that during the time of the loss this morning, Bryce *might* have had time to get to the Crowden's place over in the east end before David and his sister Mary arrived there. We've got to ask ourselves though, how do we know if Bryce even knew about those premises or that David Crowden worked there; or even that Crowden would be guaranteed to open the door of the portacabin first thing in the morning? Even if he did know about the place, it could so easily have been the sister Mary who opened up this morning and what would be Bryce's justification for killing her, other than she's a family member?'
'Begs the question then Frankie, is Bryce the true suspect?' interrupted Thomas, 'or are we looking for someone who is either working with or for Bryce; or even someone taking advantage of the situation to top the Crowden's and muscle in on old Alex's empire?'
Johnson held up his open hands and looked at the three detectives, his face grim.
'Gentlemen, I'm open to suggestions.'
Sutherland glanced around the table and then he spoke.
'This recent killing seems to suggest a third party's involvement, yet I'm not happy about dismissing Bryce as a suspect. I feel we should continue to monitor his activities; for the meantime anyway.' Again he glanced round the table, unconsciously seeking support for this suggestion.
Barry Thomas nodded his head.
'I agree with Ronnie. We can't dismiss Bryce for the two previous murders, on the basis

of this mornings killing. It is likely that he might have an accomplice and we should start looking at his known associates. One other thing comes to mind, Frankie. Don't you think that we should approach Bryce and interview him regarding Mathew Gordon and Sammy Crowden's murders? At least let him know that he is a suspect? After all, he's already compromised the surveillance – no offence Andy,' he smiled at Dawson, 'and besides, we'll be firming up on his whereabouts at the time of all three killings.'
Johnson slowly nodded his head.
'Good idea. Three killings is getting out of hand and I've got that bas….' he stopped speaking and run his tongue round his upper lip, conscious of the presence of the junior detective at the meeting.
'I have Mister Moredun requesting that we get this tied up as soon as possible.'
Neither Philips nor Sutherland caught his eye, each with a blank expression on his face. They could only guess at the hassle Johnson was enduring from the unpopular ACC.
'So,' he slapped his hands down on the table as a forewarning the meeting was concluding.
'Barry. Liase with the fire investigation and scene of crime and let's see what they've discovered about David Crowden's death.'
'Ronnie,' he turned to the DI, 'take your DS – Kevin Wilson isn't it? - with you and interview Bryce; best bring him into the office and have it tape recorded. Also see what you can dig up regarding any associates, that sort of thing.'
'Andy. Have your team continue to stick with Bryce and carry on reporting to Mister Sutherland. That's all gentlemen, so good luck.'

*

The telephonist at the temporary Fiscal's department situated within a disused office block adjacent to the motorway rang through to Richard Smyth's office.
'Call for you Mister Smythe,' she chirruped, 'from a Detective Inspector at Govan CID.'
'Mister Smyth?' inquired the youngish sounding voice.
'Ah, thank you for returning my call Inspector and the heartiest congratulations on your recent promotion. I understand from what I'm hearing it was well deserved,' he smoothly replied, 'and I can assure you I'll be keeping a well-placed eye open for any future career opportunities that might come your way. Now, about that little matter we discussed. Any joy?'
The Detective Inspector, eager to be of assistance to a senior member of the Fiscal's department who could in turn show favour when it may possibly be needed, reminded Smythe that the information he sought was currently classified and the inquiry was being handled by his senior detective, Frankie Johnson.
'Of course, my dear fellow,' replied Smyth, wishing the bloody idiot would get on with it, 'and after all, you must be aware that as a member of the Fiscal's department, anything that you might disclose is of course treated in the strictest confidence. As we discussed, I have a real interest in seeing these people convicted,' he added as a salve to the younger mans conscience.
Smythe listened intently as the detective relayed snippets that he had overhead, pieces of a jigsaw that when put together, framed a picture of the dead woman's husband, John Bryce as the primary suspect in the killing of both Mathew Gordon and Samuel Crowden.
Following the conversation, Smythe sat silently at his desk, his fingers forming a bridge

in front of his nose as he contemplated how he could use this information to force Alex Crowden to release his strangling hold upon him.
It was during this contemplation that the chilling thought occurred to him; if this man Bryce were prepared to kill Mathew Gordon for simply defending the Crowden's, what would he do to me if he should discover that I had actively assisted in having the evidence destroyed?

*

Alex sat with Mary in the lounge of their home, each cradling a large glass of brandy in their hands.
'I can't believe he's gone,' she sobbed, one hand across her mouth.
Her father had seemingly aged ten years within a few short hours.
'Tell me again what happened,' he grunted, trying to picture in his mind what had become of his beloved son.
'Well,' she started hesitantly, knowing she had to keep it simple if she were to remember the story at a later time, 'as I'd said last night at dinner; I'd that couple coming in to collect their Volvo and Davie insisted on coming with me this morning to open up. You now what he was like,' she wept quietly, dabbing at her eyes with a lace rimmed handkerchief, 'him and Sammy. Always trying to be so protective of me.'
She figured this was a nice touch. Pop would always want to think of his sons being loving brothers. Her face paled even more at the unexpected image of Davie's kind of loving; his sweaty body thrusting at her, his irritating cough as he held one clammy hand tightly across her mouth and whispered she'd not to make a sound lest she woke Pop. The rotten shit!
'Anyway,' she continued, focusing on her pretence, 'he'd opened the gate at the yard and asked me for the portacabin key; said he'd get the kettle on while I parked the car. I was walking towards the office when….' she hesitated, assuming a look of horror on her face as though remembering the awfulness of the moment, 'the place just seem to explode. I don't know what happened. Suddenly there was confusion and that young lad I employ, I think he phoned for the fire brigade.'
She smiled weakly at her father, rising and crossing to sit by him.
'I'm not much help Pop, am I?'
He placed a protective arm about her shoulder and pulled her close to him.
'I don't want to upset you, Mary, but you have to know.' He didn't relish breaking the news when she was so upset, but she was a Crowden, after all.
'I think Davie was murdered.'
She pulled free of his arm and turned to face him, her face registering shock. This, she knew, was the moment of truth; the moment for which she had practised.
'You don't think it was some kind of accident; a gas leak maybe?'
He stared at her, slowly shaking his head. He knew she'd be upset when he'd told her, not wanting to believe another of her brothers that she adored, was killed in this way.
'Remember, there wasn't any gas connection in that portacabin, Mary and there are no gas pipes in the ground nearby, either. Not according to the survey report that I managed to obtain. That's why the building company were so pleased; they could just move in and bulldoze the old place down and get on with constructing their road.'
He didn't want to add that when he had been standing over the stretcher, the place reeked of petrol.

With uncommon gentleness, he turned towards her and took hold of one hand, smoothing at her brow with his other.
'No, sweetheart, I'm sorry to have to break this to you but I'm in no doubt that Davie's death was murder.'
Careful now, she cautioned herself, forcing her breathing to become rapid. She returned his stare, her eyes as wide as she could, adopting her favourite little lost girl look.
'But who? Who would do this?'
'I've someone in mind,' he answered her, averting his eyes from her gaze. 'Better you don't know. Just be satisfied that it's someone that will regret the very day he was born.'
She stood up, staring down at her father. She experienced a sudden feeling of exhilaration; it was as she had planned. Pop believed the same man that killed Sammy, had now killed Davie.
She was free. Her secret could no longer be used to harm her relationship with her father and everything that her Pop had now? It would all one day, be hers.
Including his stable of women.

The phone rang while she was preparing tea. The caller wouldn't give his name, simply asked to speak with her father. She was in the midst of telling the caller to ring back when Pop entered the kitchen and quietly took the phone from her. She watched him as he listened, called the man Dickie, then hung up.
He stared hard at her, his eyes the look of a man who sought to destroy; her stomach heaved. Surely not? It couldn't go wrong now. Not after all her planning.
'That's it confirmed,' her father told her.
Then to her relief, he added, 'I know now who killed my boys.'

*

The death of another member of the Crowden family, surprisingly the co-accused in the case that caused such a public outcry just a few short weeks previously, was immediately seized upon by the local press; not least among them Ally McGregor of the *Glasgow News*. His front page exclusive coupled the deaths of the lawyer Mathew Gordon and Samuel Crowden with this new killing of Samuel's brother David, whose demise was now admitted by a harassed police media spokesperson to be a suspicious death and currently being investigated. In McGregor's book, *suspicious death* spelled murder. Castigating the police in his report for their failure to apprehend the killers and also inadvertently terrorising many old women who lived alone and who read his story, McGregor speculated that the three killings were the work of an unknown vigilante group. He based his theory once again on his unnamed sources, while inferring that one such source either belonged to or was connected with the police.
By remarkable coincidence rather than astute journalism, and solely based on the common knowledge of the Crowden's acquisition of Delaney's Car Sales premises, McGregor described all three victims as involved in property purchasing throughout the city. He blatantly ignored the obvious detail that Mathew Gordon, having been the family lawyer, certainly would have been involved in all of the Crowden's financial dealings. To support his story he reminded the readers of the recent and mysterious disappearance of Patrick Delaney, the former owner of the premises that had exploded and resulted in David Crowden's death and which now was owned and operated by the Crowden family. Smugly satisfied with his story, he tore the sheet of paper from the printer and presented

it to his editor.
Fully familiar with McGregor's style, the editor's main concern that none of the allegations, principally in reference to the Crowden's property dealings, would come back and bite the newspaper in the arse; litigation being constantly in his mind, particularly where McGregor was concerned and quoting his usual 'unnamed source'.
'Okay, run it,' he eventually sighed while mentally crossing his fingers that his chief crime reporter's fiction would not ruffle too many feathers this time.
McGregor raised a triumphant fist and raced away to e-mail his report to the print room. Little did he suspect at that time the far-reaching consequence his vivid imagination would bring into play.
The following morning, the published edition of the *Glasgow News* was pored over by more than one interested party.

*

The Glasgow based public relations man responsible for the good name of a well known and high profile building company, e-mailed the article to the head office of his English owned company, marking it for the immediate attention of his Chief Executive Officer. The accompanying memo suggested that their pending business association with what was now publicly known to be a notorious Glasgow criminal family could prejudice any further construction opportunities that might arise in the south west area of Scotland. Reading the article, the CEO decided he needed no further consultation on the matter and immediately ordered that negotiations for the plot of land that bridged their Glasgow site and the main road nearby, be terminated. Phoning the PR man later that day, he congratulated him on his prompt attention to the article and assured him that they would find another site. As an afterthought, the CEO instructed him that in due course, he was to advertise the sale of the waste ground behind Delaney's and dispose of it forthwith.

Glasgow District Council disappointedly received the news of this major investment withdrawal and issued an open statement to the local media, expressing their disappointment and regret that a valuable building and employment opportunity had been denied the local community.
Two councillors' who had both heavily financially invested in derelict properties in the surrounding area with the inside knowledge that the properties would have been compulsorily purchased by the council for a goodly sum, received the news with mounting dread. The councillors' investors also realised their venture was now collapsed and called for immediate repayment of their substantial loans.
This unforeseen abandonment of the project by the building company resulted in a panicked confession by one councillor to the police Fraud Squad. His statement, a plea designed to mitigate his undoubted sentence at a later trial and duly noted in the presence of his lawyer, was a full and frank admission of his activities and included the names of those who assisted or who conspired with him in the dishonesty.
Knowledge of the councillors' betrayal soon swept through the City Chambers and like lemmings, more of his former colleagues furtively contacted the Fraud Squad, hoping to make their own deals before they too become further embroiled in the scandal.
Working in secrecy, it took the investigating officers some months to collate all their evidence and finally present their case to the Procurator Fiscal's office in Glasgow.
Among those names libelled in the extensive list of charges and who featured

prominently throughout were Alex Crowden and his lawyer, the now deceased Mathew Gordon.

*

CHAPTER 23

Winding down the last shutter, Johnny Bryce was pleased another long day was over. His regular early morning rises and yesterday's visit to the cemetery had taken more out of him than he had expected.
He considered the reports he had seen, both in the newspapers and on TV concerning the death of David Crowden. He hadn't anticipated such an overwhelming feeling of relief; that someone somewhere had unwittingly completed Johnny's task. *Suspicious death*, the police spokeswoman had called it, but like most of the viewers he read into her statement; Crowden must have been murdered.
The metal shutter settled onto the mall floor with a slight bump.
He wasn't really that surprised, considering the criminal background of the Crowden family as he knew it and suspected that likely there would be more than just he out to get them; David Crowden's other illegal activities had probably caught up with him, he supposed.
He thought he might have felt cheated, that the job had been completed for him, but had to admit that now not having to settle with Crowden had lifted a huge weight from his shoulders. For the first time in months, he sensed a curious feeling, a composure that he now come to recognise as freedom.
Walking back to the control room to hang up the shutter keys, Johnny thought about the recent few weeks. He was now convinced the police had no evidence against him for killing either the lawyer or Sammy Crowden; if they had, he reasoned, they would have come knocking on his door before now. That they suspected him was obvious; the surveillance had again brought him to work at midday though to be fair, he smiled grimly, he had only spotted the one tail car. They were getting better, he grudgingly admitted.
The three female shop assistants, heads together as they discussed the latest shop gossip, smiled at him and nodded goodnight as he locked the control room and headed for the back stairs that led to the car park.
In the distance, the sun was disappearing over the high-rise flats in the nearby town of Linwood. He walked swiftly to the Micra, checking his wristwatch and noting he had twenty-five minutes to get to the Paisley College before the class began. He was still surprised at his previously hidden aptitude on the Information Technology course and eagerly looked forward to practising what he had learned. His talent had been recognised by his tutor and she recommended he apply for the instructor tutorial that was due to begin next month. He knew that their personal relationship was slowly developing and suspected she was on the verge of asking him to dinner. His reluctance to become romantically involved with another woman had been a deliberate decision; his reluctance based on his need for revenge, the need to make the Crowden's pay for what they did to Laura. And of course Karen, he guiltily added as though in afterthought.
Driving through the slowly emptying car park, he felt relaxed and calm, then remembered he had forgotten to check and see if the matchstick was in place on the tyre. To his surprise, he realised why he had forgotten.

There was nothing left for him to do. It was over.

*

Feigning a headache, Mary was lying fully dressed lying atop her bed in blouse and slacks when she heard the front door bang shut. Pop had said he was expecting a visitor and she guessed it had to do with his plan for getting even with the man whom he suspected of killing both Sammy and Davie.

She sneaked a look out of her bedroom window and saw the Renault car parked by the pavement outside, recognising it as the heap that belonged to Shooter Martin.

She lay back on her bed and stared at the ceiling, idly tracing a finger in the air above her head as she listened to the two men speaking the hallway downstairs, then the noise of the lounge door closing.

Her hand dropped to her side and she thought again about the moment on Davie's face when she had banged the portacabin door closed, recalling with a satisfied grin that his hands had been pulling at his zipper and the look of surprised look of bewilderment on his stupid face!

She marvelled that she didn't feel anything for him, no remorse at all.

She had never really liked her brother; hating him almost she was forced to admit. Since the first time her pink buds had appeared, pushing out against her school shirt, he had been at her; rubbing past her in the kitchen, shoving his prick against her and thinking she wouldn't realise what he was doing. Touching her at every opportunity. Only the threatening presence of Pop in the house had kept her safe, kept Davie out of her room. It must've seemed like a dream come true when at last she had lured him to her bed, believing she was permitting him to screw her in return for his silence since discovering her secret. That was his problem. Like most men, or at least the two she had experienced, his dick ruled his head and he believed he was some kind of stud. Her mouth twisted in revulsion and she rubbed hard at it with the back of her hand; recalling the weight of him upon her and tasting again his nicotine stained fingers as he urged her not to make a sound.

She rolled over onto her side, drawing her legs up as though to rid herself of the memory and propping her head up on one hand, her fine blonde hair falling over her eyes.

Now Sammy, he was a different kind of brother, she allowed herself a smile. He never guessed that Davie was a serial molester and even if she had complained to him, he wouldn't have believed it of his older brother anyway. But that was his problem, she sighed. Sammy never thought anything bad about Davie; he'd always idolised him and thought that the sun shone out of his arse.

Strangely, the more she thought of him; she didn't really miss him either. Maybe I'm emotionless, she frowned. But then she remembered other experiences, the pleasurable ones; and breathed a little faster, knowing that indeed she did have her moments of weakness.

She glanced at the door to ensure it was tightly closed and rolled onto her back, spreading her legs wide on the double bed; arching her spine as she rolled her buttocks into the soft mattress and closed her eyes tightly, trying again to recall that moment, the near sexual thrill it had given her when she knew she was about to kill him. She wondered what thoughts had crossed Davie's mind when she lit the rag and left him to watch the flames sneaking under the door. Eyes still closed, she slowly and deliberately slid her hand up and gently rested it on her right breast, lazily tweaking at her nipple with forefinger and

thumb through the thin material of her silk chemise. As she caressed the aroused nipple a soft, gratifying sigh escaped her when she imagined the panic he must have experienced just as the door handle came off in his hand and he knew he was trapped, that he was going to die.
It hadn't been too difficult undoing the screws and she was pleased that she had the foresight to leave them loosely in the screw holes.
She thought about the explosion; had not expected to be caught in the blast, but if anything, it added authenticity to her story. She had gotten a fright when the blast had thrown her full length onto the ground.
Mary opened her eyes now and sat upright, all pleasant thoughts dismissed from her mind as she reached down to tentatively rub at the small scab upon her left knee. Maybe a short drag at one of the cigarettes in her tin, she idly thought.
Her eyes opened wide and a sudden shiver careered down her spine. She swung her legs over the side of the bed, everything else vanquished now from her racing mind.
A cold fist gripped at her heart.
The lighter! My God, she thought, clutching with one hand at her throat. What happened to the lighter?

*

Downstairs in the lounge, Shooter Martin stared at his boss and saw that in the last day he had visibly aged. He watched with some surprise at the older mans' hand shaking as he poured the whisky into the two chunky glasses, seeing some of the golden liquid spilling onto the polished veneer table.
'I'm not myself these days, Shooter,' Alex admitted as if reading his thoughts, handing over a neat glass. 'The shock of losing Davie has taken its toll believe me.'
He sat down on the opposite armchair.
'But that doesn't mean that I've lost it. I'm still in control, I still know want I want.'
Shooter sipped at the fiery liquid, feeling it course its way down his parched throat. He wasn't usually a whisky man, but given the circumstances thought it might be churlish to refuse the drink in favour of beer.
'I had a phone call from our Fiscal friend,' Alex continued, 'that confirms what the fat man found out. The cops are watching that woman's husband, John Bryce. It'll be tricky, Shooter; but I want him dead. Do you think you're up to it?'
Shooter smiled and sipped again at his drink to allow him the few seconds to consider what was being asked of him. He had never refused Alex anything; always had done as the older man asked. It was mainly due to Alex that he had managed to salt away almost his entire earnings, all the while enduring his miserable life living in the squalid house in that depressing housing estate; driving an old car; just so that he could save everything for the day he would get away. Portugal, that's where he fancied settling down. Nor would he be taking that shrew of a wife or those two cheeky bloody daughters either, he'd already decided.
'I'm your man, boss,' he cheered Alex with his glass. 'Time and date, that's all I need.'
Alex smiled in return.
'I knew I could rely on you, old friend. But this time it will be different. This time, I'll waste the bastard myself. All I need is for you to get him to where I want him; somewhere quiet, where nobody can hear him scream.'

The man in the dark car drummed his fingers on the steering wheel. He glanced at the dashboard clock. He had seen enough for tonight, he decided, as he started the engine and drove off.

*

Impatiently she waited till Shooter Martin had left, knowing that Pop's mind would be fixed on his discussion with his henchman and she could easily then convince her father of her need to collect her Mini from the Car Sales yard. Any earlier and he'd likely insist Shooter accompany her, at this time of night.

'The cops won't be there forever, guarding the place Pop,' Mary argued. 'You know what it's like round that area. As soon as the police move on, the locals will be looting everything that isn't welded down. You've had a wee drink so I'll get a taxi, there's no need for you to drive me,' she gently patted his red cheek. Unconsciously, she wondered at his pallor and considered that maybe tomorrow she'd have the doctor call in; perhaps check his blood pressure.

Alex argued in vain. She could be so stubborn, he thought proudly; just like her mother. He grinned at her retreating back as carrying her jacket and wearing a short business skirt that best showed off her long legs, she hurried down the garden path.

The early evening twenty-minute cab journey across town was uneventful. When Mary arrived, the first sight that she saw was that the whole of the side street had been cordoned off with blue and white coloured plastic police tape. A young uniformed cop stood idly guarding the front entrance to the Car Sales plot, curiously watching the taxi as it arrived. Paying off the cab, she deliberately turned her back to the cop and leaned through the passenger door, standing with her legs slightly open and deliberately gave him a grandstand view of her skirt material straining across her perfectly rounded buttocks. As the taxi drove away, she turned and beamed at the bemused policeman, who stood gaping at her.

'Hi,' she greeted him with a broad smile, flicking back her blonde hair with one hand, 'I own this place…or what's left of it,' she sighed theatrically. 'I can't thank you and you colleagues enough for the great job you're doing; looking after it till I get the repairers in.'

The cop blushed. It wasn't often a stunning looking blonde took time to speak to him. In his three months service, he'd been assigned all the shitty jobs and he'd considered this to be just another; watching over what remained of a car sales place that looked like a parking lot for tanks. You can't do any harm just standing here, the old sergeant had told him. But this, he unconsciously shuffled upright, was an unexpected bonus.

'Just part of the job,' he grinned at her, 'er, miss…?'

'Mary Crowden,' she fluttered her eyelashes at him, flashing him a perfect white toothed smile. God! Are men so stupid?

'Do you have some kind of ID Miss Crowden?' he asked. This request he considered, made him sound professional.

'Mary, please,' she cooed. Her jacket folded across one arm, she took her time fishing her driving licence from her purse and handed it to him.

The cop pretended to examine it, his eyes predictably straying to her cleavage.

'So, what's your purpose for being here?' he asked her, then as if by way of explanation, added, 'I have to note all callers. Sorry.'

'I've come to collect that,' she pointed past him to the Mini Cabriolet.

The cop was stunned. He didn't want to refuse this absolute doll, but he had strict instructions neither to allow anyone into the scene nor anything to be removed from it.
'I'm sorry,' he apologised, his face contorting with regret, 'it's still a crime scene. I can't let you take the car without official permission. Sorry,' he lamely repeated.
His chances of nipping this bird were, he could see, fast disappearing.
Mary looked crestfallen, one hand slowly rising to her throat, lips slightly apart and eyes wide open as once more she assumed the tried and trusted little girl lost look.
'You're absolutely sure?' she asked him in a faltering voice.
He shook his head. Even the possibility of a date with this stunning blonde wasn't worth a boot in the balls from that grumpy old sergeant of his.
'Sorry, miss.'
'I don't know if you're aware,' she began hesitatingly, 'but I was here when the portacabin…exploded. It was my…. brother Davie… that was killed.'
He was gobsmacked. Crowden! Now the name rung a bell. The sign attached to the fence said 'Pat Delaney Car Sales' and that had thrown him. He kicked himself for not listening properly when the sergeant had briefed him. All he had heard was *relieved in four hours*. Of course! David Crowden, the deceased. It was a murder inquiry now, though. His mind raced. Briefly, he thought maybe he should radio for the CID, but he hadn't yet been allowed to make any decisions. Better not, he decided, fearing he would get it wrong and receive yet another bollocking.
'Look,' she place a well manicured hand gently on his chest and leaned towards him. He gulped as the scent of her expensive perfume made him giddy. He could feel his pulse racing.
'I don't want to get you into any trouble, eh…what is you name, anyway?'
'Billy,' he replied, 'Eh, Bill.' His mother called him Billy, but he thought Bill sounded more mature.
'Bill,' she sighed at him, her large blue eyes captivating him. 'When I…. when I was blown over, I lost a thin silver bracelet from my wrist. It had been my mother's; her final gift to me when she died. I fell down over there,' she pointed past him into the yard. 'Would it be all right if I have a look for it? I promise, if I find it I'll show it to you. You can decided if I you need it for your investigation. Would that be in order?' she simpered.
He swallowed hard. He was of a mind to tell her it wasn't really *his* investigation, but that might lessen him in her esteem. What would be the problem of letting her have a look? After all, he was there to assist and she *had* lost her brother. He glanced up and down the almost deserted street, fearing the sergeant was about to pounce upon him for a dereliction of duty.
'Okay,' he nodded to her, 'but be quick.'
Mary flashed him a grateful smiled and ducked as he held the plastic tape over her head. She walked to where she thought she had fallen, the earth and mismatched concrete slabs covered with a greasy mud; the result of the flood of water from the firemen's hoses when they had dampened down the remains of the portacabin, making it now difficult to be exact.
Her eyes darted back and forth. The lighter had been blue coloured, she recalled, but in the fading light with only the overhead street halogen lamps to aid her, try as she might she couldn't find it anywhere.
'Damn!' she muttered. She could see where the rivulets of water had washed through the

yard. It occurred to her that maybe the lighter, weighing just a few ounces, might have been flushed away with the mud. Tripping daintily across the uneven yard and cursing her choice of shoes, she followed what she thought was a trail of mud to the fencing, then saw the open drain the fire brigade had unlocked to allow the water to run away. Her confidence soared. If the lighter wasn't where she had fell then it was more than likely it was now where it could never be found; at the bottom of the street sewer.
Turning, she returned to the gate with a renewed confidence.
'Any joy?' asked the young cop.
'No', she curtly replied, the anxious cop already dismissed from her thoughts now that she had achieved her intention, 'where can I get a taxi from round here?'

*

DCI Barry Thomas resigned himself to another late night at the office. Using his handkerchief to polish the lenses of his reading glasses, he drained the remaining coffee from the mug. He switched on his Anglepoise desk lamp and settled himself comfortably in his chair in preparation to beginning again. His first reading of the reports was better than he had anticipated and he believed that going over them was worthwhile; it was always worthwhile checking for mistakes or anything he had previously missed. Sorting the paperwork in chronological order he began to painstakingly read over the account of the Fire Investigation officer, Martin Ferguson, who after deliberation had deduced that someone outside the portacabin and standing at the metal door, had set the fire. Ferguson's report explained that the slight charred marks discovered on the doorstep seemed to indicate that the flame had crossed underneath the door, across the threshold and ignited the petrol fumes inside. Following a thorough search, he had determined that no timing device or anything similar inside the portacabin was used to ignite the petrol fumes. Therefore, the logical conclusion was that whoever set the fire did so at the time David Crowden was inside the portacabin with the door shut and, if his sister was to be believed, wrote Ferguson, the only other person present in the yard at that time, was she.
Thomas reached for the scene of crime report and used a highlight pen to circle the paragraph that referred to the finding of a cheap, plastic butane lighter that was discovered some thirty yards from the portacabin. Highly significant was the statement from the young lad employed by the Crowden's who had indicated on a sketched drawing the position where he had seen Mary Crowden fall at the time of the explosion. Thomas compared the lad's statement with that provided by the scene of crime officer and saw the spot was almost exactly where the lighter had been found. The detective interviewing the lad had also wisely asked if he was aware of Mary Crowden being a smoker? The youth had stated that to the best of his knowledge she was not only a non-smoker, but firmly against smoking anywhere in the portacabin or the yard.
The scene of crime woman who had discovered the lighter was clearly no fool and used her initiative, for her report also indicated that fingerprints on the lighter were compared and matched to the fingerprints she had the foresight to obtain from the Mini Cabriolet; still parked within the devastation of the yard and whose registered keeper was – Mary Crowden.
Then there was the detail of the inner door handle. Idly Thomas scratched at the days stubble on chin as he read that, according the scene of crime woman, the inside door handle had been unscrewed from its position in the door; however, the laborious search of the portacabin had discovered not only the handle but all of the four retaining screws,

lying among the debris. The screws were later Forensically proven to match the holes in the metal door. Undoubtedly, the report concluded, when the door was closed, as it seemed it was at the time of the explosion, anyone inside the portacabin would not have been able to exit without the outer handle being operated from the other side of the door. With a self-satisfied smile, Thomas vigorously rubbed both his hands together and sat back to consider the evidence.

That Mary Crowden had access to the office was undisputed; it was also evident she had ample opportunity to place the petrol containers within the office and the fingerprint evidence on the lighter was in itself damning. But why, he wondered as again he scratched irritably at his chin, would she wish to kill her own brother?

He made some notations on his pad and turned to open the pathology report. Accompanied by the book of photographs obtained at the mortuary, it made grim reading and inured as he was to violent death, Thomas turned his lip down in revulsion at the graphic images before him.

One surprising piece of information revealed by the post mortem seemed to leap at him from the page and his brow knitted in concentration.

'Well, well,' he murmured to himself, 'didn't expect that.'

*

The surveillance cars spread out in the narrow streets around the Technology College. The female detective called Sheila alighted from her vehicle, hurrying to catch up with the distant figure entering the gates. Sidling in behind a group of laughing teenagers, she tested her covert radio microphone tucked into her coat collar and informed her colleagues she had lost the target, but was now beginning a search of the classrooms situated on the first floor.

Almost ten anxious moments passed before Sheila again made radio contact, her voice betraying her relief that she had discovered Bryce sitting among a group of about a dozen students within the IT Department. The single sheet of paper sellotaped to the glass window on the door, identified the tutor and the class subject. Unexpectedly impressed by the target's apparent level of IT competence, she knew there was nothing to be gained and she would only attract attention by hanging about the deserted corridor and so made her way back to her vehicle, where she joined Gerry.

'There's a large number of cars in the college car park, probably students I should think' she informed him. 'We'd not be out place parking in there and we would have an excellent view of the main door when he finishes his class.'

Gerry agreed and drove to a spot at the far edge of the car park and as far from Bryce's Micra as possible; then everyone settled down to wait.

Almost three hours later, the college began to disgorge its evening course students. Sheila and Gerry watched as singly, in two's and in groups, the students of all ages exited the main door and slowly dispersed, some making their way to surrounding vehicles while others tramped with their bags and cases towards the main gate.

Fifteen minutes passed and the crowd became a trickle.

'Are you sure that was the only door open?' asked an anxious Gerry.

Sheila bit her lower lip, praying to God she hadn't fucked up. Another loss would bring the wrath of even the normally placid Frankie Johnson down on them all.

'There are emergency doors,' she slowly replied 'but the exit signs all pointed to the main

door. It looked like there was just the one janitor on duty in the cubicle inside the main door and I'm guessing he would only open the one door that he could control. Any other entrance would be an invitation for sneak-in thieves. You know what this area is like.'
She had just finished explaining when the door opened and Bryce stepped out into the brightly illuminated steps. To their surprise, an attractive dark haired female, almost the height of the target and carrying a bundle of files under one arm, accompanied him. They stood speaking at the door and even at a distance Sheila could see they seemed to be comfortable in each other's presence. As they watched, they saw Bryce smile and the woman's head tilt slightly back as though laughing at some joke.
Almost ten minutes passed and most of the cars had by now departed the car park. Fewer students came out through the doors now and Sheila and Gerry slid down in their seats, hoping the darkness of their position would not reveal them to Bryce.
The woman leaned over and with her free hand, touched Bryce's arm. Sheila's interest peaked and her eyes opened slightly wider. She made a mental note for the log. As a female, she could appreciate just how handsome a man John Bryce was and her feminine instinct came to the fore, for she recognised that kind of touch. It was affection, a proprietorial contact between two people who were slightly more than acquaintances.
The woman shook her head, tossing her long hair and hugged the files to her body. She turned to walk down the steps, waving as she left. They watched Bryce walk to his car.
Gerry, mindful of the instruction regarding identifying all of the target's associates, reached down and depressed the radio switch.
'Four one seven to convoy,' he began, 'target towards his vehicle. "Four two nine"; there's a female now entering a light coloured three door MG Rover, registration number unknown. I'll let you know when she's exiting the main gate. Take her on and find out where's she going.'
They saw the interior light in the woman's car dim and extinguish, and then it slowly backed out from its parking bay.
'Rover now reversing, wait, wait, wait. Rover now towards the main gate,' he calmly broadcast. 'Now out of gate and left, left, left to you, "four two nine", over.'
'Four two nine, acknowledged. We've got eyeball of the Rover, Gerry.'

In the Micra, it never occurred to Johnny Bryce that the police would be interested in his tutor. He hoped the two figures in the darkened Mondeo he had seen in the car park weren't too bored as they waited for him.

*

Standing in the shadows of Annie Hall's bedroom, Andy Dawson listened quietly to the radio broadcasts as the surveillance followed John Bryce's Micra towards Glenburn. Every now and again, the officers in the vehicle designated "four two nine" interrupted the transmissions to inform Gerry they had followed the Rover through the Clyde Tunnel to the north side of Glasgow and were now travelling on the Clyde Expressway towards the west end of the city.
The Micra, Andy heard, was now being parked up in its usual place in the car park and the target was heading down the lane towards his home.
He gently moved the curtain to one side and saw the shadowy figure striding along the dark path and approaching the rear garden gate.
The crew of "four two nine" were now in Byres Road. The Rover had made a right turn

into University Avenue and stopped outside a tenement building.
Andy watched as Bryce, closing the back door behind him, switched on the kitchen light.
The woman had parked the vehicle, locked it up and was now into the close at 642 University Avenue.
Gerry instructed all stations to stand-by. Andy's mobile phone rang.
'Okay boss,' said Gerry, 'what's next?'
Andy rubbed at his chin as he considered his choices.
'Have the crew of "four two nine" check all names in the close at that address against the PNC details of the registered keeper for the Rover; see if we can tie up the woman's car with that address. Keep two vehicles on the plot to support me here, till the nightshift arrives. Then get the rest back to base and knock off for the night. I'm expecting Gracie Collins to be here anytime and when I'm relieved, I'll meet you at Paisley office before we knock off. There's a couple of things I want to discuss regarding shifts and deployments; nothing sinister, just the usual paperwork, overtime claims, rest days and crap like that. Also, Ronnie Sutherland and his DS intend,' he grinned as he recalled Sutherland's way of putting it, '*inviting*...the target to Paisley police office tomorrow, for a little chat; hopefully before Bryce sets off for work, so we'll need to be on the plot for a surveillance in case they miss him.'
'Right,' acknowledged Gerry, 'see you at Paisley then.'

The hesitant tapping on the door startled Andy, who was deep in thought. He opened it to find Annie standing there, a tray balanced in one hand and her other raised to again knock at the door.
'Sorry,' she smiled at him, 'I didn't think you heard my knock and I didn't want to barge in.'
He took the tray from her and settled it down on the small dressing table, smiling in return and pleased at her thoughtfulness. It didn't escape him she had brushed her hair and was wearing lipstick. A faint but pleasant scent of perfume wafted into the room behind her. He handed her a mug of coffee.
'This is a nice surprise. Not keeping you up, I hope?'
'No, I've a few things home from the library that I have to deal with before tomorrow morning, so I was working on my laptop downstairs,' she replied.
She sat on the edge of the bed, smoothing down her skirt, knees drawn demurely together, studying his dark silhouette as he peered through the window.
'Any idea how much longer your.... what do you call it.... your surveillance, will last Andy?'
'Could be a few days, could be tomorrow,' he replied. 'There's a move afoot to interview a... suspect... so depending on how that goes will likely determine how long we remain on this job.'
For some curious reason, Annie experienced a dread that it would end, that this tall and dark man, scruffy though he might seem, she inwardly smiled at her own description of him, should move on; perhaps without even knowing of the attraction she felt for him. It occurred to her that maybe she should say something, but what?
'Any holidays planned this year Annie?' he spoke over his shoulder, his attention still drawn to the window.
'Nothing in the wind so far, but I've never been a great one for going abroad. The friends

I have of my own age are usually married or involved, so it kind of limits me, if you know what I mean.'
'What, good looking woman like you?' he turned his head and grinned at her, his even white teeth bright against the darkness. 'I'd have thought the men would have been beating down your door to take you on holiday.'
'As if,' she replied dryly. 'It might have escaped your attention Detective Sergeant Andrew Dawson, but I'm not your typical model woman. I tend to take my work too seriously, with the possible exception of my new suit my wardrobe is about five years behind fashion, my hair,' she flicked a hand though it, 'looks like it's been blown dry by Concorde and I've always been….' she tailed off, not daring to admit her greatest weakness.
'You've always been what?' he turned to face her, the soft light from the hallway beaming through the open door, casting against his face and brightening his eyes.
'You're what?' again he softly asked her.
Annie took a deep breath and it came out, as though in a rush, pleased he couldn't see her crimson face in the darkness.
'I'm shy.'
Andy turned away, smiling broadly and trying not to laugh out loud.
'Oh, is that all?'
'Is that all!' she repeated, suddenly annoyed as she stood up and clenched her fists.
'Have you any idea,' she hissed at him, 'any idea at all what it's like to go through life, hoping against hope that you won't be singled out in the classroom, you won't be the one chosen to do this or that? Trying to constantly remain in the background?'
She sat down again heavily onto the bed.
'It might seem like a great joke to someone who has confidence, but let me tell you it's no laughing matter for us poor sods with none.'
He glanced across the way as Bryce's bedroom light came on. Good. He turned again to face her.
'Look, I didn't mean to take the mickey out of you,' he began, his voice soft and apologetic.
'And I meant what I said. You *are* a good-looking woman. Don't underestimate your achievements either, Annie. You're the head of a council department. You're a university graduate; you own your own home and I'll bet that your salary is pretty good too. I don't know how you see yourself, but I'm looking at a successful young woman. And yes, if I'm honest with you, it does surprise me that you're not…' he searched for the word, '…involved.'
Annie held her breath. She knew this was getting tense. As if in a moment of clarity, she just knew, no hoped, that Andy was going to say something special.
'What I mean is when this is all over,' he swept an arm towards the darkened window, 'I was wondering…'
She almost stopped breathing.
'…if you're not seeing anyone like…'
Come on, she silently urged, come on!
'…that maybe you would perhaps…'
She almost blurted out Yes!
'…go out for a drink with me? Dinner maybe?'

She forced herself to remain calm; took a deep breath and smiling in the dark, replied, 'Yes, that sounds nice. I'd love to.'

*

CHAPTER 24

The meeting between Frankie Johnson and Barry Thomas held within the DCI's office at Govan police office, the following morning, was to review of the evidence that Johnson intended presenting to the Procurator Fiscal in Glasgow. The front page of his report indicted Mary Crowden for the murder of her brother, David Crowden. What disconcerted both men was that try as they might, neither man could imagine what possible motive had driven her to kill her brother.
'I've read your report Barry and I heartily concur with the evidence that is available. There seems little doubt that she murdered him; the evidence seems pretty conclusive to me. Is there anything, anything at all, that might indicate another person was involved? Someone else with a grievance against the Crowden's, or Mary in particular, who could have set it up to frame her?'
Thomas stroked his thinning hair with his hand.
'It seems pretty straight forward, Frankie. The young lad has been thoroughly interviewed and he seems to be kosher and the scene of crime and fire brigade evidence is indisputable. The lassie, for some unaccountable reason, has set it up and just hasn't had an opportunity to properly dispose of the lighter. It's my opinion that she underestimated the extent of the blast she caused and when she was flung to the ground, she has put her hands out to save herself, released her grip on the lighter and gone into shock from that time. As well as that, in her own words that the first cop on the scene wisely wrote down in his book, Mary has admitted she watched her brother go into the portacabin alone and nobody else was about. In all likelihood, she probably hasn't given the lighter or the door handle any further thought and never considered that we would conduct such an extensive search of the locus.'
'You're in no doubt that it's her fingerprints on the lighter?'
Thomas paused slightly before answering.
'The prints match those taken from her car. She's not on fingerprint file, but as soon as we arrest her, then we take her prints and match them to the lighter and thereby tie up her involvement. So, to answer your question, I'm satisfied that it's her prints on the lighter.'
'This kind of puts the cat among the pigeons, Barry,' Johnson sighed. 'We've now got to consider that if Mary is responsible for her brother David's murder, does she have the strength to stab Gospel Gordon to death and hang Samuel? And more importantly, why?'
Both men sat in silence, each deep in thought as they fought for some explanation as to why Mary Crowden would kill her brother, perhaps both brothers and family lawyer.
'And before you ask, Frankie,' Thomas broke the silence, 'I've already done my homework. There is absolutely no suggestion that John Bryce and Mary Crowden are in any way connected, so that puts paid to a conspiracy by them both to do in Gordon and the brothers. Remember also, it was Mary that we suspected of delivering the key to her brothers for the vehicle that ultimately killed Bryce's family, so I don't see Bryce willing to associate with her if he ever discovered *that* little matter.'
'Do you think that maybe she suffered some sort of remorse, like a guilt trip, for the

death of Bryce's family's? Decided to top her brothers and Gospel in some kind of revenge?'
They stared at each other questioningly, then as if one, shook their heads as they replied in unison, 'Naaaaah!'
'Christ, Barry,' Johnson raised his eyes to the smoke stained ceiling, and rubbed with both hands at his face, 'this case is *really* doing my head in. I think we'll need a Philadelphia lawyer to work this bloody inquiry out.'
'So,' Johnson continued. 'How do you propose to deal with your suspect?'
'By warrant. I don't want to go and lift her outright. I'll speak to the PF tomorrow morning, present my case and have him issue me with an arrest warrant to allow me to fingerprint her first. When I've had them compared and proved her prints match the lighter, I'll arrest her and charge her with murdering David.'
'Seems like a plan to me,' Johnson nodded his head. 'Ronnie and his DS will be interviewing Bryce right now. Depending on how they get on, I'm considering standing down surveillance on him. With no further evidence on Samuel Crowden and Mathew Gordon's murders and, frankly, little chance of anything else forthcoming, it's a waste of resources; so, I'm thinking of keeping the inquiries open in name only. This is Glasgow, after all. We've got other things to be getting on with.'
He rose to his feet.
'I'll keep you informed. Good luck with the PF.'

*

As Johnson departed, Johnny Bryce was at that time sitting on a hard wooden chair, his hands clasped together in his lap as he faced Ronnie Sutherland across a table upon which Sutherland rested both elbows. He had been annoyed that they had waited till he arrived at work and then approached him as he patrolled the shop floor. He guessed the timing had been staged to put him at a disadvantage, make him ill at ease.
He couldn't know that a simple problem with a faulty starter motor had caused Sutherland to be late arriving at Paisley office and in turn, missed him at his house.
The stares and whispers of the shop assistants and his colleagues as the two detectives requested he accompany them and walking with them through the store had angered him, but he forced himself to remain calm and complied with their every request that at Paisley police office, included the indignity of having his fingerprints taken and a DNA swab from inside his mouth. His mind raced as he tried to remember anything that he might have missed; anything that might have betrayed his presence either at Gordon's car or within the Crowden's garden. Then he relaxed slightly, deciding it was just another ploy to make him believe they might have some forensic evidence.
DS Kevin Wilson sat to one side in a corner of the small and featureless interview room, ostensibly taking notes; but all three were aware the double tape machine on the table was recording everything anyway.
Sutherland loosened his tie and activated the recording machine. Johnny recognised the tie trick, a distant memory of interrogation procedures coming to mind; by visibly making himself comfortable, Sutherland was cleverly suggesting they might be some time in the room.
They waited until the buzzing noise from the machine quietened then the DI introduced himself, adding Wilson and Johnny's names as the only other occupants within the room. He further added the time, date and place of interview.

'Thanks for coming down to speak with us Mister Bryce; may I call you Johnny?' he smiled.
Johnny shrugged. 'Can I call you Ronnie, then?'
Sutherland smiled tolerantly as he nodded; touché, he quietly thought. Now it begins.
'The purpose of asking you here, Johnny is that we suspect you might have some involvement in the two deaths currently being investigated; that of Samuel Crowden, whom you will be aware was one of the accused charged with your wife Karen and daughter Laura's death and who, regretfully, was acquitted; and that of his lawyer, Mathew Gordon.'
'Will I require the services of my own lawyer?'
'Do you think you will need a lawyer?' Sutherland countered.
Johnny smiled.
'If this interview is being tape-recorded, then I suppose it's highly unlikely you will…what's the term? Fit me up. So no, I'll dispense with the services of a lawyer, for after, all as you said…. Ronnie,' he stressed Sutherland's Christian name, 'I'm only here to speak with you, not admit to something about which I have no knowledge.'
Wilson licked his lips. He tried to recall from all the interviews in which he had conducted or participated, if he had ever seen a suspect so calm or self-assured. John Bryce was either a cool and confident man or, he hesitated to even think about it, possibly innocent of their suspicions.
'On the nights that both deceased were murdered, Johnny. Can you recall where you might have been, what you were doing, who you were with?'
'No.'
Sutherland waited for Johnny to go on. When he didn't he looked at him, puzzled, his hands spread out in front of him.
'No? That's it? No?'
'Correct,' Johnny nodded his head. 'Of course, I can recall reading about the murders or watching television the following day, but I've absolutely no idea where I was on those nights. I don't keep a diary and my days are mostly routine. I get up early, go through my usual physical routine round the estate, go to work, go home, watch TV and go to bed. And so on and so on. Oh, I also attend evening classes twice a week; computing studies, so they'll have a record of my attendance, I guess. But surely,' he smile broadly at Sutherland, 'your surveillance team will have recorded my presence at the college.'
He stared hard through narrowed eyes at the detective. Time for a quick thrust, he thought. He leaned forward, palms flat down on the table in an unthreatening manner.
'According to reports that I saw on television, the other accused in the case of my wife and daughter's death, David Crowden; he's also been recently murdered, I believe. Why haven't you asked me about him? Surely if I'm suspected of two murders connected with the case, wouldn't it be logical to presume I'm suspected of his also?'
'That's something which is currently being investigated, Johnny,' Sutherland smoothly replied, 'and about which at this time I have no further knowledge.'
Nevertheless, the question had thrown him. He had expected Bryce to be completely defensive of the allegations, not to take the initiative and tie in the third murder with those of Samuel and Gospel.
Johnny wasn't letting it go.
'Seems to me that you'd want to know if I'd any involvement in the first two murders, I

must have some involvement in the third murder. No questions about it then?' he persisted and then sat back in his chair, folding his arms, an amused smile dancing about his mouth.
Sutherland refused to be fazed.
'We may, in due course,' he hesitatingly began, 'get round to speaking to you about…that…particular inquiry. However, since you raised the matter, do you have an alibi for that morning; when David Crowden was murdered?' he asked.
Johnny grinned.
'Ah, now there I *can* help you. That was the morning your lads watched me jog out of my house. I got into my car and they lost me. Correct?'
Sutherland slowly nodded. He was only admitting to something that Bryce already knew anyway.
'I drove to St Conval's Cemetery in Barrhead,' Johnny continued in an even voice. 'I sometimes…visit; though to be honest, I hadn't been up there for a while. And before you ask, I didn't see anyone while I was there. So no alibi, I'm afraid.'
In the corner, Wilson made a note on his pad and raised his eyes towards Sutherland, who nodded as Wilson slipped from the room.
'DS Wilson out of the room,' he spoke slowly for the benefit of the tape. He turned his attention back to Johnny.
'But for now, might I return to the subject under discussion. What can you tell me about Jennifer Hopkins?'
If Sutherland expected that in his change of direction, the question would upset or in any way disturb Johnny, he was disappointed.
His face betrayed no emotion as he replied:
'Miss Hopkins is my computing tutor. I met her when I began my course at the Technology College. I have had no meetings or dealings with her outside of the college.'
Sutherland had read the surveillance detective's log; her suspicions that perhaps Bryce and the woman called Jennifer Hopkins might be a little more than tutor and student. Research into the PNC had not revealed anything about her so it was fair to presume the police had no record of her. The hasty background check that morning described her as divorced, residing alone and employed full time at the college as a lecturer within the IT Department. The three photographs, hastily snapped that morning from a surveillance van as she left her tenement building for work, showed an attractive woman in her mid thirties, getting into a light coloured Rover car.
'Would she be surprised to know that you might be a murder suspect; a *double* murder suspect, even?'
'I can't say what she might or might not be surprised about. But to use your own words; I presume then that, officially, I am a suspect for the murders of these two men?'
It was Sutherland's turn to be on the offensive.
'Stands to reason, John. You've lost you wife and child to Samuel and David Crowden. Their sleazy lawyer, Mathew Gordon, gets them acquitted at court. What man in his right mind wouldn't have some sort of desire for revenge against them?'
Johnny didn't reply, simply stared at the detective. He understood now, his inference that Jenny might somehow feel differently about him if she were to learn he was being interviewed in connection with the killings. In a quiet and subdued way, Sutherland was threatening to expose him to her as a murder suspect; believing that any relationship he

might imagine they had would be compromised by this revelation.
'Of course you're right,' he began, his face pale.
The door opened and Wilson returned to the room. Having just arrived and heard Johnny's last comment, his ears perked up and he held his breath. Was this a confession, he hoped? Sutherland grudgingly updated the tape regarding Wilson's return, inwardly cursing that maybe the moment of confession had been lost.
'Please continue,' he instructed Johnny.
'Like any man, I wanted those responsible to be punished. Who wouldn't? But I always believed that was the responsibility of the police and the courts. When you and the courts failed in your job, I was naturally upset. However, being upset and angry at *your* failure doesn't make *me* a murderer, Ronnie. And if you really want to know? Then yes, I'm glad they're dead. All three of them. In some way, I believe that natural justice has prevailed. The system was unable to punish these two…bastards,' he angrily spat the word out, but aware of what he was saying, 'and their lawyer mouthpiece who conspired with them to defeat the system. I watched them on television, the day the court released them and saw them sneer and smirk on their way to their car. Then when Gordon suggested to the reporters that my wife, by being on that road at that time of night was in some way to blame for her and Laura's death? You have no idea how angry I felt.'
He was on his feet now, bracing himself on the table with his hands as he leaned forward towards Sutherland, his eyes blazing. In the corner, Wilson readied himself to intervene, hoping to hell that they weren't going to have to try and physically subdue this suddenly strong and potentially lethal, former marine.
'As for killing them?' Johnny continued, 'I've no doubt that if you've done your job properly, you will know of my background and what I'm capable of. But right now I don't think that you have a hope in hell of proving that I have committed any criminal act. If you did, I'm guessing I would have been charged and locked up long ago, rather than have to endure this pussyfooting about with you here.'
His voice quietened as he visibly relaxed, but remained standing and staring bitterly at the detective.
'The system freed those two killers and allowed their lawyer to publicly dance of my wife and daughter's grave. The same system that you and your colleagues work within also allows me the freedom to remain at liberty, without charge, unless you have evidence. Do you?'
Sutherland didn't reply, simply gazed back with blank eyes.
'I thought not,' said Johnny. He turned towards the door.
Wilson stood up to bar his path, his Adams apple working overtime as he prepared himself to take on what he now frighteningly realised was a muscular and powerful man.
'If you can't charge me, pal,' said Johnny ever so softly, 'then don't even think about trying to detain me.'
Behind him, Sutherland raised a hand and to Wilson's relief, waved the DS out of Johnny's way.
Pulling open the door, he stopped and lowered his head. Then he slowly turned back to face the still seated Inspector and quietly exhaled; his shoulders slumping as the tension in his body released itself.
'For all I've said, I don't hold any grudges against you and your guys Ronnie. But don't come after me again. Not unless you can prove me guilty of something.'

When he had gone, Sutherland reached across and switched off the tape recorder.
'Well,' he shook his head at the stunned DS. 'That wasn't too bad, was it?'

*

DI Ronnie Sutherland decided against phoning Frankie Johnson and accompanied by Kevin Wilson, travelled to Govan police office to personally report the circumstances of the interview with John Bryce. For good measure, he took the tape recording of the interview with him.
Johnson listened to Sutherland's verbal report, occasionally nodding his head but remained silent, saving his question to the end.
'Not a good result then?'
'I won't excuse myself,' replied Sutherland, 'but without any evidence I didn't really have much to go on. Listen to this.'
He activated the play button on the portable tape recorder and all three men listened in silence as the interview progressed. At the sound of Bryce standing, his chair scraping on the uncarpeted floor, Johnson raised his eyebrows; the only indication he was concentrating on what had happened within the small room.
At the sound of Bryce's voice warning Wilson to stand aside, Johnson glanced over at the DS.
'Might have proven to be a bit of a handful if you'd had to try and stop him, eh Kevin?'
'Too fucking right,' Wilson mumbled quietly under his breath, relieved that it hadn't come to that.
With a resigned sigh, Sutherland pressed the stop button and waited for Johnson's comment.
'Well,' he said at last, 'he's right about one thing. Without evidence, we've no case. The best we can do is record him as a possible suspect and leave it at that. I hate to admit it, but it seems likely that both Samuel Crowden and Mathew Gordon's murders will remain undetected. God alone knows how I'm going to write those off to the ACC,' he muttered.
'What about David Crowden's murder, boss?' inquired Wilson. 'Any developments on that?'
Johnson half grinned.
'Ah, therein lies a story,' he replied and then followed up with the result of Barry Thomas's investigation and the pending case against the sister of the deceased, Mary Crowden.
'So,' Wilson's brow furrowed, 'John Bryce has been cleared of that? But I thought that when surveillance lost him wasn't there some question that he might have been involved; that he could have had the time to get to Shettleston and kill the second brother?'
Johnson remembered then and searched among the papers on his desk. At last, he found what he was looking for. He glanced up at Wilson.
'Kevin, earlier this morning you instructed a DC Maria Lavery to go to a cemetery in Barrhead?'
Wilson stared at him, a puzzled look on his face.
'That's right sir. Bryce claimed that on the morning the surveillance boys lost him, he was visiting his wife and daughter's graves. Said nobody saw him, but I thought it should be checked out, anyway.'
'Well, when she returned to Paisley, Lavery just missed you and phoned here; asked me

to pass on the result of her inquiry. After you spoke with her, she hotfooted it up there and surprise, surprise, she dug up…' he stopped and grinned self-consciously. 'Excuse the irreverent pun. Anyway,' he continued, glancing at his spidery writing on the note, 'it seems that Lavery found a witness, some elderly lady tending her daughter's grave. The woman described Bryce to a tee, including him driving away in his Micra. Recognised the car as the same sort her sister has. She confirmed it by admitting to Lavery that her curiosity got the better of her and went to check what grave he had been visiting. She took Lavery to the headstone of Karen and Laura Bryce. In short,' he glanced at Wilson again, 'provides our man with an alibi that he didn't know he had. Good work Kevin, even if it does take Bryce out of the equation for David Crowden's murder.'
Wilson didn't know whether to be pleased with his thoroughness or disappointed that Bryce's alibi checked out.
'So what's next, boss?' inquired Sutherland.
'Nothing else for it, Ronnie; I'm going to pull the surveillance off Bryce and we'll go with Barry Thomas's case against Mary Crowden. He intends meeting with the PF here at Glasgow tomorrow morning and once the warrant is typed up, he'll arrest her. Probably find her at home now her business is gone up in smoke.'
'Anything for us to do?'
Johnson shrugged his shoulders as he shook his head.
'Not immediately, Ronnie. You did what you could with the hand that you were dealt. We can't put someone before the court without evidence. Knowing something is different from suspecting something and is different again from proving something.'

*

The mobile phone pressed to his ear, Andy Dawson listened as Ronnie Sutherland passed on Johnson's instructions.
'Once you get your team together, call in to Paisley and I'll debrief everyone in the conference room.'
'Okay, boss. So that stand down is effective immediately?'
'Immediately,' Sutherland confirmed.
He used the radio to issue his instruction, listening as one by one, the car crews acknowledged his order. From his notebook, he tore a page and wrote a brief note to Annie that would explain his absence when she returned home from work. As an afterthought, he added his mobile phone number and underlined it twice with a PS, requesting she call him.
Glancing around him, he hoped this wasn't the last time he would be visiting this particular house.

CHAPTER 25

It was still dark in the early hours of next morning when Shooter Martin drove into the Glenburn area of Paisley. He stopped in an empty bus bay and used the small torch to again examine the map. His stomach rumbled and he grimaced at the sharp stab of wind. Raising one buttock, he groaned with relief as an explosion of flatulence escaped him; screwing his face in disgust and winding down the drivers window to release the fetid smell.
All these bleeding estate roads look the same, he silently complained. At last, his finger

traced Cotton Close and he realised that he wasn't too far away. Driving slowly, he wound his way through the narrow streets and arrived in a cul de sac that opened into a reasonably sized car park. He wasn't to know that the Micra car parked just a few dozen yards away belonged to the man that he was hunting.
Pulling his woollen tammy down low over his ears, he parked his old Renault and closed the door with a soft click. He didn't want any nosey parker looking out of their window and wondering at the strange vehicle parked there.
Dressed in his usual bomber jacket and dark trousers, Shooter decided that if the coppers were watching this guy Bryce, the easy way to spot them would be walking around the area. One thing he always prided himself in; he could smell a copper from fifty yards. He rubbed hard at his midriff as though the action might also help dissipate the painful ache in his guts.
Cops, he knew, were notoriously lazy and would rather sit on their arses in a warm car than pound a beat. The target squad would likely be no different, he reasoned, particularly if they were spending long hours waiting on Bryce moving. He grinned widely; he had seen enough TV cop programmes to get some idea of their methods.
The next hour was spent in the slowly emerging light tramping the paths, streets and roads that surrounded Cotton Close. Several times he slowed his pace, approaching cars with suspicious lumps that might be heads; only to discover things such as a jacket folded on the rear parcel shelf and, on one breath stopping occasion, a plastic nodding dog whose head was moving due to a draught caused by a slightly open rear window.
But of the cops, the supposed surveillance, there was no trace, none at all.
The pain in his belly was getting worse.
Dawn finally broke in all its splendour and he yawned, stretching himself as a milk van passed, the youths eyeing him with studied indifference until with a sneer, he gave them the two-fingered salute. The jeers and catcalls that resulted caused him some alarm and he regretted his foolishness, glancing at the curtained windows of the hoses nearby lest the noise attracted too much attention.
Head down, he swiftly walked away. He had the ominous feeling that his bowels were about to erupt and needed to get home – and now.
He passed several early morning workers, trudging tiredly to their cars or nearby bus stops.
Strolling back to his car and concentrating on keeping the cheeks of his arse tight, he stopped. It would do no harm, he figured, just to have a closer look at the rear of number 39 and might prevent him having to visit the area again. For a brief instance, his attention was sidetracked from his stomach complaint as a plan formed in his head.
He found the narrow lane at the rear of the mid terraced dwellings and cautiously walked along its well-trodden path, anxious that he didn't awaken any dog in the nearby houses. Not all the rear gates had numbers attached, so he counted off until he drew near to what he presumed must be number 39 and slowed his pace. Glancing sideways, he could see a light was on in the kitchen.
As he approached the low wooden gate, he heard the key in the lock of the rear door just as the kitchen light went out and walked away a little faster. Less than a minute later, he heard footsteps behind him and half turned his head to see a man come running past. There was little doubt in his mind the man had come from Bryce's house.
'Morning,' grunted the jogger.

He watched as the man he presumed was Bryce continued running and disappeared into a nearby street. He was not to know that Johnny, grinning hugely as he pounded past him, had suspected the bald man wearing the woollen hat to be a police surveillance officer. Shooter collected his car and drove out of the estate, relieved at last to be heading home. As he drove, he flipped open his mobile phone and pressed the selected button. After a few short rings, the call was answered.
'I've had a good look at the area Alex and there's none of our friends hanging about. I don't know about your contact in the PF's, but if the parcel *is* being looked after, I can't find them that's supposed to be holding it. So, big man, when do you want to do this?'
'Can you get back there now? Maybe lift the parcel this morning?'
Alex Crowden's voice betrayed his eagerness to settle this matter, once and for all.
'Tomorrow morning might be better, Alex. I wasn't expecting any action today, so I don't have any insurance with me. I left it in its cubby hole back at my training place.'
He held his breath.
'Tomorrow morning then,' Alex reluctantly agreed. 'First thing. Take the parcel to the old farm.'

Driving across Paisley towards the motorway, Shooter felt a sense of relief that Alex hadn't pressed him. That he could handle Bryce alone? He didn't foresee any problem. That he needed his insurance? Probably, recalling how fit the jogger had looked when he had passed Shooter by.
No, his unwillingness in getting it done today was more basic…and, he clenched his teeth against the pressure in his guts, getting more urgent. He pushed his backside harder into the drivers seat, staving off the sharp pain of the flatulent wind as he pressed his buttocks tightly together and quietly prayed that he'd make it home before his bowels released their smelly cargo.
Hard man though he was, even Shooter was too embarrassed to admit to his boss that the spicy dish his wife had prepared for him last night had done more than satisfy his hunger. The stupid cow must have laced it with too much curry powder, causing his unexpected dose of the runs. For that, he promised himself, she'd feel the back of his hand across her jaw.
His discomfort might have set his boss back a day, but while he regretted not being able to comply with his request, no way was Shooter going to lift Bryce off the street while there was a risk his arse might explode. No, he needed to be fully alert when doing these kinds of jobs. Just like Pat Delaney, he recalled with a grin, remembering the skinny mans' terror on the night he shoved him in the boot of the hired car, before he killed him. The journey home through early morning motorway traffic was a wearisome nightmare for the shaven headed man. At last he turned into his short driveway and scrambled from the Renault. Bursting through the front door, his knees together, he shuffled painfully up the narrow stairs with his bowels threatening to explode before he could make it to the loo on the top landing. Dropping his trousers, he sat on the bowl and shivered at the relief.

Across the road, the man in the dark car was puzzled. Arriving earlier that the morning, he was angrily surprised to discover the Renault gone. But now the car had returned and he watched as Martin had run from it into the house. His curiosity aroused, he vowed he wouldn't make that mistake again.

*

Standing at the bus stop, Annie hall had a light spring in her step. She was thrilled when she read the note left by Andy, sure now that he really meant what he had said the previous evening. So struck was she by the thought of their future date she almost failed to realise that her neighbour, Mister Bryce was passing her by. His courteous wave took her by surprise and she thought that in some way, he too seemed pleased.
Yes, she smiled as she shoved her hand out for the bus and grinned at the driver, life was certainly on the up.

*

The modern purpose built building, located on the corner site in Ballater Street on the southside of Glasgow, a few hundred yards from the High Court that lay across the Albert Bridge, housed the Procurator Fiscal and his staff who served as the criminal prosecutors for the greater Glasgow area. The reception room was busy when DCI Barry Thomas arrived. His telephoned request for a personal interview with the PF had been received but, the pretty young receptionist bluntly informed him, was regretfully declined due to the PF's other commitments and if he waited he could perhaps meet with an Assistant? Thomas sighed and settled down in the crowded waiting room, regretting his decision to rush over and not bring a daily newspaper with him. This, he presumed, was part of the ongoing friction between the police and the PF's department. After an hour, he was ushered into the presence of a senior Assistant PF.
Sitting opposite the Assistant in the plush office, he idly noted that it seemed no expense had been spared catering for the creature comforts of the senior management.
The burly, blonde haired man, dressed in a dark blue pin stripe shirt with bleached white collar and cuffs, broad red braces matching his tie that declared his loyalty to a local rugby team, acknowledged Thomas's presence with a curt nod as he continued flicking through the stapled pages of the e-mailed document.
'I've read the report that you had sent across, Mister Thomas and the evidence seems pretty clear-cut. However, you've elected to apply for a warrant rather than simply arrest this…' he glanced at the first page, 'Mary Crowden. Why so?' he sat back behind the expansive desk, casually flipped the report onto a leather pad and placed his hands behind his head as he stared curiously at Thomas.
The detective had a sneaking suspicion this wasn't going to be as straightforward as he had hoped.
'I decided that I'd rather proceed by warrant because while I overwhelmingly believe it is indeed her prints on the lighter that was discovered at the scene, I would much prefer to have her prints irrefutably matched before I charge her with her brother's murder.'
The Assistant sat forward. He mentally considered his caseload and slowly exhaled. He was busy and really hadn't the time to discuss this case with a portly, middle aged, middle management detective; sometimes these people had to be reminded who, ultimately, they were answerable to.
'I disagree. According to the statement noted from of the young man who is employed within the yard and her own admission that she was the only other person present at the time of the explosion and in company with the fire brigade report, it seems to me to be ample evidence of her guilt. It is my recommendation that you simply arrest this woman and charge her. I really see no need for an arrest warrant to be issued. If anything, I

consider it clouds the issue; makes it seem as though you are *seeking* evidence prior to libelling charges against her rather than proceeding with what appears to me to be *sufficient* evidence.'
Thomas sat stony-faced. He recognised this statement for what it was; simply an excuse for the PF's department to avoid what he firmly presumed the Assistant considered to be extra work. Once again he felt the old frustrations; the police did all the legwork and presented what they knew to be the best evidence available while tossers like this sat behind their fancy desks poring over a good case, worrying about their budget and finding any bloody excuse to save money.
'I disagree with you,' he said at last, 'and to be frank, I am somewhat aggrieved that my *experienced* opinion is being disregarded in this matter.'
The Assistant tried to intervene, but Thomas held up a hand as he continued.
'You or someone in your department will have the evidence presented to you by my officers today, this afternoon more than likely. I am acutely aware that it is simply my duty to detect the culprit, while it is your responsibility to arrange for the case to be tried and prosecuted. However,' he sighed resignedly, 'I firmly believe that at any future trial proceedings, Mary Crowden's defence team will seize upon this issue and it might very well cause.... difficulty...to whoever should prosecute it,' he added a veiled warning, 'and if the case should fail because of this small matter?'
He left the question unanswered, stood up and shrugged into his coat, ignoring the ashen-faced lawyer.
But I'll remember this conversation, he silently vowed.
'I will of course comply with your instruction and,' he glanced at his watch, 'as her whereabouts today are not known, I'll arrest Mary Crowden first thing tomorrow morning. Good day, sir.'

*

Frankie Johnson held the phone loosely and listened with an amused smile as Barry Thomas ranted and raved into his ear. Better to let his DCI blow off steam than interrupt, he decided.
'So in short,' he said at last, 'this guy at the PF's office recommends we go for a straight forward arrest rather than proceed by warrant? Okay,' he nodded his head at the handset, 'let's get it done tomorrow morning then, Barry. Get this inquiry tied up. There's a lot of other things happening in the city right now and I need you back on track clearing up a few other matters.'
That done, he turned again to the paper that lay upon his desk. The Fraud Squad Detective Superintendent had, as a matter of protocol, informed Johnson of an ongoing and highly confidential inquiry regarding the illicit purchase of property in pursuance of corrupt practices by serving councillors within the Glasgow District Council and their various associates. The Fraud Squad boss was aware of Johnson's' high profile murder inquiry and the report had been forwarded because it seemed that the patriarch of the Crowden family, old Alex himself, was deeply involved and likely to face corruption charges. In simple terms, Johnson was being requested that if the inquiry paths should cross, he provide any information that might assist the Fraud Squad and they would in turn avail him of their findings, relative to Crowden.
He smiled again. For once, things were looking up and it seemed that they were on a roll. Not only was the daughter to be lifted for the murder, but as an icing on the cake old Alex

was finally to get his collar felt; and on corruption charges, no less. Privately, he had to admit that the death of the two Crowden brothers was no great loss to society either. Johnson only knew the boss of the Fraud Squad slightly, spoken briefly to him at the occasional social evening during the Chief Constables Dining In Night and exchanged the occasional word at criminal seminars. Their careers had followed different paths, but he was aware the soft-spoken Aberdonian had the reputation as a stubborn and determined investigator.
Poor old Alex, he mused; it really hasn't been your year.

*

Arriving home later that evening, Johnny Bryce thought of his day and had to admit, other than the man he passed in the lane this morning, he had not been able to detect any surveillance throughout the journey to or home from work. The police surveillance must be getting better, he grinned.
He wasn't to know that he was no longer being tailed.

CHAPTER 26

The team that DCI Barry Thomas assembled to arrest Mary Crowden from her home comprised of the young Detective Inspector who had initially attended Samuel Crowden's death, three burly detective constables, whose presence was to prevent any interference or obstruction by the father Alex Crowden and two female detectives in the event Mary decided to struggle. Thomas had considered it wiser to employ the women officers' rather than have the usual and hopefully unfounded allegations of groping and touching a female suspect during an arrest that always worried his male officers.
As the rest of the city awoke, the team made their way to their two vehicles and set out for the Crowden's house in Tweedsmuir Path.

*

The man in the dark coloured car parked one hundred yards from Martin's house had guessed correctly. He watched as the shaven headed man locked his front door and noisily pushed the metal door of the garage upwards, before disappearing inside. The man wasn't to know that from behind a deceiving and cleverly constructed false panel on the garage wall, Shooter retrieved his insurance; a sawn-off, single barrelled shotgun wrapped in an old towel. From a plastic box in the wall cavity, he removed six shotgun cartridges, ample ammunition he considered for what he was about to do. He loaded one cartridge into the shotgun and shoved the remaining five into his jacket pocket. The shotgun he placed in the specially sewn pocket of his trousers.
'Right,' he mumbled to himself, taking a deep breath as though preparing for an athletic competition, 'time to collect the parcel.'

*

Johnny Bryce rolled over and clicked off the alarm clock.
Something was different; something had changed.
Barely awake, he lay on his back, he stared at the ceiling. Today, he mused, was the first day of the rest of his life.
He thought about his discussion with Jenny last night, their first time together outside of college; the first time she hadn't been his tutor, but simply a good looking woman who liked him for who he was. The small restaurant in Causeyside Street with the old

fashioned booths had been an ideal choice. The background music, played so softly it allowed its patrons to speak in hushed tones and the soft lighting had created the perfect ambience for what was in reality, their first date.
It had been an awkward start to the evening; he didn't immediately relax, at least not till she had leaned over and placed her hand on top of his. The uncommon intimacy, something he had not experienced from a woman in a long time, not even from poor Karen, had brought a lump to his throat.
Now why did I think of her as that, he wondered? Poor Karen. For the first time since her death, he could remember her without resentment. During the preceding months he had unconsciously blamed her, coming to accept that her angry and petulant flight to her manipulative mother with Laura might indeed have been contributory to his daughter's death.
He rubbed hard at his face with his hands; he shouldn't really blame Karen. What happened was a tragedy and if she was in any way partly culpable, her death washed clean that wrong.
With a deep sigh, he sat upright, running his fingers through his thick tousled hair.
Again he thought of his date with Jenny. Comfortable as they were with each among the classroom students, alone together they had acted like shy teenagers.
Their conversation had been wide and varied; he relating anecdotes of his life in the Corps and she of her former husband, whose possessive obsession of her and his flat refusal to consider their having children had finally drove her to divorce.
The night had drawn to a close when at last, she cautiously admitted that she was deeply attracted to him; wanted to see more of him. He was pleased and relieved, confessing he felt the same about her and reassured her feelings for him were not based on his tragedy, but something deeper.
Walking her to her car, they had kissed; shyly at first then with a passion that aroused in him a sense of the future.
It struck him then what seemed different.
He had not had the nightmare. Last night he had not dreamed of Laura.

*

He followed Martin's vehicle as it sped west on the motorway towards Paisley, staying always at least two hundred yards distance and tucking in behind other vehicles when traffic congestion slowed the Renault. He had no idea where Martin was going, but wherever it was, he sure was in a hurry.

*

As he'd instructed them one of the burly detectives and a female colleague walked swiftly to the rear door, preventing any likelihood of escape that way.
Thomas pressed the doorbell, hearing the angry sounds as someone heavily descended the stairs.
The door was pulled open and Alex Crowden, surprisingly already dressed and curiously wearing a dark coloured boiler suit buttoned up to the neck and heavy, workman's boots, stared at the detectives. If Thomas hadn't known better, he reflected, he'd have thought old Alex was on his way to some kind of messy job.
'What the fuck do you want at this time of the morning!' he barked. He didn't need any identification. Just like Shooter, he could smell a copper from almost fifty yards.
'An invitation to come in would be nice to start with,' replied Thomas.

'Do you have a warrant?'
'Do I need one?'
He didn't fail to see the big man's eyes narrow as he swallowed hard, then shoved the door open wide and walked back into the house.
The last thing Alex needed was cops in his house, particularly when he was off to meet Shooter and the man that had murdered his sons and his friend.
Lying in her bed, but awoken by the sound of the bell, Mary Crowden listened as she heard her father stomp into the lounge and the mumbled sound of visitors following him. She leapt from her be and grabbed her dressing robe, slipping it on as she tiptoed to the top of the stairs from where she could hear what was going on.
In the lounge, Alex turned to face Thomas, his mind working overtime. Had Shooter been arrested as he abducted Bryce and then grassed him off? No. Shooter wouldn't grass anyone, let alone his old pal.
'So, what's this about?'
'Mary at home?'
It's not about Shooter or Bryce,' he felt a sudden relief.
'What do you want with her?'
'She is at home then?'
Alex took a pace forward but stopped as the two burly detectives behind Thomas did the same. He recognised that having a go at the detective would get him nowhere; not with those two bruisers backing up the wee fat bastard.
'Mary!' he suddenly shouted without turning his head.
The sound of footsteps on the stairs and the door hurled open to admit his daughter; her open robe flowing behind her, the short, almost see through nightdress showing off her full figured body to the obvious appreciation of the two detective constables. The female officer with them remained blank faced.
'Pop?' Mary gasped, her puzzled expression obvious.
Thomas turned and stared at her.
'Mary Crowden, I arrest you for the murder of David Crowden,' he began, 'you do not have to say anything….'
And at that point, as Barry Thomas later recounted to Frankie Johnson, old Alex Crowden went bleeding mental.

*

Nerves on edge, Shooter Martin drummed his fingers on the steering wheel, his eyes staring at the narrow entrance of the lane. For almost twenty minutes, he had walked round the surrounding streets, but had seen nothing that indicated the police were present. As satisfied as he could be, he finally returned to his Renault. He rubbed a large hand across his unshaven chin. Right now he had a problem. Rawlings had told him Bryce used a Micra motorcar to get to work. During Shooter's walk, he had spotted two Micra's. He was guessing, but of the two, the only Micra he could see in the near vicinity to Bryce's house was the one parked facing him. If it wasn't that car, or if Bryce took another route to work, he'd incur Alex Crowden's anger and they'd have to re-think his plan for abducting Bryce.
He glanced at his wristwatch. It was still early and only a few locals had left their homes, none of who paid any attention to the shaven headed man sat low in the drivers' seat of the Renault. None except the driver of the dark coloured car parked some distance behind

him, watching curiously from his vehicle at the corner of the street to the rear.

Johnny had decided for once, to forego his physical routine. The late night dinner with Jenny and his early shift duty, to monitor the cash tills being emptied of their takings from the previous day, had wearied him. Surprising, since I've had such a good nights sleep, he chuckled good-humouredly. Today was going to be a good day, he decided. Dressed in the security firms corporate uniform of grey slacks, black shoes, white shirt with company tie and navy blue blazer, he strolled leisurely along the lane towards the car park, indifferent now as to whether or not he was being watched by the police. Approaching his Micra, he saw the same man from the previous day walking towards him, this time without his woollen hat and his right arm hanging against the side of his body and carrying a light jacket in his hand. For one curious moment, Johnny experienced an acute sense of danger, but seeing the guy for the second consecutive morning, assumed again him to be a police surveillance officer.
That was his big mistake.
As the shaven headed man drew near, it was obvious that he was approaching Johnny, not passing him by. Suddenly, he raised his arm and Johnny could see the man was holding a gun under the jacket, a large calibre weapon he saw at once; then he recognised it, a shotgun with a sawn off barrel.
'Open the door,' hissed Shooter.
Play for time, his instincts told him. But the man stood too far away for Johnny to even consider attempting any kind of lunge at him. He knew to that if he turned and tried to run and even though the effective range of the shotgun was no more than fifteen to twenty yards, the sprayed blast from the sawn-off would likely strike him down. The man didn't need to be a good shot; he only had to point in the general direction of Johnny and pull the trigger to almost guarantee hitting him.
'Open the fucking door!' Shooter hissed again, more vehemently this time.
Johnny inserted the key and pulled over the drivers' door.
'Now the back door,' ordered Shooter.
He did as he was told.
'Get in!'
'The back or the front?' he replied.
'Don't be a smart arse,' said Shooter thought gritted teeth. This was taking far too long. 'Here or elsewhere,' he brandished the shotgun very slightly, making his intention clear. 'Do as you told or else. You're driving, dummy!'
Johnny got in and saw the man in his rear view mirror climb in behind him. The shotgun he guessed, was now pointing at his back through the seat and the seat, he knew, would offer little or no protection against a twelve bore calibre weapon at that range.
'I guess you're not a police officer then?' he asked lightly. The punch, when it came, was delivered with uncanny accuracy to the back of his head, the pain bringing tears of rage to his eyes. Stars danced before his eyes as a feeling of helplessness overwhelmed him.
'Put your seat belt on and then drive,' instructed Shooter. It had gone as smoothly as he had planned and he was in control, so allowed himself to relax slightly in his seat.
'There's a man that wants to meet you Bryce. So keep your mouth shut and just take your directions from me. Savvy?'
Johnny nodded his head, concentrating on steering the Micra from the car park.

Behind them, the man in the dark car puzzled over what he had seen. From a distance it looked like some sort of rendeavous. He started his engine and prepared to follow the Micra.

*

The charge bar at Govan police office was in a state of chaos. Even the combined efforts of the three burly detectives had some difficulty restraining the maddened Alex Crowden, who continued to lash out with fists, feet and head. While he struggled with his captors, his daughter Mary, now more soberly dressed, stood pale faced but demurely against a wall, her two female arresting officers at either side of her as Barry Thomas took himself off towards the first aid room.
Frankie Johnson appeared at Thomas's elbow, a subdued grin on his face.
'Got your woman, then?' he lightly inquired.
'Goth morth than my womenth,' stuttered Thomas, his head held back as he pinched the bridge of his nose in an attempt to stem the flow of blood. 'Goth a fuckigth broketh nothe.'
Johnson couldn't contain himself and erupted into laughter, clapping his DCI on the back.
'I'll have someone drive you down to the Southern General casualty,' he said 'and your DI can process Mary for the murder and old Alex with assaulting you.'
He walked with Thomas to the car park at the rear of the office, beckoning a detective to accompany them as Thomas's driver.
'You did well, Barry,' he told the detective. 'Here's hoping that this will be an end to it, eh?'

*

Johnny continued to obey the instructions from his rear-seated passenger. He tried to remember his military training; recalling that when captured by an enemy, the crucial time to escape was as soon after capture as possible.
Well, that's no bloody good at the moment, he inwardly sighed, stuck in the driving seat of a car wearing a constraining seat belt and with a twelve bore sawn-off pointed at my back!
'Turn right here,' came the soft voice from behind him.
Johnny did as he was told. He had tried to converse with the shaven headed man from the start, but only received another punch on the back of his head and a warning to shut up or else. Since that time his thoughts had been racing. Who was this guy taking him to meet? He certainly wasn't a cop; that was evident. The only other option was he either worked for was connected to the Crowden's and likely that's whom he was delivering Johnny to.
The road he had turned onto was an overgrown rural track, a riveted path probably used by farm vehicles he guessed. He didn't know the area, but the last signpost had indicated he was leaving the suburban town of Linwood.
The track narrowed and he was forced to slow down to avoid deep potholes.
'There's a gate coming up on your left, smart boy. Slow down and turn in there and then stop at the old barn,' instructed Shooter.
Johnny did as he was told, trying to work out what kind of advantage he might have when the guy was getting out of the car. Pity it isn't a movie he grimaced. The hero always seems to be able to tackle the bad guy and down him without getting his head blown off

his shoulders. He had seen the effects of a shotgun blast at close range and knew the devastation that the weapon could wreak to the body. For now, he decided, he had no option but to play along with his abductor and take his chance if it arose.
'Switch off the engine,' ordered Shooter. 'Take off your seat belt. Good boy, now place both hands behind your head, interlocking the fingers.'
He did as he was told. In one swift movement, his hands were seized in a powerful grip and his arms forced agonizingly back, causing his back to arch against the seat and rendering him helpless to resist. He cried out at the unexpected pain and felt a noose being placed over his wrists and tightened, cutting deep into his skin.
As suddenly as he was seized, he was released. He heard the back door open and the man was beside him, pointing the shotgun at the door.
Johnny brought his hands back over his head and saw that a large plastic tie had been used to securely cuff his wrists together.
'Get out,' ordered Shooter, pulling at the drivers door.
As Johnny tried to step from the car, he was roughly grabbed by the hair and bodily hauled from the drivers seat, falling heavily onto the wet grass, the breath being knocked from him.
Shooter pulled him by his hair to his feet and pushed him towards the derelict building, shoving the shotgun painfully into his back.
'Can you at least give me a hint what I'm doing here?' he tried again as he picked his way across the uneven ground. This time the butt of the shotgun was thumped against the back of his head, causing him to fall to his hands and knees. Stars floated before his eyes and he was hauled to his feet and manhandled towards what had been the wide doorway into the now roofless barn.
'Sit down on that rock,' Shooter told him, 'and keep your mouth shut.'
The rock he pointed to was fallen masonry; had once been part of the wall, Johnny thought.
He kept his head low, using his eyes to glance about him. He saw the gunman seemed worried or at least a little surprised.
Shooter was indeed mystified; he had expected Alex to be waiting on them when they arrived. Where the fuck was he, he wondered?
Ten minutes; then twenty turned into half an hour, but still Alex did not arrive. Shooter paced up and down the path, occasionally staring at Bryce as though he were to blame for Alex non-appearance.
The back of Johnny's head hurt and he suspected it was bleeding. But he kept his mouth shut. At the moment, his captor had all the advantage and Johnny decided there was little point at this stage in making him any angrier; possibly have him inflict more injury to him. No, when the desperate moment came, he'd need all his strength if he were to tackle the brute. It was just a question of getting him close enough.
Frustratingly, Shooter stayed clear of his prisoner, ever watchful but not near enough to either hurt Johnny or be jumped by the bound man.
As time went on, his frustration grew. He stomped over to where Johnny sat and stared hard at him, the shotgun balanced in his right hand. Deliberately, he bent down and drawing back, struck the helpless Johnny across the face with the back of his left hand, sending him crashing against the lichen stained wall. A trickle of blood run from the right side of Johnny's mouth, but the pain was overcome by a tremendous rage; a desire to beat

this bastard to a pulp and he knew that given even the slightest opportunity, that was what he intended to do.
'Think you're a hard man, sonny?' he taunted Johnny. 'If I take those plastic cuffs off you, think you could take me, eh?'
He stood back and sneered.
'When Alex gets here,' his eyes opened wide, seeing Johnny's face and realising that at last the tied man knew whom Shooter was waiting for.
'That's right, sonny. Alex Crowden; the man whose sons you murdered. You think I'm hurting you? You don't know what pain is, sonny. He'll tear your fucking arms out of their sockets and rip your head off.'
At that he spun to his left then turned quickly, swinging the shotgun; but Johnny had guessed the blow was coming and turned sideways, catching the powerful blow across his right shoulder and again sending him crashing into the stone wall with a sickening crunch. Shooter stood back and scowled at Johnny, who lay on his side, dazed from the blow.
His bladder was full and he needed to pee. The only exit from the barn was through the gaping hole where the door had once swung. Inside the walled derelict, Bryce wasn't going anywhere; he glared at the prostrate man, not without Shooter seeing him.
With uncommon modesty peculiar to men of his generation, he turned and walked to the corner of the building from where he could watch the open barn doorway, unzipping his trouser flies and balancing the shotgun under his left arm. He glanced down, took hold of his penis and began to urinate against the wall, grinning as he aimed the stream at a panic-stricken spider scuttling across the brickwork.
So intent was he on drowning the insect he failed to hear the soft footsteps in the grass behind him. His first indication that something was wrong was as the heavy blade of the spade came crashing down squarely on top of his shaven head, flattening the skin and demolishing the small blood vessels it protected while simultaneously causing shards of splintered skull to shoot downwards and into his brain.
Caught in mid-flow, Shooter's arms flew wide, the shotgun dropping to the grass beside him as his knees buckled and slowly he toppled against the wall, his penis continuing to discharge his urine down his trousers leg.
Seconds later, a slight whooshing noise as the spade was again swung through the air signalled the second blow that crushed his head, resulting in massive internal haemorrhaging and driving even larger fragments of bone into his brain.
He didn't die immediately but lay awkwardly against the rough brickwork, like a puppet whose strings have been severed. Softly moaning, his body quivering at the unexpected shock of the attack, his dribbled urine formed a puddle at his groin. Bleeding internally from the massive trauma to his head, gravity forced his blood towards the natural exits and he started to haemorrhage from his nose and his ears.
His last conscious thought was that somehow, the fucking spider had done for him.

Johnny, still stunned from banging against the wall, tried to sit up. He jerked upright as the voice came from behind the wall.
'You're safe now,' said the man, the faintest tremor in his voice. 'He won't harm you again.'
Johnny shook his head as though to clear it, trying to turn and see who had spoken, but

the man stood out of sight behind the wall. Could it be a trick, some perverse joke before his abductor assaulted him again? Maybe it was this Alex Crowden that they were to meet here.
His uncertainty played on the mans' already taut nerves.
Johnny took a chance.
'I'm tied here with a plastic strap, a cable time. I'll need to be cut free.'
'I'll let you cut yourself free,' said the voice again, but this time Johnny thought with some hesitation, 'but first you have to make me a promise.'
'Who are you? And where is he, the other guy?' Johnny asked, desperately looking abut him for something, anything that he could use as a weapon.
There was the briefest of pauses before the voice answered.
'It's not important who I am and like I told you; he won't hurt you again. I need to you promise that if I set you free, you'll wait where you are for ten minutes and let me get away. Deal?'
His mind raced. Whoever his rescuer was, he couldn't be the police and why didn't the man want to be seen? But it didn't really matter; as long as he had stopped the maniac with the shotgun, that's all he needed to know.
'It's a deal,' he replied, his throat suddenly dry.
'Hang on,' replied the voice. With shaking hands, the man took a small pocketknife from his trousers, opened the blade and then carefully wiped it and the handle with a clean handkerchief. That done, he called to Johnny.
'I'm going to toss a knife into you, so that you can cut yourself free,' he warned and then deliberately threw the knife into the opposite corner of the barn, where it fell among the tall grass growing there.
Johnny cried out, 'Thanks!' but the man carrying the spade, never heard. He was already twenty yards away and hurriedly making his way back down the farm track towards his car.

Ignoring his promise, Johnny didn't wait any time before scuttling over to the corner of the barn and stamping down the grass to find the knife. He found the old, bone-handled pocketknife almost immediately and with some difficulty, cut through the plastic. If it were some cruel trick, at least now he would go down fighting. Holding the knife as he had once taught his marine recruits, he slowly edged his way to the open doorway, his mouth dry and his heart racing. Taking a deep breath, he swung round the corner, prepared to defend himself; but there was no one there. The first sight that greeted him was the slumped form at the corner of the building, the shotgun lying uselessly by his side.
He glanced about him, but of his mysterious rescuer, there was no sign.
He could see that the shaven headed man was still alive; the faint but visible movement of his chest indicated he was at least breathing. Then, as Johnny watched, the gunman gave one slow, exhausted sigh as his body trembled with shock, then he stopped breathing.
He grimaced at the wound, curious as to what kind of weapon had inflicted such damage and almost flattened the gunman's crown. Checking for a pulse, he detected nothing and decided the shaven headed man was certainly dead. He backed off, still looking about him, but then remembered that Alex Crowden might yet arrive and like his recently

expired associate, could also be armed.
The Micra remained where he had been forced to stop, both doors still open and the key in the ignition. He slammed shut the rear door, got into the drivers seat and reversed slowly out of the yard. He stopped in the farm track and adjusted the rear view mirror. The face that stared back was pale faced and gaunt; dried blood at the corner of his mouth and a graze across his forehead when he had been struck with the shotgun and banged against the brickwork of the wall. Using his sleeve, he wiped his mouth clean, flinching at the ache in his face.
He couldn't go to work now. The logical move would have been to contact the police, report what had happened. After all he frowned, he was the victim here. But that would lead to more questions, perhaps even unwittingly causing the arrest of his rescuer. No, he was going home.
Johnny Bryce decided he had had enough excitement for one day.

*

When finally he had calmed sufficiently down to nothing more than a silent rage, the police bailed Alex Crowden later that afternoon and informed him he would be summonsed in due course to answer the charge of assaulting a police officer.
His first action on being discharged from Govan police office was to contact Gospel Gordon's firm, demanding the services of their best brief to represent his daughter Mary, been arrested on a trumped up murder charge.
'No,' he growled into the mobile phone, 'I don't have time to come into your office. Just get your arse across to Govan and find out what the fuck's going on! Once you've done that, phone me!' he instructed the perplexed and extremely nervous lawyer.
That done he pressed the button to contact Shooter, but the phone rang out before switching to the answer service. Alex never usually left messages other than instructions to contact him; he didn't trust them and never knew who might listen to it.
Several times over the next few hours, he phoned Shooter, but each time his call was answered by the automatic answer service. By evening, the unthinkable occurred to him that perhaps the collection of the parcel had not been as straightforward as Shooter had foreseen.

*

Three days later, a farm worker searching for loose stone to repair a section of wall that divided his field from a neighbour, drove his tractor along the narrow track to the old barn and there discovered a corpse lying against the wall. His frantic phone call was first responded to by the local station constable who, more used to dealing with straightforward fighting drunks and road accidents, panicked and called for immediate assistance. Within the hour, the discovery had escalated into a full-blown major inquiry that later established the dead man, a Glasgow criminal called Thomas Martin who went by the nickname 'Shooter', was a trusted associate of the notorious gangster Alex Crowden. In due course, Frankie Johnson was informed of the discovery and apprised of the circumstances.
Ronnie Sutherland, the investigating DI, contacted Johnson to regretfully inform him that a heavy fall of rain two nights previously had washed away any chance of forensic evidence that might have otherwise been available. The lack of eyewitnesses or any other evidence seemed to indicate the murder was just another gangland revenge killing; particularly in view of the discovery of the shotgun that bore Martin's prints and lay

beside his body
Sutherland was no fool. From his days in the serious crime squad, he knew better than most about Shooter Martin and his allegiance to Alex Crowden. He thought again of the aborted case against the Crowden brothers and something occurred to him, an idea so startlingly clear that after he briefly toyed with it in his mind, he almost as quickly dismissed it, believing that it was better to work with evidence rather than supposition.
Later that week, while visiting Paisley police office and reviewing the case with Ronnie Sutherland, Frankie Johnson studied the scene of crime photographs. He could see the heavy rain had completely soaked the corpse and the surrounding ground. Curiously though, the same heavy rain had been unable to destroy a spiders' web that stretched from the nearby wall, across the narrow gap and attached itself to Martin's waxy face.

EPILOGUE

As the cool autumn disappeared and winter of that year approached, many changes occurred in the lives of those persons who had been primarily or peripherally involved in the tragic circumstances that had begun and resulted in the death of Karen Bryce and her daughter Laura.

*

A page three article by a junior reporter in the *Glasgow News* reported the finding by police of a partially clothed and badly beaten man in a back street adjoining St Vincent Place in Glasgow city centre. The area was renowned for being frequented nightly by young male prostitutes and vicious thugs who preyed upon the weak men that engaged such youths. The victim, almost unconscious when he was discovered, was conveyed to the casualty ward of the Glasgow Royal Infirmary, but succumbed to his injuries shortly after his admission. The young policewoman who had accompanied him in the ambulance later provided a statement to the CID that the man repeatedly mumbled how sorry he was, that he didn't intend killing such a beautiful boy. Attempts by the young policewoman to speak to the man and elicit more information were denied by the ambulance crew, whose sole priority was keeping their casualty alive.
An empty wallet located not far from the scene of the attack was later proven to belong to the victim, whose identity was revealed as Richard Smyth, Depute of the Paisley Procurator Fiscal and known throughout the judiciary as 'Devious Dickie'.
Smyth's rambling statement within the ambulance was never investigated.

*

The late and unlamented Patrick Delaney is still missing.
The murders of Mathew 'Gospel' Gordon, Samuel Crowden and Thomas 'Shooter' Martin remain unsolved.
Missus Gordon is enjoying her new-found wealth in Monaco with a twenty-five year old male companion.

*

Annie Hall's relationship with her policeman boyfriend developed rather more slowly. Her reluctance to comply with his macho, rugby style of living led to more than one heated argument. Gradually, the couple reached an understanding and compromised; an agreement that suited both, for they discovered that neither wanted to lose the other.

Eighteen months later on the tropical island of Barbados, Andy Dawson surprised his librarian girlfriend by presenting her with an engagement ring.

*

The High Court trial of Mary Crowden, who was charged with the brutal slaying of her brother David Crowden, begun within three months of her arrest. During this period, bail had been refused, the Crown arguing that her obvious association with a well-documented criminal family might prejudice the proceedings, particularly in regards to prosecution witnesses.

Acting for the accused, her distinguished counsel successfully argued that his client had been arrested on the strength of fingerprint evidence and, outwith the hearing of the jury, pointedly made His Lordship aware that as Mary had never previously been fingerprinted and there was at that time nothing with which to compare the incriminating fingerprints found on the lighter, the arrest was therefore illegal; albeit her prints subsequently taken after arrest did indeed match those found on the incriminating plastic lighter.

His Lordship agreed with the learned counsel for the defence and threw out the fingerprint evidence. To the obvious delight of the smiling Miss Crowden and the fury of the Crown prosecuting counsel, the case proceeded with the remaining evidence but it quickly became apparent that it seemed this evidence standing alone might not be sufficient to convict the accused. Most of the nine men, and at least one admirer among the six women, and who together comprised the jury, were secretly delighted for the extremely attractive, blonde and buxom Mary.

Ally McGregor of the *Glasgow News,* in his storyline that night drew a parallel between Mary and the infamous nineteenth century case of Madeline Smith; the young Glasgow woman accused of poisoning her lover within her basement apartment rooms in the affluent family home at 7 Blythswood Square. It didn't escape the attention of the jurors who read the article that Madeleine Smith, like Mary Crowden also a blonde beauty, and who reputedly bewitched the all-male jury, received that verdict peculiar to Scottish Law - *Not Proven;* a verdict that neither convicts nor totally acquits the prisoner, but does release the accused back into society and free from ever again facing trial on the same accusation. In some minds McGregor's article sowed the seed of a possible decision for the lovely young woman.

It was during the evidence presented by the pathologist, when she graphically detailed the deceased's injuries and presented her post mortem examination results that caused the accused to turn pale and faint. Those listening naturally assumed the horror of her brothers' injuries were too much for her to bear. However, Mary was the only person to whom a relatively insignificant piece of information that had no particular bearing on the case, caused real concern. The trial was briefly suspended to allow her to compose herself, but when it resumed, it became clear to the observers in the public gallery that the self-assured Mary Crowden was no longer the bright and confident young woman she had previously portrayed.

The jury were out less than two hours. When they returned to the court the foreman announced that by a majority verdict, they found the case to be *Not Proven.*

The former accused paid little attention to the muted congratulations offered by admiring well-wishers, for her counsel had arranged her hurried departure from the rear door of the court.

Only she knew that the pathologist had already announced the verdict. It seemed to her

that David had the last laugh. She had not anticipated the seduction of her brother that culminated in his murder and was calculated to silence him, had not only kept her secret, but also revealed his.
For David's secret had been something so dreadful that he had never dared admit it to another.
For David was HIV positive.

*

Alex Crowden quickly became a broken man. Following her arrest, he instructed the lawyer acting for Mary, and whom he was after all paying, to keep Alex fully apprised of the details of the whole, sordid business. At first he had been unable to accept or comprehend why the police would charge her with David's murder, but slowly as the truth emerged, he had come to acknowledge what he knew in his heart to be true. Mary had murdered him. Without compassion or remorse, she had killed her own brother. Greed was the motive, he soon learned and was not surprised.
Because, after all, she was her father's daughter.
He knew shortly after the verdict was announced that she had been set free. But even if he had wished, he was unable to greet his daughter when she was finally released from court, for by that time he was languishing in the harsh confines of HMP Barlinnie remand wing, awaiting trial with a number of others on public corruption charges.
His prostitution empire quickly disassembled as other less scrupulous criminal figures took advantage of his absence to move in and commandeer his assets. The fortune he had amassed during the years was soon used, paying the heavy fees demanded by his and Mary's defence teams. By foolishly releasing these funds to their legal counsel's and without the benefit of the financial advice he had previously enjoyed from Gospel Gordon, Her Majesty's Inland Revenue took an interest in his illicit bank accounts and, with no record of tax payments to accompany this fortune, his accounts were frozen and monies seized pending further investigation.

*

It quickly became apparent to Johnny Bryce that the police no longer had any interest in his movements. The day following his abduction, he was visited at home by Jenny Hopkins who, shocked at his battered appearance, accepted without question his explanation that he had fallen; there were some things, he privately decided, that Jenny should never know.
Her gentle ministrations to his bruises became a little more heated and, waking the next morning with the lovely Jennifer asleep by his side, Johnny discovered that life had perhaps more to offer him than he had expected.
The coming months saw their relationship develop into love. Six months later, the pregnant Missus Bryce and her new husband boarded the plane that would take them on the first leg of their journey to Wellington, New Zealand. Their new life as immigrants begun in earnest when at last, they opened their own IT training and computer business. Shortly after, the devoted couple were blessed by the arrival of twin sons.

*

It was November of that year, while their daughter and her fiancée were house hunting and Archie Crichton and his wife were minding their adored grandson as they happily strolled round their local Super-DIY store.
Missus Crichton again marvelled at the change in her husband. His fit of depression

seemed to have completely lifted and he was once more the man she knew and loved. She often wondered if the impromptu surprise party she had arranged for Archie at the local bowling club had been the turning point; particularly when his old friend and colleague, Ronnie Sutherland, had arrived and insisted on making a speech. Curiously, he never revealed what the two of them had discussed during the ten minutes they had quietly spoken together, but she knew whatever had been said had lifted her mans' spirits. Later, Archie had whispered to her the wee lad was safe now and that was all that mattered. The memory of that evening still caused her throat to tighten and bring tears to her eyes as she recalled the kind things he had said about her Archie. She didn't need to know anymore.

'We're in the presence of a man who has diligently served his community for thirty years, never failing to give his all and making me proud to be his friend,' Ronnie had told the assembled crowd. The happy cheers for Archie at the end of that special night had brought them both to tears.

She watched her husband and grandson walking ahead of her, laughing together; the large man swinging the wee chap round by his arms, the two of them sniggering like school kids, bless them.

That's when she saw it, a steal at fifteen pounds. She glanced ahead, but her two favourite men were busily engrossed in having a good giggle, the boy pointing gleefully at the brightly painted garden gnomes and tormenting his protesting grandfather to buy him one.

Sliding it from its rack she hurried to the till, intending to put it in the boot of the car before Archie could complain at the cost, silly man that he was. She beamed, pleased with her bargain. As if spending money on him was any kind of waste.

He needed it anyway, she knew. A new spade. It was still a mystery she frowned; his old flat bladed one mysteriously disappearing like that from the garden shed.

*

Needless to say, this story is a work of fiction.

If you have enjoyed the story, you may wish to visit the author's website at:
www.glasgowcrimefiction.co.uk

The author also welcomes feedback and can be contacted at:
george.donald.books@hotmail.co.uk

Printed in Great Britain
by Amazon.co.uk, Ltd.,
Marston Gate.